LEGACY OF SHAME

LEGACY
OF SHAME

Nora Kay

Hodder & Stoughton

A CIP catalogue record for this title
is available from the British Library.

ISBN 0 340 75150 9

Typeset by Hewer Text Ltd, Edinburgh
Printed and bound in Great Britain by
Clays Ltd, St Ives plc

Hodder and Stoughton
A division of Hodder Headline
338 Euston Road
London NW1 3BH

For Bill and Raymond

Chapter One

'Your mother was my mistress. You knew that, of course you did?'

Kate McPherson shook her head. 'I didn't know that, Uncle Edwin.'

He frowned. 'That must stop, addressing me as Uncle Edwin.'

'Why?'

'Because, my dear, I am not your uncle, we are in no way related.' He made an arc of his fingers. 'For reasons of her own your mother wished you to call me that and my mistake was agreeing to it.'

'I see.' She didn't, but it was better to pretend she did.

'In future you will address me as Mr Hamilton-Harvey.'

Her attention was wandering the way it did these days.

'Are you listening?' he said sharply.

Kate jumped. 'I'm sorry. Yes, I'm listening.'

'Then tell me what you are to call me?' He sounded like a school teacher with a particularly slow pupil.

'Mr Hamilton-Harvey.'

'Good, we have that settled. How old are you, Kate? Eleven isn't it?'

'No, ten, I'm ten and a half.'

He nodded. 'Nearly grown up. In a few years you will be old enough to get a job and look after yourself.'

'Yes.'

He was frowning again. 'You do realise that you are not my responsibility?'

'Yes,' she whispered.

'Nevertheless, something will have to be done about you. The problem is what.'

Kate was trying to hide her panic. What was going to happen to her?

'Please, can't I just stay here with Mrs Lennox?' Mrs Lennox had been kind. Kate had wept into her soft bosom and been comforted.

'Certainly not. This is my house, Kate, and I have – plans for it. As far as Mrs Lennox is concerned, the woman was only engaged to see to the running of the house after your mother fell ill. Where is the woman?'

'In the village, she said she had some shopping to do.' The awful choking sensation was back in her throat but she fought it. Suddenly it had become very important to Kate not to break down.

He nodded, dismissing Mrs Lennox. The girl was not his responsibility but even so he did feel duty-bound to make some arrangements. He had never been drawn to the girl, possibly because when he might have made a fuss of her, she had remained unresponsive. Mildred had blamed it on shyness and it was possible that she had been in awe of him. Fortunately the girl was intelligent and Edwin Hamilton-Harvey wondered how much of the situation she really knew or guessed. Better to find out now.

'Kate, I can't believe that you didn't know your mother was my mistress.'

Kate remained silent.

'You do know what a mistress is?'

Kate felt a flash of anger that he should think her ignorant. The head teacher of a school was called a head-mistress and a woman was mistress in her house. Fancy him thinking she didn't know that!'

'Yes, I do know,' she said louder than necessary.

He breathed more easily. For one horrible moment

2

Edwin Hamilton-Harvey had seen himself trying to explain and deuced awkward that would have been.

'Good, I felt sure you would.'

They were sitting in the comfortably furnished sitting-room in the stone-built house known as The Rockery. The front of the house lived up to its name with rockery plants and heathers covering the huge stones and making an attractive, colourful display. It occupied a secluded position about half a mile from the village of Lamondhill in Angus. The man had been smoking but put the pipe aside. He wore a tweed suit with leather buttons on the jacket and was sitting in the easy chair with his legs stretched out before him and crossed at the ankles. Kate was sitting nearer to the window in a straight-backed chair. She was pale and her fingers kept pleating and unpleating her blue cotton skirt. There was no fire and a plant with a great deal of greenery hid the empty grate. The September day was pleasantly warm though by evening it would be much cooler and Mrs Lennox would light a fire. Kate looked around her at the familiar scene and thought how different it had looked when her mother had been its mistress. There was that word again. Her mother had made it a home, now it was just a house. Mr Hamilton-Harvey's house. Hanging on the wall were framed watercolours of the local beauty spots and one rather dull oil painting of a table with a bowl of fruit and a vase of pink roses, one of which had shed some of its petals on to the circle of lace. On the wall above the bureau hung a calendar with a view of Balmoral Castle and showing very clearly that this was the year 1930.

Edwin Hamilton-Harvey was irritated to find himself in this position. Shortly after they had met, Mildred told him that she and the baby were alone in the world. It hadn't mattered then, probably he had thought it an advantage that Mildred had no one. Thinking back to that time brought an unexpected lump to his throat. She had been so lovely with her ivory smooth skin, her honey-coloured hair and those magnificent deep blue eyes. The years had not taken away her beauty but rather they had enhanced it. The lovely girl

3

had become a poised and beautiful woman and the times spent with Mildred had been the happiest of his life.

One day he imagined Kate would be quite lovely. She was very like Mildred with the same colouring, only her eyes were violet blue rather than that deep wonderful shade. He only wished his own daughter was as pretty as Kate. Heads had turned for Mildred and the wonder of it was that she hadn't appeared to notice. She had seemed to be perfectly happy to be his mistress though he guessed and it was an accurate guess, that the house in its isolated position and the security it gave was the main attraction. He had loved Mildred from the time they met but he knew she hadn't shared those feelings. Not that he could fault her in any way, Mildred had always been warm and loving but without giving all of herself. Occasionally he had wondered about the husband who had died so young but he never asked and she never volunteered any information. He had a wife and family who were dear to him and Mildred had Kate and her memories. It had worked out very well. His wife, Gwen, had hated the intimate side of marriage and had been quite unable to hide the fact from Edwin though, to give her her due, she had tried.

Edwin was a good-looking, stockily built man of forty-seven. He had a small moustache, slightly receding hair and pale blue eyes. His home of which he was very proud, was in Broughty Ferry where many of the wealthy folk of Dundee chose to live. The Rockery was his love-nest and at twelve miles from Dundee was far enough away from his home to avoid gossip and near enough for frequent visits. Craggy Point, the family estate belonging to the Hamilton-Harveys, had become Edwin's on the death of his father together with a distressing amount of debt which had been the result of his father's weakness for gambling. If the estate was to remain in the family then those debts had to be settled and soon. Marrying into money was the obvious solution, indeed Edwin saw it as the only way out of his difficulties, and to this end he courted the plain but wealthy Gwen Morton who was a few years his senior. Gwendoline Morton was no fool, she knew the reason for Edwin's interest but since it suited her she gave him every encouragement. Her dearest wish was to marry into an old and respected family and when Edwin proposed she had no hesitation in accepting. The marriage had taken place quickly and without fuss and there were some who thought it must be a shot-gun marriage. It wasn't. Gwen did her duty as she saw it and once she had produced a son and heir and a daughter besides, she saw no reason to continue sharing a bedroom. She told her husband that she had no objection whatsoever to him keeping a mistress provided he was discreet about it. With that side of their marriage taken care of, Gwen and Edwin became good friends. She having the better brain was always consulted before any decisions were made. As well as keeping an eye on the estate, Gwen continued to safeguard her own interests. Years before, fortunes had been made in the Dundee jute mills but those richly prosperous days were all but gone. India with its cheap labour had been a distant threat which had become grim reality. Many mill workers were without jobs and, a sign of the times, corner shops could no longer afford to give credit. A few, including the Hawkhead Mill, continued to make a profit though nothing like the good old days. The Hawkhead Mill had been established by the Morton family and, with no male heir to succeed, it had come to Gwen. For the sake of appearance, Edwin was in charge but it was widely known that he knew very little about the jute trade and that his wife was the true manager.

In time the son, Roderick, would take over. Roderick got his intelligence and his business sense from his mother and from his father his good appearance. His height, six feet of him, came from Gwen's side of the family.

Edwin Hamilton–Harvey had been silent for some time and Kate kept looking across.

'A sad business, Kate.' He sighed. 'She was a fine woman, your mother.'

5

'Yes.' She couldn't stop them, couldn't hold back the scalding tears.

'Now! Now! Kate, that won't help, you know.' Edwin couldn't abide tears, even tears of grief. It was fourteen days since Mildred's untimely death and in his opinion that was long enough for an outward show of grief. What good did tears do? They didn't bring back the dead. He couldn't remember grieving for very long when first his mother and then his father had left this world. The death of his mistress was affecting him much more. Still life had to go on and he was already thinking of installing someone else in The Rockery. Not a refined, gentle creature like Mildred, this one was a little on the coarse side but she was young with a voluptuous body and he was seeing the promise of exciting times ahead. The matter of Kate McPherson would have to be settled and soon.

Kate sniffed, dried her eyes, mumbled an apology and gave her full attention to the large porcelain bowl on the rosewood table. It was empty and that didn't look right. Her mother had loved arranging flowers and it had always been filled with fresh blooms from the garden or with bits of greenery or red berries when the flowering season was over.

The man got to his feet. 'I must be on my way, Kate, and don't worry things have a habit of working out.'

She watched him go, heard the door shut and a few minutes later a car starting up. What would he do about her? Where would she be sent? She wasn't going to be allowed to stay at The Rockery, he had made that clear. Kate wondered what plans he had made for it. Perhaps he was going to sell the house. He had never liked her, she had sensed that. When he came it was only her mother he was interested in and Kate had always felt left out and unwanted. What if he just washed his hands of her? He had said she wasn't his responsibility and made sure she understood that. The thought of being alone and forgotten sent a chill down her spine and suddenly the silence of the house became oppressive and frightening. The knuckle of her hand went into her mouth to stop the scream and then she heard the key turn in the lock. Mrs Lennox was coming in the back door with her shopping bag. She put it down on the table with a thud as though glad to be free of it. With a strangled cry Kate rushed into her arms.

'There! There! Kate, my little pet,' she said drawing her close. 'I wouldn't have left you if I'd known you'd get into this state. You could have come to the shops.'

'No, I didn't want to, I didn't want people saying things and making me cry. I can't help it, Mrs Lennox.'

'No harm in a good weep, my little lamb, in fact it does a lot of good. To my mind you haven't done enough of it. Sit yourself down and we'll have a cup of tea in a wee while. I bought a doughnut for you, freshly made. You can always tell with a doughnut. If the sugar has disappeared then it wasn't made that day.' She began putting away the shopping.

'He was here, Mrs Lennox,' Kate said holding her sodden handkerchief balled up in her hand.

'Your Uncle Edwin?'

'He isn't my uncle, he told me that and he wants me to call him Mr Hamilton-Harvey.'

'I shouldn't let that worry you. Lots of children call adults who come a lot about the house aunt or uncle, then when they are older it stops.'

'I didn't know that.' Kate thought there was an awful lot she didn't understand.

'That's the kettle boiling I'll make the tea.' The woman busied herself, then sat down at the table opposite Kate. 'Eat your doughnut and I'll have a piece of sponge to keep you company.'

Mrs Lennox was small and dumpy and a kind-hearted soul who was deeply concerned about Kate. Life could be so cruel. The bairn wasn't yet eleven and an orphan. Had there been a husband? She thought so but others weren't so sure. No one knew much about the lady who had lived at The Rockery but all agreed she was pleasant and nice-looking which made it difficult to understand why she should have a man arriving in his car and staying overnight. Kate called him her uncle but not many believed he was a relative.

Mrs Lennox wished she could do something but it was impossible. There was barely room to swing a cat in her small house and although they were happy enough the overcrowding did bring out the bad temper and raised voices. These few weeks away from her demanding family had been like a holiday. Her eldest, Peggy, was coping. She was a bossyboots at the best of times and the young ones would know better than disobey or answer back. It would do the rascals no harm. Her sailor husband seldom came home and she had a suspicion that there was someone else. She didn't ask him. The money arrived regularly and that was something for which she should be thankful.

Jessie Lennox would have made a good nurse. She had had plenty of practice with her own family, nursing them through measles, chickenpox and more worryingly, whooping cough. She had looked after elderly relatives stubbornly holding on to a life that had little meaning until at last came the merciful release. Seeing a young child slipping away, cheated of life, made the woman angry as well as sad. There seemed no sense to it but then as she would tell herself it would all be made clear one day. Watching Kate's mother getting ever weaker yet managing to remain cheerful was hard to bear yet the carers had to remain strong. Folk needed someone on whom they could depend.

'Mrs Lennox, what about school?'

'What about it, Kate? No, keep pouring – I like a full cup of tea. Thanks, lass.'

After the funeral Kate had gone back to school. Her teacher and Mrs Lennox had been in agreement that it was best. The routine and being with her school friends would help to keep her mind off losing her mother. The children had been told to be especially kind to Kate because of her loss. Those same children who could at times be cruel were capable of showing sympathy. The thought of how they would feel if it was their mother who had died brought it home to them how Kate must be suffering.

'Mr Hamilton-Harvey said I couldn't stay here and if I have to go away that will mean a new school, won't it?'

'Yes, if you leave Lamondhill you'll have to go to another.'

Kate's lips were quivering. 'I don't want to leave, I like my school.'

'You could like your new one even better.' Mrs Lennox popped the last of the sponge into her mouth and then gathered up the crumbs and ate them. 'What were we talking about? Ah, yes, school. Don't worry your head about that, one is very much like another. You do well at school, so your teacher said and she should know.'

'Did she really say that?' Kate looked pleased.

'She did.'

'Sometimes I'm top of the class and sometimes Jane Cummings beats me,' Kate said shyly.

'You stick into your lessons, lass, and make something of yourself. My lot haven't been blessed with brains but then again we can't all be clever. You, Kate, are going to be one of the lucky ones with brains and beauty.'

'I'm not beautiful. My mother was.'

'Yes, your mother was a lovely lady and one day you will be the same.'

Kate smiled. 'Do you know what he, I mean, Mr Hamilton-Harvey, asked me – and that's another thing,' she said as if it had just occurred to her, 'why has he got two names?'

'The Lord only knows, one is enough for most folk. A bit of swank, I'd say, and he is a toff after all. What did he ask you?'

'He asked me if I knew what a mistress was.'

Mrs Lennox gave a start. 'And do you?' she said cautiously.

'Of course.'

'You do?'

Kate frowned. Mrs Lennox didn't think she knew either.

'Yes, I do. Do you want me to tell you?' Was it possible that Mrs Lennox didn't know?

'No, lass, I don't think so.' The woman paused trying to weigh her next words. She didn't want Kate to lose respect for her mother. 'Remember, Kate, there are times when some of us are driven, through no fault of our own, to do what we know to be wrong.' Picking up her cup she drained the last of the tea and wondered just how much the child understood or pretended to understand.

For her part Kate was puzzled. 'Miss McGowan is a headmistress,' she said slowly and waited for Mrs Lennox to say something.

Mrs Lennox didn't know whether to laugh or cry. Poor little innocent, she hadn't the faintest idea about the accepted meaning of mistress. Should she enlighten the child or would that be cruel? Losing her mother at that age was dreadful enough without finding out that her beloved mother had been mistress to that man – and for all those years. No, she couldn't do it. On the other hand to hear it from someone else, someone less sympathetic . . . she would have to sleep on it.

Chapter Two

When Kate opened her eyes there was a faint glimmer of light coming through the crack between the curtains. About to get out of bed, she stopped herself, realising this was Saturday. No school today and Mrs Lennox had told her to have a long lie and only to get up when she felt like it. It should have been nice snuggling down and for a little while it was. Then the familiar ache for her mother and knowing she would never see her again, brought a rush of tears and in an effort to stop them Kate turned on to her stomach and buried her face in the pillows. How long she lay like that Kate didn't know, she must have exhausted herself and then drifted back to sleep. Rubbing her eyes she yawned then got up and pulled on her dressing-gown, the warm pink one that had replaced the yellow one with the white rabbits on the pocket. Kate went downstairs, her slippered feet making no sound on the carpeted stair. The kitchen door was slightly ajar and she was about to push it open when Kate heard the voices. One belonged to Mrs Lennox, the other she didn't recognise. Should she go back to her bedroom and come down again when whoever it was had gone? Undecided, Kate lingered a few moments and then she didn't want to move. They were talking about her and surely she had a right to hear what was being said. Kate wasn't fully convinced that she was doing the right thing but the need to know was stronger than her willpower.

As for Mrs Lennox, that woman could have seen her early-morning visitor far enough.

'It's you, Mrs Petrie,' she said resignedly and made no attempt to invite the woman in. She just hoped that whatever talking there was could be done on the doorstep. It was not to be.

'That's a chill wind,' she said giving a shiver. 'I'll just step in for a few minutes.'

Mrs Lennox sighed and moved aside to let her unwelcome visitor enter, then shut the door.

'Fine and warm in here, that's the thing about kitchens. The bairn, she's not here then?'

'Kate's in bed and asleep I hope.'

'Best place for the poor lass.' She tut-tutted. 'It's just that I'm worried, we all are. What's to happen, Mrs Lennox? What's to become of Kate?'

Mrs Lennox was trying to make allowances. There was no harm in the woman she knew that. She just had a need to have her curiosity satisfied.

'You know as much as I do.'

Vera Petrie folded her arms and her expression said that she didn't believe that, not for a single moment.

'There's nothing to tell.'

'I can't believe that and surely you can tell me. You must know it won't go any further.'

Mrs Lennox knew nothing of the kind.

Vera Petrie lowered her voice. 'That man, the one Kate calls her Uncle Edwin, I saw him here yesterday. Will he take her do you think? No, on second thoughts he wouldn't be likely to do that, not unless the bairn is his, of course.' Her eyes were bright and curious.

Mrs Lennox pursed her lips. 'Kate's father died when she was little more than a baby, Mrs Petrie, I do happen to know that.'

'There you are then.' She nodded her head several times. 'You can rest assured that he won't take responsibility for his mistress's bairn. Someone was saying, and I'm inclined to agree, that there will be another woman taking up residence in The Rockery before too long.'

'I've work to do, Mrs Petrie, you must let me get on.'

'Oh, there's plenty of that waiting for me. A woman's work is never done.' She took a step towards the door Mrs Lennox had already opened then stopped to have her final say. 'Always thought Kate's mother to be a superior kind of woman. Makes you think doesn't it why a woman like that would belittle herself to be a mistress to that man, to any man come to that, and for it to go on for all that time. Poor Kate, it's to be hoped she will be spared the truth.'

'We don't know the ins and outs of it and we never will. Goodbye, Mrs Petrie. Kate will be down any minute and I must see to her breakfast.' She saw the woman out and then shut the door firmly.

Kate went quickly back upstairs then came down a few minutes later. She said good morning to Mrs Lennox and sat down at the scrubbed kitchen table.

'There you are, lass, get that into you,' the woman said putting down a steaming plate of porridge in front of her.

Kate picked up her spoon and forced down a few mouthfuls. She had been trying to make sense of what had been said. It had something to do with mistress and Kate was finding that confusing. How could her mother have been Mr Hamilton-Harvey's mistress? Unless that was another name for housekeeper. Kate didn't really think that. It had sounded as though her mother had done something shameful and Kate would never believe that.

'You're very quiet, pet.'

Kate put her spoon down and pushed aside the unfinished plate of porridge. 'I'm sorry, I'm not hungry.'

'A slice of toast, how about that?'

She shook her head. 'I heard you both talking,' Kate burst out. 'Don't scold, I know I shouldn't have been listening and I meant to go away only I didn't.'

'You were outside the door listening?'

'Yes.' Kate licked her dry lips. 'Has mistress got another meaning, a bad one?'

Mrs Lennox was using the bottom of the table to roll out pastry and she was giving it all her attention.

'Has it got another meaning?' Kate persisted.

'Yes, Kate, it does have another meaning. Let me get this apple tart in the oven and you can get yourself washed and dressed, then we'll talk about it, if that is what you want.'

'I should know, shouldn't I?'

'It might be better but I won't find it easy to explain.'

'You'll try?'

'Yes, I'll try. Off you go then. Put on a clean blouse and bring the one you had on yesterday down and anything else that needs washing.'

Kate did as she was told and came down looking fresh in her pleated skirt and pale blue blouse with its pretty mother-of-pearl buttons and carrying the clothes for the wash-tub. Mrs Lennox was putting the final touches, fluting the edges before brushing the pastry with egg yolk and popping the tart in the oven.

'We had better sit here and talk or else I'll forget I've something in the oven and it'll be a burnt offering I'll be serving.'

Kate smiled. She knew that she had put Mrs Lennox in a spot, that the woman didn't want to talk about whatever it was. And Kate was sorry, only it was so very important that she learned the truth and she would get that from Mrs Lennox.

'Before I begin, Kate, and whatever you are to hear . . .' She stopped, not having the words to complete what she wanted to say.

'I know what you mean,' Kate said hastily. 'Nothing you tell me will make any difference. I loved my mother and I know she wouldn't have done anything wicked.'

'Neither she would. Your mother was a very fine lady and she would have been quite incapable of doing anything bad. Some of us are called on to make very difficult decisions, Kate, and in my opinion not one of us is in a

14

position to judge another. Faced with a similar situation we don't know what we would have done.'

'Like when you haven't got any money?'

'Like that, Kate. Poverty, real poverty, not knowing where the next penny is coming from, is hard to bear especially if there is a child to feed and clothe.'

By the time she had finished there were beads of perspiration on the woman's brow. Someone else, better educated, might have made a better job of the telling but she had done her best.

'My mummy liked him, I'm sure she did,' Kate said quietly.

'Yes, she would have and he was probably in love with your mother, she was a lovely lady.'

'Why didn't he marry her then? My daddy died when I was a baby.'

'I thought I explained that to you. Mr Hamilton-Harvey will no doubt have a wife and family.'

'He must have liked my mummy best.'

'No question about that.'

Kate was looking thoughtful. 'Mummy was a pretend wife?'

'You could say that.'

'What about his real wife? Would Mrs Hamilton-Harvey have been angry if she'd known?'

'None too pleased,' Mrs Lennox said drily. 'There again the gentry have their own funny ways.'

'Is Mr Hamilton-Harvey gentry?'

'Lass, I don't know anything about him but I would be inclined to say so.'

'Thank you for telling me, Mrs Lennox,' Kate said politely. 'You didn't want to and I made you.'

The woman was close to tears and to cover it up she spoke brusquely.

'You've had no breakfast worth talking about and if there is one thing I cannot abide it is a child who picks at her food.'

'The porridge will be cold now but I'll take a piece of bread and jam, please,' Kate said, anxious to please.

'Bring me the loaf over and I'll cut you a slice. Two slices, I rather fancy a piece of bread and strawberry jam myself.'

Mrs Lennox made fresh tea and they were both eating their bread and jam. 'Kate, don't you have someone? Didn't your mother mention any of her family?'

'She didn't have anyone, I know that.' Kate frowned and tried to think back. 'A long time ago she told me I had an Aunt Sarah, my daddy's sister, but she said there was no—' Kate stopped and screwed up her face trying to remember the expression.

'No coming and going?' Mrs Lennox suggested helpfully.

'Yes I think it was that.'

'Do you know where this Aunt Sarah lives?'

'No.'

'Maybe the address is somewhere in the house. Look, lass, I don't want to interfere with what is none of my business but that bureau in the sitting-room—'

'All the furniture and everything in the house belongs to Mr Hamilton-Harvey, he told me that.'

'I don't doubt that's the case but there could be papers and the like in that bureau that are yours by right. You never know, Kate, your aunt's address could be there.'

'Do you really think so?'

'It's a possibility and you won't know if you don't look.'

'I won't get into trouble if I do?'

'How could you? There's only you and me in the house, I don't see anyone else.'

Kate giggled nervously. Maybe she wasn't alone in the world after all and surely Daddy's sister would give her a home if she made it clear she wouldn't be any bother.

'You think I should look and not wait and ask Mr Hamilton-Harvey?'

'No need to ask permission, Kate. You have every right to your mother's personal property.'

'Even the gifts she got – from him?'

'Even those though I was thinking more of old letters and documents.'

'Will you come and help me look?'

'No, Kate, you should do that yourself and take your time about it.'

'Please come,' Kate pleaded, 'I don't want to do it on my own.'

'Very well.' Mrs Lennox got up slowly, wishing she had taken after her father who had been as thin as a rake instead of her mother who had always had a weight problem and especially so in later years. No doubt about it, the rolls of flesh slowed you down.

Kate knew the key was in the jug on the sideboard and went to get it. Very carefully she turned the key in the lock and brought down the lid of the bureau. The lid had a leather insert with gold markings round the edge. This was where her mother had done her writing. There were little drawers down either side and one at the bottom that stretched the length of the bureau. Kate brought out this one and found it to contain documents tied together and a collection of letters in their envelopes. The one on the very top had Kate gasping. She hadn't expected anything and here was one with her name on it. Wordlessly she showed it to Mrs Lennox who smiled as though she had known there would be something.

'Close the desk, dear, you can have a good look another time.' She gave the thin shoulders a reassuring squeeze. 'Take that up to your bedroom, Kate, whatever your mother has written is for your eyes and your eyes only.'

Kate's were huge in her small face and her heart was beating wildly. She was both excited and afraid.

'On you go, dear,' the woman said kindly. 'I'm down here when you need me, but this is something you have to do yourself.'

Clutching the envelope, Kate went slowly up the stairs and once in her bedroom shut the door and sat down on the bed. Her teddy bear, neglected for years but still occupying a place on the shelf beside her dolls, had slipped and fallen to the floor. Kate went to pick him up. The teddy bear had been a comfort when she was tiny and she felt the need of comfort now. She cuddled the soft toy knowing it was babyish but it didn't matter since nobody could see her. Maybe her mother could see but she would understand.

Kate opened the envelope and withdrew several sheets of notepaper in her mother's small neat handwriting. There was no date. The letter began:

My dearest Kate,

I hadn't realised until now just how difficult this was going to be, to explain in a letter what brought me to do what I did. Yet I must try. I owe it to you, my darling child, and to myself. I have known for quite a long time that I am not to get better, yet I have been more fortunate than some. There have been long periods when I have felt almost my old self and daring to believe that I had been cured. It was then I thought I should write a letter to you just in case I slipped away before you knew about your mother. Had you been older perhaps we could have talked woman to woman. On the other hand had you been older the truth would have been obvious.

When you read this, Kate, I shall have gone to a better place and where I expect to meet my Maker. I know He will be merciful. What I did was wrong and against all the teachings yet, even so, faced with a similar situation I know I would have done the same. Poor Kate, you are puckering your brow. I'm not making much sense am I?

Several times I tried to tell you about Edwin, or your Uncle Edwin as you called him, but I just couldn't. Your eyes would have reproached me. For all his annoying ways, Edwin is a good man and I shudder to think what kind of life we would have had if he hadn't offered a way out. More about that later. Sadly you two never hit it off and I thought it better to accept that, rather than try to alter things and perhaps make matters worse.

Now we come to the story and one could call it that I think. My one and only love was your father, Robert, always remember that, Kate. For the time we were together we were gloriously happy and when you were born we were so proud. We felt our happiness was complete. If anyone tries or dares to suggest that you are illegitimate do not believe them. In the sight of God and not only God but witnesses, Robert and I were declared man and wife or I should say husband and wife. We were married at the end of a dreadful war, they called it the Great War, I often wonder why. Your father had been married before and I knew all about it. Ruth was a nurse and they met in France. As so many did in those dangerous times, they married without really knowing each other. That was the way it was, Kate, it was important to snatch happiness when one was in constant danger, never knowing what another day would bring.

Robert always said I was the love of his life and I know that to be true. Even so, he must have loved Ruth. The hospital where Ruth was working suffered a direct hit and Ruth was among those reported missing believed killed. In the midst of such confusion it was difficult to account for everyone. Miraculously Ruth wasn't in the hospital when it was bombed, she had been in the house of friends nearby. Their home had been badly damaged and the occupants killed. Only Ruth survived though she was at death's door. No one knew who she was and when she did regain consciousness she had no memory, no recall whatsoever. Can you imagine what that must have been like, Kate, not to know who you are or anything about your early life? There is a great deal I don't know or maybe I have forgotten. I think a French family took pity on Ruth and gave her a home when she left hospital. I do know there are cases where the memory never returns and it was feared that this was to be Ruth's fate.

If I were to go into all the details I know this letter would just go on and on and apart from that I tire very easily now and a paragraph or two is all I can manage at a time. Where was I? Ruth? Yes, this is about Ruth, thinking about her makes me so sad, so bitter and yet I shouldn't let myself be bitter.

Ruth did at long last get back her memory and eventually she set about searching for her husband. Apparently the only address she could recall and that vaguely, was Robert's sister, Sarah's. You can just imagine the scene, Kate. Ruth returning to this country to look for her husband only to discover that he had remarried and there was a baby. We were all distraught. Sarah blamed Robert. He should, she said, have made more enquiries about Ruth. Missing believed killed by enemy action was not the same as a death certificate. They had words, Sarah and Robert. Your Aunt Sarah, Kate, is a lot older than Robert, twelve years or thereabout. They were never close, indeed they hardly knew each other because when Sarah left school she was sent to care for her ailing aunt after whom she had been named. This, Robert told me, did not please Sarah but there was no question of her disobeying. In the event things turned out well for your Aunt Sarah. Her aunt died and left her niece the house and a large sum of money or I believe it to be so.

I can't say other than that Ruth behaved very well. She and Robert had an awkward meeting in Sarah's house. Ruth wanted Robert, he was her husband, but she accepted that he needed time to put his affairs in order. In other words, Kate, what was to be done about us.

We were all worried and miserable and Robert, poor darling, was nearly out of his mind. He couldn't eat, he couldn't sleep, his work was suffering. Your father was an engineer, Kate, and held down a responsible position but with so many sick absences his firm eventually paid him off. That was the final blow. After that Robert just went steadily downhill and a few months later he died. That was a dreadful time and I was heartbroken. Then came the shock of finding myself virtually penniless. I was not Robert's legal wife and therefore I had no claim, no widow's pension — nothing. By then, of course, the whole sorry business was out in the open. My marriage was declared null and void. In the eyes of the law Robert had committed bigamy, a serious offence that could have meant a prison sentence. There was no question of that with your father since it was readily accepted that he had believed himself free to marry when we took our vows.

Friends were helpful and sympathetic but I had no family, no immediate family that is. No one to turn to in my time of need. The savings didn't last long — you have to remember we had been living on them. Your father had not been earning a wage before he died.

We, you and I, had to move to a smaller, cheaper rented house and I managed to get a job as a waitress. Out of my wages I had to pay someone to look after you. What I was getting was a pittance and not enough to keep us. Are you wondering why I didn't ask help from your Aunt Sarah? Had it been offered I would have been only too happy to accept but I wouldn't ask, I couldn't bring myself to do that. Her sympathies were entirely with Ruth or so I thought. She blamed her brother and had left him in no doubt that she considered him a fool. As she kept pointing out, he should have had enough sense to make further enquiries. There was no death certificate and without that he had not been free to marry again and he ought to have known that. She blamed me too. Your father had been completely honest with me, Kate, and like him I never thought it possible that Ruth could have survived. If she had surely he would have heard?

And this, my child, is when Edwin Hamilton-Harvey entered my life. The tea room where I worked was clean and pleasant but not the kind of place a man like Edwin would be likely to frequent. He had, he told me, been too early for an appointment and had decided to pass the time by

*having a light refreshment. I served him and he left a
substantial tip (a tip, Kate, is what is left below the plate
for good service) for which I was grateful. I didn't expect to
see him again. However, he came back several times and
always sat at one of my tables. When the tea room was
quiet we would talk and I told him I was a widow with a
baby daughter. It was a shock when he asked me to have
dinner with him and I was all set to refuse. Then I thought
how lovely it would be to have one night out. There was no
shortage of volunteers to look after a baby provided one
could pay. I could ill-afford the money but I excused myself
by believing I deserved one treat.*

*I still remember that evening, the evening that was to
change our lives. I dressed carefully and Edwin compli-
mented me on my appearance. In the high-class restaurant it
was the best table and excellent service. Wine loosens the
tongue especially when one is not used to it. I blame the
wine but there was a great need in me to unburden myself
and Edwin's was a sympathetic ear. He told me what he
lacked in his own life was the warmth of a woman's love
though he stressed that his home life was happy. If I was
prepared to supply what was lacking in his marriage then
he would settle me and my baby in a pleasant house and
give us a comfortable living.*

*I was deeply shocked, Kate, but I was also tempted. The
run-down area where we were living and the hand-to-
mouth existence was depressing. I saw no way out of it,
Kate, other than to accept Edwin's offer. You may not
approve of what I did, indeed I'm sure you don't but before
condemning me remember this, my dear. You never had to
do without. You never went hungry or sat cold and
shivering in an unheated house or attended school in shabby
clothes. Think on that, Kate, and don't judge too harshly.
And now to the final part before I close the envelope for you
to find when I am gone.*

*Edwin, and one cannot blame him, will be unwilling to
take responsibility for you and it will come as a great relief*

to him to learn that you have an aunt on your father's side. There isn't a lot I can tell you about your Aunt Sarah but I do have her address. I found Sarah to be a strange woman and set in her ways as people living alone often are. Yet I do believe she will give you a home if you write and explain that you are alone in the world. I thought long and hard about writing to her myself but came to the conclusion that the letter should come from you. She considers herself to be a good Christian and you, after all, are her only family. Or I believe that to be the case. I can't be sure. She may have married late in life and have her own family. I think not. There are some women who are not the marrying kind. They value their independence too much and I would put your aunt firmly into that category. It could be and I trust this to be the case, that Sarah will be glad of your company.

Be brave, my darling Kate. I pray that you will be blessed with true happiness. Leaving you makes me very, very sad but Robert is waiting and at last we shall be together.

From your loving mother

Aunt Sarah's address is:
  Miss Sarah McPherson
  Oakdene House
  Silverbank
  Near Dundee

I forgot to mention, my darling, that there is no money, maybe a few pounds in my purse but no more. Edwin paid all the accounts and the small monthly allowance I received did not allow me to put anything aside. That did worry me but there was nothing I could do about it. I just prayed that Edwin wouldn't grow tired of me. Had he done so we, you and I, would have managed somehow. A housekeeping position provided I could have you with me! A baby would have been a problem but not a sensible girl of ten. Fortunately it never came to that.

Chapter Three

When she finished reading the letter, Kate was pale and shaken. Closing her eyes she could imagine her mother sitting at the bureau, her head bent over the page. How had she felt writing the words that would only be read when she was gone? Had she been afraid? Kate didn't think so, sad but not afraid. Her daddy was already in heaven and had waited all these years to have her mummy join him.

She would treasure her letter and keep it safe from prying eyes. She didn't know whose prying eyes, but Kate would take no chances. A good hiding place would have to be found. She was quite sure that Mrs Lennox wouldn't look at what was not meant for her eyes. And she didn't think Mr Hamilton-Harvey would bother either. Then again she couldn't be sure about him. He might be curious to know what his pretend wife had written to her daughter. Kate felt guilty calling her mother a pretend wife but it was better than mistress now that she knew what that meant. Mrs Lennox had tried her best not to make mistress sound bad but she hadn't altogether succeeded. Kate had heard the faint disapproval in her voice.

Thinking back to the letter she knew she hadn't understood everything in it. She would read it again at night in bed and read it very slowly. One part did worry her. Hadn't she been taught that if something was wrong then one did not do it, it was as simple as that? Maybe she would have to wait until she was a bit older, then she might understand. Mrs Lennox kept saying that. Instead of worrying about that she should be thinking about what she was going to say in her letter to Aunt Sarah.

Downstairs Mrs Lennox was becoming concerned. Kate had been upstairs for a long time. Had the letter distressed her and was that why she hadn't come down? Going to the foot of the stairs she called up.

'Kate, are you all right?'

'Yes, Mrs Lennox, I'm all right. I'll be down in a minute.'

Kate folded the pages and put them back in the envelope. Where to put it for the time being? Not back in the bureau, that was the last place. The bureau along with everything else belonged to Mr Hamilton-Harvey and he might consider he had a right to see what was in it. Kate's eyes went to the bed. She had been making her own bed for a few months now and tidying her room. Her mother had said that now she was nearly grown-up, she was entitled to her privacy and that meant knocking at her bedroom door and only going in when invited to do so. Kate crossed to the bed and put the precious letter under the pillow. Then she went downstairs.

'There you are, Kate.' There was relief in the woman's voice. The lass didn't look upset, a little pale perhaps but no sign of tears.

'Were you worried, Mrs Lennox?' It was nice to think that someone cared about her.

'Starting to be. You'd been up there a good while.'

'I know.' Her voice dropped to a whisper. 'It was a long, long letter.'

'You'll need to take great care of it. That was a lovely thought, writing you a letter.'

Kate smiled happily. 'It'll be like a keepsake, won't it?'

'Yes, that's exactly what it is.' She paused. 'Could you do with a glass of milk and a biscuit?'

'Yes, please.'

'Be my legs and bring the milk from the cold slab.'

Kate giggled. 'You say some very funny things, Mrs Lennox.'

'Old expressions handed down. Might stop with me, I don't see mine making use of them.'

Kate sat down at the kitchen table, drank some milk and began munching her biscuit. Mrs Lennox was sitting opposite.

'I've got my Aunt Sarah's address. She lives in Silverbank.'

Mrs Lennox looked relieved. 'Now isn't that just grand. Silverbank isn't that far away and it's a bonny wee place. I was there, oh years and years ago when I was just a slip of a girl.' Her body shook with laughter. 'I was just a girl it is true, but I was never a slip of a thing though I would have liked fine to be.'

'Were you always—' Kate stopped herself and hastily drank some milk.

'Was I always fat you were going to say? Not like I am now. Comfortably rounded was how my mother used to describe me and, though I say it myself, I had my chances with the lads. Not all of them go for the skinny type. That said, Kate, think yourself lucky you're slim. Likely you'll take after your mother and she was a fine-looking woman.' She stopped and frowned. 'How did I get on to that? What were we talking about?'

'Silverbank, where my Aunt Sarah lives.'

'So we were and I told you it was a bonny place.'

'How long would it take to get there?'

'Couldn't rightly say, lass. You'd need to get the bus into Dundee then catch another one at the bus station in Lindsay Street. There's no telling how long you'd have to wait between buses. I'd say it would more than likely be an hourly service so if you just miss one you'll have a long while to wait.'

'Mr Hamilton-Harvey will be pleased when I tell him about Aunt Sarah.'

'I've no doubt but, give the man his due, Kate, I don't see him abandoning you altogether.'

'He doesn't like me very much.'

'I'm sure that's not true.'

'It is true, I know it is. I was a nuisance, he just wanted Mummy to himself. My mummy was the same as you, she wouldn't believe me either.' Kate was nearly in tears. 'She got cross when I said it but I still had to keep out of the way.'

'What did you do?' Mrs Lennox was curious. Children were quick to know if they were welcome or not.

Kate pouted. 'Went up to my bedroom and read my books.'

'What about going out to play?'

'My mother didn't like me bringing my school friends to the house.'

'You could have gone to play with them. Not when you were very young,' the woman said hastily, 'but by the time you were nine I would have said you were old enough to have some freedom.'

Kate shook her head. 'My mother said she would just worry all the time I was away.'

'So she would, you being her one and only.' Mrs Lennox could understand the dead woman's reluctance to have Kate mix with the village children. There could be talk about the man whose car was often to be seen beside The Rockery and who didn't leave until the morning. Children were quick to pick up what wasn't meant for their ears as she well knew. That poor soul had only been trying to protect Kate for as long as possible. 'You'll be fine with this Aunt Sarah,' she added.

'She never wrote to my mother.'

'That could go both ways. Maybe your mother didn't write to your Aunt Sarah.'

Kate nodded. 'Maybe they didn't like each other.'

'She could get on with you.'

'Why?'

'You being a relative and your mother only related through marriage.'

'That would make a difference?' Kate was trying to be very grown-up and ask the right questions.

'A big difference I would say.'

'What if Aunt Sarah doesn't like me?'

'She will.'

'But what if she doesn't?' Kate persisted.

'Then you'll have to try and make her like you.'

'How can I do that?'

'You'll find a way. I would advise you, lass, to get a letter off this very day, don't delay. Write what you are going to say on a scrap of paper then copy it out carefully on to notepaper.'

'Yes. There's notepaper and envelopes in the bureau and I saw some stamps.'

'Off you go then and make a start.' She smiled. 'The sooner it's away the sooner you'll get a reply.'

'When Mr Hamilton-Harvey comes back I'll be able to tell him I've written to my Aunt Sarah.' Kate thought she was looking forward to that. She wanted him to know she wasn't alone in the world.

'You might have a reply by then if your aunt decides to answer your letter by return of post.'

'If she says yes—' Kate stopped and her heart began to pound. What would she be like, this strange aunt?

'That'll be you settled, lass, and I'll be getting my walking ticket.'

'Will you mind?'

She seemed to be pondering. 'I'd like fine to be living in a house like this but there's times it's on the quiet side. I didn't think I'd miss all the noise but I do and the clutter. Comes of being more comfortable with what you're used to. Maybe my lot will appreciate me when I get home.'

Kate went through to sit at the bureau and write her letter. It wasn't easy writing to someone you didn't know. After several attempts she screwed the paper into a ball and threw it into the wastepaper basket. She tried again and thought she had it right. She would ask Mrs Lennox before copying it out on the good paper.

Mrs Lennox went through to the sitting-room and sat in the chair favoured by Mr Hamilton-Harvey. She put on her spectacles and took the single page from Kate.

'Will that do?' Kate asked uncertainly.

'Let me read it then I'll tell you. Very neat writing and I like to see that. It'll show your aunt that you have taken care.' She began to read.

> *Dear Aunt Sarah,*
>
> *My mother died, I don't know if you know that. She left me a letter and your address. She said that since my father was your brother you might be kind enough to let me live with you. I wouldn't be in the way and I'm not noisy. I can make my own bed and keep my room tidy and I promise to help in any way I can.*
>
> *Please let me know as soon as possible if I can come.*
> *Yours sincerely,*
> *Your niece Kate McPherson*

'Will that do?' Kate asked anxiously.

'It's perfect.' Mrs Lennox swallowed the lump in her throat and thought to herself that only a hard-hearted woman could say no to that.

On Friday the reply arrived with the first post and was addressed to Miss Kate McPherson. Kate picked up the cream envelope from the mat behind the door. The writing was large with heavy down strokes.

'Open it, love, it'll be the same news whether you open it now or later.'

'I know.' Kate took a deep breath and tearing a little of the flap put her finger inside and opened the envelope. It was very brief, Mrs Lennox could see that from where she was standing.

Kate was beaming. 'I can go and live with her, she says so and I can tell that to Mr Hamilton-Harvey.' Kate read it out aloud:

Dear Kate,
Your letter came as a surprise. I suppose I must offer you a home if you have nowhere else to go. Let me know when to expect you.
Aunt Sarah

'I know what you are thinking, Mrs Lennox, that it isn't very welcoming but she is only being honest. I'm only going to her because I have no choice and she probably thinks she has none either.'

Out of the mouth of babes, Mrs Lennox thought. Kate could be so childlike one minute then come away with something very grown-up. She eased her bulk out of the chair but Kate had got to the window first. A car had stopped outside.

'He's here, Mrs Lennox. That's Mr Hamilton-Harvey getting out of the car.'

'And that's me off to the kitchen.' The woman had become remarkably fleet of foot. 'You answer the door.'

'I don't have to, he has his key.'

'Of course, I wasn't thinking. I'm all of a dither, his kind always get me that way.' The kitchen door closed and a moment later there was the sound of a key turning in the lock. Edwin Hamilton-Harvey stepped inside and saw Kate at the sitting-room door.

'Good morning, Kate, on your own?'

'Mrs Lennox is in the kitchen. Do you want her?'

'Not at present, I came to see you.' He said no more until he was seated and indicated rather irritably that she should be seated too.

Kate sat down.

'I may have a solution to the problem of what to do about you—'

'You won't have to do anything,' Kate interrupted. 'I'm going to live with my Aunt Sarah, she has just written to say so.'

'Indeed!' He seemed annoyed. 'I'm glad to hear that, but had you told me this before it would have saved me a lot of trouble.'

'I'm sorry but I didn't know before today.'

He frowned. 'May I enquire how you did come to know about this aunt since I was of the opinion that you had no one. Indeed I distinctly remember your mother saying so.'

Kate prepared herself for an explanation. 'Aunt Sarah was my father's sister although they didn't know each other very well. That was because she was a lot older. My mother and – and my Aunt Sarah didn't get on very well.'

'I understand, relations were strained.'

She nodded. If that was the same as not getting on and she supposed it was. 'I found my aunt's address in the bureau.'

'Where does this woman live?'

'In Silverbank.'

'Not a great distance.' He was tapping his knee and pondering. 'No doubt there is an adequate bus service but you will have your possessions to remove from The Rockery which rather puts paid to public transport. There must be one or two suitcases about the house and you have my permission to use them, in fact to keep them.'

'Thank you.'

'Get Mrs Lennox to assist you with your packing and we'll arrange a time to have you and your belongings delivered to this aunt of yours.'

'Mr Hamilton-Harvey?'

'Yes?' He smiled, relieved that she had dropped the Uncle Edwin seemingly without effort.

'What were your plans for me?'

'You are curious?'

She nodded. He was very approachable all of a sudden.

'Arrangements were under way to have you cared for in a foster home.'

'A foster home,' she said fearfully.

'Kate, I am not talking about an institution although that could have been your fate. No, my dear, I wouldn't have had that. I was prepared to pay to have you live in a good foster home with other children like yourself. These are kind people, Kate, who do this for a living.'

'I see.'

'Still it isn't to happen and I'm glad about that.'

'Have you got a family, Mr Hamilton-Harvey?' When the words were out she wondered how she had dared and he looked very surprised.

'Yes, Kate, I have a son and a daughter.' She heard the pride in his voice.

'Grown-up family?' She was getting very daring.

'Just about,' he smiled. 'Roderick is almost fourteen and Alice is two years older.'

'That's nice,' she said politely.

'I think so too.' He got up. 'And now, my dear, I must go. As regards Mrs Lennox once you are with your aunt there will be nothing for her to do. She'll know that herself but you can mention it. As for the remuneration I shall deal with that in a day or two.'

'Thank you.'

They were standing facing each other. 'This will probably be the last time I see you, Kate. I hope you settle down but I have no doubt you will.' He was smiling as he held out his hand. She looked at him gravely and then shook his hand.

The packing was almost complete. The clothes, shoes, her clock, her mother's jewellery box, which Mrs Lennox said was hers and she must take it, and other small items were divided between the two suitcases. They were leather and heavy before anything went into them. Her winter nap coat would be carried over her arm and her school books were in her schoolbag.

'Is that the lot, Kate?'

'I think so.'

'Don't you want to take any of your mother's clothes? I mean small things like scarves, gloves and hankies.'

'No. I have the jewellery and the little ornaments from her dressing-table,' Kate said unsteadily, 'that will do.'

'That's fine then, don't go upsetting yourself. We'll shut the cases and that will be that. You can close that bag if it will close.'

'My dolls are in it and teddy's going to be horribly squashed.' She bit her lip. 'I couldn't leave them behind.'

'Of course you couldn't. One day when you have a wee girl of your own she'll play with them.'

'I'm going to cry, Mrs Lennox. I wish, oh, I wish I wish—'

'We all wish things could be different, Kate, but we just have to do our best with the way things are. And don't you dare start crying or you'll set me off. No, love, even if it kills us we are going to part with a smile.'

When the car drew up at the gate they managed the parting without breaking down. The driver was a young man with a ready smile. The cases went in the boot and all the rest on the back seat.

'A lot of luggage to take on holiday,' he laughed.

'I'm not going on holiday, I'm going away for ever.'

Hearing the break in her voice he looked at her quickly. 'You want to sit with me in the front, you'll have more room?'

'Yes, please.'

'In you go then. It'll be nice to have a bonny wee lass to talk to on the journey.'

Kate was wearing a summer dress, her buttercup dress. Her mother had said when they bought it, that the buttercups looked so real she wanted to pick them. Kate had four summer dresses with her but she was wearing her favourite. Mrs Lennox had wondered if she would be warm enough. September could be on the cool side.

The car moved off slowly. Mrs Lennox was standing at the gate and they waved until they were lost to sight. Kate sat with her hands in her lap and stared straight ahead as they drove through the village and out on to the main road. The lad gave her time to recover then he spoke.

'What's your first name?'

'Kate.'

'Mine is Dave. Want to talk about it?'

'Talk about what?'

'Whatever is making you sad. Don't if you don't want to but sometimes it helps talking to a stranger.'

She glanced at him sideways. 'I don't mind telling you. My mother died and that's why I'm sad.'

'I'm sorry, Kate,' he said quietly. 'That's awful for you and tough on your dad.'

'He's dead. He died when I was a baby. I can't be sad about him because I never knew him. But I wish he hadn't died, I wish I'd known him because being told about somebody isn't the same is it?'

'Not the same at all.'

Poor kid, he thought, this was probably her being dumped on some relative. He hoped whoever it was would be good to her.

'Look under the dashboard, Kate, and you'll find a bag of caramels.'

'A dashboard is that what it's called?' She found the bag and took out two caramels. 'Shall I unwrap yours for you?'

'Yes, please. It can be tricky doing that and driving. Don't want to land in the ditch do we?'

'Want me to pop it into your mouth?'

'No, I think I'll manage that.'

'I'm going to live with my Aunt Sarah. She doesn't know me and I won't be very welcome.'

'That I do not believe, anyone would welcome you.'

She shook her head. 'I wrote and asked if I could come and live with her because I had nowhere else to go. She said I could come but it wasn't a very – a very—'

'Welcoming letter,' he finished for her.

'I told her I wouldn't be any trouble.'

'There you are then. I bet she'll give you a big hug when she sees you.'

'She didn't like my mother, they didn't get on.'

'Happens in families, but you can't be blamed for that.'

Kate brightened. 'Maybe we will get to like each other.'

'You're a brave wee soul.'

Kate looked at him seriously. 'I'm not brave, I've got a scary feeling inside. Mr Hamilton-Harvey—'

'He a friend of yours?'

'No. He – he was a friend of my mother's. Is he a friend of yours?'

'Hardly! You must be joking. His kind and mine don't mix. He knows my employer and it was my luck to land for this job. I like driving and I like it even better when I have someone like you to talk to. Especially since you are bonny.'

'Am I really?' She sounded coy but she wanted to know. If Dave thought her pretty then she must be.

'A wee smasher.'

'What does that mean?'

'A lass who takes the eye. Thought you would have known that.'

She shook her head.

'Wolf whistle. Ever heard of a wolf whistle?'

'No.'

'You will when you are a bit older. How old are you?'

'Ten and a half.'

'In a few years you'll forget about that half.'

'How old are you?'

'About twice your age. If you're moving you'll have to go to a new school.'

'Yes,' she said a little fearfully.

'Don't worry about that, one is pretty much like another.'

'That's what Mrs Lennox said.'

'That the old dear who was seeing you off?'

'Yes. She looked after me when my – when my mother got ill.'

He was a kind-hearted lad and he wanted to take her mind off her troubles.

'Bet you were top of the class.'

'Sometimes but not always.'

'Must be great to have brains. Me, I was nearer the bottom of the class.'

'You are only saying that.'

'All right, I was about the middle. You know, not brilliant but not quite a dunce.'

'We'll soon be there,' Kate said in a small voice. 'That road sign we passed said three miles to Silverbank.'

'Saw it too. Once we reach Silverbank we'll have to stop and ask directions to this house. What is it called?'

'Oakdene House.'

'Sounds posh.'

'I don't know whether it is or not.'

'You'll soon find out.'

'Where do you live, Dave?'

'Invergowrie. Now that's a grand wee place.'

Kate was sure he would have a kind mother. Maybe he had sisters and brothers and they were a real family. It must be nice to belong to a big family and never be lonely. She wondered what Aunt Sarah would be like and the funny fluttery feeling was back in her stomach.

'Here we are, Kate, my little princess, just approaching the village and that woman with the shopping bags is bound to be local and probably knows everyone.' He stopped the car, leaned across Kate and wound down the window. 'Excuse me.'

She came over. 'Needing directions?'

'Yes, please. How do we get to Oakdene House?'

'Home of Miss McPherson?'

'Yes,' Kate said.

'Keep on right through the village then take the left turn at the church. There are four houses and the one you want is the last, next to Alf McKenzie's field.'

37

'Thank you very much.'

'You're welcome.'

Dave started up the car. 'Clear directions and believe me you don't always get them. I've seen me being directed miles out of my way.' They turned left at the church and to Dave this was a very posh area: no one was short of a bob or two or they wouldn't be living here.

The houses were solid, stone-built and each was given privacy by the tall trees separating them. Oakdene was the smallest though a good size. The manse belonging to the church at the corner was huge and the other two were large family houses.

Dave had slowed down to a crawl to give Kate a chance to see where she would be living. Kate thought Oakdene House looked very nice. Dave thought the front garden was much too perfect. A garden should be natural looking and this one wasn't. It looked to Dave like a forbidden area and only needed a 'Keep Off' sign like they have in parks. It would be a brave weed that raised its head. Dave grinned thinking of their garden at home. None of them had green fingers and it was left to his poor mother to keep the weeds down and plant a few bulbs. They did, however, have to take turns with the lawn mower and there was a rota on the back door to make sure his brother, his two sisters and himself took their turn. His father was excused since he had a bad back which played up at the mention of outdoor work.

'Here we are,' he said switching off. He got out, went round to open the door for Kate and at that moment the door of the house opened and a tall, thin, straight-backed woman came into view.

Kate's heart sank. The woman looked so forbidding in her plain grey dress. She had read lots of school stories and her Aunt Sarah, it couldn't be anyone else, looked like the worst kind of schoolmistress, the kind that had you shaking in your shoes even when you knew you had done nothing wrong.

Dave's thoughts were running on similar lines. Poor kid, posh district or not, there wasn't likely to be much laughter in Oakdene House.

Chapter Four

The woman stood for a moment or two then came down the gravel path pausing briefly to uproot a weed then leaving it to wither. Kate watched and her first thought was that her Aunt Sarah was in no hurry to meet her niece or she wouldn't be worrying about a weed. Biting her lip she smiled nervously. Her hands felt hot and sticky and she wished she could wipe them on her handkerchief only her handkerchief was in her coat pocket. If she wiped them on her dress they might mark it. Maybe they wouldn't shake hands, wasn't it more likely that she would get a kiss on the cheek? Not a hug as Dave had suggested, she didn't look like someone who hugged. It was awful not to know what was expected of her. Dave had been so kind and helpful. Should she tell her aunt that? If it had been her mother the driver would have been thanked in the charming way she had and invited to have a cup of tea before setting off on the return journey. Somehow Kate didn't see her aunt offering tea. She hadn't shaken her hand or kissed her cheek, she had done nothing but look at her coldly. How severe she appeared but she mustn't make hasty judgements. Some people who looked as soft as marshmallows turned out to have a hard centre. Maybe her Aunt Sarah was the opposite and was hard on the outside and soft inside. The thought wasn't particularly comforting since she didn't believe it.

Dave had the cases out of the car and was opening the

boot to get the canvas bag. He looked up when the woman spoke.

'Young man, you can make yourself useful and take that baggage into the hall.'

It sounded like a command which it was and Kate was both embarrassed and fearful when she saw the glint of anger and the tightening of the lips. Dave was riled. He had been about to suggest that he carry them indoors but to be ordered to do so was a different matter. There had been no if you please either. If it hadn't been for Kate, and the poor kid looked scared to death, he would have left the suitcases where they were and driven off.

'I'll carry one of the cases, Dave,' Kate said quickly.

'Too heavy for you.'

'No, honestly I can manage.' And to show she could, Kate picked up one of the cases and staggered along the path with it. The woman watched but offered no assistance. Dave came behind, a case in his hand and the canvas bag under his arm. Without a word he relieved Kate of her burden and went ahead, through the vestibule and into the hallway. He stacked the cases and the bag against the wall without actually touching it so the besom wouldn't have cause to complain. He remembered Kate's coat was still in the back of the car and hurried down to get it and the schoolbag.

'That do you, missus?' he said cheekily.

'Yes, that will do and it happens to be Miss,' she said looking at him down her thin nose.

'Should have known it would be.' He turned to Kate and she saw the sympathy in the brown eyes. 'Best of luck, Kate,' he said quietly. The poor kid would need it, he thought, having to live with that long streak of misery.

Kate didn't want him to go and she had a sudden urgent need to throw her arms around Dave's neck and beg him not to leave her. If he asked his mother nicely she might let Kate live with them. Then she thought how silly she was, how pathetic. Dave had done the job he was paid to do and he was probably anxious to be on his way.

'Goodbye, Dave, and thank you for being so kind to me.'

Lifting his hand in farewell he nodded coldly to the woman, winked and smiled to Kate and went away whistling. A moment or two later Kate heard the car move off, she turned and watched and then he was gone. It left her feeling bereft, as though her last friend had deserted her.

The woman went to close the outside door then the glass door.

'A very uncouth young man. We'll leave the cases meantime and go into the sitting-room.' Kate followed her aunt and once inside the room her eyes went quickly round it. A big room with a high ceiling, much bigger than the sitting-room in The Rockery and Kate had thought it big. Pictures in heavy gilt frames hung on the walls which were covered in a cream embossed paper. Donkey brown velvet curtains hung at the bay window and in the centre of the window was a stand with a brass pot holding healthy looking ferns.

'Take a good look.'

'It's very nice, Aunt Sarah.' Kate took a further look since it seemed to be expected. The floor was covered with a carpet patterned in shades of brown and fawn with a surround of linoleum also brown and it shone from constant polishing. Kate was astonished at so much brass. There was a high brass fender with a brass poker on one side and firetongs on the other and nearby a brass tidy with another smaller poker and firetongs. The large brass log box was empty but it shone like everything else. And all around was the faint but pleasant smell of furniture polish. Kate wondered if her aunt did all the polishing herself or if she had someone to come in and help.

'Very nice,' Kate repeated. 'You have a lot of brass ornaments.'

'That isn't the half of them.'

They were standing and the pretty summer dress suddenly seemed out of place. She should have worn her dark

43

skirt and blouse. Kate felt ill-at-ease and worst of all she
didn't know what to do with her hands. In the end she put
them behind her back.

'You take after your mother, there isn't much of Robert
there.'

'No.'

The pale eyes were assessing her and Kate didn't think
she was coming off very well.

'Since we have dealt with the formalities we can be
seated, I think.' She sat down carefully on the chair with the
curving wooden arms and the lovely tapestry seat. Kate,
after a small hesitation, sat on the edge of the sofa.

'Thank you for letting me come and live with you, Aunt
Sarah,' she said politely.

The woman inclined her head. 'To be honest and why
should I not be, your letter came as an unpleasant shock.'

'You didn't want me?'

'That is correct.'

'I do understand and it is better to be honest,' Kate said
earnestly, 'I didn't want to come here either.'

'What do you mean?' her aunt said sharply.

The sharpness unnerved Kate. 'All I meant was, I didn't
know you and I wanted to stay in Lamondhill with Mrs
Lennox, only she has a big family and a tiny house and there
wouldn't have been room for me.' She was breathless when
she finished.

'Who is this Mrs Lennox?'

'The lady who looked after me when my mother took
ill.'

'A servant woman,' she said dismissively. 'And tell me –
about this man.'

'You mean Mr Hamilton-Harvey? He didn't want me.'

'Which is what one would expect.' She paused and her
eyes bored into Kate. 'Agreeing to have you here was not an
easy decision to make. At my age I do not welcome an
upheaval in my life. Nevertheless, Kate, I accept that it is my
Christian duty to give you a home. The Lord works in

mysterious ways and it would have been His wish that you should be taken from that sinful house and put into my care.'

Kate couldn't let her go on. She was going to talk about her mother being a mistress and she couldn't bear that. Her eyes were brimming with tears.

'You are not to say anything about my mother,' she said unsteadily. 'She was good and she was kind and—'

'Stop that snivelling. I accept that you had some love for your mother but certainly not respect. Nothing can alter the fact that in the sight of God she was a sinner and in the most shocking way. Bad enough that she should bring that upon herself but you were there. It was a perfectly dreadful upbringing for any child.'

'She didn't have any money, that was why,' Kate said desperately.

'The Lord always provides.'

'Well He didn't. I know it all better than you do. My mother explained it, she explained everything. It wasn't her fault, Aunt Sarah.'

The hand went up silencing Kate. 'Let me get this right. Your mother wrote you a letter, presumably to be opened after her death. Is that so?'

Too late Kate realised what she had done. The colour drained from her face and she shivered feeling the goose pimples on her arms. The letter that was to be her secret, that no one but Mrs Lennox knew about, was no longer a secret and it was all her own fault. She had no one to blame but herself.

'Is it the case? Answer me girl.'

'Yes.'

'As your guardian I must have it.'

'No, I'm sorry but you can't. My mother wrote it to me and no one else has a right to see it.'

'I beg to differ. I have every right. You are in my charge. Calm yourself, girl, this is not a very good beginning, is it?' She looked at her niece coldly.

'I know and I'm very sorry but—'

'But nothing. You will do as you are told.'

Kate knew she had lost and felt a cold anger. Her aunt was hateful. How could her father have had a sister like this? Her mother had always told her that he was a kind and gentle man and she would have known. Kate thought there was nothing nice about this woman. She didn't even look nice with her broad shoulders and thin body. Her neck was scrawny and her face was the colour of – the colour of a suet pudding. Kate felt better when she'd thought of that. It was a good thing thoughts were your own. No one could force you to tell what you were thinking. They might think they had but they couldn't be sure.

'I will show you to your bedroom. Take the canvas bag and whatever else you can manage.'

'Yes.' Kate put her schoolbag on her back and managed the canvas bag and her coat. Her aunt carried one case upstairs then went down and brought up the other one. Kate thought she must be very strong.

'Thank you,' Kate said when the second case was on the floor.

'That outburst of yours was unfortunate but I shall overlook it this time. No doubt you are hungry,' she ended surprisingly.

'Yes, a little bit.'

'Do you like scrambled eggs on toast?'

'Yes, I do.'

She nodded. 'What do you think of your room?'

'It's very nice, Aunt Sarah,' Kate said truthfully. There was a single bed with a pretty pink bedcover and matching curtains at the window. The walls were white making the room look bigger and brighter. The floor was covered in linoleum but there was a rug beside the bed, one beside the dressing-table and another at the window.

'There are coat-hangers in the wardrobe.'

'Thank you, I have some with me. Mrs Lennox thought I should bring them.' Kate opened the bag.

'What on earth have you there?'

'My dolls, my teddy bear and books.'

'Dolls and a teddy bear at your age! Going on eleven, aren't you?'

Kate was surprised that she knew. 'Yes, I'm ten and a half. I don't play with them, I know I'm too old for that but I just like to keep them.'

'That is very childish. The Bible tells us that when we are older we put away childish things.'

Kate wished her aunt would stop quoting the Bible and she didn't think that was what it said at all.

'I want to keep them for always,' Kate said stubbornly.

'Nonsense, you are being silly and selfish. The church will be having a sale-of-work in the near future and those should bring in a few shillings.'

Kate felt as though her whole life was collapsing. 'Please, Aunt Sarah, let me keep them.' Her eyes were pleading.

The woman sighed. 'What a baby you are, Kate, I can see I am going to have trouble with you. However, since it seems to upset you so much we'll leave it for the time being.'

'Thank you.' It was a small reprieve.

'Start on your unpacking and I'll go down and prepare a meal. I'll give you a call when it is ready. The bathroom is next door. Remember to wash your hands before you come to the table.'

'I always do,' Kate said indignantly.

'And don't think I have forgotten the letter because I haven't. Leave it out for me.'

'And if I don't?' Kate said very daringly.

'You will, my dear. It is a big mistake to cross me as you will come to realise. Somehow I don't think you will. And now I'll go and see about the tea.'

Kate opened the wardrobe door then crossed to the chest of drawers. She opened the three drawers and saw that they were neatly lined with paper. The bottom drawer was quite deep and she thought it would be a good place to put the dolls and teddy. She would cover them with a cardigan and Aunt Sarah might forget all about them. Kate had one case empty and had started on the other when the call came. She washed her hands and went downstairs.

'In here, Kate, this is where we dine.'

There was a small fire burning and a half-moon rug was in front of the fireplace. On the mantelpiece was a marble clock and at either end was a pewter jug.

'Sit down.'

Kate brought out the chair and sat down. The scrambled egg looked lovely and fluffy, just the way she liked it. Kate wondered if grace would be said and made no move to start until she was sure. When her aunt picked up her knife and fork, Kate did the same.

'Cooking and baking are what I enjoy most and it is easy to excel at something one likes doing.'

'I can't cook but I would like to learn.' It wasn't true, she hadn't thought about it until this minute but Kate was anxious to please.

'One day, perhaps. You are quite a big girl and should be capable of doing housework. How much help did you give your mother?'

'I didn't do any real housework,' Kate said honestly.

'What do you mean by real housework?'

'I made my bed and kept my room tidy.'

'And that was all?'

'Yes.' Kate bit her lip. 'My mother said there would be plenty of time for that. She wanted me to – to enjoy—' She gulped and stopped.

'Presumably what you are trying to say is enjoy your childhood. That is the sort of silly thing I would have expected from your mother.'

'Why didn't you like her?' Kate finished her scrambled egg and put her knife and fork neatly together on the plate.

'I don't recall having said I disliked her!'

'You never say anything nice about my mother.'

'Because, Kate, I deplore weakness. Your mother couldn't face up to – oh never mind, that is history now and not your concern. Help yourself to what you want. You will find me to be a strict disciplinarian but fair. I am always fair.'

Kate didn't have an answer to that so she nodded her head.

'You, my dear, will get good nourishing food and plenty of it.' She gave a ghost of a smile. 'That should please a growing girl?'

'Yes.' Kate smiled and reached for a scone. Aunt Sarah pushed the butter dish nearer. 'Take jam as well, that is home-made strawberry.'

'Thank you. Strawberry is my favourite jam.' She had been about to say her mother made it then decided not to.

'In return for taking you in and giving you a good home, I shall expect assistance in the house.'

'I said in my letter that I would help.'

'So you did. You and I have a lot to talk about. First let me tell you a little about myself. When my aunt, your Great Aunt Sarah died, she left me this house and the contents. Her money also came to me, not great wealth but enough to keep me in reasonable comfort.'

'That was good of her.'

'No more than I deserved. I have a good head on my shoulders and I had the sense to take professional advice and invest the money wisely.'

Kate was wondering why she had to hear all this.

'Help yourself, you've nothing on your plate.'

'No, thank you, I've had enough.'

'Where was I?' She frowned. 'The house, I was telling you about the house. Over the years I have made some changes and got rid of the pieces of furniture I disliked. Not the brass though. Oh, no, not the brasses, they have always been my pride and joy. There is nothing like brightly shining brass.'

'It does look nice.'

'Mrs Adamson, my cleaning woman, comes to me three mornings a week and one of those mornings is devoted to cleaning and polishing the brasses. At the end of the month I shall inform the woman that two mornings a week will do me. From then on you will take over the cleaning of the brasses.'

'Yes.'

'That will do to begin with, later on you will take over completely from Mrs Adamson. No use paying out good money when you are here. We shall manage everything between us.'

'Yes,' Kate said with a sinking heart.

'We must discuss school. As soon as I had your letter I went to see the headmistress at Westhall School and enrolled you. Miss Wilson knows the reason for you being here. I explained to her as much as I thought she should know.'

Kate wondered how much that would be. Surely she wouldn't have said anything nasty about her mother.

'Up you get. You can help me carry the dishes through to the kitchen,' she said getting up herself. 'Be careful, we don't want breakages, do we?'

'No. I'll be very careful.'

The kitchen was well-fitted and like everywhere else it was tidy and spotlessly clean. Her mother had kept a clean house but not like this. This was too tidy and it made Kate feel uncomfortable. Like visiting a showroom and not having to touch anything.

Aunt Sarah washed the dishes and Kate was given a clean dish towel to dry them. She was slow because she was trying to be extra careful.

'By the look of you you haven't done much of this before.'

'I'm being very, very careful, that's why I'm slow.' Kate put the dried dishes on the scrubbed table.

'This is my everyday china, Kate, and kept in the dresser. The plates and saucers are kept separate and the washed ones put on the bottom, not the top. That way they all get washed regularly and there is no danger of dust gathering. I'm very particular.'

'Where do the cups go?'

'On the hooks and the cutlery box is in the drawer. Cleaning the cutlery, Silvo for that, will be one of your jobs.'

'I've never done that before.'

'You won't learn younger. It would appear you have done very little, but all that will change. Not immediately so don't look so alarmed. You'll get a little time to settle in.'

They returned to the dining-room which was also the living-room. The sitting-room or lounge was used only when there were visitors, Aunt Sarah was telling her. Kate didn't think there would be many visitors. Aunt Sarah went over to sit at one side of the fireplace and indicated that Kate should occupy the chair on the other side.

'May I go upstairs for a book, please?'

'No, you may not. I shall take out my embroidery and do a little of it. Can you sew?'

'At school we used to get one period a week of sewing, but I wasn't very good.'

The woman sighed. 'Something else I see I shall have to teach you. Hands should never be idle – that was something I was taught at an early age. What does that clock say?'

'Quarter past seven.'

'When do you usually go to bed?'

'Half past nine.'

'That is reasonable for your age. Early to bed and early to rise, I'm a great believer in that.'

'On school days I got up at eight o'clock and about half past eight or sometimes nine o'clock on Saturday and Sunday.'

'That won't do here. You will get up at seven o'clock just as I do. After breakfast and before you leave for school you will clear the breakfast table, dry the dishes and make your bed.'

Kate was aghast. 'I'll never waken at seven o'clock.' To Kate it sounded like the middle of the night. Even at eight o'clock she had had difficulty leaving the warm bed.

'There is a spare alarm clock which I shall set for you and if that doesn't waken you then I'll come in and shake you awake.'

Kate stared. Her aunt was a monster. She couldn't stay in this house, she couldn't. She did have a little money. It was what had been in her mother's purse. Mrs Lennox said it wouldn't go far but it was nice to have something for an emergency. Kate thought this was an emergency. When Mr Hamilton-Harvey had spoken about a foster home she had been afraid but maybe it wouldn't be too bad. She wouldn't be alone; there would be other children. She couldn't though because she didn't know how to get in touch with Mr Hamilton-Harvey and he might not want to help her. He had been glad to know she was going to live with her aunt. There was nothing else for it, she would have to stay with Aunt Sarah until she left school and got a job.

'Kate, have you gone deaf? That is twice I have spoken to you and you haven't answered.'

'I–I'm sorry, I was dreaming.'

'Then stop dreaming and pay attention, I don't like talking to myself. I was telling you how I came to get Oakdene House.'

'You did tell me, Aunt Sarah.'

'It is worth repeating since you have been paying so little attention. Your great-aunt left me everything, it was in return for the years I spent looking after her when she was a semi-invalid. I was young, too young for such a demanding task and it went on and on.' She seemed to have forgotten Kate. 'I was a handsome lass, better looking than some of my friends who considered they had made good marriages. I saw them married one after another and raising children while I was tied to a selfish, cantankerous woman who threatened to cut me out of her Will if I left her. But if I stayed then everything she had would become mine. By the time she was taken from this world my youth had gone, I was a middle-aged spinster.'

'That was awful for you.'

The voice made her start, she had forgotten the child. 'What was awful?'

'Missing out on everything and never having any fun.'

'How wrong you are. I didn't miss out, I used to think I had but I was wrong. You see I won in the end. Those I once envied have had a struggle to make ends meet. Jobs were scarce and there was the constant worry of their husband not being able to hold on to his job and all those mouths to feed. No, Kate, I was the lucky one. I am beholden to no one and those same women whom I once envied now envy me. Marriage wasn't the picnic they had expected. I am the winner,' she said triumphantly, 'and history has a habit of repeating itself. You are here for me just as I was there for my Aunt Sarah.'

'It's not the same, you aren't an invalid.' Kate sounded shocked.

'Indeed I am not, I enjoy good health but none of us knows what lies ahead.' She smiled the first real smile Kate had seen. 'It never ceases to surprise me how our lives are mapped out. To have you, Robert's child, here in my house is something I never imagined.'

'You didn't want me,' Kate reminded her.

'Neither I did but I think I have changed my mind. You will give me peace of mind for my old age.'

Kate was looking bewildered.

'Don't you understand, child,' she said slyly, 'I'll have you to look after me.'

'I might get married.' Kate thought of Dave. It would be nice to be married to someone like Dave.

'No, Kate, you won't get married. You will be unable to turn your back on this, just as I was all those years ago. You like this house, don't you?'

'It's very nice.' Kate wondered how often she had used the word nice but she couldn't think of another with the same meaning.

'One day if you do right by me, it will all be yours.

Think about that, Kate, and how lucky you will be not to
have to worry about the future.'

Kate was more worried about the present. Her mother
had found Aunt Sarah strange, she had said so in her letter.
Kate had thought strange just meant peculiar. It seemed
more than that to Kate. There had been a woman in the
village who had gone off her head and Kate wondered if that
was what was happening to her aunt.

She could hardly keep her eyes open and stifled a yawn.

'It is not yet half past nine but if you are tired you have
my permission to go up to bed.'

'I am tired.'

'Take a cup of milk before you go up.'

'No, thank you, I don't want anything,'

'Off you go then, sleep well.'

'Good night, Aunt Sarah.'

'Good night child.'

Her aunt sounded perfectly normal. It was all in her
imagination, she was overtired – that was what her mother
would have said. Maybe living here wouldn't be too bad.
She would just have to do what she was told and it would be
all right.

Kate went wearily upstairs, undressed and put on her
nightdress. She didn't kneel to say prayers. Her mother said
it wasn't necessary, you could pray just as well in bed. God
wouldn't be too worried just so long as you didn't forget to
say your prayers. Folding back the cover on the bed she
slipped between the cool sheets and was asleep almost
immediately. One case was empty, the other only half
unpacked. Her mother's letter was on the dressing-table.

An hour later the woman climbed the stairs to her own
bedroom but before going in she went along to Kate's room
and quietly opened the door. The curtains hadn't been
closed and she tut-tutted at that and the half empty case
on the floor. Then she saw the letter on the dressing-table
addressed to Kate and a satisfied smile crossed her face. The
girl was learning obedience.

Sarah closed the curtains and Kate turned in the bed but she didn't waken. The woman waited a moment or two then with the letter in her hand went out closing the door behind her. Her spectacles were downstairs. She would go into the living-room and read the letter Mildred had thought necessary to write to her daughter. Judging by the thickness it was a long letter. It would make interesting reading.

Chapter Five

After the overnight rain the air was pleasantly fresh. September was drawing to a close and the first of the leaves, lightly touched with red and dull gold, were fluttering to the ground only to be lifted and borne away in the breeze. Kate wished she could have gone to school on her own. She wasn't a small child and was perfectly capable of reporting to the headmistress.

'Lucky for you that you can get home for lunch,' her aunt was saying.

'Yes.'

'Ten minutes should bring you back if you don't dawdle.'

'I won't dawdle.'

'Much better than taking sandwiches, wouldn't you agree?'

'Yes.' They had been through all this before but Kate had the good sense to keep the weariness out of her voice. She was looking smart in her school uniform and picking up her bulging schoolbag put her arms through the straps. Not knowing which of her books would be required she had decided to take the lot. If Westhall School was like her other school she would be able to keep them in her desk.

'I don't approve of schoolbags, they are far too hard on the clothes.'

'Why?'

'Because, silly child, the straps wear the material thin and blazers are not cheap. We must get you one to carry in your hand. An additional expense but no doubt worth it.'

Kate brightened. She was in favour of that. The senior girls carried satchels and she would soon be going to the senior school. She looked at her aunt and wondered why she had thought it necessary to put on her Sunday best to go along to the school. Sarah McPherson was wearing a bottle-green costume with a brooch in the lapel and a bottle-green hat with a small brim and two black feathers. Her shoes, sensible laced shoes, were black as were her handbag and gloves. Kate thought she looked like a grandmother and hoped nobody would think that was her mother. She wished she could think about her mother without wanting to cry. Kate wondered if her Aunt Sarah had ever cried in her whole life. She just couldn't imagine it.

After crossing the deserted playground they went into the school and let the door swing shut. The janitor spotted them and came over.

'Can I help you?' he said pleasantly.

'No, that won't be necessary. I know my way to Miss Wilson's room.'

He was small, round and jolly-looking and Kate smiled hoping it would help to make up for her aunt's brusqueness.

'You a new girl?'

'Yes, I am.'

'Don't worry, you'll be fine here.'

Kate nodded and hurried after her aunt who had stopped at a door further along the corridor.

'Remember, Kate, don't mumble, you have a bad habit of that. Whatever questions you are asked answer clearly.' She used the knuckle of her hand to give a sharp rap.

'Come in.'

Miss Wilson had been sitting behind the desk but she got up and came forward. She was smiling.

'Good morning, Miss McPherson, and good morning, Kate.' They shook hands.

'Do take a seat. Miss McPherson over there.' She indicated a chair. 'Kate, you come nearer to me, it will be easier for us to talk.'

Kate put her schoolbag on the floor then picked it up and opened it. 'That's my Record Card,' she said shyly and handed it over.

'Report Card, Kate,' her aunt corrected.

'No, Kate is quite right in calling it a Record Card. Some of us do. After all it is a record of one's work over the term.' She looked at the card for a few minutes. 'Well done, Kate. This is a very good report and will please Miss Hunt who is to be your teacher.'

Kate blushed at the praise. She thought Miss Wilson was lovely. The headmistress was in her late forties. She was small and slim and the navy dress she wore with its touches of white showed her neat figure to advantage. Her dark brown hair was cut short and had a soft wave and her shoes had quite high heels to give her extra height.

Doris Wilson had been studying the child and thinking how strange it was that members of the same family could be so different. Miss McPherson might well have her good points but she was not the kind of person one took to. This lovely child, recently orphaned, was in need of love and understanding and it was unlikely she would get those from this severe looking woman. On the other hand, she could be quite wrong and perhaps there was a softer side to Miss McPherson. She hoped so. In any case she would keep an eye on Kate, and Miss Hunt could be depended on to do the same. Westhall School was a friendly school, Miss Wilson prided herself on that. She believed that happy children were easier to teach. Poor Kate had just lost her mother and she had the anxious look of a child uncertain and a little afraid as to what lay ahead.

The headmistress had informed Kate's new teacher that Kate McPherson had lost both parents, her father when she was a baby and her mother only very recently. That was all she had said, the rest she would keep to herself. Miss Wilson had been appalled. There had been no necessity, none at all, for Miss McPherson to talk about family matters, especially of that nature. Why had she thought it necessary to do so? Most people would have kept quiet.

'You should know something about my niece, about Kate,' the woman had said. 'She was my brother's child and he died when Kate was a baby.'

'How sad.'

'Yes, indeed, and tragic as it happened.' Her lips pursed disapprovingly and she leaned forward her voice dropping to just above a whisper. 'The details are complicated and I won't go into them. Suffice to say that Kate's mother was an unfit person to be in charge of a child.'

'In what way? Perhaps a mental illness, a breakdown brought about by the shock of her husband's death?' Miss Wilson suggested sympathetically.

'Nothing to do with her health,' Miss McPherson said dismissively. 'Easier to accept had it been that. No, Miss Wilson, Kate's mother took up with a man, a married man and became his mistress.' Her voice rose and hardened. 'A shocking home in which to bring up a child you must agree?'

'Far from ideal,' the headmistress said quietly, 'but none of us can judge another without knowing the full facts.'

'It would take too long—'

'I have no wish to hear them, Miss McPherson. Your niece has lost her mother and the poor child needs our sympathy and understanding.'

'You can rest assured that the girl will get from me what has been lacking in her life. Kate will have the benefit of a proper Christian upbringing. I shall see to that,' Sarah McPherson said grimly.

'Poor child,' Miss Wilson murmured and the woman shot her a sharp look, not quite sure how she should take that.

The headmistress had been talking quietly to Kate, telling her about the school and putting her at ease. Kate thought she was going to be happy in her new school. If only Aunt Sarah was nice like Miss Wilson. It would be easy to love her headmistress but she could never, never love her aunt.

'Any questions, Kate?'

'No, I don't think so but thank you for telling me all that.'

'That's fine then. I'll take you along to Miss Hunt and don't worry, Kate, you'll make friends very quickly.' She got up and so did Kate. Miss McPherson did too but reluctantly. Once Kate had been taken along to this Miss Hunt, she had expected to have another talk. It wasn't to be.

'Thank you for bringing Kate, Miss McPherson,' the younger woman said extending her hand, 'and don't worry, your niece will soon settle down.'

Kate almost laughed with relief when her aunt had gone. She knew she would settle down at school, settling down at Oakdene House was the problem. It would never be home.

'Here we are, Kate, this is to be your classroom.' Miss Wilson gave a light tap, opened the door and they both went in. There had been some noise but it stopped immediately. The children had been told to expect a new girl and here she was. They had a good look.

'Miss Hunt, this is Kate McPherson.'

'Hello, Kate,' the teacher smiled. 'Nervous are you?'

'A little.'

'Everyone is on their first day in a new school.'

'I'll leave Kate's Report Card with you.' Miss Wilson smiled and left the room.

'Girls and boys,' Miss Hunt spoke very clearly, 'this is Kate McPherson, our new girl. I'm sure you are all going to be kind and helpful to her.'

'Yes, Miss,' they chorused.

'Margery, you take Kate beside you.'

'Yes, Miss.' Margery moved along the seat to give Kate plenty of room.

'Put your books in your desk, Kate, and once I give the class something to do I shall go over them with you. Very likely you will be ahead of us in some subjects and behind us in others but we'll soon even things out.'

Miss Hunt wasn't as pretty as Miss Wilson but she was very pleasant. She had a round, happy face but those who thought she might be a soft mark were in for an unpleasant shock. She could be very strict, very strict indeed, when the occasion demanded.

'Open your arithmetic jotters and do the sums I have prepared for you on the blackboard.'

'All of them, Miss?' came a shocked voice, a boy's voice.

'All of them, William. Put your thinking cap on and go over them again when you have finished. And tidy work, remember. Margery, go and sit beside Jean for a few minutes, I'll join Kate.' It was a tight squeeze for Miss Hunt getting in behind the desk but she managed.

Kate waited anxiously as the teacher went over her work.

'Good, Kate, we appear to be at roughly the same stage which is fortunate. From your Report Card I would expect you to be in our top row but that can wait until the next test.' She struggled out of the seat and getting a nod, Margery returned to her own desk.

'Shall I do the sums, Miss Hunt?'

'Yes, Kate, but I shan't expect you to finish them,' she said with a smile.

Twenty minutes later the bell rang for playtime.

'Margery, look after Kate, will you?'

'Yes, Miss.' Margery flushed at the honour of being singled out.

'Have you got a playtime piece?' Margery asked when they were in the playground.

'No, but it doesn't matter,' Kate said hastily.

'My mummy gave me two biscuits, only plain ones,' she said gloomily. 'You can have one.'

'No, thank you.'

'Well, half of one then?' she said, beginning to sound offended.

'All right, thank you.'

'Didn't you take a playtime piece in your other school?'

'Yes, I did.'

'Your mummy just forgot this time?'

Kate felt like crying. 'I haven't got a mother, mine died.'

Margery looked on the verge of tears herself. 'It must be awful not to have a mummy.'

'I haven't got a daddy either but he died when I was just tiny.'

'Who looks after you?' Margery said in a hushed voice.

'My Aunt Sarah.'

'Is she nice?'

Should she be honest or should she tell a little lie?

'No, she isn't,' Kate said going for the truth then immediately wishing she hadn't. Margery would tell everybody and they would all be sorry for her. She didn't want that, she just wanted to be like everybody else.

'Is she cruel?' Margery's eyes were wide.

'No.'

'Just not nice?'

'Strict.'

'Is that all? Lots of grown-ups are strict.'

'That's your first day in your new school, Kate.'

'Yes. Everybody was very kind, Aunt Sarah.'

'Mollycoddling is what I would call it. Not like my day.' She frowned. 'Go and change out of your school things.'

'I was going to, I always did that at home.'

'This is your home now.'

'Yes.'

'Go on then, upstairs with you and don't take all day about it.'

Kate went upstairs and wondered how her aunt could say something and sound cross when someone else could say the same words and it would be funny. She opened the drawer and took out a pink blouse, one that was getting too tight under the arms and her brown pinafore dress out of the wardrobe. It had yellow binding and Kate smiled when she looked in the mirror. She knew what her mother would have said – that the colours screamed at each other. Mrs Lennox had said that her mother had good dress sense. More than could be said for Aunt Sarah. Her clothes were all dull and drab but then she was a dull and drab creature. Kate felt a little afraid of where her thoughts were going. It was wrong to think bad of someone. Her mother had told her that there was good in everyone, only sometimes it was very well hidden.

'There you are. Sit down,' Aunt Sarah said as she poured the tea into the white cups with the thin gold rim. 'Have you homework to do?'

'Not today, but I will have some after this.'

'Then you'll do it before commencing your other duties.'

'What duties, Aunt Sarah?'

'Housework, you will have to do your share of that.'

'Yes.' Kate paused to take a sip of tea and put the cup carefully back on the saucer. 'Aunt Sarah?'

'What is it?'

'May I take a playtime piece with me? One of the girls, she's called Margery, gave me half of her biscuit.'

'You had no right to take it. Don't you get a good breakfast?'

'Yes.'

'That should do you until lunchtime. I do not approve of eating between meals.'

Kate wasn't surprised, the answer was more or less what she had expected.

'Have you finished? Have you had enough to eat?'

'Yes, thank you.'

'You should be grateful for the good food you are getting.'

64

'I am grateful,' Kate said dutifully.

'Then you should try showing it.'

'I don't know how to do that.'

'Then you should know. You should be helpful and obedient at all times.'

'That's what I'm trying to be.'

'I suggest you try a little harder. A girl of your age should be a big help about the house.'

'What do you want me to do?'

'You could start by clearing the table and washing the dishes. In future do it without being told.'

Kate got up and began putting the dirty dishes on the tray. Her aunt was putting away the food and it was she who folded up the tablecloth and put it away in the drawer.

'When you finish that you can clean the cutlery.'

'You want me to wash the spoons and things – but they aren't dirty!'

'No, stupid girl, you clean the cutlery with Silvo. Silvo for silver, Brasso for brasses.'

Kate looked blank.

The woman gave a huge sigh. 'I'm certainly going to have to take you in hand. Finish what you are doing and then I'll show you how silver should be cleaned.'

'I'm ready,' Kate said quietly when the dishes were away.

'Get an old newspaper from the bundle in the cupboard next to the pantry and spread it over the kitchen table.'

Kate did that and waited for further instructions.

'Bring the cutlery from the drawer and put it down. Yes, there will do. Now watch carefully,' she said, picking up the tin of Silvo and giving it a good shake before uncapping it. 'Put a little on the cloth and I mean a little. Give each piece of cutlery a rub with the Silvo then once you have done that take cloth number one and give them a good polish. Look at that, see how bright I get it?'

Kate looked at the shining spoon. 'Yes.'

'Cloth number two is used for the next polish.'

Kate nodded. 'Is that it finished?'

'No, it is not. The next and final stage is for all the cutlery to be washed in hot soapy water then dried and put away.'

Kate thought it was going to take for ever.

'That used to be my Friday morning job. You can do it on Mondays after school and at the end of the week it will be the turn for the brasses. That will take you longer since I have such a lot.' She said it proudly.

'When do I get to play?' Kate said in a small voice.

The eyebrows shot up. 'Play? You are far too old to play. As for school friends you will not bring them here nor will you go to their home. It is quite enough that you have their company during the day. Which reminds me. Did you attend church?'

'Not church but I went to Sunday School.'

'You will attend both.'

'Both?'

'That is what I said. You will accompany me to church then stay behind for the Sunday School.'

'When do I get to do what I want?' Kate burst out.

'You have had far too much of your own way.'

'I didn't get all my own way,' Kate retorted, 'but my mother was fair and you are not. You want to have me working all the time.'

'Work never killed anyone. I should know, I did plenty of it.'

'But it was different for you,' Kate said desperately. 'You were older, you had left school. That was your job instead of going out to work.'

'How dare you talk to me that way. I would never have spoken back to my parents.'

'You aren't my parent, you're only my Aunt Sarah.'

'Yes, I am only your Aunt Sarah. I didn't have to take on the burden of your upbringing but since I have, you will do as you are told and obey me at all times. Have I made myself clear?'

Kate nodded.

'This is all for your own good as you will find out one day.'

The days turned into weeks. Kate had done well in her school test and was moved to the top row. Margery continued to be her friend but she had made other friends as well. Kate had been asked to two birthday parties with proper invitations to be given to parents or in Kate's case, Aunt Sarah. Miss McPherson declined on Kate's behalf. She never knew what her aunt had written but whatever it was there were no more invitations.

Kate looked up from the embroidery her aunt had insisted she do. She had struggled and mastered stem stitch and lazy daisy. The tray cloth, when finished, was to be sold at the next church bazaar. There were two tiny blobs of red from the time she had pricked her finger. No doubt it would be washed but, even so, Kate was quite sure nobody would buy her work.

'We have a visitor coming tomorrow and you, Kate, must hurry home from school.'

Kate was curious. There had been no visitors apart from a few church ladies who had spoken kindly to her. One had slipped her a small bar of chocolate unseen by Aunt Sarah. Kate had enjoyed a playtime piece the next day.

'Who is coming?'

'My sister-in-law.' She said it slyly and kept looking at Kate.

Kate looked puzzled which she was.

'Ruth. Robert, my brother's, widow.'

Ruth! The name of the woman in her mother's letter. Kate knew exactly who this Ruth was but chose to continue to look blank.

'She particularly wants to meet you.'

'Why?'

'Curiosity I suppose. You are Robert's child after all.'

'I don't want to meet her.' She emphasised the 'her'.

'Her?' A raised eyebrow.

'Ruth then.'

'You will address the lady as Mrs McPherson. Ruth was Robert's legal wife.'

'My mother was Mrs McPherson,' Kate said stubbornly.

'Unfortunately for you she wasn't. To avoid the shame I have made no mention to anyone that you are illegitimate. You may not know the meaning of that word but I shall tell you. It means that you were born out of wedlock, your parents were not legally married.'

'They were,' Kate shouted. 'You are telling lies.'

'Watch that tongue of yours, my girl.'

'You hate me and that is why you say these horrible things. Well, I hate you too. I know what my mother said in her letter and you know as well because you forced me to give it to you.' Kate was flushed and angry and not the least bit scared. Later she would be. Just now she felt more than a match for her aunt as she defended her parents.

'You are a wicked, ungrateful girl.'

'You say wicked things about my mother.'

'I speak the truth. Your mother had no strength of character, she was a weak woman who sold herself. Sadly you appear to be taking after her.'

'I hope I do.'

'That is quite enough from you,' Sarah McPherson said in an icy voice. 'Ruth will be here tomorrow afternoon. We will have a meal together and you will be polite. Is that understood?'

Kate kept silent, her lips pressed together.

'There are special institutions for wicked and difficult girls. Is that what you want? It can be arranged, you know.'

Kate shook her head.

'Answer me properly.'

'No, I don't want that,' she whispered.

The voice softened a fraction. 'All that is required of you, Kate, is that you behave yourself. Is that beyond you?'

'No.'

Chapter Six

Kate slept badly. In her dreams she was being chased by a wicked witch with a face that reminded her of Aunt Sarah's. And when she thought she was safe it was only to discover that she was trapped in a room that appeared to have no door and no window. How had she got in? Kate awoke coughing as though she couldn't breathe properly. After a few panic-stricken moments the dream faded and Kate drifted into a sound sleep.

All too soon the strident sound of the alarm clock awoke her and Kate immediately remembered that this was the day she was to meet Ruth or Mrs McPherson as she was expected to address the woman. Kate made up her mind to call her nothing at all. It was possible to do that, possible to have a conversation without once addressing the person by name.

'Sharpish home, Kate!' Aunt Sarah called after her.

'Yes.' Kate went quickly down the path carrying her satchel. Her morning chores were not the trial they used to be. She was into a routine. Her aunt had been right about that. Practice, she was fond of saying, made for perfection. Little was said in the morning, indeed there was very little said at any time. To begin with Kate had tried to tell her aunt about her school day but she hadn't seemed interested. All she wanted to know was whether Kate had finished her homework and was free to do whatever job required to be done. Kate tried to show a willingness, to be helpful but she could never disguise her loathing when it came to cleaning the brasses. There were so many of them, her hands got into a mess and worst of all it was so monotonous.

'No matter how hard I rub my hands just won't clean, Aunt Sarah.'

'Nonsense, plenty of soap and hot water will do the trick. Or you can try using an old pair of gloves.'

'I tried but I was all thumbs.'

'Full of complaints as usual.'

'I'm not, I'm just telling you that's all.'

'You have no cause for complaint.'

'I never said I had.' Kate waited for the usual and it came.

'Many a girl would be glad to change places. Haven't you got a comfortable home?'

'Yes.'

'Good food and plenty of it?'

'Yes,' wearily.

'I clothe you, don't I? And that's a big item. Shoes last you no time.'

'I can't help that, I can't stop my feet growing.'

'Granted. No more than you can stop outgrowing your clothes. This is just to remind you of the debt you owe me.'

As if she needed any reminding – hardly a day went by without some reference to her total dependence on her aunt's generosity or Christian charity.

'Kate, you are not paying attention,' Miss Hunt admonished gently. The girl looked worried as though there was something on her mind.

Kate gave a start. 'I'm sorry, Miss Hunt.'

'We'll take that passage again—'

The school bell rang signalling the end of another school day. For Kate it was too soon. Why did time fly when you didn't want it to? Miss Hunt took her aside.

'Kate are you feeling unwell?'

'No, Miss Hunt, I'm all right.'

'Nothing worrying you?'

Kate shook her head.

'If you should be worried, Kate, tell me about it and I don't mean just about school.'

'It's just – just—' She stopped.

'Just what, Kate?'

Kate swallowed. 'Someone is coming to see me, I have to hurry home and I don't want to see her.' As soon as the words were out Kate felt embarrassed.

'Oh, dear, Kate, I do know the feeling.' She smiled. 'It can be quite awful to have to make conversation and be polite to someone you dislike. There are a few people I'd run a mile from.'

Kate giggled at the thought. She was only saying it but it was nice of her.

'Joking apart, dear, You only have to answer when spoken to and remember too that the person you don't want to meet may be a little apprehensive about meeting you.'

Kate knew that not to be true. Ruth wanted to meet her or so Aunt Sarah had said.

Kate nodded. 'Thank you very much and I must go,' she said anxiously.

'If you are a few minutes late tell Miss McPherson that I kept you.'

She must hurry if she was to avoid a scolding and what was the use of dragging her feet. The hateful Ruth wouldn't disappear. Kate wondered why she thought of the woman as hateful. Her mother was the one who had been wronged and in her letter she hadn't said anything nasty about Ruth. Kate understood a little more now and saw them both, her mother and Ruth, as victims. Deep down she knew what she wished. Kate wished that Ruth had died or that she hadn't regained her memory. It was sinful and quite dreadful to wish another person dead but not getting back her memory wouldn't be so bad. If she hadn't none of this would have happened. Her father wouldn't have died with the worry and her mother might not have taken ill either.

There would have been no Mr Hamilton-Harvey and no Aunt Sarah. If only wishes came true.

The back door was unlocked and Kate let herself in. She didn't make a noise and had intended slipping upstairs to leave her school satchel and change out of her uniform. She might have known she wouldn't get away with it. Aunt Sarah had sharp ears.

'Is that you, Kate?' The sitting-room door opened.

'Yes, it's me,' Kate called back. 'I'll go upstairs and change.'

'No, do that later. Come and meet our guest.'

With a sinking heart Kate left her satchel at the foot of the stairs and went along to the sitting-room. She took a deep breath, pushed the door further open and went in. Both women were sitting in easy chairs. Aunt Sarah remained sitting, the other woman had got to her feet.

'So you are Kate?' She had a lovely smile and took Kate's hand in both of hers.

'Yes, I'm Kate,' she whispered.

'Robert's daughter. Oh, my dear, I have thought of you so often.'

'Have you?'

'Yes, I wondered what you would look like, whether you would resemble Robert in some way.'

'Kate is like her mother,' Aunt Sarah said with a sniff of disapproval, 'and sadly not only in appearance.'

'Your mother was a very lovely young woman when I saw her and you are going to be just as lovely.'

Kate smiled foolishly, not knowing what to say. This wasn't at all what she had expected. Ruth was friendly and best of all she had said something nice about Kate's mother.

'Off you go, Kate, and get changed. Tea will be ready in ten minutes and I do mean ten not fifteen.'

'Yes, Aunt Sarah.'

'Sarah,' Ruth laughed. 'You sound just like our matron, we have to do everything at the double.'

Kate had her hand on the door knob. 'Are you a nurse

Mrs McPherson?' She remembered then that the letter had said that Ruth was a nurse during the war.

'Yes, Kate, I'm a nurse. And please, dear, not Mrs McPherson.'

'I won't allow her to call you Ruth.'

'No, maybe that wouldn't be suitable. Kate can address me as Aunt Ruth if she would like that.'

'I would like that.' It was true she would like to call this very nice woman Aunt Ruth.

She was of medium height and slightly plump with a lovely pink and white complexion. Her dark hair was cut short and was very thick, and she had dark eyes. Her mother had been taller, fair-haired and elegant. The two women in her father's life could not have been more different in appearance.

'Kate?' her aunt said warningly.

'Yes, I'm just going.' She almost bounced up the stairs. After washing her face and hands she changed quickly not wanting to miss any of the conversation. Looking fresh and pretty in a tartan skirt and green jumper Kate ran downstairs and into the dining-room. Aunt Sarah wore a black and white striped blouse with a black skirt. Ruth also wore a black skirt but hers was shorter. The blouse she wore was in a lovely shade of turquoise.

As was her custom when she entertained, Sarah had prepared everything beforehand. The dining-room table had been set ready with a stiffly starched white tablecloth and the best bone china teaset was being used. A dainty napkin and a tea knife were on the three plates. The covering cloth, gossamer thin, had been removed to show a mouth-watering display of tiny sandwiches with the crusts removed. There were fruit scones, plain scones, sponge cakes and triangles of shortbread.

'Sarah, this is absolutely lovely but you shouldn't have gone to all this trouble.'

'No trouble I assure you, I enjoy baking.'

'Lucky you, Kate,' Ruth smiled.

'Kate doesn't appreciate how lucky she is.'

'I'm sure that is not true.'

'I'm afraid it is. One day I intend teaching Kate how to cook but she doesn't show much enthusiasm for anything. All that young lady wants to do is to sit and read, in other words to be idle.'

'I have to confess to being like that when I was Kate's age.'

'That I very much doubt, Ruth. I do insist that Kate does her share of the housework but she doesn't do it at all willingly. Hands should never be idle and at the moment I am trying to teach her simple embroidery.' She raised her eyes as though to show this was well nigh impossible.

Kate said nothing, just helped herself to another scone.

'Sarah, aren't you being just a little hard, perhaps expecting too much? She's only a child.'

'My mother had me working hard before I was Kate's age, then I was sent to look after my ailing aunt. I am not asking Kate to do any more than I did myself.'

There was an awkward silence.

'This sponge is lovely and light, Sarah.'

'It's there for eating, help yourself.'

'No, thank you, I can't afford to put on any more weight. Not like you, Sarah, you've never had that problem.'

'I've never been one for sitting about which probably explains it. Then again it must be the same with you – a nurse is never off her feet.'

Ruth smiled. 'Much as I love my job there are times when I would welcome an easier life.'

'Would you give it up?' What Sarah wanted to know was whether or not her sister-in-law could afford to do so.

'Not entirely. I'm seriously thinking of leaving the hospital and doing home nursing.'

'Private nursing?'

'Yes.'

'What is private nursing, Aunt Ruth?'

'Caring for patients in their own home, Kate.'

'Is there a demand for that?'

'Yes, Sarah, there is. I have already been approached but I won't commit myself just yet,' she smiled. 'I'm a canny Scot and don't rush into anything until I've given it a lot of thought.'

'Elderly folk who can pay?'

'In the main, yes, though I wouldn't say no to a person in need.'

'You could be taken advantage of.'

'I don't think so, I can usually recognise that type.' She turned to Kate. 'There are some who would like to keep their loved ones at home instead of in hospital, but feel unable to do so without a qualified nurse coming in for a few hours.' Ruth looked at the time. 'I hadn't realised it was so late. If I am to catch that bus I really must make a move.'

'Where do you live, Aunt Ruth?'

'In Muirfield just a few miles from Dundee. One day soon you must come and visit me. Your Aunt Sarah won't be persuaded, having to take two buses puts her off. There again perhaps you will get her to change her mind.'

'I'm not likely to do that, Ruth. As you know I am one for my own fireside but you are very welcome to visit me.'

Kate stood with Sarah at the door to say goodbye and Kate was enormously pleased when Ruth kissed her on the cheek.

'I am just so happy to have met you at last and I know we are going to be good friends,' she whispered when Sarah's attention was elsewhere.

Kate smiled happily. They had just met yet it was as though there was a cord between them.

Ruth closed the gate, turned to wave, then walked briskly away.

Sarah tapped Kate on the shoulder. 'Come along, Kate, there is the table to clear and everything to put to rights.'

'Yes.'

'Put on an apron before you begin.'

'I forgot,' Kate said cheerfully as she went to the drawer for a tea apron. 'Aunt Ruth is nice, really, really nice and I never expected her to be.'

'And why was that?' Aunt Sarah asked as she carefully put the cakes into a tin.

'I don't know, I just thought I wouldn't like her.'

'Ruth is a sensible woman. Poor soul she has come through a lot.'

'Like nearly dying and losing her memory.'

'Yes, she was very brave. We have kept in touch since Robert died.'

'She can't have been here for ages or I would have met her.'

'An occasional visit, that is all. She does come to Silverbank fairly regularly to visit friends of hers.'

'She has friends in Silverbank? Whereabout do they live?'

Aunt Sarah's heavy eyebrows shot up the way they did when Kate had said something wrong. 'How should I know? It is no business of mine and most certainly none of yours. I imagine they live at the other end of the village where most of the houses are but then again I could be wrong.'

The thought of having made a new friend and a grown-up one at that made Kate feel much happier. She didn't feel so alone. If she ever needed help Aunt Ruth was there. All the same Kate couldn't help wondering what her mother would have thought about it. Even in her wildest dreams she couldn't have imagined Ruth and her daughter together. Different altogether for her father, if he was looking down from heaven Kate rather thought he would be pleased. He must have loved both of his wives but her mother rather more than Ruth. Kate knew that she was bound to think that. She was also beginning to understand how difficult it must have been for him. As her mother had said in her letter an impossible situation.

Kate had celebrated her eleventh birthday in March and now it was almost Easter. Celebrate was hardly the word. Her birthday had been a day like all the others. There had been no party which was no disappointment since she hadn't expected one. Jollification and Aunt Sarah didn't go together. Kate had, however, hoped for a birthday card or even a small gift but there was neither. The pleasant surprise, on her return from school, was to find a lovely birthday card and a neat package which turned out to be a beautiful jumper in pale blue with white at the neck and the cuffs. They had come from Aunt Ruth along with a note to say the jumper could be exchanged for a different size or colour. There was no need for that. The size was perfect and she loved the colour. Kate ran upstairs to try it on and came down wearing it to let Aunt Sarah see.

'Far too pale a colour. How long will that stay clean?'

'I'll be very careful.'

'Go and take it off, you can keep it for a Sunday.'

Kate went back upstairs and wondered if deep down her aunt wasn't ashamed. There was no excuse about not knowing the date, Kate had reminded her several times. She hadn't wanted to remember.

Christmas was celebrated in a quiet way. There was a special cake with icing and mince pies but no gifts. Kate got no pocket money and she couldn't buy a gift without money. New Year wasn't even mentioned. Strong drink was the root of all evil and New Year was just an excuse to partake too freely of intoxicants.

Maybe she was just getting used to it but Aunt Sarah seemed to be less fault-finding these days and Kate felt happier. She was humming a tune when she went upstairs then her happiness evaporated. It all went sour. Kate had gone to the deep drawer in her bedroom for a cardigan and immediately on opening it knew that something was wrong. There was too much space and then she saw that her dolls and teddy bear had gone. Frantically her eyes searched the room, she looked inside the wardrobe, on top of it and everywhere but there was no sign of them. Shocked and distressed she flew downstairs and into the living-room where her aunt was sitting beside the fire, sewing on her lap.

'Where are they, Aunt Sarah?' Kate demanded. 'What have you done with them?'

'Control that temper of yours at once and don't dare to address me in that fashion.'

Kate tried to calm herself. 'My dolls and my teddy bear, where are they?' Her voice was shaking.

'Where I should have sent them in the first place. I was too soft. A great big girl of over eleven years of age—'

'It doesn't matter how old I am, they are my dolls and my teddy bear. My mother bought them. Where are they?'

'I don't have to answer that but I shall. I imagine them to be in the church hall along with other goods collected for the various stalls. Next year you must give some assistance. You, Kate McPherson, should be pleased that your toys,' she emphasised toys, 'are to be sold in such a good cause. You heard what the minister, Mr McLaren, had to say about the state of the church hall roof and the large sum of money required to put it to right.'

'I don't care about any old roof. I want my dolls and my teddy bear, they weren't yours to give away.'

'You, my girl, have said too much.' There was a spot of angry colour high on each cheek. 'Go up to your room and only come down when you are prepared to apologise.'

'That'll be never,' Kate shouted. 'I hate you and I wish I'd never come to live with you.' Inside her bedroom with the door shut, Kate threw herself on the bed and gave in to a storm of weeping. She wouldn't go down and she would rather die than apologise.

Kate had missed her tea and that was quite awful because she had a healthy appetite. Worn out she must have fallen asleep. The room was quite dark when she opened her eyes and she was lying fully dressed on the bed. Kate shivered, the room was cold. Undressing as quickly as she could Kate put on her nightdress and slipped below the bedclothes. Her feet were freezing and she pulled up her knees so that she could wrap the nightdress around her feet. There was no sound and she didn't know whether her aunt had retired for the night or not. To attempt to see the time on the clock would mean getting out of bed and it didn't seem worth that effort.

In the morning she awoke starving. This was a schoolday and she couldn't miss school. She would have to go downstairs and face whatever had to be faced. In a strange way she was welcoming the confrontation and was not in the least afraid. Her aunt was hateful but her only weapon was her sharp tongue and one got used to that. With her head held high she went downstairs.

'Good morning, Aunt Sarah.'

'You've decided to put in an appearance then?'

'I have to go to school.'

'You do and I am waiting for an apology.'

Kate remained tight-lipped.

'Very well, you haven't heard the last of this, young woman. I could make you go hungry but I won't. Hurry up and eat your breakfast.'

Kate didn't need a second telling. She ate hungrily, did her chores in complete silence and set off for school. At four o'clock there was the usual rush but Kate didn't hurry. What was there to hurry for? she thought gloomily. Then her face brightened. It was Aunt Ruth at the gate and she hurried over. 'Are you waiting for me? Are you going to visit Aunt Sarah?'

'Yes to the first and no to the second,' Ruth laughed. 'This is an overdue visit to my friends Rachel and John and I thought I would leave them for half an hour or so and hopefully catch you at the school gate.'

'I'm so glad.'

'Sarah knows I visit friends but perhaps it would be better to say nothing of our meeting like this.'

'I won't say a word. Don't you like her?'

'Of course I do. Sarah is Sarah and she'll never change. That said I have to confess that a little of her company goes a long way. There, that was unkind of me.'

'No, it wasn't. She's the one who is unkind.' Kate's eyes filled with tears.

'My dear child, what is the matter? Come on, I'll walk part of the way with you and you can tell me what is troubling you.'

'Nothing.'

'You're crying for nothing?'

'You'll think it's nothing.'

'I don't think so. Come on, Kate, out with it. I don't like to see you unhappy.'

Kate swallowed. 'When I came to live with Aunt Sarah I brought my dolls and my teddy bear.'

'Of course you did. We all like to hold on to our possessions, particularly dolls and a well loved teddy.'

'Aunt Sarah said keeping them was babyish but honestly I never played with them I just like to keep them.'

'Then do that and make Sarah understand how much they mean to you.' She smiled. 'Is that really all this is about?'

'She's given them away without telling me.'

'Given them where?'

'To the church sale-of-work.'

'Surely not?'

'It's true. They were in my bedroom and they've gone. When I asked her she told me what she had done. I hate her.'

'No, Kate,' Ruth said severely, 'you do not hate your Aunt Sarah, you do not hate anyone. We can be angry with someone, very, very angry but we must never hate. That is soul-destroying.'

Kate looked down at her feet.

'It was very wrong of your Aunt Sarah to do what she did and I am angry too. When is this sale-of-work or don't you know?'

'This Saturday.'

'Then we must do something about it.'

'No, it won't do any good,' Kate said miserably, 'they will be sold by now.'

'Not necessarily. In fact I think it would be frowned upon to sell anything before the day of the sale. Shall I see what I can do?'

'Would you Aunt Ruth?' Kate brightened.

'Of course.'

'Thank you. Thank you very much but how will you manage it?'

'My friend, Rachel, takes an active part in church affairs and knowing Rachel she'll do her best.'

'Even if you do get them back, Aunt Ruth, she'll just send them to the next sale or something.'

'Not if they are in my house.'

Kate beamed. 'Would you? Would you really?'

'Of course. We'll keep our fingers crossed but I'm nearly certain that your precious dolls and teddy will be safe.' She stopped. 'I must leave you now and get back to Rachel's house.'

'Thank her for me.'

'I will. Cheerio love.'

'Cheerio, Aunt Ruth.' Kate blew her a kiss.

Ruth didn't know when she had been so angry. It was monstrous of Sarah. What harm was there in Kate keeping what was precious to her? Poor child she wasn't very happy living in that house, but then again she could have fared worse. Ruth sighed then cheered up. When she explained to Rachel she would be just as anxious to have Kate's dolls and teddy bear returned. Quietly done there would be no need for Sarah ever to know.

Chapter Seven

To Kate's great joy her dolls and teddy bear were now in Ruth's house for safe-keeping. A few of the church ladies had been disappointed. They had admired the dolls and intended arriving early on the day of the sale to make sure of getting one and putting it away for a birthday or Christmas gift. Although in excellent condition the dolls were still second-hand and the price would have to reflect that. No one paid more for an article bought at a church sale than they would in the shop. Far too many came looking for a bargain. One woman had pleaded for the doll in the pink dress to be put aside for her since she would be unable to arrive early. This was refused by the woman in overall charge. There would be none of that she had said severely.

When the story of Kate's dolls got around and having gained something in the telling, there was a lot of sympathy for Miss McPherson's niece. The poor, orphaned lass should have her dolls and teddy bear returned to her. There wasn't a murmur of dissent.

Sarah McPherson was tireless in her work for the church and was much respected for it. That didn't mean to say she was well liked, she wasn't. No one went out of their way to seek her company. She had a sharp tongue, was very opinionated and clung to old-fashioned values and old-fashioned ways, believing that anything new must of necessity be bad. When Kate arrived at Oakdene House there had been a great deal of talk. The ladies were finding it hard to believe that this very pretty girl could be related to the plain and austere Miss McPherson. Nevertheless credit must be given where credit was due and it did say a lot for a maiden lady set in her ways to take on a child and bring her up.

Kate became a regular churchgoer and afterwards went along to the church hall where the Sunday School was held. Folk began to notice how seldom Kate was seen in the company of her peers. Their concern grew when word got around that Miss McPherson's cleaning woman was no longer working at Oakdene House. The woman's three mornings a week had been reduced to two and before they could be reduced further Mrs Adamson had given in her notice. It was feared that Kate was having to do the work. They felt sorry for the girl but were reluctant to interfere lest it only made matters worse. One woman, rather more concerned for Kate's welfare than the others, had taken her worry to the minister. She could have saved herself the trouble. That gentleman had shaken his head and assured her that Kate was perfectly all right. Miss McPherson might be strict compared to some modern parents but she was a good Christian woman and Kate would come to no harm. The truth was that Miss McPherson was generous to the church and any interference by him might spoil that. He wasn't prepared to risk it. The girl was quiet, not much to say for herself but she appeared to be quite happy.

Each Sunday after the service the minister would take up his stance at the church door and shake the hands of his flock. He made a point of having a kind word for Kate but would immediately spoil it by telling Kate how lucky she was to have such a devoted aunt who looked after her so well. Sarah McPherson would give her tight little smile and nod in agreement. Kate had to smile but hers was forced.

Aunt Sarah had her own seat in church for which she paid an annual fee. The pews were long benches made of shiny wood. Most church members had cushions made to fit but not Sarah McPherson. She did not approve. The hard wooden seat was more appropriate for a church. One went to hear the word of the Lord and not for a comfortable seat.

Going to church every Sunday was no hardship. Kate enjoyed the hymn singing and made an attempt to understand the sermon, but when that failed, and it usually did, she studied the lovely stained-glass windows. Her particular favourite was the one with an angel in each corner as though guarding the central figure. This was a man dressed in a robe and with sandals on his feet. He had the gentlest of smiles and Kate thought it might be Jesus. If not then it had to be one of His disciples. Kate fell to wondering which one – she knew they hadn't all been true friends. One way to find out was to ask Aunt Sarah who was very knowledgeable about the Bible. She was forever quoting bits out of it to Kate. She wouldn't ask though. One day she would find out for herself.

The proposed visit to Ruth's house had been put off again and again. A nurse's hours were difficult and the shifts awkward but, even so, had there been a willingness on Sarah's part something could have been arranged. Ruth had come to the conclusion Kate had reached a long time ago that Sarah, for reasons of her own, didn't want Kate to be away from Oakdene House even for a day. She had, however, made it perfectly clear that Ruth would always be welcome at Silverbank.

Ruth could see the change in Kate. She had become withdrawn, the fight seemingly gone out of Robert's daughter. She was wrong. The fight hadn't gone out of Kate, she had just come to realise the futility of fighting what could only be a losing battle. She thought only of a time when she would be free. Kate was very determined that her Aunt Sarah's fate would not be hers. She wouldn't be bought with the promise of a house and money. Once she was old enough to leave school she would get a job, any job, just so long as it took her away from Oakdene House. Until then since she couldn't change anything she would just accept her lot and make the best of it.

Sarah saw the change and was pleased. The girl had been tamed, her firm handling and patience had paid off. Oakdene House would be in safe hands when the Lord called her.

On one occasion Ruth had voiced her fears.

'Kate is quiet, Sarah, much too quiet. It is almost as though she were shut away in a world of her own.'

'How fanciful you are, Ruth,' Sarah chided. 'Kate has changed but changed for the better. To me there is nothing worse than a chatterbox. Kate was inclined that way but she is getting more sense. I'm pleased to say she is much more biddable and becoming quite a help to me.'

Ruth was far from satisfied and determined to see Kate when possible. It could only be for a short time at the school gate and though it was at great inconvenience she made the effort.

She was there in her serviceable tweed coat and Kate's face brightened when she saw her. Leaving her friends she hurried to where Ruth was standing.

'I thought my eyes must be playing tricks, but it really is you?' Kate laughed.

'As real as I'll ever be.'

'Is this you visiting your friends and coming to see me at the same time? Or are you visiting Aunt Sarah?'

'Wrong on all counts,' she smiled. 'I came to see you. Would you believe a bus came along and I just got on. Come on and we'll walk slowly in the direction of Oakdene House but I won't see Sarah. Better to keep that to an occasional visit.'

Kate nodded.

'Kate, forgive me asking this, and it is none of my business, but does Sarah give you pocket money – what in my day we called a Saturday penny?'

'No.'

'Nothing? Ever?'

'I don't need pocket money, Aunt Ruth. All my needs are taken care of,' she said stiffly.

And there speaketh Sarah, Ruth thought grimly.

'I have no doubt your needs are taken care of but that isn't the same as having a few coppers to spend as you wish. Surely Sarah's friends occasionally slip you something?'

'Sometimes, yes, and that goes in my moneybox. It goes towards buying clothes.'

Ruth took sixpence out of her purse. 'Kate?'

'No, thank you. It's kind of you, Aunt Ruth, but I wouldn't be allowed to spend it.'

Ruth dropped the sixpence into Kate's blazer pocket. 'That is for spending, my child.'

'Six whole pennies,' Kate said flushing with pleasure. 'I feel rich.'

'What will you spend it on?'

'Oh, I won't do that.'

'Yes, you will. Your Aunt Sarah doesn't have to know, this is between us. Heavens! I'm doing little enough for Robert's child. At least let me give you pocket money.' Ruth sounded almost exasperated.

'If Aunt Sarah found out she would call me deceitful.'

'Believe me, I am not encouraging you to be deceitful, though you are right – Sarah would call it that. She probably doesn't realise it, but she is far too strict with you. Children need freedom and you appear to get precious little.'

'Would you buy something for me?' Kate asked hopefully.

'No, I would not. The joy of a few pennies of your own is in the choosing.'

Kate nodded happily then flung her arms round Ruth's neck. 'I love you, Aunt Ruth, and if you ever went away I would want to die.'

Ruth was upset. She had to swallow the lump in her throat before she could speak.

'No, you wouldn't, Kate, and don't talk like that even in jest. Life is very precious and only when we are in danger of losing it do we realise just how precious.'

'I'm sorry. You're saying that because you nearly died.'

Ruth was taken aback. 'Sarah told you that?'

'No, my mother did,' Kate said quietly.

'Your mother spoke to you about me?' Ruth said incredulously.

'She didn't speak about you, it was in her letter. She wrote me a long one and left it in the bureau for me to find when she – when she—'

'Oh, my dear . . .'

'A lot of it I didn't understand then, but I think I do now.' Kate's voice hardened. 'Mrs Lennox, you won't know who that is, but she was a very nice lady who looked after me when my mother took ill and then after she died. She sort of thought there might be a letter and she helped me to look. When we found it she told me it was very special, like a keepsake and that it was only for me to read.'

'Mrs Lennox was right,' Ruth said gently.

'Aunt Sarah didn't think so. It was my own fault, Aunt Ruth, I didn't mean to mention it but I must have or else she wouldn't have known. She made me hand it over. She said she had a right to know what was in it.' Kate gulped.

Ruth was shocked. 'That was wrong of your Aunt Sarah, she had no right to do that and I must say I'm surprised. It would have been different if you had wanted her to read it.'

'I didn't. She gave it back to me though.'

'Did she make any comment – I mean did she say anything about what was in it?'

Kate shook her head. 'There was nothing bad about anyone in the letter. My mother always saw the best in people,' Kate said proudly. 'She did say one thing – that she found my Aunt Sarah strange but then she is, isn't she?'

'Yes, Kate, Sarah is a strange woman.' And I'm only beginning to realise just how strange, she added silently.

'I wouldn't mind you reading my mother's letter, Aunt Ruth.'

'That's sweet of you, dear, but I would never do that.'

'She couldn't help it, you know, I mean doing what she did. That was what she was trying to explain to me in the letter.'

'That was very brave of Mildred.'

'You think so?' Kate looked pleased.

'I do.'

'Aunt Sarah didn't think so. She said both my parents were weak, that neither of them could face up to – up to the – the situation.'

'Which only goes to show how wrong she was to have thought that of Robert and Mildred. The gentlest people are very often the bravest.'

'Why?'

'Not easy to explain.' She was thoughtful. 'Perhaps they feel things more deeply.' Ruth smiled. 'How very like your mother you are.'

'Am I?'

'Yes, in appearance.'

'Am I like her in other ways? I can't ask Aunt Sarah these things but I can ask you.'

'Remember, dear, I didn't know Mildred very well but I would say you are like her in some ways. Perhaps it comes of having lost your parents, but I would say you are stronger than Mildred and possibly Robert too.'

'You are strong, Aunt Ruth.'

'Yes, I believe I am. And, darling, to go back to the letter. Keep it safe. When you take it out and read it, and I'm sure you do, it must bring your mother very close?'

'Yes, it does.' Her voice shook and she swallowed.

'I've kept you and now you are going to be late.'

'Yes and I'll get a most awful raging,' she said cheerfully.

'My fault, I shouldn't have delayed you so long. I can't even take the blame since it is better she doesn't know we meet like this. Will Sarah be very angry?' she said worriedly.

'Very likely, but you don't have to worry about me, Aunt Ruth. Honestly you don't. I used to cry like a baby when she got in a rage with me but that was because no one had ever given me a row before. My mother scolded sometimes but it was nothing and was quickly forgotten.' She gave Ruth her sunny smile and a quick hug then she walked away with that lovely long-legged grace. Then she began to hurry.

Ruth stood and watched and was looking thoughtful as she moved away and walked towards the bus stop. She had been responsible for such a lot of unhappiness. Had it not been for her return from the dead so much heartbreak would have been avoided. Ruth was nothing if not honest with herself. She could have spared herself too. There had been the awful, numbing shock of discovering that Robert, her beloved husband, had remarried believing he was free to do so. She had never got over that and never would. On top of that had been the shameful jealousy tearing at her. That she had been replaced by someone far more beautiful. There had been the dark days when she had wished herself dead, lying there with her friends in the tangled wreck of the hospital. So much suffering and heartbreak would and should have been avoided. Had Robert in the deep recesses of his heart wished that too? Poor gentle Robert to find himself a bigamist and not knowing what to do for the best. Where did his duty lie, with his legal wife or with Mildred and her baby? Meeting Mildred for the first time in Sarah's house, Ruth had been ready to hate her and no doubt Mildred had felt the same way. Yet it hadn't been that way. They had been uncomfortable with each other, which was only to be expected, but they had also known that meeting in different circumstances they could have been friends.

Had she been the selfish one? Others would probably have thought so. Sarah, Robert's sister, had always despised weakness. Her brother was weak, Mildred was weak, that was how she saw them. In her eyes Robert had been stupid, criminally negligent, in not making more enquiries. Ruth didn't believe that. Robert would have done all that he could and no one could have guessed that her memory had gone.

Perhaps if she hadn't loved Robert so much she could have disappeared, made a new life for herself and left a family complete. Poor, poor Robert, how he must have suffered and he would have taken all the blame. He couldn't bear to hurt anyone and someone had to be hurt. Being a trained nurse she should have seen what was happening, recognised the signs of someone in torment, and eased that suffering. She should have gone away, that was all it had needed but she hadn't been prepared to sacrifice her own happiness. Robert had lost the will to live. Had it been the easy way out – just to let go? Or had he thought about it long and hard? Without him there they would make their own way.

No one would ever know what had gone on in his head.

Had she been given this chance to make amends for her selfishness, to watch over and protect Robert's child?

Chapter Eight

Kate was now fourteen and enjoying senior school. She had been sorry to leave Miss Hunt and Miss Wilson who had been so kind to her, but it was exciting to go up to the 'big' school. A bit scary to start with as everything was so strange though not too scary since she was with her friends. Perhaps the most exciting part was leaving the classroom at the end of the lesson and all of them going along to another, where a different teacher would be waiting. After a week or two the novelty of change faded as everyone became used to the new system.

March was living up to its reputation with howling winds, scattered showers and occasional glimpses of the sun. By the middle of the month when better weather was hoped for, winter put in a brief appearance. People got up to find two inches of snow lying that thankfully disappeared by early afternoon in a surprisingly warm sun. Scottish folk accepted the vagaries of the weather and many of the older ones paid heed to the old saying – never to cast a cloot till May be oot.

Both in the cold weather and when rain was a possibility, Kate wore her navy blue trenchcoat. She liked to wear it with the collar turned up but she could only do that when she was out of sight of Oakdene House. Aunt Sarah saw to it that it was down when she left. For Kate it was a very small step in defying her aunt.

The four o'clock bell couldn't come soon enough and Kate was the first in the cloakroom to collect her coat. Aunt Ruth was coming to Oakdene House for afternoon tea. Six months ago she had finally resigned from her hospital job and was enjoying the freedom that gave. Not that she was idle, Ruth was presently employed for three days a week looking after an elderly gentleman who was difficult and demanding. Or so he had been with his daughter, who hated the thought of her father returning to hospital yet knew she couldn't carry on as things were. Nurse Ruth McPherson had proved to be a godsend. She was kindly and efficient and would stand no nonsense. Once her patient realised this he quietened down. If he didn't, he was told, the alternative was hospital and since he'd had a taste of that life and found it not at all to his liking he had no wish to repeat the experience. He became very nearly a model patient.

Kate let herself in with her key. After hanging up her coat on the coatstand, she climbed the stair to freshen up. That done she ran downstairs and into the room where the table was set and Aunt Sarah and Aunt Ruth were in armchairs on either side of the fire. Logs had been added and they crackled sending out sparks but none that reached beyond the brass fender.

'Hello, Kate,' Ruth smiled.

'Hello, Aunt Ruth—'

'Kate, I've turned the gas down but the kettle should be near the boil. Make sure it is, then make the tea.'

Kate didn't need to be told. She knew perfectly well how to make a pot of tea; she'd had plenty of practice.

'Yes, Aunt Sarah,' she said and disappeared into the kitchen.

'Kate is growing up, Sarah, I see quite a difference. She is a young lady now.'

'She's fourteen.'

'I know, that's really half woman and half child isn't it?'

'I was grown-up at fourteen, there was no half child about me at that age.'

'I find that sad, Sarah. Robert did tell me on one occasion that his mother was very strict with you. He thought too much had been put on you at an early age.'

'What did he know about it?' Sarah said harshly. 'It was having him, a late baby that ruined Mother's health. She was never the same after that and most of the work was left to me.'

Ruth looked surprised. 'Yet she sent you to look after her sister-in-law?'

'She didn't, that was my father's doing. There was the promise of money if I was sacrificed.'

Kate had come through from the kitchen and was putting the teapot under the peach-coloured, satin-quilted tea-cosy.

'Did you consider you were sacrificed?'

'At first, of course I did. I *was* sacrificed but in the end I was handsomely rewarded.'

'As long as you think so,' Ruth said doubtfully.

'Come to the table, that's Kate with the tea.'

Ruth got up. 'This looks delicious as usual. Baking isn't my strong point and I excuse myself by saying that I never had the time. Or the inclination one should add.'

Kate smiled. Ruth knew how to butter up Aunt Sarah.

'Kate, I was just saying to Sarah how grown-up you look and all of a sudden.'

'Have I changed?'

'Oh, yes, Kate, you have changed. The lovely long-legged child has become a tall, elegant young lady.'

'Don't fill her head with nonsense, Ruth, and Kate, pay attention to our guest, see that she has something on her plate instead of looking so pleased with yourself.'

'A sandwich, Aunt Ruth? The white bread is ham and the brown has—' She looked at her aunt.

'Dates. I thought it would make a change.'

'Lovely! Thank you, Kate, I'll have a ham sandwich.' She smiled as she lifted one from the plate. Sarah took the brown bread with the dates and Kate, who wished the sandwiches were bigger ate her ham one in two bites and reached for another.

'Kate,' her aunt said reprovingly, 'I never deny you food but I've told you before to eat slowly. Bolting your food is rude as well as being bad for you.'

Kate flushed feeling shame that her table manners were being criticised. She was hungry and a thick piece of bread and jam would have gone down well instead of these dainty little bites.

Ruth saw Kate's discomfort and sympathised. She could remember coming home from school and being absolutely starving and her mother cutting thick slices of new bread.

'Kate's a growing girl, Sarah. Just be thankful she wants to eat. I know mothers of girls just a little older than Kate who are worried sick about their daughters not eating. It isn't lack of appetite, just a fear of getting fat and feeling they won't be attractive to boys.'

'I have no time for the modern young woman, she doesn't seem to have the sense she was born with.'

'Sarah! Sarah! They are not all the same,' Ruth laughed. Then she turned to Kate. 'Have you decided or given any thought to what you want to do when you leave school?'

'No.' She looked to Aunt Sarah who had taken a sip of tea and put down her cup.

'Kate is fourteen and could leave school now but I am allowing her to stay on another year. Isn't that so, Kate?'

'Yes, Aunt Sarah.'

'I'm very glad to hear it but I hope she will stay on until she gets her leaving certificate.' Seeing Sarah's shocked face she went on. 'Kate is bright and think how proud Robert would have been to know his daughter was to get a good chance in life.'

'I have no idea what Robert would have thought.' Sarah's tone of voice made it clear that she didn't care much either. 'Kate will leave school at fifteen, that has been decided. There is nothing to be gained by staying on,' she added.

'Oh, but there is. I must beg to differ. There will be a better paid job and one with prospects at the end of it.'

Sarah looked smug. 'Kate is in the fortunate position of not having to go out and earn her living.'

'But Aunt Sarah, I want to.'

'Be quiet, Kate, I know what is best for you,' her aunt said crushingly.

'Sarah,' Ruth said gently, 'no one would dispute but that you want the best for Kate but the world is changing. This is the thirties, girls want a taste of freedom and some independence before they settle down to marry and have children.'

'Aunt Ruth is right, Aunt Sarah, that is what I want. To get a job, earn money and stand on my own two feet,' Kate said desperately.

'You talk nonsense, be quiet Kate. Ruth, you mean well but with due respect this is none of your business.'

'I feel it is, Sarah, I feel some responsibility. Kate is Robert's child.'

'But not yours.'

'Sadly, no, she's not mine,' Ruth said quietly.

Kate felt a warm glow. Aunt Ruth had said that, she had actually said she was sad because Kate wasn't her child. Just for a moment Kate allowed herself to wonder what it would have been like to have Ruth for her mother. Then she felt guilty, such thoughts were disloyal to her own mother.

Sarah's back was rod straight. 'Ruth, you do not fully understand the situation. I did not ask Kate to come here, she chose to and since I have had the burden of her upbringing the decision concerning her future will be mine.'

Kate's heart sank. It was true, she had asked to come and live at Oakdene House but, even so, surely she should have some say in her own future. Her aunt was talking again in that measured voice that dared anyone to disagree with her. 'That said, Ruth, I accept that you have an interest in her welfare.' She paused for another sip of tea. 'Thanks to my training, Kate is accomplished in household tasks and sadly as I am getting older, I am becoming less able to do all I would like. Have no fear, I shall make Kate a suitable allowance and within reason she shall have free time to follow her own pursuits.'

Kate stared at her aunt not believing a word of it. She would be a maid-of-all-work working for a pittance, and as for following her own pursuits that was laughable. Any time she wanted out with a friend something would stand in the way. Well she wasn't going to let that happen. Somehow she would make her bid for freedom.

'And,' Aunt Sarah continued, 'when my time comes and provided Kate has done her duty by me, she will become a young woman of means.'

Kate broke the silence that followed by quickly talking about school.

'We've got new typewriters and we are learning short-hand and typing.'

'Very useful,' Ruth nodded. 'I often wish I could type. Some office jobs can be very rewarding, Kate, particularly those that offer advancement to the more able.'

'That would mean having very high speeds,' Kate said doubtfully.

'Not always. There are offices where they like to train their own staff. In any case, dear, there are colleges in business studies and, of course, evening classes.'

'Ruth, I am not hurrying you away but if you want your usual bus . . .'

'Oh, goodness, I'm glad you reminded me of the time. I prefer this one since the next, for some unknown reason, isn't very reliable.'

The three of them got up. 'Aunt Sarah, may I go to the bus with Aunt Ruth?'

Sarah hesitated then looked at her coldly. 'Yes, you may.'

Kate smiled, glad that there had been no objections. 'I'll see to clearing the table when I get back.'

'The dishes will be left for you, I shall clear the table.'

They were in the hall and Ruth was being helped on with her coat.

'Thank you, Sarah.' She fastened the buttons and picked up her black velvet beret. 'This one has seen better days,' Ruth smiled as she checked the angle in the gilt-edged mirror above the coatstand, 'but don't we all cling to something we feel happy in?'

'Yes, I would agree with that.'

Kate had her coat on and was carrying her woollen gloves. There was a hole in the finger of one which ought to have been darned and Kate didn't want it to be seen.

'Thank you again, Sarah, that was just delightful.'

'I'm sure you're very welcome.' Her eye caught the small packet on the hall table. 'What is this you've left?'

'Nothing really, just home-made tablet. Not mine I hasten to add,' she said with a smile. 'One of my married friends makes it and sells it in aid of funds for the scout camp. It comes highly recommended.'

'That was kind of you, Ruth, but unnecessary. You don't require to bring anything as I have told you before.'

'I know that, Sarah. The tablet might be too sweet for you, but I'm sure Kate will enjoy it.'

They were outside and the full force of the wind made them catch their breath then laugh.

'The shock of leaving a warm house. I often think that March weather is colder than we get in the depth of winter or maybe it feels that way because we resent it with spring so close.'

'Thanks for trying to help, Aunt Ruth, I do appreciate it.'

'I didn't do very much. I didn't want to offend your Aunt Sarah and as you gathered she was annoyed at me for interfering. That said I thought she was coming round a bit. I mean, Kate, she isn't forcing you to leave school at fourteen and she could.'

'I know and I find that puzzling because she definitely isn't in favour of giving me another year.' Kate paused. 'I think, and I could be wrong, but I have this feeling that she wants to please me in this and then it will be easier to get me to do what she wants.'

'Keep her company in Oakdene House instead of going out to work? Yes, it's possible,' Ruth nodded thoughtfully. 'Would you give that serious consideration if, as she said, you would receive an allowance and, of course, the freedom to spend time with your friends?'

'No, I would not,' Kate said firmly. 'That was just talk for your benefit, she wouldn't keep her word. I have to get away, Aunt Ruth, and when I'm fifteen I'll apply for an office job in Dundee.'

'Kate, that is still a year away and a lot can happen in that time.'

'My position won't alter. Don't think I am against helping Aunt Sarah, I'm not, but there is a happy medium. You know what her main trouble is?'

Ruth smiled at the earnest face. 'No, but you are going to tell me.'

'This sounds daft but I truly believe it to be true. She wants me to have the same dreary kind of life she had and she keeps dangling this carrot before me. That if I do right by her then everything she has becomes mine. And then she adds as though she is terribly proud of it, that I'll come off far better than she did because her careful management of the money, the investments she has made have increased her bank balance substantially.'

'Well done, Sarah,' Ruth said and meant it.

Kate was just a teeny bit annoyed. 'You aren't taking me seriously.'

'Kate, I am taking you very seriously. I do want what is best for you and what would make you happy. What I don't want you to do is to throw away what should rightfully be yours.'

'Don't you understand I don't want her money. She can leave it to a cats' home for all I care.'

'You can say that now but you might not always think that way. In fact talking like that is just silly.'

Kate looked stubborn. 'I won't change, Aunt Ruth,' she said quietly. 'Oakdene is a lovely house but that is all it is. It has never been home to me and it never will. I don't hate Aunt Sarah, we are not allowed to hate, but I have no affection for her, none at all. I did try to get closer to her when I first came but it was obvious to me that she didn't want that.'

'She is a deeply unhappy woman.'

'If she is then she has only herself to blame.'

'Kate, dear, Sarah may have her regrets. Money doesn't make happiness but when it is in short supply, and I do mean short supply, then the road can be hard to travel. You should know that.'

'Meaning my mother and Mr Hamilton-Harvey? See I still remember his name though I'm not so sure I would recognise him if I saw him.' Kate was silent for a few moments then she said slowly, 'However hard life turns out to be I can't imagine myself doing what she did, yet I can understand why Mother did it. It was desperation. She could have coped if I hadn't been there.'

'Yes, that is probably true.'

'You wouldn't have done what she did either, but don't you see we wouldn't have been required to. You are a trained nurse and in time I'll have qualifications. Poor Mother had nothing to offer, no skills and all she could hope to get was a poorly paid job.'

'Mildred was in a worse position than most and to this day I feel some guilt.'

'Why?'

'As Robert's widow the pension came to me.'

'It was legally yours, my mother had no claim and she accepted that.'

'Even so, Kate, her need was greater than mine and once my health was fully restored there was a hospital job waiting for me. I honestly didn't know your mother was in such dire need.'

'She wouldn't ask Aunt Sarah for help,' Kate said

proudly. 'She said that in her letter and she also said that had it been offered she would have swallowed her pride and taken it. If she had, Aunt Ruth, and she must have known Mother's circumstances, there would have been no Mr Hamilton-Harvey. Maybe that is another reason why I could never come to like her.'

'If you don't mind me asking when did you . . .'

'Know that my mother was Mr Hamilton-Harvey's mistress?'

Ruth nodded. 'Only tell me if you want to.'

'I want you to know everything. Mrs Lennox—' She looked at Ruth.

'Yes, I know who you mean.'

'She was a lovely person and I asked her to explain. Some of it is very funny and I have to laugh thinking about it now. I thought a mistress was like a headmistress or the lady of the house. Then things I was hearing weren't making sense. Poor Mrs Lennox did her best to explain. She didn't want me to lose respect for my mother and at the same time she thought I should know.'

'Rather than hear it from someone else?'

'That was probably what she thought.'

'Very good of her, and her not even a relative.'

Kate nodded. 'Once I knew, or thought I knew, what mistress meant I was terribly embarrassed. If I'm honest I was ashamed though I wouldn't admit it to myself. I couldn't use the word mistress. Instead, into myself, I called my mother his pretend wife.'

'Oh, Kate!' Ruth felt a lump in her throat. Poor brave little lass, what a lot she had come through. 'A pretend wife, that was lovely.'

'Aunt Sarah called my mother wicked and that was just so untrue and cruel. She was good and she was kind. No one got hurt, Aunt Ruth. That man's wife didn't mind at all and Mrs Lennox told me that the aristocracy and some of the very rich people have a different way of living.'

'How true, but then it takes all kinds,' Ruth said with an

attempt to lighten things. 'And, precious child, shouldn't we be walking a little faster if I am to get that bus?'

They increased their pace. 'Aunt Ruth?'

'Yes, dear?'

'Once I leave school and if I manage to get a job in Dundee, may I come and live with you?'

'I answered that before, Kate. I said you would always be very welcome, but I'm still hoping something can be worked out to keep you in Sarah's good books.'

'That would make a change, I don't think I have ever been in her good books.' Kate's face hardened. 'I'm not exaggerating but I don't think a day has gone by when I haven't been reminded about how well off I am. And about how much she has done for me. What sickens me most is telling me I am totally dependent when I know that to be a lie.' Kate swallowed and when she continued her voice was shaking. 'Aunt Sarah has been getting money for me, an orphan's allowance, I only found out by accident.'

'I'm aware that there is such an allowance but I never imagined Sarah would apply for it though she was entitled to do so.'

'Which means I am far from being dependent on her charity. Maybe it didn't amount to much but she wasn't losing out. She had that and an unpaid servant. Before I came she had a cleaning lady to pay and she came for three mornings a week. Then she decided there was no good paying out good money when there was me to do the work,' Kate said bitterly.

The bus was in sight when they reached the stop.

'Things will work out, Kate, just keep smiling. I'll see you soon.'

The bus had drawn up. 'You two intend taking this bus?' the conductor said irritably.

'Sorry.' Ruth hurried on to the bus, gave a wave and the bus moved away.

Chapter Nine

Kate was anxious and uneasy about the strange feelings she was having and had haltingly tried to explain them to Aunt Ruth.

'Darling, those strange yearnings or whatever are all part of growing up. Down one moment and up the next, all terribly upsetting, but you'll be thankful to know this awkward stage passes quite quickly.'

Kate smiled. It was reassuring to know she had nothing to worry about. Funny though to feel happy and carefree then a little later to feel sad and weepy and no real cause to feel either.

Sarah was watching the changes in her niece and finding them disturbing. The girl was so moody. Her age could have something to do with it if one could believe the nonsense written these days. Sarah didn't. Kate was difficult and always had been. What alarmed her most was seeing that her scoldings were largely ignored. And it incensed her to see a quirk of a smile playing round Kate's mouth as though she was amused when she should have been ashamed.

Ruth was to blame for this and Sarah would have dearly loved to forbid the visits but was wise enough to know that such an action would be counter-productive. They would meet despite her. The nerve of the woman to treat the girl as though Kate was her own daughter. Sarah didn't analyse her own feelings or she might have recognised jealousy. Instead she fumed at Ruth for encouraging Kate to work hard and get good qualifications when it was a complete waste. If she had anything to do with it, and she had everything to do with it, there would be no office job or any other kind of employment. Without Ruth's interference Kate would have come round and accepted what was best for her. A lucky girl not to have to earn her living – but to get her to understand that.

It was really too bad of her sister-in-law but folk had short memories. They remembered what they wanted to remember and conveniently forgot the rest. Hadn't she taken Ruth's side and ignored Mildred's plight? And this was the thanks she was getting.

Her eyes clouded over, the niggling worry wouldn't go away. Her health was giving Sarah cause for concern. She who had always had an abundance of energy, was finding that she tired easily and although she got through the usual amount of work, it took her longer. Those tonics advertised, that promised so much were less than useless. Sarah didn't have much confidence in doctors either. She would have to be very ill indeed before she sent for one and by that time, Sarah thought grimly, she would probably be beyond help. The woman held firmly to the view that small ailments could be treated successfully by oneself or by one of the medical profession but when it was our time and God called us, then no medicine on earth would alter or delay that. Maybe she was wrong about delay, but if there was no quality to life what was the use of postponing it?

Oakdene was a big house to keep clean and Sarah liked everything just so. The girl was a good worker thanks to the training she had received. Perhaps, Sarah mused, she should have given Kate a little praise now and again but that hadn't been her way. She had given her niece a good home and she should be getting the benefit. It was unthinkable that Sarah should lose her. She needed Kate. Of course she could pay for someone to come in and do the work but how many of those women were satisfactory? Take your eyes away for a few minutes and they would be cutting corners and leaving jobs only half done. Kate knew how she liked things and Oakdene House was her home.

As for Kate she was aware that she wasn't the only one changing. The iron grip was easing, the prison door opening, not wide but sufficiently so to give her some freedom. And she was getting bolder. Kate felt she could afford to be, since there was no danger of her being without a roof over her head. Aunt Ruth had made that clear. She had also made it clear that Kate would be all kinds of a fool if she upset her Aunt Sarah enough to have her rushing off to the solicitor to change her Will.

Kate now had two evenings a week to call her own and most of Saturday. Pocket money had been a thorny point. Her wants were seen to, Aunt Sarah said, so where was the need for pocket money? The cinema was for heathens and Kate was forbidden to enter one. Sweets were bad for the teeth, did she want to ruin hers? Kate held out, she wasn't going to give in and if all else failed she had one card up her sleeve.

'It's just money to have, Aunt Sarah. My friends get pocket money and I want to be like them. Sixpence would do.'

'Would it indeed? Sixpence is a lot of money, my girl, but then you don't know the value of money. You've always got things too easily.'

What things? Kate wondered. Aunt Sarah didn't know that Kate got money from Ruth and she wouldn't get to know either. Kate wanted the chance to save and if she could save sixpence a week it would soon mount up. Some of her school friends got sixpence and others had to do with threepence but extra could be earned by doing jobs about the house. When it came to jobs about the house Kate thought she should be in line for a lot more. Still she wouldn't be greedy. Sixpence would do very nicely and if she got it Kate would consider that a victory.

The victory had been hard won and only came when Kate played her trump card.

'Aunt Sarah, I am not dependent on you.'

'But you are, my girl, totally dependent.'

'No, I am not. You have been receiving an orphan's allowance for me and when you add that to the amount of work I do, I would say you have been very well paid for giving me a home.'

Her colour was high. It was clear that Aunt Sarah was taken aback.

'May I enquire how you came by this information?' she said haughtily.

'By accident.'

'That I do not believe.'

'It happens to be the truth and that is all I am going to say.'

Kate had been in the post office for stamps when she overheard Miss Gibson, the postmistress, saying to her assistant that Miss McPherson's new book had just arrived. Kate, more to be helpful than out of curiosity, had offered to take the book.

'If that is for my aunt I can take it, Miss Gibson?' She had the book in her hand and Kate could see it clearly.

'Thank you, Kate, but I'm afraid you can't. The old one has to be surrendered before the new one is handed over. Rules, dear, we have to abide by them.'

Kate left the post office deep in thought. That had been an orphan's allowance book. Why had her aunt kept that a secret? Was it because she wanted Kate to go on believing that she was dependent on her aunt for everything? Yes, that would be it. Should she tackle her with it? Should she ask her straight out about the allowance? No, better not. Aunt Sarah, being the kind of person she was, might report the postmistress for divulging confidential information. Not that she had but it might look that way. How awful if she got Miss Gibson into trouble and she was such a nice woman. She would keep the information to herself and the day might come when she could put it to good use. Kate felt that time had come.

Sometimes Kate would think back and weep for that ten-year-old arriving at Oakdene House desperately in need of love and tenderness and finding only harshness. She had known it would be difficult to love this severe woman but deep down she had been insecure enough to want to try. And she had tried, tried very hard only there had been no pleasing her aunt. Kate could never do anything right. Even so she had gone on trying because if she hadn't she might have found herself homeless and that was a terrifying thought.

How vulnerable she had been and so easily wounded. Sometimes in bed she would lie gazing up at the ceiling and feel the rage and the overwhelming sense of injustice. A child's early life was supposed to be the happiest time. Her happiest hours had been in the classroom, it had been returning to Oakdene House that brought misery. How she had envied her school friends secure in the love of parents, returning to a home full of fun and laughter. And even when there was trouble or sadness they would be together to face them. Once, it seemed so long ago now, she had known that kind of love with her mother but it hadn't been perfect because Mr Hamilton-Harvey had spoilt it.

Ruth reached the school gate just as the pupils were spilling out. Being tall, Kate was easily spotted and Ruth felt the pride of a mother with an outstandingly pretty daughter. The gawkiness, common to so many schoolgirls, was missing. It had never been there, Kate was one of the lucky ones. The early signs of development were beginning to show but not embarrassingly. A few of her contemporaries, who pretended to be proud of their bosoms, were secretly ashamed, feeling eyes on them, and wishing themselves flat again. Those others who showed absolutely no signs of approaching womanhood were worried in case somehow they were different.

In a few years Robert's daughter would be beautiful just like her mother had been. She was very like Mildred in appearance but that was all. Kate was a fighter and Mildred had never been that, though that wasn't to say she gave in easily. It was harder for the gentle ones who had to make a greater effort. Ruth knew all about that. She had seen it in her husband. Yet between Robert and Mildred they had produced a daughter with a strength of will she recognised as similar to her own. Kate should have been her daughter. She practically was.

Seeing Ruth, Kate waved, said something to her friends, then quickly walked over to join her aunt at the gate.

'Hello, darling.'

'Hello, Aunt Ruth.'

They hugged each other and Kate wondered if Ruth knew just how much that show of affection meant to her. For so long she had been starved of warmth and affection, receiving none from her Aunt Sarah. Did that stem from her aunt's early life? Had she, too, been denied love, the right of every child, and was the lack of it responsible for the sour person she was today? If it was then Kate thought it incredibly sad. Perhaps Aunt Sarah deserved some pity. She had asked Ruth.

'What was Aunt Sarah like when she was a young girl?'

'I don't know, I didn't know her then.'

'Did she ever have a boyfriend?'

'Not to my knowledge. And if you are thinking she was unattractive you would be wrong. She was good-looking in a severe sort of way.'

'Meaning she scared them away?'

'No, I wouldn't say that,' Ruth smiled.

'She once told me she'd been a handsome lass.'

'Did she? Well I suppose that was true. There might have been someone in her life that none of us knew anything about.'

'Sad, isn't it?'

'Depends, Kate. We sometimes have choices and if we choose the wrong one then we have no one to blame but ourself.'

'Hello, Kate.'

Kate turned. 'Hello,' she said abruptly and blushed furiously.

Ruth watched in amusement as the boy, tall and gangling with the hunched look of a boy not yet at ease with his height, went on ahead to join another friend.

'Kate, you've gone all rosy red.'

'Oh, don't, Aunt Ruth, I feel such a fool when I blush.'

'Well you shouldn't.'

'You don't blush,' Kate said accusingly.

'I'm too old but I'd be thrilled to bits if a tall, dark, handsome young man smiled at me. Oh, darling, blushing is nothing to be miserable about, you are a lovely girl and it is only natural that boys are attracted to you.'

'David Morton isn't attracted to me, he's not the least interested,' Kate said scornfully. 'Goodness he'll be leaving school shortly and going on to university, to medical school. He's going to be a doctor. All the girls like him and he doesn't just smile at me.'

Ruth said no more, she was trying to remember how she felt at that age. Not as easily embarrassed as Kate, that was for sure.

They had almost reached Oakdene House. 'What am I to do, Aunt Ruth?' Kate said despairingly. 'No matter what she says I am not staying in Oakdene House to be a servant which is what I would be. I mean it, Aunt Ruth, I have to get away so please, please, don't you try to make me change my mind.'

'I would never do anything to make you unhappy, dear. What I worry about is you being impulsive. Things are not as they once were, you are able to meet your friends. That is a beginning and there could be other concessions. Sarah needs you and is making no secret of the fact.'

'How wrong you are. She does *not* need me,' Kate said almost angrily. 'All she has to do is to engage a woman to come in and do the work. She can afford to and makes no secret of that either.'

'In her own way she could be fond of you, Kate.'

'Don't give me that, Aunt Ruth,' Kate said grimly, 'she never has a kind word for me and I'm the one who should know.'

Ruth sighed. She wasn't going to win this one.

Kate closed the gate behind them and they walked along the path. Sarah had just opened the door.

'Good afternoon, Sarah, it's a lovely fresh day and we enjoyed the walk.'

'Come in, Ruth, and Kate, I've washing on the line, take them in before they become too dry for ironing. I'll see to making the tea and then we can sit down.'

Kate went through the house to the back garden collecting a clothes basket on the way. She unpegged the clothes and rolled them up the way she had been taught. The ironing would be her job once Aunt Ruth had gone.

Sarah was saying very little and Ruth was doing her best to fill in the silences that were becoming awkward. She could be amusing about her patients but in the nicest way. Kate laughed but Sarah could barely summon up a smile. In an attempt to ease the strained atmosphere which she couldn't understand Kate started talking about school. She had done well in her school work and especially in commercial subjects. In the near future she could start applying for jobs. Aunt Sarah stared at her coldly and Kate lapsed into silence. Buttering a scone she thought back to the schoolday. They had received instructions on how to apply for a job. The letter, they were told, was the first thing a prospective employer would see and if it was to create a favourable impression then it must be neatly written, be grammatically correct and contain the information required. Only then could they hope to be asked to attend an interview. And for that, appearance was all important.

Quiet colours, a dark skirt and a freshly laundered white blouse would be seen as businesslike. Only when asked to do so should you sit down. Keep your back straight and don't cross your legs. Feet should be together. Answer questions in a quiet confident manner. 'Remember all that,' Miss Mollison, teacher of commercial subjects, had said, 'and you will have an excellent chance of securing the job. Good luck, all of you.'

'We'll need it,' a disgruntled voice said, once Miss Mollison had departed and the keen ones were back practising their typing on the now much used Underwood type-writers.

Maeve Baxter gave a mock yawn. 'All that for ten bob a week, office juniors that's all we'll be.'

Kate giggled. 'What did you expect?'

'A lot more,' auburn-haired Veronica drawled, 'I expect to be someone's secretary before long—'

'Girls,' Miss Mollison was back, 'don't you have homes to go to? Cover those typewriters then take yourselves off.'

Kate's mind jerked back to the present. She had put it off long enough. Sitting here at the table with Aunt Ruth for support would be better than another unsuccessful attempt to talk over her future with Aunt Sarah.

'Miss Mollison was being very helpful—'

'Ruth, a piece of sponge?'

'Thank you, Sarah,' Ruth took a piece and put it on her plate, 'Kate, what were you saying about Miss Mollison?'

Kate gave her a grateful look. 'She was telling us how to conduct ourselves at an interview, what to wear and just being generally helpful.' She picked up her cup and drank some tea.

'I would have expected girls of fifteen to know how to conduct themselves.'

'They do, of course they do, but she meant when we were being interviewed.' Kate glanced at Ruth but she was taking a great interest in the sponge she was cutting up into ridiculously small pieces. She didn't raise her eyes.

Taking a deep breath, Kate spoke slowly and clearly and said the words she had prepared. 'Aunt Sarah, I know this won't please you, but I am quite determined to make my own way in life. I am going to apply for an office job.'

'I forbid it.'

'You can't keep me here against my will. Aunt Sarah, I don't want to quarrel with you—'

'Your place is here, Kate. You know it and I know it. Ruth is to blame for filling your head with nonsense.'

'No, Sarah, I am not to blame. Kate is a very mature fifteen-year-old and you, I think, can take the credit for that. Kate knows her own mind. This is her life and she has the right to live it her way.'

'Without guidance?'

Ruth smiled. 'Forgive me, Sarah, but I think Kate has had more than enough guidance. What she needs now is to spread her wings.'

'After all I have done for her is this the way I am to be treated?'

'Sarah, look at it another way. You were a lonely woman before Kate came into your life. She has given you companionship and it is you who ought to be grateful. Sarah, Kate has given you so much can't you find it in your heart to be generous now?'

Sarah looked at Ruth with eyes as cold as glass. 'I have made you welcome in my house but not after today—'

'Please, Aunt Sarah, don't quarrel with Aunt Ruth. She only wants to help me.'

'I am the one who knows what is best for you.'

'No, Aunt Sarah,' Kate said her voice shaking, 'you are only thinking of yourself. And,' she gave a short laugh, 'it's funny you know, it really is. Anyone listening to this would believe that you cared for me and it is so far from the truth. You don't care whether I go or stay, all you care about is getting your own way. You can't bear to be thwarted.'

'Ruth, get your coat and go.'

'I'm sorry, Sarah.'

'It is too late for that.'

Ruth looked distressed. 'I'm sorry it has ended this way, Sarah, we are sisters-in-law and families should keep in touch.'

'Keeping in touch is one thing, interfering with what is none of your business is quite another. Kate has led a sheltered life. If she is not here with me where is she going to live and more to the point how is she going to survive on a few shillings a week?'

'I'm going to stay with Aunt Ruth,' Kate said quietly.

'If you do, and listen to me very carefully, Kate, if you leave my house and take up residence with Ruth then that is the end. I shall be in touch with my solicitor for the purpose of making a new Will. Your loss will be someone else's gain.'

'I don't want your money, I've told you that before.'

'You have. I didn't believe you then and I don't believe you now. You, Kate, will come to rue the day you crossed your Aunt Sarah.'

'I am going but surely we don't need to quarrel about it. You won't have any difficulty getting a woman to do the cleaning and I'm prepared to stay here until you do.' Unless you take too long about it, Kate added silently.

For Sarah it was a glimmer of hope. Ruth could expect no further invitations and without her bad influence Kate would come to her senses. She was smart enough to know that it could be a bleak future without her Aunt Sarah's money.

Chapter Ten

It was a calm, still day and the lovely month of June was drawing to an end. For some it was also the last days of school. Along with the excitement of leaving came a little sadness. The girls were standing in the classroom solemnly shaking hands with each other as though it was the parting of the ways when in all probability they would be bumping into one another in the village Main Street or even more likely in the Rainbow Café. The owners of the café were very accommodating to the young of Silverbank and only when a table was required would they be politely told to remove themselves. Nobody objected or made a fuss – how could they when for the cost of a glass of lemonade they had been occupying a table for an hour or sometimes longer? Many of the locals wondered at the tolerance of the owners. Where was the profit? they said, in allowing the young ones to sit so long, not to mention the noise they made? Others said where was the loss when no one wanted the table?

On a Monday and Wednesday evening Kate would join her friends in the Rainbow Café or perhaps just stroll along the street with them. Aunt Sarah, had she known, would have been horrified. Well brought up young girls did not parade the streets – only those who were not as good as they should be would make an exhibition of themselves.

Tonight Kate was joined by Moira McGlashan. She could have had a special friend, a best friend, but Kate hadn't wanted that. There was no reason for her to feel shame yet that is what she would have felt. How to explain that she was seldom available after school? And worse to know that everyone was feeling sorry for her. The freedom she was now enjoying had been a hard fought fight.

'Have you started applying for jobs, Kate?'

'Not yet. How about you?'

Moira McGlashan was a plain girl until she smiled, then her whole face lit up to show perfect, even white teeth.

'I'm applying for everything even those I haven't a hope of getting. And it pays, Kate, I've two interviews. One on Thursday and another on Friday.'

'That's great.'

'I thought so too,' she said gloomily, 'until I discovered at least half a dozen others have got an interview as well.'

'You've as good a chance as any of them.'

'I suppose I could look at it that way.' She paused. 'Time you were getting your skates on, I mean there aren't too many vacancies in this area.'

'I know but it's a bit complicated. You see I promised my Aunt Sarah I wouldn't start applying until she is fixed up with a cleaning woman.'

'You mean a char?'

'My aunt calls them cleaning women.'

'She might take her time about it. It is true, isn't it, that she wants to keep you at home?'

'Yes.' Kate wondered how everybody seemed to know her business.

'If you don't make the effort, Kate, you'll never get away.'

'Oh, I will but it might take a little time.'

'By then you'll be lucky if you get a job, in an office I mean.'

'Not if I go to Dundee.'

Moira's mouth fell open. 'How could you manage that? The bus service is pathetic.'

'I wouldn't be travelling, I'd stay with my Aunt Ruth.'

'Does she live in Dundee?'

'Not exactly in Dundee, just a little bit out.'

'That your Aunt Ruth who comes to meet you sometimes?'

'Yes.'

'She looks nice.'

'She is nice,' Kate smiled.

'Kate McPherson, you're a dark horse, do you know
that.'

'It hasn't happened yet, Moira.'

'Then make sure it does.'

'Kate was well liked and there was a lot of sympathy for
her but not to her face. They knew she wouldn't want that.
The girls didn't know Miss McPherson but they had heard
their mothers talking about the proud, sharp-tongued woman who was bringing up her niece. Moira didn't feel in the
least sorry for Kate. How could she feel sorry for someone
who looked like Kate? The beautiful people in this world
had it made for them. They could be assured of having doors
opened for them. They didn't have to try hard to attract
boys, their problem and it was one Moira wouldn't mind
coping with, would be warding them off.

'I wouldn't mind working in Dundee, there's plenty to
see and plenty to do but the buses are hopeless. My dad
agrees it is an absolute disgrace and that it shouldn't be
beyond the powers-that-be to organise a through service
instead of all the bother and waste of time changing buses.'

'Why doesn't your dad do something about it?'

'Don't think he hasn't tried, he has but he hasn't got that
kind of authority. Mind you, he brings up the matter at
every opportunity and gets some support but not enough.'
She shrugged. 'That's how it is.' They walked along the
street and stopped outside the café. 'I've the price of a coffee,
sorry it doesn't stretch to two.'

'I've sevenpence.'

'Great, we'll go in then.'

'You did say coffee?'

'I did.'

'Do you like it?'

'Not 'specially but I feel I've gone beyond lemonade.'

'Expect I have too. I'm going to try and acquire a taste for coffee. Tea is better—'

'But so ordinary and we are just about to go out into the big, big world.'

They giggled and went over to join the others at the table.

'Aunt Sarah, you are making no attempt to get a cleaning woman.'

'It isn't easy, I am not having just anyone in my house.'

'But are you even trying?'

'Don't you start to question me,' Sarah said sharply.

'I'm not,' Kate said wearily, 'I only want you to be settled with someone so that I can start applying for office jobs.'

'What kind of life would that be for you, stuck in an office all day pounding a machine?'

'I don't know but I want the chance to find out.'

'You don't know when you are well off.'

'I don't think I am well off, in fact I know I'm not. Oakdene House may be home to you, Aunt Sarah, but it is – is—'

'Is what?'

'It's like a prison to me,' Kate burst out and before she lost her nerve went on, 'I've never had any freedom and I couldn't even have a best friend because I didn't want anyone to know that I wasn't allowed out.'

'You exaggerate.'

'No, I don't.' Kate knew she was getting desperate. She couldn't spend the rest of her life washing, ironing, dusting, cleaning brasses, yet that was what loomed ahead if she didn't show some spunk. How easy to be caught in this web, the fight slowly but surely being knocked out of her. The years would go on, Aunt Sarah would then be old and in genuine need of being looked after. The longer she put it off the more difficult it was going to be to get away.

'You can't keep me here against my will.'

'I'm your guardian.'

'That doesn't give you the right to ruin my life. I'm young and I want some fun. Maybe you were different when you were young—'

'I had some sense.'

Kate took a deep, shaky breath. 'The last thing I want, Aunt Sarah, is to quarrel with you but I am determined to make my own way. I'm going to live with Aunt Ruth and get a job in Dundee.'

Her aunt finished the row she was knitting then put the work down and looked at Kate for a long time without speaking. She had never had much colour in her face but whatever was there had gone. Her face was grey and her eyes at their coldest.

'If you leave here, Kate, and make your home with Ruth, then that will be the end as far as I'm concerned. You will never enter my door again and when I'm gone not a penny piece will go to you.'

'I *am* leaving you,' Kate said quietly, 'my mind is made up and I shan't change it. That isn't to say I wouldn't like to come and visit you occasionally but if I am not to be made welcome then I won't trouble you. As for your money I have told you before and I'll tell you again that I don't want it.'

'You want it all right. You are no fool, Kate, money and security mean a lot to you, how could they not? You have your mother as an example of how low—'

'I think we can leave my mother out of this,' Kate interrupted furiously. 'You made no effort to help her in her time of need though you could easily have done so. In a way, Aunt Sarah, you were to blame for forcing her to – to—'

'No one, no matter the circumstances, is forced to take that road.'

'Maybe I agree with you but neither of us has, or is likely to be placed in such a position.'

'No amount of hardship would have forced me to do as she did.' She gave a shiver of revulsion. Then seeing Kate's face she said suspiciously, 'Why are you smiling?'

Kate was smiling at the thought of anyone wanting Aunt Sarah as their mistress. 'I didn't think I was,' she said innocently.

'Mildred was a weak woman—'

'Don't say any more, I won't listen. I've had enough, I'm going up to bed.'

'Is the kitchen tidy?'

Kate gave a short, brittle laugh. 'I don't know, Aunt Sarah, and what's more I don't care. Good night.' She turned away and missed the shocked look on her aunt's face.

Kate wasn't so brave as she sounded and when she reached her bedroom she was shaking with nerves. How had she dared to say so much? And had it been too much? What if she was shown the door before she had a chance to contact Aunt Ruth? Kate had never been in Aunt Ruth's house, all she had was the address. For some time Aunt Ruth had been talking about having the phone put in to make it easier for her patients or their families to contact her. Still that was no help since it hadn't happened. It would have to be a letter and she must get it in the post as soon as possible. Kate sat on the bed chewing her thumbnail as she wondered what to do for the best. Then a glimmer of an idea presented itself. Aunt Sarah slept soundly and made plenty of noise about it. Why not wait until she was asleep then creep downstairs for stationery and a stamp? It wouldn't take her long to write a few lines to Aunt Ruth and beg her help.

Passing her aunt's room on her way back there had been a particularly loud snore and Kate froze in case she awoke. She listened for a few moments then moved swiftly and silently to her own room and closed the door softly.

So far so good. She began her letter.

Dearest Aunt Ruth,

Things have come to a head and are as bad as they could be. I had a horrible row with Aunt Sarah. It started when I accused her of not trying to get a cleaning woman and it just got worse after that. Maybe I said too much. Please, please Aunt Ruth, come to Silverbank, not Oakdene House, you would never get over the door. I'll wait where we usually meet and around the same time. I'm so sorry if this puts you about but I need you desperately.

My love,

Kate

With the letter now written, Kate felt calmer but she would only fully relax when it was in the post and getting out to post it could be awkward. Could she risk leaving the house now and running to the postbox? If she did the letter would be lifted in the early morning. Worth risking? Yes, it was. She would be as quiet as a mouse. The back door made a bit of noise when opening it but not the front if she was terribly careful. Or she didn't remember it doing so. Everything was so much louder in the night, Kate hadn't thought of that until now. With the letter in her hand, Kate crept downstairs and after a nerve-racking few minutes she was outside. The moon was out showing the way clearly and after turning the corner the sight of the red pillarbox was like seeing a friend. She gave the letter into its safe-keeping and ran all the way back to Oakdene House. The door was off the snib and she pushed it open. As she did, Kate heard the flushing of the toilet and stopped dead, not daring to breathe. Would Aunt Sarah come downstairs or would she just return to her bedroom? It seemed an age before the bathroom door opened and then, blessed relief, the bedroom door gave a click and Kate breathed more easily. Not daring to move until she thought it safe to do so, the wait seemed endless, but finally she was ready to risk it. Carrying her shoes she climbed the stairs quickly and silently and let herself into her own bedroom. In less than five minutes she was undressed, had put on her nightdress and was under the bedclothes. Not to sleep, she was too wide awake for that. Instead she went over the day's happenings and congratulated herself on taking this first important step. Very soon now she would be away from Oakdene House and out of Aunt Sarah's clutches.

'Oh, Aunt Ruth!' Kate was almost weeping with relief when she saw her aunt and wordlessly Ruth took the girl in her arms and held her until she recovered. 'I'm sorry,' she whispered.

'Nothing to apologise for.'

'It was the relief you see. I was so afraid you wouldn't manage.'

'Well, here I am as you can see.' Ruth used her no-nonsense voice. 'We need to talk and that is best over a cup of coffee. Where do you suggest we go and don't dare suggest the Rainbow Café.'

'I wasn't going to though there is nothing wrong with it.' Kate gave a shaky laugh. 'The Bluebird Tearoom in Duncan Street would be more to your liking.'

'Then that's where we'll go.'

The tearoom was popular with the matrons of Silverbank though some thought it rather expensive. Two middle-aged sisters ran the tearoom. The home-baking was delicious, the premises spotless and if the service was slow, which it usually was, not many complained since it gave them plenty of time for a chat.

They hadn't been long seated when the waitress, dressed in a snowy white apron over a dark dress, came for their order.

'I'm having coffee. You prefer tea, don't you, Kate?'

'I'd rather have coffee, please.' Ruth smiled to the waitress. 'Two coffees, one black and one white.'

'Biscuits or shall I bring the cakestand?'

'The cakestand, I think.'

The girl went away. 'Have you acquired a taste for coffee?'

'No, I haven't but I think I ought to like it. Don't you?'

'It is nice to be able to take anything but given a choice it is better to ask for what you prefer.' Ruth put her elbows on the table and leaned forward. 'Begin at the beginning, Kate, and tell me exactly what has been going on.'

Kate did and in the middle of the telling the coffee and the cakestand with scones, fruit loaf and sponges arrived. 'What should I do, Aunt Ruth?'

'Clearly you are very unhappy where you are, I hadn't realised it was so bad.'

'It is bad.'

'Then, of course, you must leave Oakdene House and make your home with me. As long as you understand that Sarah does mean what she says. You will be cut off without the proverbial penny.' She raised her eyebrows.

Kate was impatient. 'I've told you, Aunt Ruth, I don't care. All I want to do is get away from her, get a job and start earning money.'

'No hurry for that. And don't run away with the idea that since Dundee is a big city there will be no scarcity of vacancies. Of course there will be some and a great many girls after them.'

Kate's face fell.

'No need to look so glum. Half of those seeking employ-ment have no skills, you have something to offer which puts you in a much stronger position.'

Kate cheered up. 'I've often wondered about your house, Aunt Ruth, and isn't it awful that I've never been there?'

'I couldn't agree more but Sarah made it impossible.' Ruth frowned in concentration and absentmindedly reached for a piece of buttered fruit loaf before noticing that Kate had nothing on her plate. 'Do help yourself and don't wait to be told. How is that coffee?'

'Not bad.'

'Add more sugar.'

'I think I will.'

'Let us be practical about this. Have you cases to hold your belongings?'

'Yes, I do. I have those I arrived with. They belonged to Mr Hamilton-Harvey but he said to keep them. Two cases and a canvas bag. The canvas bag may have belonged to my mother, I don't know.'

'Good. And you can get hold of them?'

'Yes, I know where they are. In the cupboard at the top of the stairs.'

'Fine, you go ahead and see to the packing of the cases and I'll arrange transport. Malcolm, an acquaintance of mine, drives a van, it doesn't belong to him but I imagine he could work something out. I'll ask him.'

'You will come with him,' Kate said anxiously.

'I'll have to. He'll need directions though I daresay he could manage on his own. Don't worry, dear, I'll be there. You, Kate, will have to share the back of the van with your luggage and whatever else is there. I'll remember to take a cushion and you shouldn't be too uncomfortable.'

'I don't mind, honestly.'

Kate informed her aunt of the arrangements but she made no comment. Not an unnecessary word had been spoken but Kate didn't let that bother her. She had too much to think about.

On Thursday morning Kate reminded Sarah that she would be leaving the house in the afternoon.

'I did not require to be reminded.'

Kate bit her lip. 'Is there anything you would like me to do before I go?'

'No.'

'I do wish you had done something about a cleaning woman.'

'That has nothing to do with you.'

'I know it hasn't, I only meant I wish you had. There is

such a lot of work.' She was in no danger of changing her mind and the thought struck her that perhaps her aunt thought she might. In which case she would not have required a cleaning woman. Aunt Sarah had failed. Kate was going no matter what.

After a silent lunch prepared by Aunt Sarah, the woman got up from the table, climbed the stairs and reappeared in her coat and hat. She stood at the living-room door, tall and straight.

'What time are you to be leaving my house?'

'About three o'clock.'

'Then I shall return after that.'

Kate watched her go and felt a fleeting sense of loss. It could have been all so different. There was pity in her heart for this friendless woman. Did she see happiness as a weakness and to be despised? How very sad if that were so.

Kate had the cases and the canvas bag just inside the front door. She would take them out when she saw the van. In the meantime she would take up her position at the front window and watch for them coming. When the shabby van did splutter to a halt at the gate, Kate was putting her luggage on the front step.

Malcolm was a small, middle-aged man with a ready smile and a broken front tooth.

'This the lot?'

'Yes, leave something for me to carry.'

'No need, you see to the locking of the door.' He went away whistling tunelessly to where Ruth was waiting to give a hand.

Kate double-locked the door as usual then put the keys through the letterbox. She would have no further need of them. Kate didn't turn for that final look, instead she hurried down the path, tears blinding her. She was being stupid, stupid, stupid. Why tears when all she wanted was to get away? Ruth, as though she understood didn't say a word. She got into the passenger seat and left Malcolm to settle Kate in the back.

She was more composed now. 'Sit yourself down on the cushion and if you lean against the side there'll be room, or just about, to stretch your legs.'

'I'm fine, thank you.'

A longer journey in such cramped conditions would have been extremely uncomfortable but Kate had too much on her mind to worry about her comfort. Did Aunt Ruth really want her or was she just being kind? Kate thought that might be it. She didn't want to be a nuisance and maybe that was what she was.

Muirfield turned out to be a smaller village than Silverbank. It was attractive in a quaint sort of way. Changes would pass it by because the inhabitants liked things the way they had always been. Those who would have it different could move to the town, the village wasn't going to change for them.

'My home, Kate, and now it is yours as well,' Ruth said softly.

'I can't even begin to tell you how grateful I am.'

'Then don't. The word grateful is forbidden in this house. Why should one person, and in particular a young person, have to show gratitude for what another takes for granted?'

'Everybody isn't kind-hearted like you.'

'Ah, Malcolm, there you are. Many, many thanks. You'll find an envelope on the seat.'

'No need for that,' he said gruffly. 'You didn't seek payment when you looked after the wife.'

'That was different. Off you go before your boss discovers what you are doing in his time.'

'Och, he's no' that bad.' Even so he hurried away.

'What a nice, obliging man.'

'Oh, my dear, the world is full of them.'

Ashgrove Cottage was one of a straggle of little houses, roses round the door type of places. Each well-spaced cottage had its small front garden and a large area of ground to the back. Part of which was taken up with a drying green and the four posts required to hold the washing line. There was a cellar where coal and logs were stored and another that might hold a mangle or just be used for storage. Nearly everyone grew their own vegetables and some had berry bushes. In the season blackcurrants and raspberries would be picked and the jelly pan would be in constant use until enough jars were filled to last the whole year.

Kate stepped into her new home. The passageway was narrow but the cream paint on the walls made it seem wider.

'We'll leave the cases where they are for the time being and after a cup of tea we can get organised. This is very modest compared with Oakdene House.'

'This is a home, Aunt Ruth.'

'Bless you, darling, it certainly isn't a showpiece,' she laughed. 'I'm not the least bit houseproud, Kate, not too many nurses are. Don't ask me why.'

'Maybe they realise that there are more important things in life than polishing.'

'Meaning all that brass?'

'It was the job I hated most.'

'I must remember when you get married to let everyone know that brass ornaments will not be well received.'

Kate laughed delightedly. 'This is what I am going to enjoy most of all. Someone to laugh with and share a joke.' She gulped. 'I really do feel sorry for Aunt Sarah. I could never bring myself to like her and I did try.'

'I know you did and for your peace of mind and mine, you have to stop thinking about Sarah. She is well able to look after herself and, as my mother used to say, there are those who do not need our sympathy because they enjoy being miserable.' She walked ahead and opened a door. 'This is to be your bedroom.'

Kate went in. 'This is lovely.'

'It is nothing of the kind. It is functional as is mine. Do whatever you wish, alter the position of the furniture, I shan't mind in the least.'

'I wouldn't do that.' Kate looked about her.

The eiderdown on the bed was in a deep shade of blue and the curtains at the window were also blue but a washed-out blue as though faded from the sun.

'I've given you two pillows but if one is what you are used to, put the spare on top of the wardrobe and I'll get around to removing it. Sorry about the carpet, I hadn't realised how worn it is in parts. We'll go together and choose another.'

'No, you mustn't put yourself to that expense,' Kate protested.

'Darling, stop concerning yourself with money. We won't starve, I have been very lucky with two of my patients, my former patients, remembering me in their Will. Wasn't that sweet of them? I did worry in case the relatives were upset but they assured me they weren't. I'm far from wealthy, just reasonably comfortably off if I can put it that way.'

'I'm glad for your sake, but I am not going to be a burden to you.'

Ruth was frowning. 'Kate, you really don't understand, do you? I want you here and I wished you could have come before but I didn't want to spoil anything for you.'

'You really and truly want me?'

'Kate, you are Robert's child and I just wish that you could have been mine. You were the child I should have had.'

'I – I—'

'You can't say anything to that. Mildred adored you and you loved your mother dearly. Mind you,' she said with a laugh, 'it was lucky you had Mildred for a mother and not me. You have her to thank for your looks. Be grateful for that – I can use grateful in this context – but be careful.'

'Why? Be careful of what?'

'Admirers, my dear, you'll have more than your share of those which means you have to choose carefully.'

Kate was looking embarrassed.

'Early days, I know, but just a timely warning.' She

moved away. 'Next door is the bathroom. The cistern makes a dreadful noise and the plumber has been back and forward but so far hasn't been able to discover the source of the trouble. Next to that is my bedroom. Have a quick peep in,' she said opening the door. 'Not very tidy but I have an excellent excuse today since my niece-cum-adopted-daughter was expected. She shut the door. 'As you can see the cottage is small and compact. There is a good-sized scullery off the living-room. Edna, my neigh-bour, calls hers a kitchenette because she considers scullery to be an ugly word.'

'So it is.'

'From now on my scullery is a kitchenette.' They were in the living-room and the open door showed a new-looking gas cooker, a double sink, a small table and numerous wall cupboards.

Kate thought the living-room very inviting in a shabby, homely way. There was a dining-room table and chairs set into the bay window. Against one wall was a dresser with drawers below. The top half had glass doors and was where the china was kept. Much of it was blue and white and in the very popular Willow pattern. There was a sofa, slightly sagging in the middle, with a crocheted cover over the back and removable armcovers. On a low table was a newspaper carelessly folded and Kate was shocked to feel her fingers itching to fold it properly. Aunt Sarah's training would not be so easily forgotten and she must take care not to offend Aunt Ruth by tidying up. A book was open and face down on the coffee table. Surprisingly there was an ashtray and a packet of twenty Capstan.

'I didn't know you smoked, Aunt Ruth.'

'You are discovering my bad habits. I'm not a heavy smoker and it is no great hardship to do without. Just occasionally I feel the need to unwind and a cigarette helps. Take my advice and don't start. Incidentally I forgot to mention there is a bicycle in the shed. Use it whenever you wish. I seldom cycle now that we have a bus every half hour.

This,' she said going ahead, 'is the sitting-room. It doesn't get much sun and I'm very rarely in it.'

Kate grinned. 'It has a Sunday look about it.'

'Shades of Oakdene House?'

'A wee bit.'

'The heavy furniture came from my mother's house. I didn't want it and then again I couldn't see all her prized possessions going to the auction rooms. One day, Kate, we'll get rid of the lot and start again. It'll be fun doing it together.'

'Maybe you should hang on to them. Aunt Sarah had a visit from a church member, her Elder I think he was, and he advised her not to let anything go, that one day they could be worth a great deal.'

'What had Sarah to say to that?'

'Only that she was well aware of their value.'

'Tea, I'm parched, we'll get that kettle on.'

'Let me help.'

'Cups and saucers in the dresser, cutlery in the top drawer. Fruit loaf suit you? We'll have a proper meal later.'

'Lovely.'

'After we have our cup of tea I'll help you unpack and please, please, make yourself at home. You don't have to ask permission to do anything. Do what you want. I have to keep reminding myself that you are only fifteen but a sensible fifteen so there are no rules, only those you make for yourself.'

'I promise I won't go mad.'

'I know you won't,' Ruth said seriously. 'Oh, good, that's the kettle boiling, I'll make the tea.'

At Ruth's suggestion Kate had emptied everything on to the bed and Ruth had removed the cases and bag to a cupboard.

'We must decide where everything should go.'

'I don't have all that much.'

'Go and open the wardrobe door.' It was a command.

Kate did as she was told and gave a cry of pleasure. 'My

dolls and teddy,' she laughed giving teddy a hug, 'it's like meeting old friends.'

'I gather Sarah never discovered what happened to them?'

'They were never mentioned.'

'We'll have to find another home for your family but we'll think about that later. I've just had a thought, Kate, how about you enrolling for a course at Pitman's College? That would give you better qualifications than the average school-leaver. From what I gather it isn't just shorthand and typing, the course includes business routine whatever that means. I'm not saying you lack confidence—'

'I do and I know it.'

'Then a course at Pitman's should take care of that.'

'Won't it be expensive?'

'Not all that much I shouldn't think and even if it was I wouldn't grudge a penny of it. Kate, I wish you would get that into your head.'

'Thank you very much I really would love to go to business college.'

'Fine, we'll look into that right away. In all the excitement I forgot to tell you that the engineers are coming to put in the phone.'

'That's great, I won't be afraid of answering the phone when I get that office job. You're going to find it a big help.'

'Tremendous help. Up to now I have been obliged to the postmistress or Fergus Mackie, the grocer. I paid for the calls, of course, and they didn't mind but it was all rather public and folk around here are just as bothered with their nose as anywhere else.'

Chapter Eleven

At sixteen, Kate was quietly confident and looking forward to taking her place in the business world.

'You've done very well, Kate, and I'm proud of you.'

'All thanks to you, Aunt Ruth. I've thoroughly enjoyed my year in college and I've made so many friends.' To begin with Kate had felt on the outside, very alone and overawed. Most of the girls were older, a few had reached eighteen and Kate thought them so sophisticated. They wore quite a lot of make-up and talked about the latest films as though they knew the film stars personally. They also frequented the dance halls where they met boys and giggled about their conquests the next morning. Kate wasn't too bothered about dancing and boys but she did think it was time she saw the inside of a cinema. There was no Aunt Sarah to stop her.

Aunt Ruth spoke about the pictures not the cinema. 'I wouldn't like to say how long it is since I was in a picture house.'

'I would like to go.'

'Nothing to stop you, you could have been before this.'

'I know.'

'Go with your friends or we could go together.'

Kate smiled. 'I'd like the first time to be with you, then I wouldn't have to admit to never having been in one.'

Ruth nodded thinking she should have done something about this before.

'Mind you they show a lot of rubbish, rubbish to me that is, but as soon as there is something half decent we'll go. We do have quite a choice of picture houses but I've only been to the La Scala and The Kinnaird. To be honest I prefer a good variety show.'

'When were you last at one?'

'That I couldn't tell you. It's waiting around for a bus that puts me off. These very modern young ladies you know will go dancing?' She raised her eyebrows.

'Yes, I'll wait a bit for that, in any case I can't dance.'

'Of course you can.'

'Only if you count Country Dancing, we did that at school. This is very different, Aunt Ruth, I've seen them practising the steps and it looks very complicated.'

'Everything does until you know how to do it.' Ruth worried her lip. 'I'm all for you having freedom and I did say there would be no rules, that doesn't mean I won't be concerned if you were to stay out late.'

Kate came round the table to give Ruth a hug. 'I have no intention of staying out until all hours so you need have no worries on that score. I'm not going to do things just because everyone else appears to do them.'

'I see I have a very sensible niece. Kate, love, I have a bit of spare time this week and we must do something about clothes. Not just you, I could do with something new myself.'

'What did you have in mind?'

'Summer is behind us and we could both do with a warm winter coat. I'm thinking about a dressy two-piece as well. Jersey cloth is warm without being bulky and if I see something that appeals to me I'll just buy it. As for you, my dearest, you need a complete new rig-out.'

'I do not.'

'Yes, you do. What you have makes you look like an overgrown schoolgirl.'

'What a cheek,' Kate said laughing. She knew it was true and that she would love new clothes but felt guilty about taking so much from her aunt. The thought niggled her that perhaps Aunt Ruth wasn't as comfortably off as she made out.

'We'll have a whole day going round the shops and I intend getting our coats in Draffens.'

'Won't that be horribly expensive?'

'Very likely but, as the saying goes, you get what you pay for and something that keeps its shape is usually cheaper in the long run. I'm hoping you won't grow any taller, you are just lovely as you are.'

'I hope I don't. Do you think I've stopped growing?'

'Yes, I'm nearly sure. We'll risk it anyway and get you a coat you really like and are happy in. Of course I'll have to agree that it suits you, we can't afford to make expensive mistakes.'

They were to look back on that as a lovely, carefree day and they came home laden with parcels.

'I'm dying to get home to try on my new clothes,' Kate said flushed and happy. 'I love everything and as for that pink jersey suit I'm so glad I managed to persuade you to buy it.'

'Pink at my age!'

'Pink suits any age. The assistant said that.'

'Well she would, wouldn't she? She wanted a sale.'

'You aren't old, Aunt Ruth, and you certainly don't look old. Pink is perfect with your colouring.'

'You've convinced me.'

The bus conductor was a cheerful man. 'You two been buying the shop?'

'Just about,' Ruth laughed as he assisted her off the bus.

They were laughing and talking and spoke briefly to a neighbour. Then they were home. Ruth had her keys ready and gave them to Kate to open the door. The first post had arrived before they left and the letter lying on the mat must have come with the second. Kate looked at it and felt her happiness drain away.

'Move, darling, I can't get in until you do. Is that a letter for me?'

'No, for me,' Kate said, moving to let her aunt in then stooping to pick up the letter.

'What's the matter? You've gone quite pale.'

'I know that writing,' Kate said tonelessly, 'it's from Aunt Sarah.'

'And why should a letter from your Aunt Sarah put you in this state?'

'I don't know but it has.'

'First things first, we'll go and drop these parcels on the bed then you can open your letter. I can't imagine why you should be afraid. You live here, this is your home for as long as you need it so stop worrying.' She paused and frowned. She wasn't exactly worried more curious. 'More than likely she is wondering how you are getting on.'

Kate looked at her, neither of them believed that. Her hand was shaking as she opened the envelope and drew out a single sheet of notepaper. It was very short.

> Dear Kate,
> I need you. Please come home.
>   Aunt Sarah

Kate handed it to Ruth.

'She doesn't waste words.'

'I'm not going, Aunt Ruth, and she can't make me.'

'Of course she can't. You know that, I know that and so does Sarah.'

'What can she want with me – I mean after all this time? What do you think, Aunt Ruth?'

Ruth was silent for a few moments. 'Knowing Sarah as I do I would say it must have cost a lot to write that letter.'

'Hardly a letter.'

'She said all she wanted to say. I can't be sure but I think Sarah is ill.'

'She's never ill.'

'Perhaps she is now.'

'What you are saying is that you think I should go.'

'I am saying nothing, the decision must be yours.'

Kate was getting angry. Angry because she was frightened.

'And if I don't know what to do, what then? I'm asking you to advise me.'

'Then I advise you to go.'

Kate's face fell showing her shock.

'You didn't expect me to say that?'

'No, I didn't.'

'That is my advice, you don't have to take it.'

'Will you come with me?'

'No. I'm not wanted, you are. Try to remember, dear, that you are sixteen years of age with a mind of your own.'

'In charge of my own destiny,' Kate said with a touch of sarcasm. Everything had been going so well and now this had to happen.

'We all are up to a point. It can't do any harm, Kate, going to Oakdene House to see what the position is. Sarah will see a very different girl from the one who left her aunt's house a year ago.'

'Will she?'

It was Ruth's turn to get annoyed. 'Perhaps I only imagined the change. I thought this year had given you confidence in yourself.'

'Don't be angry with me, Aunt Ruth. I am a different person, it was just the shock that's all. Coming home and finding the letter.' She forced a calmness she wasn't feeling. 'Better to get it over, I'll go tomorrow.'

'Good girl. The ten o'clock bus would be your best one. Don't forget me anxiously waiting so do take time to slip along to the phone box and give me a ring.'

'I'll do that.'

'With that settled we'll try on our new clothes.'

They did and admired each other but some of the joy had gone.

Next morning Ruth and Kate had breakfast together and looked out at the rain running in rivulets down the window.

'That should clear soon.'

'I'll wear my old trenchcoat.'

'It's too short, put on your new one and take an umbrella to keep your hair dry.'

'My coat isn't all that short, it'll do today.'

Ruth didn't argue. Girls could be moody and if Kate wanted an argument Ruth wasn't going to oblige.

'Time you were getting a move on, Kate. I'll do a little shopping in the forenoon and remain in for the rest of the day. That way I'll be here for your phone call.'

By the time Kate reached Silverbank the rain had given way to blinks of sunshine. She got off the bus and walked the familiar route to Oakdene House without meeting anyone she knew. The garden had the end of season look but was neat and tidy. Walking up to the front door, Kate took a deep breath and rang the bell. It seemed strange to be doing that. After a few moments the door opened and Aunt Sarah stood there. Kate looked for signs of change and thought perhaps Aunt Sarah had lost a little weight. Her face was an unhealthy grey or had it always been like that?

'Come in, Kate. It was good of you to come so promptly.'

'I wondered what you wanted, your note didn't say much,' Kate said, as she stepped inside.

'Enough to bring you which was all that was intended. I think you have grown. You must have, that coat is far too short, far too much leg showing. I would never have had you going about like that.'

'It was raining and I didn't want to put on my new raincoat.'

'Keeping that for the dry days, are you?'

Kate looked taken aback then laughed. One up for Aunt Sarah.

'We'll have a cup of tea. No home-baking, what is the use of baking for one especially when I eat so little?'

'Why is that?'

'Eating so little? No appetite. There's biscuits though.

Take off your coat and if you want to make yourself useful you can set a corner of the table. There's plenty in the larder for a meal later on.'

Kate went to hang up her coat on the coatstand then proceeded to do as she had been asked. She could see that everything was clean and tidy but nothing shone as it once had. Standards had certainly slipped.

Sarah put biscuits on a plate then poured the tea. Kate drank some of hers and waited for her aunt to speak and when she didn't thought she must.

'Why did you send for me, Aunt Sarah?'

'I'm ill.'

'You don't look ill to me,' Kate said brutally then was immediately ashamed. 'Maybe you are just a bit run down,' she suggested.

'If it were only that. No, Kate, I am quite seriously ill.'

'I'm very sorry to hear that, Aunt Sarah, but I can't come and look after you,' she said gently.

'Why not, I looked after you?'

'You used me, Aunt Sarah. I was very unhappy here.'

'Ruth had no right to take you away.'

'She didn't. I left because I wanted to get away and I knew the longer I put it off the more difficult it would be. Aunt Ruth has been wonderful to me and if you must know I love her very much.'

'Think you do. You could be happy living here.'

'Never. You'll just have to pay for someone to look after you.'

'It wouldn't be like it was. It would be very different, you have my word for it.'

That couldn't be Aunt Sarah pleading.

'No.' Kate shook her head vigorously.

'I do have a cleaning woman, not a particularly good one but the best of those available. You see, Kate, you wouldn't have much to do. A nurse comes in in the morning—'

'What for?'

'I did tell you I was ill.'

'But not ill enough to be in bed.'

'I'll fight it as long as I can,' she said grimly and showing some of the old fighting spirit. 'I know my trouble, it is the same as my mother had, and Dr Lamond merely had to confirm what I already suspected. The silly man didn't want to come straight out with it.'

'You can't blame him for that, Aunt Sarah, he would be trying to be gentle.'

'I don't need that, I face facts. You are here because you are my nearest and I am prepared to overlook the shocking way you repaid my generosity.'

Kate kept silent.

'I did what I said I would and changed my Will. Do right by me, Kate, and I can put that to right.' She paused and took out her handkerchief to wipe her mouth. 'All I ask of you is to be here in Oakdene House for the time left to me.'

'I–I—' Kate stopped. What could she say? How could she refuse? Then again how could she stay? What about her own future, her rosy future? With her qualifications she had a very good chance of finding a worthwhile position. Why did nothing ever work out the way she wanted? And why should she give it up for Aunt Sarah who had treated her so harshly?

'You'll stay with me, that's settled, I knew you would.' She got up. 'Forgive me but I must rest now. I'll go upstairs and lie down.' Kate thought she sounded exhausted.

'Will you manage?'

'Yes, thank you.'

'I have to go out for a few minutes,' Kate said remembering the phone call she had to make.

'That's all right and, of course, you'll have to go back and bring some clothes with you. Your bus fare, I'll have to give you that.'

'No, you don't, I have money.' Kate put on her coat and took coppers from her purse. The phone box was quite near to the letterbox and Kate remembered creeping out at night and posting the all important letter to Aunt Ruth. And after all that she was returning to what? The phone box was empty and she got in and closed the door. The procedure was still strange to her but she read the instructions, inserted the coins, and in a moment or two the voice came across clearly.

'Hello, this is Ruth McPherson.'

'It's Kate, it's me.'

'Thought it might be.'

'Just listen and I'll tell you everything as quickly as I can. It is upsetting,' she gulped. At the end of it Ruth said, 'Sarah isn't inventing an illness to get you there, Kate, and it is true about her own mother. Poor Sarah.'

Kate could hear that she was shocked and upset. 'Why don't you come? You're a nurse, you would know what to do. I'm going to be completely useless.'

'Sarah doesn't want me and I can understand that. She would prefer her needs to be seen to by a stranger.'

'I don't know what to do,' Kate wailed. 'She's resting just now.'

'Kate, you don't really have a choice do you? You have all your life ahead of you and Sarah hasn't long to live.'

'I know,' Kate said resignedly. 'I'm being dreadfully selfish thinking of myself.'

'It is asking a lot of you and no one would blame you for walking away.'

'You would,' Kate said accusingly.

'Pop in a few more coppers or we are going to be cut off.'

Kate did so quickly.

'I wouldn't blame you, dear, but I would be disappointed. It is only natural that you are anxious to get a job and enjoy the independence that would give you. On the other hand, Kate, if you refuse to stay with Sarah, and I repeat, as you have every right to do, then you may never forgive yourself.'

'Thank you, I needed you to say that. I'll get the bus

home and pack some clothes then I'll return to Oakdene House and stay for as long as necessary.'

'Good girl.'

'I do wish you would come and see her.'

'I would and willingly but I know Sarah. She can forgive you but she won't forgive me. Without my influence she truly believes that you would never have left her. And think about it, she could be right, Kate.'

Kate had no answer to that. 'I must go, I'll see you later. Bye.' Kate put the phone on its cradle and hurried back to Oakdene House. All was quiet, Aunt Sarah hadn't come downstairs. She had been lying on her bed for two hours with the eiderdown over her. When she joined Kate she looked better.

'Have a good rest?' Kate smiled.

'I wish I didn't need them. I never had time for other people's illnesses and I have even less for my own.'

'Is it bad some days?'

Sarah looked surprised at the question. She was surprised and strangely moved. 'It can be but I do get something to help.'

'I phoned Aunt Ruth.'

'Dear me, she's going up in the world. A phone indeed.'

'She finds it useful. Aunt Sarah I'm going back home,' she stressed home just so there was no misunderstanding, 'to pack a case and I'll come back to Oakdene House some time tomorrow afternoon.'

'There's a ten-shilling note on the dresser, take it.'

'I don't want it.'

'Take it I said,' she said sternly. 'I have no wish to have Ruth pay your fares. When you are here you will have an allowance just as I said you would, though you chose not to believe me.'

The nurse was now coming twice a day and Kate had been shown how to keep her aunt comfortable. The weeks turned into a month and then two. After three months it became clear that Sarah was wasting away. She had stopped taking food, only accepting a sip of water. It was heartbreaking for Kate to watch the change. The woman had so little flesh left that she looked wizened, and the hands, those once busy hands, were like claws. The bones of the skull showed through the lank, sparse hair.

Kate was very pale. The strain of looking after Aunt Sarah was telling on her and Aunt Ruth was worried too. There was nothing she could do to relieve Kate since she wasn't welcome. Guilt stabbed at her. Had she done wrong in encouraging Kate to take on such a difficult task? It was a question she asked herself but had no answer.

When the end did come, Kate blamed herself for not being with Aunt Sarah. She had gone in as usual in the morning and had believed her aunt to be sleeping. Kate had tiptoed out and left her. The nurse arrived when Kate was doing some washing and had called to her.

'Kate, you had better come.'

Kate dried her hands and hurried upstairs. She would have gone into the bedroom but the nurse stopped her.

'What's the matter? Has Aunt Sarah had a bad turn?'

'She's gone, Kate, Miss McPherson must have died in her sleep.'

Kate went white. 'I was in, I thought she was sleeping.'

'Best way to go, her suffering is at an end.' The nurse spoke kindly but matter-of-factly and Kate wondered if that was for her benefit or did nurses get used to seeing death? 'I'll get in touch with Dr Lamond, he'll see to the death certificate.'

Kate nodded without taking any of it in.

'Come on downstairs, a cup of sweet tea will help. You're very young to be dealing with this.'

'She didn't have anyone else.'

'I'll see to making the tea and I'll wait until the doctor arrives. Can you get in touch with someone to keep you company?'

'Yes, I'll let my Aunt Ruth know – she's on the phone.'

'That's handy.' She turned back to the cooker. The gas was fully on. 'A kettle takes an age to boil when you are waiting for it?'

Kate was shivering and she was glad of the cup of sweet tea when it was handed to her. She couldn't help thinking that Aunt Sarah had gone to her death unloved and made that last journey alone. If only she had been there to hold her hand, but she hadn't.

She hurried to the phone box to find it was occupied. The woman was smiling foolishly and in no hurry to finish her conversation. There were bursts of laughter that grated on Kate. High spirits and laughter seemed so out of place when someone had just died and that was ridiculous. There were sad times for all of us just as there were happy times.

At last the door opened. 'Sorry to keep you waiting.' She was still smiling.

'It's all right,' Kate mumbled and went in quickly. The phone was answered almost immediately.

'Aunt Ruth—' Kate began to cry.

'It's over, dear, is that what you're phoning to tell me?'

'Yes. Aunt Sarah is dead. Aunt Sarah is dead,' she repeated.

'Kate, I do have one or two things I must do before I can get away, but just as soon as I see to them I'll be on my way.'

'You'll stay?'

'Yes, I'll pack a few clothes. You aren't alone in the house are you?'

'No, the nurse is here and has been very kind and helpful but she'll have other patients to see.'

'Yes, she will have. Call on a neighbour to sit with you.'

'No, I won't do that. I have a feeling Aunt Sarah wouldn't have wanted it.'

'Probably not. You sound a bit more like yourself.'

'That's because I know you'll soon be here.'

'The sooner I ring off the sooner I'll be with you. Be brave, darling.'

Kate put the phone down and let out a shaky breath. Aunt Ruth was one of those wonderful people who just took charge and calmed fears.

It was all over, people had called to express their sympathy, a surprisingly large number of folk. And the funeral was well attended.

For those first few days Kate found herself crying, sometimes she hardly knew she was crying until she felt the salty taste at the corners of her mouth. Aunt Ruth had tried to explain that grief took people in different ways. One could love a person and grieve deeply, that was natural. To grieve for someone not loved in her lifetime was much harder. Regret and guilt got mixed up. Being a nurse, Ruth had seen a lot of grieving people and she told Kate that when she was young she had been appalled at the way some behaved. They had actually been smiling and she had only understood later that they couldn't help it. Something to do with nerves and the wrong signals getting to the brain. Life was very strange and we were no nearer understanding it than they had been hundreds of years ago.

Kate was recalling the last conversation she had with Aunt Sarah. Her aunt had woken up to find Kate sitting at her bedside with a book.

'You're there?' Her voice was croaky.

'Yes, Aunt Sarah, I'm here.'

'The solicitor, I never got—'

'Don't talk, save your strength.'

'For what?'

Kate smiled. That had been true Aunt Sarah, only the sharpness had gone.

'I – never – had – any – intention—' she stopped for a moment then went on – 'of changing my Will. That was to bring you to your senses. Kate, it is all going to you, everything.'

'I don't know what to say, Aunt Sarah, except thank you. But truly I meant it when I said I didn't want it.'

'You thought you did. I'm wearied, Kate, I'll be happy to go.'

'Don't talk like that, please.'

'Why are the young so afraid of death? It comes to us all, there is no escape.' Her eyes closed then opened. 'What rubbish is that you are reading? No, don't tell me.' She closed her eyes and when Kate was sure she was asleep she got up and left the room.

After the funeral Kate went to see Aunt Sarah's solicitor. Aunt Ruth had refused to accompany her, been adamant about it, saying that the business was between Kate and the solicitor.

Matthew Brand, the senior partner, was a man of few words. He expressed his sorrow at the passing of Miss McPherson and proceeded at once to inform Kate that she was the sole benefactor, apart from a few small bequests.

'Your aunt was a very astute woman who had the happy knack of making wise investments.' They both smiled. 'You are to inherit a substantial sum and there is also the question about Oakdene House and what is to be done with it. Have you given any thought to that? I mean would you contemplate living there or would you wish to sell the property?'

'I won't live there, Mr Brand.'

'You want it put on the market?'

'Yes, please.'

'I foresee no problems. The house is in a desirable area and the property itself has been well maintained.' He stopped and Kate made to rise believing he had finished with her. 'A few minutes longer, Miss McPherson, there is the question of money for your immediate needs. Would you allow me to make a suggestion?'

'Please do.' Kate felt in need of advice. It hadn't as yet sunk in that she was a young lady of independent means.

'Then let me suggest you take a monthly allowance. You can afford to be generous to yourself.' He smiled.

'That would suit me very nicely,' she said shyly. 'I

shouldn't need much for myself but I live with an aunt and I owe her a great deal. Would it be possible to make over a sum of money, a generous sum, to her?'

She bit her lip when she saw his frown.

'Not a direct withdrawal for that purpose. Your late aunt left few instructions but one was that no other person was to benefit. I have to carry out my instructions.'

'I do understand.'

'Do I gather that this lady has been looking after your welfare?'

'Yes, she has. She has been very good to me. Apart from giving me a home she has paid my fees so that I could attend college.'

He nodded thoughtfully. 'Obviously you wish to repay that kindness?'

'Yes, I do.'

'Again this is just a suggestion. A very generous monthly allowance should take care of your own expenses and leave enough to adequately pay for your bed and board if I can put it that way. There would be a bit over besides.'

'Thank you very much. You've gone to a lot of trouble and I do appreciate it.'

'It has been a pleasure. Any time you wish advice of any kind do get in touch.'

'I will.'

Kate left the solicitor's office feeling almost light-headed. All this money and she didn't deserve it. She hadn't liked Aunt Sarah and there was no use denying it now. Only in the last few weeks of her life had they struck up a warmer relationship. Kate brushed away angry tears. She could have been kinder, she could have tried harder. Did she really believe that? Kate wasn't sure and it was too late for regrets.

Aunt Ruth had arranged for another nurse to take over her patients. She only had two. Old Mrs Hardy required her services one day a week to allow her daughter some time to herself. As for Mr Deuchars he was coming along fine and would very soon be able to do without a nurse.

'Where do we start, Aunt Ruth?'

'I would suggest the bedroom and get that over first.'

Kate nodded and they went upstairs. Kate had not been idle. She had the bed stripped and the sheets and pillowcases were at the laundry. The blankets had been washed and dried outside. A good wind had helped to dry them quickly. Kate had put them in the kist along with the spare ones already there. The eiderdown covered the mattress.

Kate looked at the dressing-table and her eyes filled with tears. How sad it was having to dispose of another's possessions. More than sad it was like intruding. Going over to the dressing-table she saw the tray and two silver-backed brushes and a tortoiseshell comb. A few grey hairs were showing in one of the brushes and she found that upsetting. There was the square wooden box Kate had often seen and had wondered about its contents. Rather disappointingly it turned out to hold no more than hairpins, a selection of hair-slides and a black velvet hairband that must once have been worn by the young Sarah.

'Kate?'

'What?' She didn't turn round.

Ruth was emptying the wardrobe and putting the clothes on the bed.

'Try not to think about it, just see it as a job that has to be done.'

'I'll try but it isn't very easy.' She turned round then. 'Sorry I'm not being much help.'

'It'll get easier and if you keep busy that'll help to take your mind off it.' She paused and stopped what she was doing. 'Kate, put aside what you want to keep. As for the clothes they can go to the Salvation Army or some other organisation. They are always glad of good, cast-off clothing.'

Kate was shaking her head. 'I won't take much. Maybe the silver hair-brushes and the wooden box. What about you, Aunt Ruth, please take something.'

'No, I won't. And the reason is that I honestly don't need anything. My house is cluttered enough already. You should leave the furniture in place, I think, it suits the house and will help the sale. Whoever buys might be interested and if not the best pieces can go to the auction rooms and the rest to the saleroom.'

'Will someone see to all that?'

'If they are paid for it,' Ruth smiled.

'That won't be a problem. Just thinking about all that money embarrasses me, Aunt Ruth.'

'You'll get over that and before long you will get used to being a young lady of means.'

'I have to be pleased, it would be plain silly not to be. I do wish though that it could have been shared between us. You were her sister-in-law and Aunt Sarah was very fond of you at one time.'

'Darling, I am just so pleased for you and I have given in to your pleading. Really what you are paying me for your board and lodging borders on the ridiculous. You could have the comfort of a hotel for that.'

'It wouldn't be home and that is what I have with you.'

'Bless you.' Ruth was on her knees opening drawers. 'Fancy anyone having that kind of money and darning. There again that is how some folk have it.'

'Aunt Sarah used to have me darning my school stockings and if it wasn't neat enough I had to take it all out and start again.'

'Poor you. Never mind, no more of that ahead of you.' Ruth had opened another drawer. Inside were winceyette nightdresses, two never out of their folds. Next to those were woollen vests, petticoats and elastic-legged knickers. 'Kate, find a case or something for this lot.'

She went in search and came back with a large cardboard box. 'This do?'

'The very thing, we'll label it and put it aside.'

There was one surprise discovery that had them looking at each other. In among scarves, gloves and other small items was a box, very old and held together by a ribbon. Ruth gave it to Kate to open.

'Look at this, Aunt Ruth, a bundle of letters.' Beside them was the faded photograph of a young man in soldier's uniform and under that a brooch, a cheap little brooch that would have cost no more than a shilling or two. Kate was trying to make out the writing on the photograph and had taken it to the window.

'Can you read it, Kate?'

'Just about. It's got love Harold on one corner and it looks like the name Sarah above but only the Sa is readable.'

'I think we can safely say it is Sarah.'

'She must have had a boyfriend,' Kate said softly.

'Looks like it.'

'Perhaps she had to choose?' Kate said.

'And the soldier boy lost. We'll never know.'

'Funny, isn't it, but somehow I could never think of Aunt Sarah with an admirer. Yet as a young girl she must have had the same hopes and dreams that we all have.'

'Maybe there was no choice for Sarah,' Ruth said quietly, 'her soldier boy might have been killed in action.' It brought back memories of her own painful wartime experiences.

'Yes, that could have been it.' Kate had the bundle of letters in her hand.

'Are you going to read them?'

'No, I wouldn't do that and I'm just surprised that Aunt Sarah didn't destroy them.'

'Perhaps she couldn't bring herself to do that.' She smiled. 'I'm glad you've decided not to read them.'

'Did you think I might?'

'No, not really but many would. They would want their curiosity satisfied.'

'Ours won't be. They will go on the fire and we shall watch them burn.'

'And the photograph?'

'That's different, I'll keep that and the brooch. It is of no value and she must have kept it for sentimental reasons. I have a feeling that if Aunt Sarah is looking down she would approve.' Kate began studying the face on the photograph. Below the army cap the features were indistinct, as though wreathed in mist. Where was he now, that soldier boy? Dead and buried in a foreign country or alive and well, maybe living not so many miles away with a home and family of his own? Or, poor soul, was he in a home for the maimed and wounded with others like himself? Young men who had given so much for their country and were now old and largely forgotten. People were too wrapped up in their own lives to spare a thought for those who had given so much. Poppy Day was Remembrance Day – one day in a year when for a few minutes folk did remember, put their hand in their pocket and bought a poppy, Flanders poppies sacred to the dead of the 1914 to 1918 war.

Chapter Twelve

Kate had found employment with a firm of solicitors, Stephenson, Smith & Methven who had their offices in Crichton Street, Dundee. Aunt Ruth had been very impressed at her being successful so quickly. It had been Kate's first interview.

'You really do want to work and not join the ranks of the idle rich?'

'I really want to work and make use of my hard won qualifications. What a waste if I didn't.'

'A shocking waste I have to agree,' Ruth smiled.

Kate was serious. 'No one need know about the money?'

'Not unless you tell them.'

'I won't.'

'Then rest assured no one will guess. You haven't exactly gone mad though we do live very well.'

'We always did.'

'I think so but without the luxuries which, I fear, we are now taking for granted.'

'Only very small luxuries, Aunt Ruth.' Kate was glad she could supply those. There was so much more she would have liked to do but Aunt Ruth would have none of it.

Kate looked very businesslike for her interview. She wore a dark skirt and a long-sleeved white blouse with a neat collar. Over it she wore an oatmeal-coloured jacket with large pockets. She had seen it the previous week in D.

M. Brown's window and Kate couldn't resist going in to try it on. Apart from the one on display there was another in stock, in Kate's size and she decided just to buy it.

Mr Wilfred Methven was to do the interviewing. He was sallow-skinned with grey hair covering a dome-shaped head and intelligent eyes. When Kate entered his office he put down his pen and leaned back in his chair.

'Do be seated, Miss—' he looked down at the letter which Kate recognised was her application for the job – 'Miss McPherson,' he finished with a smile.

'Thank you.' She sat down in the chair he indicated which was opposite his and remembered those early instructions to sit up straight and keep knees together. He appeared to be lost in thought for a moment or two and Kate had time to take in her surroundings. The chairs were leather with brass studs down each side of the back panels. The shelves were covered with files and a floor to ceiling glass case held what she imagined to be law books. More files were on a low table. Plain beige curtains hung at the window and at the centre of the windowsill was a healthy looking plant. She knew they were facing Crichton Street, a wide, pleasant thoroughfare in the heart of Dundee.

The interview had gone well and Wilfred Methven, one of the partners, had been suitably impressed. Here was a quietly spoken, confident young girl with excellent qualifications. A lovely young woman was an asset in any office; the only drawback being that they might not have her for very long. Such an attractive girl must have a string of admirers. On the other hand maybe she was in no hurry to enter into matrimony. Young girls of today didn't rush into it as their mothers had. They wanted a taste of freedom first. He would offer her the position and then there would be no need to bother with the other applicants. Miss Howard could deal with those.

'Am I right in thinking, Miss McPherson, that you are available to start right away? By that I mean could you start on Monday first?'

'Yes, I could.'

'Splendid. I do believe you would suit us very well.' He paused. 'The wages, hours and conditions are all acceptable to you?' With each question the bushy eyebrows shot up.

'Yes, quite acceptable,' Kate said quietly.

'That being so I am offering you the position of short-hand typist, Miss McPherson,' he said a little pompously.

Kate smiled broadly hardly daring to believe it had been that easy. 'Thank you very much.'

'Your appointment will be verified in writing but please report to Miss Howard on Monday at nine o'clock.'

He got up and Kate did too. They shook hands and he saw her to the door.

When she went downstairs and out into Crichton Street, Kate was smiling to herself. Aunt Sarah's money had changed her. Without it she would have been very anxious to get the job and her anxiety would have shown. Her confidence must have impressed him. How else would she have got the position ahead of the other applicants? And there must have been others. This would be a very sought after position with the office being in the centre of Dundee and the chance of advancement.

Kate hadn't needed to take the earlier bus but just in case the unexpected happened and the bus was held up, she decided to do so. Rushing in at the last minute wouldn't give a good impression. She arrived before a quarter to nine happy and excited to be one of the band of workers hurrying to their shops or offices. When she climbed the stairs to the offices of Stephenson, Smith & Methven, Kate turned the knob and the door opened. No one was around. The broad passage she remembered from her interview had a number of doors leading off it and there was the reception desk with the sliding panel closed. Kate was looking about her when an elderly woman came out of one of the doors and looked at Kate enquiringly.

'Good morning,' Kate smiled, 'I'm Kate McPherson. Mr Methven told me to report to Miss Howard.'

'I am Miss Howard,' she said in a clipped voice. 'So you are Geraldine's replacement. The poor girl was most reluctant to leave but had no choice. Her father's promotion meant the family moving away.'

Kate nodded and wondered why she was being told this seemingly unnecessary piece of information.

'I'll miss her, she was very efficient.'

'I'll do my best, Miss Howard.'

'Of course you will, I meant nothing by that.' She smiled. 'We'll miss her was all I meant. Come and I'll show you the cloakroom.'

The woman had fine grey hair scraped back from her face and secured into a tight bun. She was tall and thin, shapeless really, with a very good complexion that many a younger woman would have envied. Kate was to find out that the woman had a disconcerting habit of looking at someone with disapproval then walking away leaving the person uncertain as to what had brought on that look. Miss Howard, Kate was also to learn, was a lonely woman who lived for her work and dreaded each day that brought her closer to retirement.

'The other members of staff will be in shortly.'

The cloakroom was small with pegs along one wall. There was a door and behind that Kate was informed was a toilet and wash-hand basin. The furniture consisted of a gate-legged table and three wooden chairs. Kate hung up her coat next to a donkey brown one which, she imagined, belonged to Miss Howard. A stout pair of brogues were neatly together on the floor below.

'If, like me, you prefer your coat to be on a coat-hanger then you must supply that yourself.'

'I'll bring one in.'

'We have a woman who comes in to clean the offices and the cloakrooms and I impress upon the staff the need to be tidy and not give the cleaner more work.'

Kate nodded and just then a door burst open and laughter carried to them.

'The others arriving. Come and be introduced. Good morning, Amy,' Miss Howard said to a plump girl with frizzy fair hair and a lovely warm smile. 'This is our new member of staff, Miss McPherson.' The two shook hands and smiled. Then Miss Howard turned to Kate. 'As soon as I am free, I will explain what will be required of you. Meantime Amy will show you your desk and help you settle in.'

'Thank you.'

'What's your first name?' Amy asked when they were alone.

'Kate.'

'Your predecessor will be a hard act to follow.'

'So I have been led to understand.'

'You know about the wonderful Geraldine?'

'Only that she was very efficient.'

'She was, I'll give her that.'

'You didn't like her?'

'No, I didn't and I wasn't the only one. I can't stand folk who keep in with the bosses and she certainly did. It wasn't safe to say too much when she was around.' Amy was studying Kate. 'I'll tell you this for nothing, with your looks and figure I wouldn't be slaving in an office. I'd be gliding down a cat-walk.'

'Wouldn't do for me, Amy, I'd feel all kinds of a fool parading up and down with everybody's eyes on me. Probably fall over my own feet.'

'In here,' Amy said pushing the door wider. 'This is where you will be working. The partners as you would expect all have their own office and so does Miss Howard. We lesser souls are herded together. In case you haven't been informed you will have to take your turn at reception. Not to worry, it's a doddle. Just a case of directing clients to the waiting room until whoever they have to see is available. Most of them have to wait but that's normal for a solicitor's office.'

'Is that all there is to it?'

'Not much more. Answer the phone and the usual, you know,' she said off-handedly.

Kate didn't but she nodded. 'Is there a Mr Stephenson and a Mr Smith?'

'Not any more, long gone. Law firms tend to keep the same name for obvious reasons.'

'People get used to them?'

'That's right. The Methven side is still alive and kicking and likely to be for some considerable time since Mr Methven has two sons and one is already preparing to follow in papa's footsteps.'

The office was large and airy and contained four desks and two tables. A cupboard door was open showing shelves of stationery and various other items. Filing cabinets covered most of the walls and Kate saw three Remington type-writers. 'Which desk is mine?' she asked.

'The one next to mine.' Amy sat down at hers and pointed.

'Thank you.' Kate put her handbag on the floor beside the chair.

'You can take Geraldine's typewriter. I have my own and the other is for anyone's use. Stationery is in that cupboard as you can see. It's Netta's job as office girl to keep it tidy but it seldom is. Miss Howard occasionally feels the need to show her authority and comes in to read us the riot act.' She grinned. 'We all look suitably apologetic and humbled and that sends her away happy. On the whole, Kate, we haven't much to grumble about. We lead a quiet but busy life. If we do have a slack day it is a Monday.'

'What do you do, Amy?'

'Good question. Typing and filing mostly. Shorthand was beyond me, I was quicker writing in long hand.' She stopped when they heard running footsteps and then the door was flung open.

'Ah, here she comes, late as usual. Good morning, Netta.'

'Only five minutes late.' Netta put out her tongue. 'So there.'

'This is Kate.'

'Hello,' Netta grinned. She was a small, cheeky girl with short, straight hair worn in a fringe and with that auburn hair came the usual crop of freckles. 'Think you're going to like working here?'

'Give her time, she's hardly five minutes in the place.'

'If everybody is as friendly as you two then the answer is a definite yes.'

The buzzer sounded and Netta gave a huge sigh. 'Just in the door and would you believe it her highness wants me already,' Netta said glumly. 'Trouble I expect, it follows me around.' She went out taking her time about it.

'Probably is trouble. Netta will have forgotten to do something. She is a great trial to poor Miss Howard and it is a miracle Netta is still in a job.'

Kate laughed. 'I'm going to like her.'

'We all do, that's how she gets away with so much.'

'How about the bosses or should I say partners? Are they easy to work for?'

'Most of the time. Mr Methven and Mr Maitland are of the old school, very proper you know. They expect a high standard of work but they always say thank you and I have to say I like that.'

'How about the other partner?'

'Mr White is a lot younger, middle or late thirties I would say but I'm not all that good with ages. Like the other two he expects a good standard of work but he also likes a bit more if he can get it,' Amy said dropping her voice.

'Amy, I'll need that explained to me.'

'Wouldn't have mentioned it on your first day but with your looks you will need to be careful. Andy White can't resist a pretty girl or a pair of shapely legs and he has a huge opinion of himself.'

'Is he good-looking or does he just think he is?'

'Some would call him handsome I suppose but then

everyone has different ideas about what makes a man good-looking. Providing he isn't actually ugly I'm more attracted to brains.'

'You appreciate an intelligent conversation?'

'Yes, I do but that isn't what we were talking about. I was putting you on your guard. Mr White happens to be married with a couple of children but that doesn't seem to cramp his style.'

'Has he made a—' Kate stopped and looked confused, she hadn't meant to say that.

'No need to look embarrassed and the answer is no. I'm not his type.'

'Thanks for the warning.'

Amy smiled. 'I have a feeling you would be able for him. Sadly, Eva wasn't. She was a pretty little thing and very shy. Poor thing she would have done almost anything rather than take dictation from Andy White. She left as it happened.'

Kate looked shocked, she was shocked.

'I did ask her but she said her leaving had nothing to do with Mr White but I didn't believe her. Certainly she was going to another job but I wouldn't have said to a better one.' Amy had taken the cover off her typewriter and was feeding into it a headed sheet of paper, two plain ones and two carbon papers.

'If that was the reason she left why on earth didn't she speak to someone senior, to Miss Howard? Surely someone could have done something.'

'Not so easy, Kate. Miss Howard wouldn't hear a word against the partners. She thinks they can do no wrong. And reporting one partner to another –' Amy shook her head – 'heavens no, just not done. If you tried it, it would probably cost you your job.'

'Fight your own battles?'

'That's it, Kate.'

Netta had returned carrying a bundle of papers. 'Amy, you have to file these,' she said dumping them on her desk.

'I'm busy as you can see. Why can't you do it? Or are you incapable of such a simple task?'

'Not at all,' she said with a toss of her head, 'my morning is to be spent tidying that stationery cupboard which you and Milly mess up.'

'Who is Milly?' Kate asked. 'Another member of staff?'

'Milly works three days a week,' Amy explained and stopped typing. 'You'll like her, Kate. Millicent Barclay is the daughter of a close friend of our Mr Maitland which is the reason she is here.'

Netta had started on the cupboard but turned round to put in her contribution. 'Milly doesn't have to work, Kate, the family have pots of money.' She shook her head in disbelief. 'Fancy anyone being daft enough to work when they don't have to. I told her she needs her head examined.'

'Madness and I bet Kate agrees with that.'

Kate smiled but felt uncomfortable. What would they say if they knew she didn't have to work for her living, that it was her choice? Kate thought it might make a difference, like a barrier. She would cease to be one of them. They would lump her with this Milly Barclay and although they liked her she was just that bit different.

Netta got off her knees. 'Two shorthand pads for you, Kate.'

'Thanks. Shouldn't I be doing something?'

'Can't wait to get started,' Amy grinned. 'Enjoy these idle moments when you can, there won't be many of them. Any questions before Miss Howard arrives?'

'No, I don't think so. Or maybe one if you don't mind me asking?'

'Ask away.'

'This Geraldine you are all talking about, did she have problems with Mr White?'

'Delicately put I must say.' She snorted. 'Geraldine wasn't around when looks were given out so she was never in any danger. Neither am I come to that. Apart from not being his type I don't take dictation.'

'He doesn't know I'm living,' Netta said mournfully.

The door opened and immediately Amy began pounding the keys of her typewriter and Netta looked very busy.

Miss Howard came into the office and smiled to Kate, 'Are we to address you as Miss McPherson or do you prefer to be Kate?' She was smiling as though the answer was a forgone conclusion.

'Kate, please.'

'This is a good time, Kate, for you to be introduced to the partners. We can leave out Mr Methven since you met him at your interview and in any case he has a client with him.'

Kate got up and followed Miss Howard. They went a short distance along the passage, then Miss Howard stopped and gave a light tap before opening the door. She signalled for Kate to come in, then in a quiet voice made the introductions. Even seated, David Maitland had the appearance of a very tall man. He was thin and haggard looking and his mousy hair could have done with a trim. He wore spectacles well down his nose and pushed them up as he rose from his chair and came round.

'Our new member of staff, I'm pleased to meet you Miss McPherson and I do hope you will be happy working for us.' He had a deep, pleasant voice and his smile was tired but kind.

'I'm sure I shall,' Kate smiled and liked him on sight.

'Nothing like throwing you in at the deep end.' His smile was for both of them. 'My morning is taken up with clients, that is so isn't it Miss Howard?'

'Yes, you have a full morning, Mr Maitland.'

'After lunch come along, by then I shall have some letters to dictate.'

'He's very pleasant,' Kate whispered once the door was shut.

'Mr Maitland is a perfect gentleman,' Miss Howard said in a tone of reverence. They continued along the passage. 'This is Mr White's office.' Kate could see that for herself.

The partners had a brass plate on their door giving their name. Kate noted that Miss Howard knocked then waited until invited to enter before doing so.

They went in, the introductions were made rather hurriedly.

'Thank you, Miss Howard, I needn't detain you.'

Knowing herself dismissed the woman went out closing the door quietly behind her.

'Do sit down, Miss McPherson. Miss Howard didn't say your Christian name.'

'Kate.'

'Kate! I like that, a short no-nonsense name. Am I to call you Kate?'

'If you wish.' She didn't wish it at all but could hardly say so. She sat down. Even without knowing his reputation, Kate would have disliked Mr Andrew White on sight. There might be those who would call him handsome, Netta had appeared to think he was. For the minute or two he stood Kate saw that he was quite tall and broad-shouldered with thick light brown hair brushed back from his forehead. David Maitland's suit had been slightly crumpled but not Andrew White's. He had the tailored look of a man obsessed with his appearance and his bold eyes were making Kate feel uncomfortable.

'So you are Geraldine's replacement?'

'I believe so.'

'Very, very efficient our Geraldine, but not nearly so decorative.' The smile broadened and he leaned forward. 'I hope your shorthand is up to the mark, Kate.'

'The examiners seemed to think so, Mr White,' she said coolly and thought she had scored a small victory when she saw his start of surprise.

'Very well answered, my dear. I do like assurance in a young lady. I think, no I don't think, I know we are going to get along splendidly.'

Andrew White was very taken with this outstandingly good-looking girl. Life was dull and he could do with a bit of excitement. He was bored with his wife, had been for a long time and he could only take so much of his boisterous children. How foolish he had been to marry and settle down. Like so many others he should have brazened it out instead of doing the honourable thing when he'd got the girl pregnant. In those days Marian had been pretty with good legs and a nice figure but she'd let herself go. Had the nerve to blame it on him and the children. Said she never had a minute to herself. Others in their position had a cleaning woman but she had no help at all. Following that would come the usual complaint about money. If he was a bit more generous with the housekeeping she could doll herself up and get her hair styled properly. He hated it when the tears gushed and the shouting began. What was the use of bothering with her appearance when he never took her anywhere? Babysitters, she spat at him, were not hard to find but they had to be paid. Come to think about it he had a lot to put up with.

Now this glorious creature had arrived like a gift from heaven. Cool and proud, just his type. He enjoyed a challenge and the coolness he felt sure was just an act. Underneath that cool exterior was a passionate young woman and one, he felt sure, who would appreciate the attentions of an older and experienced man. He would take it slowly and before very long she would be agreeing to have dinner with him. Andrew White's thoughts were leaping ahead, dinner was only the beginning. In the fullness of time or hopefully long before that, it would be more than just dinner.

'Do you live in town, Kate?'

'No.'

'Where do you live?'

'Muirfield.' There was no use trying to avoid the question. If she didn't tell him he could very easily find out where she lived.

'Pretty little place. Not much of a bus service though.'

'I find it convenient.'

'Perhaps not so convenient if you were to be later in leaving.' He saw her start and shook his head. 'I put that badly. Let me stress that the occasions would be rare when I would require you to remain behind for half an hour or so. That said it would distress me to think of you waiting about in a bus station. Indeed I would consider it unsafe for such a lovely young lady to be hanging around. No, my dear Kate, it would be my pleasure to drive you home.'

'How very thoughtful of you, Mr White, but you won't have to go to that trouble. When it comes to extra work I shall be happy to do my share and I have no objections to coming in earlier in the morning or working through my lunch time should it be necessary.'

'Wouldn't do, the letters would have to be posted that evening.'

'Sorry, Mr White, but I wouldn't be able to oblige. You see I live with an aunt who is old-fashioned and very proper. She would be horrified if I were to remain behind when the rest of the staff had gone home. You do understand, it is just her way.' Kate raised innocent blue eyes.

Andrew White was angry. He couldn't make up his mind whether the girl was telling the truth about a difficult aunt or if it was a warning that she would stand no nonsense from him. Damned if she would get the better of him – he didn't give up that easily. Women liked playing games and she could well be one of those. Success with this girl lay in not rushing his fences.

'Sensible old lady.'

Kate had difficulty in holding in her mirth. Aunt Ruth would have something to say about that description.

'Will that be all, Mr White?'

'Yes, run along, I have work to do and I've wasted enough time as it is.' Your fault not mine, Kate said silently.

'Kate?'

She was at the door and turned round. 'Come back after lunch I have letters to dictate.'

'Sorry, Mr Maitland wants me then.'

He frowned. 'We could do with another full-time short-hand typist. Milly coming in three days a week isn't enough.' His head went down and Kate fled.

Amy broke off her typing. 'I have to introduce you to our filing system. Is it my imagination or are you looking a trifle flustered?'

Kate touched her cheek. 'Perhaps I am, this is all new remember. After lunch I have to take dictation from Mr Maitland. He's nice, I liked him.'

'Dictation holds no horrors for you?'

'Not unless he goes off like a runaway train.'

'More likely to have a snooze between every sentence. Come on, I'm waiting to hear what you thought of you-know-who.'

'Not much. In fact I thought him odious.'

'Which he is. Appearance wise what did you think of him?'

'All right, I suppose, if you like his type. Personally I thought him forward and arrogant.'

'Don't tell me he's blotted his copy book already?'

Kate smiled grimly. 'Thanks to your timely warning I went in prepared. And no before you ask, he didn't make a pass or try to make one.'

'Come on put us out of our misery. What did happen behind those closed doors? Bet Miss Howard had to make herself scarce.'

'She did and it's no laughing matter, Amy, this is my first day in work.' Kate swallowed. She would try to treat it light-heartedly and not show that the man had upset her. 'Nothing happened behind those closed doors other than a casual remark.'

'Which was – come on, Kate, this is worse than pulling teeth. Or don't you want to tell us?'

'Nothing much to tell. He wanted to know where I lived and when I said Muirfield he suggested that on the occasions when I may have to stay late he would be happy to drive me home.'

'Oh ho!' Netta said and stopped the half-hearted cleaning of the stationery cupboard. 'I hope you had your answer ready.'

'My poor aunt got the blame. I made her out to be terribly old-fashioned and strait-laced and that she would be deeply concerned if I was to miss my usual bus.'

'Is your aunt really like that?' Netta wanted to know.

'Anything but, Netta, she is an absolute darling and I have all the freedom I could wish. Maybe because of it I never want to take advantage.'

Amy nodded. 'I can understand that. She sounds nice, your aunt. What about Andrew White? Did you make it clear enough that you want nothing to do with him – outside business?'

'I sincerely hope so.'

Chapter Thirteen

Kate was alone in the office when the door swung open and a young woman breezed in. Her eyes shot up in surprise to see Kate.

'Well, aren't you the early bird. I'm usually in first.' She was smiling showing perfect teeth and held out her hand. 'Millicent Barclay but call me Milly and you must be Kate McPherson our new member of staff?'

'Yes.' Kate could barely take her eyes away from this stunning girl. She was dark-eyed, petite and looked as fragile as a piece of Dresden china. Which made her handshake all the more surprising.

Milly laughed outright. 'Not quite what you expected? My handshake takes everyone by surprise. You see, Kate, I may look a weakling but I am not. In fact I'm as strong as a horse. The parents, poor darlings, didn't expect me to survive since I was such a puny wee scrap and I'd only to sneeze to have the doctor dragged out. He did try but never managed to convince them that I am a perfectly healthy specimen.' Like a lot of young people Milly spoke too quickly, the words falling over each other in her eagerness to get them out. Kate found it out of place in someone so sophisticated and polished and because of that all the more endearing.

Millicent Barclay had delicate and neat features in a small pointed face. Her skin had the soft bloom of good health and was as smooth as ivory. Her blue-black hair was swept up high in the front then rolled to form a perfect 'V' at the nape of her neck. The style would have done credit to an experienced hairdresser but Milly did her own. Not many believed that the only time she saw the inside of a hairdresser's establishment was when her hair required to be cut.

'Think you're going to like it here?'

'Yes, I'm sure of it.'

'Amy and Netta would give you a good welcome?'

'They did, couldn't have been more friendly.' Kate was thinking that Milly had excellent dress sense, knowing how to set off her petite figure to advantage. The bright red costume went well with her dark colouring. Chic was the word that sprang to mind. The jacket was softly tailored with a nipped-in waist.

'Don't know about you, Kate, but before I came here my idea of a solicitors' office was of grey people going about quietly and talking in hushed voices. Mind you when clients are around we are almost as quiet as the grave. My father had serious misgivings about me coming to work here, well he would wouldn't he the way I talk non-stop?'

Kate grinned, she really liked this girl.

'He warned Mr Maitland that I would never fit in but here I am to prove him wrong.'

'You would have been judged on your work and I'm sure that was to everyone's satisfaction.'

'Thanks, Kate. Actually I am a good worker possibly because I enjoy what I'm doing. The alternative would have been staying at home and finding something to occupy myself.'

'A bit boring?'

'The understatement of the year.' Milly had wandered over to look out of the window and Kate was sitting at her desk and getting everything arranged to start the day's work. 'Amy is clever though she is at pains to hide it. Mr Maitland takes quite an interest in her. He told me that Amy would have made a good lawyer, she has that kind of brain but the family didn't have the money to put her through university.'

'Sad. There must be a lot like her who never get the chance to make use of a good brain.' Kate laughed and shook her head. 'She told me shorthand was beyond her.'

'It wouldn't have been beyond her, she just wouldn't have been interested. When Miss Howard retires Amy will most likely get the promotion. The job will change and she will be given a different kind of responsibility. I know all this because Mr Maitland is a friend of ours.'

'Amy could get married.'

'There's always that, isn't there? Mr Maitland would call that a horrible waste of a superior intelligence. He's a bachelor and I imagine that is from choice.' She giggled. 'When I was a little girl I used to call him daddy-long-legs. They seem to go on for ever don't they – his legs I mean.'

'He's certainly very tall and I would say painfully thin. Ah, look what the wind has brought in,' Milly interrupted. 'Good morning, Netta, what brings you in this early?'

'Trying to keep in Miss Howard's good books. Good morning, Kate.'

'Good morning, Netta.'

Just then Amy came in the door sounding breathless. 'Missed my usual bus. It went ahead of its time, I'm sure of it.' She sank down on the nearest chair to get her breath back. 'Milly, have you and Kate introduced yourselves?'

'We have. Incidentally you didn't tell me our new recruit was a tall, elegant blonde.'

'How could I? Kate only started yesterday and I haven't seen you have I?'

'No, that was stupid of me. The brain doesn't function properly at this time of the morning.'

'It is after nine o'clock,' came a crisp voice from the doorway and they all turned. 'Good morning girls, less talk and more work if you please. What would a client think if he came in just now and a babble of voices coming from the office.'

'The first appointment isn't until nine fifteen,' Netta said.

'I am aware of that, Netta, and it is very nearly that now. And might I bring it to your attention that careless filing causes a lot of unnecessary trouble and a needless waste of time. One does not expect to find the papers for Galloway in the section for M. Be more careful in future.'

'Sorry, Miss Howard,' Netta mumbled. She waited until the door was closed before saying in an aggrieved tone, 'How does she know it was me, I don't do all the filing?'

'An educated guess,' Amy said and ducked her head to avoid the flying rubber.

The time for talking was over and they settled down to work conscientiously until the break at half past ten. Before then Netta collected the money and went to the baker's shop only a few yards down the street. She returned with four iced biscuits, made the tea, handed round the cups and the ten-minute break began.

'With that figure Kate could have been a model, don't you agree, Milly?'

'First thought that came into my head when I saw her. Heavens! What I'd give to be tall and blonde and have lovely long legs.'

Kate was embarrassed, she didn't like to be the centre of attention and she had never been conceited about her appearance. 'I would have loved to be dainty like you,' she said. 'Men always rush to help petite girls—'

'And we tinies could see them far enough at times. Believe me, Kate, tall girls, especially those blessed with a good figure, have it made for them, they have most of the advantages. Models are nearly always tall, since clothes look better on them. Seen close up many of them are just plain skinny but they carry themselves well and that is what it is all about.'

'There goes the voice of the expert,' Netta grinned as she gathered up the crumbs on her desk and popped them into her mouth.

'I beg to differ,' Kate said firmly. 'You, Milly, look absolutely marvellous in that red outfit, doesn't she Amy?'

Amy gave a huge, exaggerated sigh. 'You are both gorgeous and would you kindly shut up about appearances and spare a thought for your ugly sisters.'

'Cut that out for a start,' Netta said indignantly, 'and anyway looks are only skin deep.'

Kate drank the last of her tea and reached for her shorthand pad. 'Mr Methven wants me. Is he fast or slow can anyone tell me?'

They were all laughing including Kate. She hadn't worded that very well. 'You know what I mean.'

'Of course just a slip of the tongue. Mr Methven is a bit of a ditherer, always having second thoughts and changing what he said. Not to worry, he doesn't rush. If, however, it is a fast worker you want then look no further than Andy White—' Milly stopped. 'Did I say something wrong?'

'Kate has met Mr White,' Amy said warningly, 'and she was not impressed.'

'No, I wasn't.'

Milly nodded and was silent.

It had been a busy day and they had been kept hard at it. For all the light-hearted banter they were good workers, Netta included. Amy and Netta left together and Milly waited the few minutes until Kate was ready.

'Where are you heading, Kate?'

'Lindsay Street bus station. I live in Muirfield.'

'My home is in Broughty Ferry.' Milly paused. 'Forgive me I'm always asking questions.'

'I don't mind.'

'Have you a steady boyfriend?'

'No. Have you?'

'Not at the moment. How about us meeting for a coffee some time? Easier to chat over a coffee than in the office.'

'I'd like that.'

'Good, we'll arrange something. I always make snap

judgements about people and I'm seldom wrong. I have a feeling that you and I are going to be good friends.'

Kate smiled. 'Funny, I feel exactly the same way.'

Kate had kept up with a few of her college friends and was enjoying a pleasant social life. There were boys but none she would want to be serious about. She found that parting at the bus station took any awkwardness away. Kate didn't quite know what was expected and she could never bring herself to ask. This way it was just a quick kiss before she stepped on and a wave when the bus moved off.

The Tayview Restaurant in Union Street was a favourite with the young people and was where Kate and Milly met. Tonight they were sitting enjoying a coffee and a cream cake. The contrast in their appearance drew glances from both male and female. Both were strikingly attractive girls, the one so fair and the other dark, the one tall and the other petite. Milly strongly objected to being called short since, she said, the word was associated with something missing and not necessarily inches.

'My mother suggested I invite you for a meal, Kate. Mr Maitland has been singing your praises and my mother is anxious to meet you, so is Daddy.'

'Thank you, I'd like to meet your parents, then you must come and meet my Aunt Ruth.'

'Your Aunt Ruth?' Milly sounded puzzled.

'I live with my aunt, both my parents are dead.'

'Oh, how awful for you, I had no idea, Kate.' Milly looked distressed. 'We all moan, I know I do, about the restrictions and our parents being hopelessly old-fashioned but to lose them – Kate, I don't know if I could survive that.'

'You would, you would have to. My father died when I was a baby so I never knew him.'

'Your mother, how old were you when she died?'

'I was ten.'

'Old enough to remember,' Milly said softly.

'Yes, though faces fade and that's worrying. I don't want to forget my mother so I often go back on old photographs.'

'She would have been very lovely, I'm sure of it.'

'Yes, she was. But I'm terribly lucky with Aunt Ruth, she is just like a mother. We get on famously and I love her dearly.'

'Is she a maiden lady? That's my awful curiosity again.'

What would Milly think if Kate was to tell her the truth, that Ruth had been her father's first wife? Legally his only wife.

'No, she is a widow, a childless widow,' Kate said firmly.

'She has you now.'

'Yes, we have each other.'

They were silent for a little while each with her own thoughts.

'Getting back to the office,' Milly said as she daintily licked the cream from her finger, 'how do you find the partners? I'm in a slightly different position with Mr Maitland a personal friend of the family.'

'Yes, that must make a difference.'

She nodded. 'I'll always be grateful to Mr Maitland for making it possible. The parents were dead against me working but I was determined to get some qualifications.'

'Which you did, so you must have won the argument.'

'For the simple reason they didn't think I would finish the course.'

Kate smiled. 'Which you did.'

'And, Kate, I did rather well. Daddy, I think, was quite proud of my achievement but tried to hide it from Mummy.' Milly paused. 'Family friend or not if my qualifications had not been of a sufficiently high standard Mr Maitland wouldn't have offered me the position. Full time was what he had in mind and so had I but in this my mother was implacable or should I say adamant – whatever she would not budge. Three days a week that was it, take it or leave it.'

'Maybe your mother will weaken in time.'

'That is my hope.'

'Your father will be on your side?'

'Let us say his sympathies are with us both. He would never do anything to hurt my mother and I wouldn't put any pressure on him. How could I, Kate, it wouldn't be fair. Wife or daughter? How does a man choose?'

'His wife probably,' Kate smiled, 'but not easy for him.'

'Impossible. The days at home I'm hauled to tea with this aunt or this friend. I mean, Kate, how do you raise a smile when you are almost bored out of your mind. They talk about such trivial, such unimportant things.'

'Important to them.'

'Then poor souls. The shopping trips aren't so bad. I like to be in fashion but I am not a slave to it.'

'Me neither.'

'We've gone off the subject, I was asking your opinion of the partners.'

'Mr Maitland and Mr Methven are very nice,' Kate said carefully. Mr White could be a friend of Milly's though she didn't think so. Better to be careful though.

'Which leaves Andy White and I gather there was a spot of trouble there.'

'I wouldn't put it as strong as that.'

'You don't like him?'

'That's right, I don't.'

'Made a pass at you, did he?'

'No.'

'Heavens! the man's slipping. Andy's weakness is beautiful young women.'

'Have you had to fight him off?'

'Gracious no. He knows better than try.' She paused and frowned. 'Must have done something to have you dislike him.'

'He was dropping hints that I would be expected to stay behind if something urgent came up.'

'How did you answer that? Come on, I like to hear of

someone getting the better of Andy. It's his poor wife I feel sorry for; it can't be much fun to be married to a womaniser.'

'I made my poor aunt the dragon. Told him she was very strict and would be horrified to think of her niece being in the office with a man after the rest of the staff had gone home.'

'You didn't really say that?'

'Not in those words but the meaning was clear.'

'Andy's face must have been a study.'

'I'm not sure he believed me.'

'Then, my friend, you'll have to be on your guard.'

'Why should I have to?' Kate burst out.

'You shouldn't and provided you aren't tricked into staying behind I can't see what harm he can do you.'

'I know. I'm making a mountain out of a molehill.'

'No, I don't think you are. If Andy becomes awkward or unpleasant you must tell me. I can help. A little word to Mr Maitland—'

'No,' Kate said sharply, 'I wouldn't want that, I'm a big girl and I'll fight my own battles.'

'No harm would be done, Kate. Andy wouldn't want to be in Mr Maitland's bad books—'

'I would be blamed.'

She shook her head. 'Men are not like women, they don't hold grudges. It would be quickly forgotten. A quiet word man to man that's all it would be.'

'Thank you, Milly, but no.'

'All right I won't interfere.'

The days passed and Kate had settled into office life. Mr White usually asked for Milly when he had dictation and only rarely was Kate in his room. On those occasions he was distantly polite and very businesslike. Kate felt a little ashamed. She had made a fuss about nothing.

'Mr White wants you, Kate,' Amy said coming in the door.

Kate picked up her shorthand pad and a pencil and went

along to his office. She knocked, heard his 'come in' and entered.

'Sit down, Kate.'

She did with her shorthand pad on her knee and her pencil ready.

'Damn! Sorry, pardon my language, I must leave this until later.' He got up and hurried out. Kate shrugged and returned to her office and her other duties. She was very busy and the time passed quickly. This wasn't one of Milly's days and both Amy and Netta were in a hurry and had left smartly. Kate finished off and was preparing to go to the cloakroom. Miss Howard said good night to Mr Methven who was talking to Mr White.

'Kate, you're not in a tearing hurry are you?' Mr White had interrupted his conversation to call to her.

'No,' she said before she could stop herself.

'Good. I have an important letter which must go off tonight.'

Miss Howard had departed.

'I'll say good night to you both,' Mr Methven said, and followed that with, 'Don't keep the poor girl too long, they do a long enough day as it is.' He was frowning.

'Oh, I shan't.'

What could she do but follow him?

'Your shorthand notebook, Kate.'

'I'll get it.' She hurried away to collect it very much aware that they were the only two left in the building.

'Sit down, Kate, this won't take long,' he said briskly.

'I hope not, Mr White, I don't want my aunt worrying about me.'

'A big girl like you! Is this aunt the ogre you make her out to be or is this just for my benefit?' He laughed. 'Be truthful now.'

Kate found herself smiling. 'I never suggested that my aunt was an ogre, Mr White, she certainly isn't that. She would, however, have expected to be informed if I was to be later than usual. Otherwise the meal would be ruined.'

'Not a great tragedy surely.'

'Hardly but certainly an annoyance.' She flipped over a page to show she was ready for dictation. He dictated a short letter which, Kate knew, could have waited until the next day. There was no urgency and she had been tricked. 'Read it back, Kate, if you please.'

She did.

'Fine that deals with that.'

'I'll get this typed,' Kate said getting up.

'No, not just yet. What a lovely girl you are, my dear,' he said softly. Leaning forward he looked into her eyes. 'Has anyone taken you for a meal at that new place – the Burnside Hotel?'

'No.'

'Well worth a visit and I'd like to be the one to take you.' His voice was persuasive. 'That will be a treat for the near future.'

'Thank you, but—'

'We can go for a drink before then. How about a small one before I drive you home? Don't worry we'll keep it to one, I wouldn't want you to overindulge.' He gave a laugh.

'No, thank you,' she said coldly. She didn't think she had anything to fear from him but even so she was alarmed and her heart was beginning to race.

'A lady always says no when she really means yes.'

'Not this one, Mr White, when I say no I mean it.'

'Andrew, call me Andrew, I prefer it to Andy.'

'I gather the letter isn't urgent?'

'Tomorrow will do. This was an opportunity to further our acquaintance and that I couldn't resist.'

'Mr White I want to leave now, this minute.'

'No, you don't you are just a tease, you gave yourself away, my dearest one.' He was breathing heavily. 'You could have made an excuse not to remain behind but you didn't, did you?'

She stared at him.

'No answer to that have you?'

Kate got up almost overturning the chair in her haste to get away. She made a rush for the door but he was there before her and had his back to it.

'Not so fast, young woman, you've led me this far . . .'

Tall though she was he had the advantage in height and strength. Screaming would be pointless, there was no one to hear her and it would be so humiliating, a last resort. How strange that one could be faced with danger yet be reluctant to add to the humiliation. And she was humiliated. Suddenly his arms were about her and his mouth pressed on hers. Kate struggled but she was no match for his strength. To keep up this useless fight would only exhaust her. Then she remembered a girl in college, a slight, small girl, who had managed to escape from a similar situation by a knee to the groin. When Andrew White slackened his hold believing that Kate was responding she took her chance. Raising her right knee she drove it into him. She heard the gasp then saw him double up with pain. A wave of panic came over her. Had she hurt him badly? Should she go for help? Then the uttered obscenities reassured her. The man would live and this was her chance to get away. Running out of the room Kate dashed to the cloakroom for her coat, collected her handbag and flew down the stairs, only breathing freely when she was in Crichton Street and became one of a crowd going home from work. Once she looked behind her, fearful that he might be following but, of course, he wasn't. Perhaps he was still incapable of moving.

Calmer now Kate made her way to the bus station and caught the bus just as it was moving off.

'Timed that a bit neat, lass,' the conductor said as she jumped on and he punched her a ticket.

Sitting with her eyes turned to the window, Kate's mind was clearing and she began to consider her position. With money not a consideration leaving her employment would be no hardship, only why should she? She enjoyed the work and had made friends and most important of all she had done no wrong. Why then did she feel so humiliated and guilty?

Could she have avoided it? With hindsight, yes, but she had been taken by surprise, off her guard. If she had refused to stay behind would Mr Methven have thought her disobliging? Not if she had said it was inconvenient. The fact was she had been given no time to think up an excuse.

No, she would not leave. He wouldn't have that satisfaction. Furthermore she would tell no one, put it down to an unpleasant experience. Better by far to forget it ever happened. Mr White wouldn't report her. How could he, what would he say? Now that she was safe, Kate had an overwhelming desire to giggle. Whatever damage was done to more than his pride he would have some difficulty in explaining it to his wife.

Kate was right that no one would hear about it. There was no more trouble for Kate McPherson, it would be strictly business from now on. For nearly an hour Andrew White had sat behind his desk in excruciating pain. The humiliation he was feeling was nearly as bad. He had made a big mistake with Miss Kate McPherson, one that he wouldn't repeat in a hurry. The bitch had won. God, he hoped she wouldn't tell anyone.

Chapter Fourteen

Large raindrops were splashing the pavements and the darkening sky gave warning of a downpour. Workers, anxious to avoid a soaking, were hurrying to their offices or shops. Milly had left home prepared for rain and was wearing a raincoat and carrying an umbrella. Turning the corner from the High Street she was just in time to see Kate disappearing into the close in Crichton Street. A superior close with a tiled entrance and shining brass plates. Milly took the stairs in a rush and arrived as Kate was going in the door. She turned round.

'Thought that might be your fairy footsteps,' Kate said holding the door open. Early though they were, Miss Howard was ahead of them, her coat already in the cloakroom and her 'office' shoes on her feet.

'Good morning girls, not a very pleasant one. Did you hear the thunder during the night?'

'I didn't but my mother mentioned it at breakfast.'

'Quite frightening it was.' Miss Howard gave a shiver. 'I do hate thunder, it has such an eerie sound. God's anger my mother used to call it. Did you hear it Kate?'

Kate shook her head.

'How nice to be young and able to sleep through anything.' She walked away and they heard her office door close.

Kate and Milly continued to the cloakroom, hung up

their coats and gave a quick glance in the mirror. Milly took out her compact and powdered her nose. Kate pulled a comb through her hair.

'Miss Howard isn't the only one scared of thunder and lightning. I'm not so bad about thunder but I hate those flashes of lightning.'

'You shouldn't be. When you see lightning you are safe, the damage is done before you see it. According to Daddy you'd be struck dead—'

'Before you knew what hit you,' Kate smiled, 'that's comforting I'll try and remember that.'

They sauntered along to the office. Milly sat down on a chair and smothered a yawn. 'Excuse me, I didn't get my full quota of sleep.'

'So it would appear.'

'Actually I'm fully awake and dying to give you the news. First though, have you anything arranged for the evening of Friday the sixteenth?'

'Of this month, the one we've just started?'

'Two weeks tomorrow if you need that information.'

'Not that I recall. No, I'm sure I haven't.'

'Good.'

'Why?'

'We, you and I, have been invited to a party, well more of a dance really – no silly games you understand and with a proper band.'

'The invitation includes me? Why?'

Milly crossed her slim, well-shaped, silk-clad legs. 'All will be revealed in a moment just have patience will you? Friends of ours, the Matthews, are giving a party for their son.' Her voice had picked up speed and animation and her eyes were bright with excitement.

'A birthday party?'

'No, not a birthday party. Mr and Mrs Matthews are just so happy and relieved I suppose, that Tony has done so well in his exams. It came as a very pleasant surprise.'

'Tony passing them you mean? He wasn't expected to.'

'Perhaps to scrape through but not to pass with distinction. His parents despaired of Tony ever getting down to some hard work but the bold boy must have taken a thought to himself and decided, in his own interests, to get the head down.' Milly giggled. 'When he was a schoolboy and supposed to be upstairs doing his homework, he would be making paper aeroplanes and flying them out the window. One of the neighbours opposite told Mrs Matthews, not to get Tony into trouble but because she and her husband had thought it hilarious. Tony's mama was not amused.'

'No more paper aeroplanes,' Kate smiled. 'He sounds fun your Tony.'

'He is fun but sadly he isn't my Tony.'

Kate detected a wistfulness in her voice. 'You like him a lot, don't you?' she said softly.

'I've always adored Tony. He's two years older than me and when I was little I used to follow him around everywhere. Proper little pest I must have been. At least he noticed me then, now I don't think he does.'

'Then make sure you dazzle him at this party. Let him see that you can have your pick of young men and there is no use shaking your head Millicent Barclay and denying it. Incidentally why aren't you invited with a partner, a male partner? Why me?'

'Believe it or not the boys are slightly outnumbering the girls. You have my mother to thank for your invitation. She apparently told Tony's mother that I have a charming girl friend who might like to come.'

'How very kind of Mrs Barclay.'

'She also suggested and I agreed that you must stay overnight with us and save any bother with transport.'

'Thank you very much and for the all-important question, what do I wear?'

'A long dress.'

'I don't have one. I do have two evening skirts but this will be a lovely excuse to splash out on an evening gown. Goodness you've got me all excited.'

'I have absolutely nothing to wear,' Milly said gloomily.
'Just a wardrobe full of clothes.'

'And nothing suitable. Surely you don't expect me to
appear in something everyone has seen before?'

'That would never do,' Kate laughed.

'Daddy will foot the bill if I ask him nicely. He'll be
happy to do that provided I don't go mad and buy something frightfully daring. Fathers are bad enough but mothers
can be the absolute limit. Mine will be trying to persuade me
into something ghastly like puffy sleeves and little bows.
Ugh!'

'Don't exaggerate.'

'I'm not, Kate. Neither of them can get it into their head
that I am not a child. Sometimes I'm nearly at screaming
point. Still,' she said cheering up, 'it isn't so bad if I manage
to get the shop assistant on my side. Mind you, I have to face
the fact that I couldn't get away with anything daring, it
would look ridiculous on me. Not on you, Kate, you could
get away with anything.'

'No I could not, I'm much too self-conscious. And you
are wrong, it isn't height that counts, it's style and you
certainly have that.'

'Thanks, it was what I was longing to hear,' she said
mischievously.

'I'll get Aunt Ruth to help me choose. She is rather clever
about it. I mean all the time she is telling me to choose what I
want, she is somehow managing to steer me away . . .'

'From plunging necklines and the like.'

'Exactly.' They were both laughing when Amy and
Netta arrived.

'What's the joke, can we share it?' Netta asked.

'We were only discussing evening attire,' Milly said.

'What to wear in bed? Pyjamas are more comfortable, I
much prefer them. Nightdresses are prettier and a bit more
glamorous but they have a horrible habit of creeping up,
with me they do anyway. What's the problem, no one of
any importance is going to see you in your nightie.'

'How do you know?'

Netta's mouth fell open. 'You wouldn't – would you?' She clapped her hand over her mouth.

'Just Milly's little joke, Netta,' Kate said, 'we weren't discussing that kind of nightwear and like you I prefer pyjamas. We were talking about evening dresses.'

'Going to a ball?'

'Heavens, no, not a ball, infant, this is a party where there is going to be dancing that's all.'

'And boys?'

'Young men, of course young men, what kind of a party would it be without them?'

Amy was combing her frizzy hair and trying to flatten it. 'When and where are we talking about?'

'Friday the sixteenth, Amy, and to be held in the Sidlaw Rooms in the Perth Road, know them?'

'Of course I know them, I *am* a Dundonian but I confess to never having been inside. I suppose you could say that I've never really lived.'

'I haven't seen the inside of them either, Amy. Milly will have though.'

'Several times and, contrary to what you might all think, they are not particularly grand although that said they are very nice. They happen to be popular for the smaller functions.'

'Pardon my ignorance but what does small mean?'

'A company less than a hundred, Netta, usually sixty or thereabout.'

'Very nice.'

Miss Howard was standing in the doorway. 'It would be very nice if I could see you girls behind your desks and doing some work. You can save your chatter for your tea-break, this is the firm's time.'

The three of them moved quickly. Covers were removed from the typewriters and work began.

★　　★　　★

'As you know, Kate, shopping isn't something I usually enjoy but I must say I have enjoyed this and particularly so since it has been so successful.'

'Thanks to a very helpful assistant, nothing seemed to be a trouble to her.' Kate was flushed and happy. She was carrying the dress box rather than have it sent and Ruth was carrying a shoe box and other small packages.

'Most shop assistants are helpful and pleasant and it is nearly always the awkward customer who complains about poor service. No, darling, you do not cross in front of traffic,' Ruth said taking a grip on Kate's arm.

'Plenty of time we could have been across.'

'Maybe you could with your long legs but I am not so fleet of foot. Remember this, it is better to arrive late than not to arrive at all.'

Kate grinned.

'My dear, you look very lovely,' Ruth said with a catch in her voice. 'You'll be—'

'The belle of the ball? Not a chance, I bet there are some gorgeous gowns and Milly will look stunning as always.'

She won't outshine you, Ruth said to herself, I don't see anyone doing that.

Kate was turning this way and that to get a proper look at herself in the mirror. She wasn't conceited about her appearance, far from it, but she couldn't help being pleased. The delicate shade of turquoise was perfect with her honey-blonde hair. She wore very little make-up, just a touch of pink lipstick and a dusting of powder over her nose. The rouge she had bought wasn't necessary, excitement had put enough colour into her cheeks. A dab of perfume had been the finishing touch. It had been a Christmas present that hadn't been opened until now. The magazines Kate read suggested a little to wrists, behind the ears and at the throat.

'Not too much, Kate. A little is appealing, too much can be embarrassing.'

'How do you know so much about it?' Kate teased.

'Trial and error in my younger days,' Ruth laughed.

'Does my mother's gold chain look all right or would I be better with a necklace?'

Ruth shook her head. 'You have a lovely, long neck, Kate, a necklace would detract I think. The chain is enough.' Kate saw a fleeting sadness.

'What's wrong, Aunt Ruth?'

'Nothing. What could be wrong? I was just thinking that if Robert and Mildred could see their daughter now how proud they would be.'

Kate turned from the mirror to give Ruth a hug. 'I hope they know how lucky I am to have you.'

'Thank you, darling,' she said tremulously. She mustn't allow herself to become too emotional. Ruth recognised the danger in herself. She had taken Mildred's place more completely than she had any right to do. It was as though she and not Mildred had given birth to Kate and it was so easy to think that with her own late husband Kate's father. Mothers would kill to protect their child, it had been so from earliest times. Ruth had never expected to feel this way, hadn't appreciated the fierceness of mother love until now. She would do well to remind herself that she wasn't Kate's mother. To become overprotective could drive the girl away.

'Kate?'

'Mmmm?'

'Let me know if I become one of those dreary over-protective females.'

'You never could. What on earth brought this on? To be honest it wouldn't bother me in the least, you becoming overprotective I mean. It's nice to be loved and I'm very happy the way things are. You are both my mother and my friend and what girl could ask for more. Oh, for goodness sake look at the time, Mr Barclay will be here any minute. Are you sure, really sure, about the cape, Aunt Ruth? My coat would do very well you know.'

'Certainly not, what a let down. And tell me when am I likely to be wearing a velvet cape?'

'Oh, I don't know. Now that you have joined the Bridge Club there will be occasions—'

'None for which I need be dressed up to the nines. It's yours Kate. I'm just glad that after all these years it still looks like new. My pleasure will be seeing it on you,' she said adjusting the cape then they both stopped to listen. 'Is that a car drawing up?'

Kate flew to the window. 'It is.'

'Have you everything?'

'Yes,' Kate said picking up her overnight bag.

'Have a lovely time.'

'Sure to.' She blew a kiss then left closing the door noisily. There was the sound of hurrying footsteps then a moment or two later the car door slamming. Ruth watched from the window as the car moved off and then was out of sight as it turned the corner.

How quiet the house would be without Kate and what a difference the girl had made to her life. Ruth had thought herself reasonably contented with her lot. Nursing had helped, caring for others was always rewarding though she was glad to ease up now. Over the years the bad memories had largely faded and most of the pain was gone. It could still return at unexpected times but these times she could manage. Ruth wouldn't have described herself as a religious person, rather as a believer. She believed in God and how he worked in mysterious ways. How could she not when she considered her own life? Who would have believed that Robert and Mildred's child, the fruit of their union, would be sharing her home?

Desmond Barclay was out of the car and had the door open for Kate. His pleasant face was wreathed in smiles. 'Let me relieve you of that,' he said taking the overnight bag.

'Thank you.' Kate felt shy and envied Milly her easy confidence in any company. She had already met Mr

Barclay and had found him to be pleasant but a man of few words.

Desmond Barclay was the owner of a string of grocery shops throughout the county of Angus. From a corner shop in his grandfather's day, the business had grown until the Barclay chain of shops had become a household name. The shops mainly catered for the top end of the market and charged accordingly for the quality goods. Those who had to watch the pennies were not forgotten and cheaper lines were also stocked. Desmond Barclay was well liked for his quiet friendly manner and his generosity to various charities.

'Comfortable?' he asked once Kate was seated and himself back in the driving seat.

'Yes, thank you.'

'May I say how very lovely you look. I don't see you or Milly being wallflowers.' The car moved off smoothly. 'My wife tells me I am hopeless with small talk so you must make allowances.'

'My problem too,' Kate smiled and immediately felt at ease. They were two of a kind and able to sympathise with one another.

'At a dance in my day the ladies were given little cards to be used to note down the partners for each dance. They don't do that nowadays which is maybe a good thing.'

'A bit embarrassing for those with a blank card.'

'Indeed.' He began to chuckle. 'Milly's mother must have decided I was much too slow.'

'She handed you her card?' Kate smiled.

'She did, to have me put my name against one dance but I decided to fill in the lot. Serve her right for being so pushy.'

Kate was laughing. 'That was the beginning of the romance?'

'I think you could say that.' They lapsed into silence but one comfortable for them both.

Milly had the door open. She was looking excited and Kate thought her breathtakingly lovely.

'Come in! Come in! Kate you look absolutely wonderful. Doesn't she Mummy?'

'Very lovely. Nice to see you again, Kate. Sit down for a few minutes until Milly is ready.'

'I am ready, just to get my cloak that's all.'

The door was pushed open and a golden Labrador came in, looked disdainfully around the room then lumbered across the room to flop down in front of the fire.

'No question about who is boss in this house,' Mrs Barclay smiled.

Milly's home reminded Kate a little of Oakdene House, the lay-out was similar but there the similarity ended. This was a lovely house with homely touches. The furniture was a mixture of old and modern and the surprise was that it blended so well. Things were left lying about and Mrs Barclay didn't seem to mind. Most of all Kate loved the kitchen and promised herself that one day she would have one just like it. A country kitchen she called it with the blue and white china on display above the Welsh dresser. Down the middle of the floor stretched a long, well-scrubbed table and when Kate first saw it there was a huge bowl of fruit in the centre and a cheeseboard. Over on the dresser was a bowl of brown eggs and at the wide window with its colourful curtains were several pots of African violets.

'Kate, where did you get that wonderful cape? Black velvet, it's gorgeous.'

'Not mine. It belongs to Aunt Ruth but I think I am getting it for keeps.'

'Lucky you.' She made a face. 'My cloak is ancient.'

'Milly, you only got it last year.'

'If it comes to something ancient I wouldn't like to say how old this is. Aunt Ruth got the cape when she was young but she hardly ever wore it and it's been in tissue paper all these years.'

Mr Barclay had been poking the dog with the toe of his shoe.

'He won't move for that, Daddy.'

'Nor should he, that's his rightful place. You girls ready?'

'Yes.'

'Off you go then, your father wants back to get his feet up.' Mrs Barclay shared a smile with her husband. 'Have a lovely time and I'll see you both at breakfast.' She went to the door to see them off.

'We'll both go in the back, Daddy.'

'Fine by me.'

'That's a gorgeous shade of red.'

'Nearly a stand-up fight in the shop. Mummy was desperate for me to choose another colour. Why is that Daddy, what is wrong with red?'

'You've heard of the scarlet woman?'

'Daddy!' Milly tried to sound shocked.

'Your mother is a little old-fashioned I daresay, though for God's sake don't say I said that.'

'I won't.'

'Red was considered rather daring in our day.'

'Why?'

'I haven't the faintest idea.'

'Yes, you do, you don't want to say that's all.'

'All I know is that you look lovely and so does Kate. Just remember and behave yourself young woman. I'm not so sure I approve of the Matthews organising a party and not being there to supervise the proceedings.'

'Supervise the proceedings indeed, you sound like a lawyer and Kate and I get enough of that all week. Don't you trust us to behave ourselves?'

'Of course, sweetheart, but all those high spirits.' He was shaking his head.

Milly, as usual, was exaggerating about the stand-up fight but there had been a quiet argument in the shop.

'Not red, Milly, you ought to have a change.' Her mother was fingering the material of one of the dresses brought out for their consideration. 'This is such a pretty shade of hyacinth blue.'

Milly made a face.

'Then how about pale gold? Not yellow, I dislike yellow myself.'

'That is honey gold,' the assistant said helpfully.

'Honey gold, pale gold or canary yellow, call it what you like I wouldn't be seen dead in it. Mummy,' Milly said in exasperation, 'I do know what suits me.'

'The delicate shades are so pretty and red is so hard,' Mrs Barclay said despairingly.

'Some reds are I agree but this one isn't.' Milly gave the gown a loving look then turned to the assistant, a woman in her thirties who was anxious to make a sale and dreaded to hear those words – thank you but I'm afraid you don't have what I'm looking for. 'What do you think?' Milly asked her and shot the woman a look that plainly told her what was expected.

'Madam, the young lady is right. That is a lovely soft shade, you could almost call it a deep rose pink. Not too many can get away wearing that colour, but your daughter can with her lovely blue-black hair and dark eyes.' She smiled. 'That is my opinion.' Her little speech finished she looked from one to the other and waited hoping she hadn't overdone it.

Milly's radiant smile was her thank you and Mrs Barclay sighed. She would give in gracefully, she hadn't expected to win, she seldom did with her strong-willed daughter.

'Daddy, you just get back home, there is no need for you to come in. This will do very nicely,' she said as the car stopped outside the Sidlaw Rooms. 'Unless, of course, you particularly want to come in?'

'Not really. I'll wait until you are both safely in then I can tell your mother in all honesty that I saw you inside.'

'Thank you very much, Mr Barclay,' Kate said as Milly slammed the door.

'My pleasure, Kate. Enjoy yourselves.'

Kate had gone past the Sidlaw Rooms on many occasions giving them little more than a glance. There was no impressive entrance to catch the eye but once inside she could see that it spoke of quiet good taste. The wide carpet runner in the hallway was red and gold and several elegant chairs were set against the wall. No one ventured to sit on one, they didn't invite that sort of familiarity nor did they offer comfort. They were there purely for show.

A footman or flunky as Milly called him, opened the door and the happy sound of voices and laughter floated out. A woman was at the entrance to the cloakroom and relieved Milly and Kate of their cloak and cape.

'This way, Kate,' Milly said proceeding to the reception room where the guests were being welcomed. 'Heavens! I thought Tony would be doing this and not his parents,' she whispered.

Mr and Mrs Matthews were having a word with everyone. Neither of them was dressed for an evening of dancing. The woman caught sight of Milly.

'Darling Milly, you look positively enchanting,' she said bestowing a kiss on each cheek. 'Doesn't she, Philip?'

'Pretty as a picture, makes me wish I was twenty years younger.' He gave Milly a hug and a smacking kiss.

'This is my friend, Kate.' She made the introductions.

'How nice of you to come, my dear.'

'Thank you for inviting me, Mrs Matthews.'

'That's all right,' she said patting her hand absentmindedly. 'As we are telling the guests, Milly, we are not staying or rather we are staying just long enough to welcome everyone and to see the party started.'

'Then we can go home,' her husband said.

'Where is Tony?'

'Good question, Milly, I was wondering that myself.'

'Philip, you know perfectly well where Tony is. You asked him to check the buffet and see if everything is there.'

'So I did but he's taking his time about it.'

'We'll just go in.'

'Do that, dear, and mingle, you'll know most of them.' She turned away to greet another couple.

The dance hall was square and large. Four musicians

were on the raised platform. The subdued lighting gave a warm pinkish glow and a few couples had taken to the floor. Someone called a greeting to Milly and two young men appeared smartly to sweep both girls on to the dance floor. Kate was quite a good dancer and was quickly into the quickstep. She could have done without the extra twirly bits her partner kept putting in but she still managed to follow.

'Thanks,' he smiled when the music ended. 'You're pretty good.' He was applauding loudly and asking for an encore which was granted.

'Not allowed, Howard old boy, you know what Tony said, circulate and give all the girls a twirl. May I?' a man said to Kate.

'The cheek of some folk,' Howard grumbled then dashed away to find a new partner.

Kate was laughing.

'You don't mind?'

She shook her head.

'I'm Brian and you are?'

'Kate.'

'Not one of the crowd are you?'

'No. Milly asked me.'

'I'm glad she did. May I say how lovely you look, Kate. Sorry, did I stand on your toes?'

'It's all right.'

'Should give all my attention to my feet they don't always do what is expected. I'm not much of a dancer, I'm afraid.'

'I'm nothing special myself.'

'Nonsense but it shows you are a kind-hearted girl. Go away you two,' he said as Milly and her partner got close.

'Kate, meet the host,' Milly said happily, 'this is Tony.'

'Hello Kate,' Tony was looking at her admiringly, 'save a dance for me will you?'

'Of course,' Kate smiled back at him before Brian steered them away.

'Your friend is a stunner. Where has she been hiding?'

Milly had never known what jealousy was until now. 'Why should she be hiding?' Milly said coldly.

'Haven't seen her around, that's why.'

'Hardly surprising since you haven't been around yourself.'

'Nippy, decidedly nippy, Milly,' he said laughingly.

'I'm not.'

He was suddenly serious. 'Look, Milly, the parents have left it to me. We are to enjoy ourselves but within limits was what they said before they left and since we are such pals you wouldn't mind helping me would you?'

'Not at all since we are such good pals,' she said sarcastically.

The sarcasm was lost on Tony. 'Great! Knew I could depend on you. Incidentally—'

'What?'

'You look terrific.'

'Thanks, I'm surprised you noticed,' Milly said but she was cheering up. His arm tightened round her as they continued with the dance.

'May I have this one, Kate?'

It was a slow foxtrot and not a favourite of Kate's. 'Thank you.'

Tony was only a fraction taller than Kate. He was slim-built, nice looking with dull blond hair in need of trimming and he had an infectious grin. Kate liked him on sight and could see why Milly was attracted.

'Enjoying yourself?'

'Very much.'

'Thought a couple of stunning girls like you and Milly would have come with partners. All the same I'm glad you didn't.'

'If Milly had come with a partner I wouldn't be here.' She smiled. 'I'm helping to balance the numbers.'

'This is one dance I've never mastered,' he said as he apologised yet again.

'Not my favourite either.'

'Muted applause then and we might get something better.' The dance finished. 'Kate, you won't mind if I steal Milly, I need a bit of assistance and she—'

'Will be delighted to help out.'

'I hope so. Between you and me I got quite a shock. I mean the Milly I knew was a proper little pest and spoilt rotten—'

'And she isn't a bit like that any more,' Kate laughed. 'Between you and me, Tony, I think you should tell her that.'

'Thanks, Kate, I might just take your advice.'

Milly joined her later and did she imagine it or was there a coldness?

'You and Tony seemed to have plenty to say to each other.'

Kate was amused. Heavens! Milly was jealous.

'I like him, Milly, I like him very much but it was you we talked about.'

She bristled. 'What were you saying about me?'

'Singing your praises. Milly, don't be so silly. Tony can't believe you are the same girl he used to find such a pest. Seeing you in all your finery has bowled him over.'

'That'll be right.'

'Please yourself but he said you were really something.'

'And what is that supposed to mean?'

'You aren't usually so slow. Tony is seeing you as a very desirable young woman and that is all I am going to say.'

'Thanks, Kate. I was jealous you know. I thought he had taken a fancy to you.'

Kate was shaking her head when Tony appeared.

'Milly, may I have the pleasure?' he said formally.

'Yes, Tony, you may,' and once in his arms she winked to Kate.

Kate was never without a partner and then there was silence for Tony to make the announcement that for those with their tongue hanging out the buffet was now open. Orderly please, no shoving and no ungentlemanly behaviour. There was general laughter and when the door opened all eyes turned to it.

'Ah, here he comes,' Tony said, as a tall, dark-haired young man stood in the doorway looking about him. Did their eyes meet across that crowded room or was that Kate's imagination?

'Sorry I'm late, Tony.'

'Never mind, just glad you could make it. Buffet is open after this dance for those who didn't hear me the first time.'

'May I?' He had come straight across to where she was standing and Kate was looking into a pair of the bluest eyes she had ever seen. The band was playing a dreamy waltz and their steps fitted perfectly. Neither of them spoke until the dance ended. His arm remained around her. 'Do you want to eat now or shall we have the next dance?'

'The next dance,' she whispered.

She didn't want the dance to end, she wanted it to go on for ever and when the music stopped was it only her sigh she heard?

Hand-in-hand they made their way to the buffet. The tables were spread with mouth-watering delicacies. There were various types of sandwiches, sausage rolls, fruit tartlets, assorted cream sponges and cakes and then biscuits to finish off with.

They each put a selection on their plate and managed to find two vacant chairs, not together, but they soon were.

'We should introduce ourselves I think.'

'I'm Kate. Kate McPherson and if you are wondering why I am here it is only because I am a friend of Milly's.'

'Nice girl, Milly, and very popular.'

'We work in the same office.'

'I didn't know Milly was a working girl, good for her. I'm Roddy Hamilton-Harvey.'

Hearing that name Kate felt her heart almost stop. It was a name she had never expected to hear again. Someone had slapped Roddy on the back and he had missed the shock in her face. Those few moments gave Kate time to recover or if not recover at least time to compose her face.

Chapter Fifteen

After the first shock of hearing that name, Kate decided she wasn't going to let it or anything spoil this evening. She accepted that Hamilton-Harvey wasn't a name one came across every day nevertheless she reasoned that there was more than an even chance that Roddy and the man she had once called Uncle Edwin could be no more than distant relatives. Their paths might not even have crossed, though that was unlikely with them both living in a small place like Broughty Ferry. She was clutching at straws and Kate knew it.

The food was delicious and when they finished what was on their plate, Kate and Roddy got up to return for more. Others with the same idea were ahead of them and there was a good deal of laughing and joking as arms got in the way and good manners were temporarily forgotten. A short time ago the table had been groaning under its weight of food and even after great inroads had been made there was still plenty left to satisfy young, healthy appetites. Soft drinks were poured and ready on another table but no alcohol was available, a disappointment to some and a relief to others. Kate had left her evening bag resting between the two chairs to show they were returning. Not that it was a guarantee of them remaining unoccupied but happily they were. Kate and Roddy sat down to eat and continue their conversation.

'Kate, you are going to let me see you again, aren't you?'

This was the chance to make some excuse and avoid any future embarrassment. How easy it should be to say there was someone else in her life but how difficult to make that sound convincing. She should have the good sense and the willpower to be sensible. Only she hadn't, not with Roddy looking at her with eyes that had gone anxious.

'Perhaps,' she smiled.

'Won't do, Kate, I need something a lot more definite than that.'

'In that case, thank you and yes, I would like to see you again,' Kate said softly.

'You would? Great! Heavens, you had me worried, I thought you were going to make some excuse.'

Kate shook her head. That's what she should have been doing but it was too late now.

Roddy smiled to show his relief. 'With that settled I can relax and you, Kate, can begin by telling me why I haven't seen you before and how you happen to know Milly.'

'Easy enough to explain why we haven't met. I live in Muirfield and Milly and I know each other because we work in the same office, Stephenson, Smith & Methven of Crichton Street. What about you?'

'What about me? Nothing much to tell. I'm just completing my education before taking up my place in the family business.'

'Which is?'

'Jute,' he said sounding glum. 'My mother is a Morton.' It wasn't said to impress but rather with a hint of apology. Everyone, or just about everyone, knew that the Mortons were jute. Their mill, the Hawkhead, was the biggest and most prosperous in Dundee.

'You don't sound very enthusiastic.'

'I'm not. I think, no, I'm fairly sure that jute has had its day and is on the way out.'

Kate thought there could be some truth in that. She was thinking of the unemployment. 'Quite a number of mills have closed down or are working short time.'

'The smaller firms are always the first to go to the wall. We haven't much to complain about, not at the moment.' He sighed. 'With me being the only son I'm expected to take over but by that time if we are to survive, we may have to diversify into something else.'

'What does your father think about it?' Kate said carefully. 'Does he think jute is on its way out?'

Roddy grinned. 'Dad doesn't give the matter much thought. To tell you the truth my old man is happiest acting out his role of lord of the manor. Mother is the one with the business head and what she doesn't know about jute isn't worth knowing. She doesn't admit to being worried because she can't believe, won't believe, that a time is coming when the jute mills will be history. I shouldn't be talking about my parents this way,' he laughed, 'but it is the case that Mother makes the money and Father spends it.'

Kate smiled.

'They are chalk and cheese yet they get on wonderfully well together and I'm very fond of them both.'

'As well as being an only son, are you an only child?'

'No, I have a sister, Alice, married to Iain. They live in Carnoustie. Iain is a farmer and I expect to become a proud uncle in the very near future.'

'Very nice.'

'Yes, we're all delighted.'

Kate vaguely remembered Edwin Hamilton-Harvey telling her he had a son and daughter and the son could be ages with Roddy . . .

'Enough about me, your turn, Kate.'

'That can wait, shouldn't we be going up to dance?' she said hopefully. 'We've missed a few.'

'No hurry and I trust that wasn't an excuse to get out of telling me about yourself?'

'It wasn't,' she lied. 'I did tell you my home is in Muirfield?'

'You did.'

'My parents are both dead, Roddy, and I live with my Aunt Ruth.'

She saw the quick sympathy. 'Sorry, Kate, that must have been tough for you.'

'It was but that was a long time ago. I'm very happy with Aunt Ruth.' She got quickly to her feet and pretended to haul him to his. 'Come on we can't miss this, it's a waltz and they are playing my favourite tune.'

Soon they were circling the floor. The evening was drawing to a close, the party would soon be over. Couples were dancing cheek-to-cheek. Milly and Tony glided by with eyes only for each other. Roddy was holding Kate very close, so close that she could hear the beating of his heart.

'You are so very lovely, Kate,' he was murmuring in her ear, 'and I'm just so terribly, terribly glad I came. How awful if I hadn't made it and I very nearly didn't.'

'Why?' Her voice was husky.

'It was all such a mad rush, I knew I was going to be late and I wondered if I should bother.'

'But you did?'

'Yes, I did.'

'You didn't want to let Tony down?'

'That's true and look at my reward. I find the girl of my dreams.'

Kate wasn't so strong-willed as she'd thought. It was always going to be the next time and then the time after that. The longer she put it off the more impossible it became. How did she end it? What could she say? I find I don't love you, Roddy. That wouldn't do. He knew very well that she did. In a few short weeks Roddy had become her whole world. This could only be love, this feeling of drowning in happiness whenever they were together. And hadn't Roddy said they were meant for one another? That had been the wonder for Kate, that he could be as much in love with her as she was with him. Her mind was refusing to dwell on the difficulties that could lie ahead. Maybe they would go away. Perhaps she was worrying needlessly.

Before Roddy got his car there had been the last bus to catch and their farewell witnessed by those others waiting for transport. Kate was shy about a public show of affection. She hadn't realised it but Aunt Sarah's strict upbringing had left its mark, it hadn't all been in vain. For as long as she had been travelling Kate had always looked away from a couple in a passionate embrace, unlike some who found it amusing and perhaps a way of breaking the monotony of standing about a bus station. A few of the older women tut-tutted and were clearly embarrassed. Aunt Sarah would have said there was a time and place for everything and a bus station was not that place. Kate was inclined to agree.

Roddy was not so easily embarrassed but he had to content himself with a quick hug and a kiss before she boarded the bus.

On a Sunday and if the weather was fine they often went walking. Sometimes into the country and at other times just wandering the streets of Dundee and usually finding their way to the docks. This was a day for the docks.

'How is your knowledge of Dundee's history, Kate?'

'Nothing to write home about but kindly remember I am not a born and bred Dundonian.'

'Your loss and that's a poor excuse since you didn't live all that far away.' They had reached the Royal Arch and stopped. 'What do you think of this?'

'I quite like it,' Kate said squinting into the sun.

'So do I. My father doesn't, like so many of his generation, he thinks of it as a waste of money.'

'It's decorative.'

'That's all though, it serves no purpose. Want to hear more about it?'

'I'm going to say yes since you're dying to tell me,' Kate laughed as she took the wrapper off a bar of chocolate, carefully broke it into two and handed one to Roddy.

'Thanks, I'll have this first.' Roddy popped the whole

four squares into his mouth while Kate broke hers. For a few moments silence reigned while they enjoyed the rich, creamy taste of the chocolate. 'That was good. What was I going to say? Ah, yes, a short history lesson.' He adopted a pompous voice. 'The Victorian Royal Arch, to give it its proper name, was built to commemorate the visit of Queen Victoria. She probably made it a short stop on her way to Balmoral but I could be wrong about that.'

'Was the queen impressed?'

'Whether she was or not politeness would have forced her to sing its praises and congratulate those responsible. Pretty awful if they went to all that trouble and she didn't show some appreciation. You aren't listening?'

'I heard it all it's just I was thinking—'

'Thinking what?'

Kate's attention had moved from the Royal Arch. She would have to broach the subject and not keep postponing it. Aunt Ruth was sounding hurt that she had still not met Roddy.

'When am I going to meet this young man of yours, Kate?'

'Soon.'

'When is soon, I've been hearing that for a while. Don't you want me to meet him?'

'Of course I do, I don't want to rush things that's all.'

'No one could accuse you of that,' Ruth said drily.

The last thing Kate wanted was to hurt Aunt Ruth.

'I didn't want Roddy thinking – well you know what I mean,' she said desperately.

'Oh, my dear, you mean he might take fright if he thought you were serious and he wasn't?' She was smiling broadly, relieved that that was all it had been.

'It could have looked that way.'

'I really don't think so.' Ruth paused. 'Mind you I could imagine your Aunt Sarah asking his intentions.'

'If Aunt Sarah had been alive and me living at Oakdene House there would have been no young man. She would have seen to that.'

'Your life is very different now, Kate,' Ruth said gently. 'I want your happiness above all else but I would never interfere or if I do you must remind me that I have no business to do so.'

'You've been marvellous about everything and I *am* going to bring Roddy to meet you.'

'Good! Incidentally what is Roddy's surname, you've never said?'

'Haven't I? Hamilton–Harvey. Roderick Hamilton-Harvey,' Kate said slowly and distinctly and looked at her aunt for any reaction. There was none. That shouldn't have surprised Kate. Aunt Ruth freely admitted to a shocking memory for names which was getting worse with advancing years.

'A double-barrelled name no less, that's impressive. Is this young man gentry?'

'No, he is not. His is a known and respected family but there is absolutely no swank with Roddy.'

'Nor would I expect there to be. The real toffs have no airs or graces. They can look like tramps but with that something that tells you they are not.'

'Roddy's mother is a Morton, he told me that.'

'The jute Mortons?'

'Yes.'

'Not short of a bob or two then but neither are you.'

Kate burst out laughing. 'Do you know this, Aunt Ruth, you are absolutely hopeless.'

'Thinking what, Kate?' Roddy repeated.

'My Aunt Ruth wants to meet you,' she said abruptly, 'and I don't know if you want that.'

'Why not?' He was looking at her in astonishment.

'Just – well – I wasn't sure,' she said lamely.

'Of course I want to meet your aunt, I was wondering why it was taking you this long to introduce us.' He paused before continuing. 'Seriously, Kate, I want our relationship to be on a proper footing – I'm not explaining this very well. What I'm trying to say is that once I've met your aunt then it will be in order for me to invite you to meet my family. My mother knows there is someone special in my life and she would very much like to meet you.'

Kate managed a smile she hoped would pass for eagerness to meet his family. That could have been true. It was only Roddy's father she was afraid to meet. Her stomach churned with nerves whenever she thought about it.

Roddy was very proud of his car and unlike some of his friends didn't show off by going too fast. At least not when Kate was a passenger. They had been to the cinema and he had driven her home.

'Roddy, come in and meet Aunt Ruth.'

'Now? Isn't it a bit late for a social visit?'

It was but Kate had the feeling she should do it now with no more excuses.

'A chance to meet then you can come for a proper visit. Unless you'd rather not?'

'It was the late hour I was concerned about. Come on.'

Kate felt a little ashamed to have sprung it on Roddy like this. She could see he was a bit nervous and that surprised her. Or there again that could be her imagination, Roddy was a very confident young man or so he always appeared. She had the door key in her hand and went ahead to open up. Once inside Kate called out, 'It's me, Aunt Ruth and Roddy's here.'

The living-room door opened and there was Aunt Ruth. Not in her dressing-gown as she might have been but fully dressed and a little flushed from the heat of the fire. She came forward smiling a welcome to Roddy.

'Roddy, my Aunt Ruth.'

'How do you do, Roddy. How very nice to meet you,' she said as they shook hands.

'My pleasure, Mrs McPherson.'

'Sit down both of you and I'll put the kettle on.'

'Please don't go to that trouble for me, Mrs McPherson.'

'No trouble, Roddy. It'll be a quick cup because I know you have to get back to Broughty Ferry. Next time you must come and have a meal with us.'

'Thank you, I'll look forward to that.'

Ruth left them and went into the kitchenette to make the tea and cut a piece of sultana cake. She was smiling happily. There was no cause for worry. Roddy was just the kind of lad she would have chosen for Kate. A well-mannered, gentlemanly boy and nice-looking. She liked the firm chin, showed strength of character she always thought. Not too handsome and Ruth was glad about that. The very handsome ones were all right to swoon over at the cinema but in real life it was wise to avoid them. Most were weak and with all that adoration was it any wonder that they had such a high opinion of themselves?

The awkwardness so often present at a first meeting didn't last long and in a very short time they were laughing and talking and enjoying themselves so much that it was Kate who drew attention to the time.

'I *am* sorry,' Roddy said springing to his feet, 'what must you think of me? I do apologise, Mrs McPherson, for keeping you up so late.'

'You haven't, I'm not an early bedder. Don't apologise, Roddy, time flies when folk are enjoying themselves. I'm so glad you came in.'

'So am I. Good night, Mrs McPherson.'

'Good night, Roddy, and go carefully.'

'You sound just like my mother. She's always convinced I'm going to wrap myself and the car round a lamp-post.'

'Heaven forbid.'

Kate went with Roddy to the door and for a few minutes they were kissing and hugging.

'I like your aunt, she's great and so easy to get on with.'

'I think so too,' Kate said proudly. 'Mind you had you not come up to her expectations your reception could have been decidedly lukewarm.'

'Glad I made the grade. No question about your reception, my mother will love you. I'll get her to fix up something very soon.' After another snatched kiss Roddy hurried down the path and Kate stood at the open door until the car pulled away. She waved and then he was gone. Kate was smiling to herself. The evening had been a success but then no one could fail to like Roddy. He was so friendly, so easy to get along with. A happy person who had a serious side to him as well.

How wonderful life would be if Roddy could be Roddy Smith or Roddy White – any name but Hamilton-Harvey. It was like fate having a bad joke. Kate had no doubt in her mind that Roddy's father and the man she had addressed as Uncle were one and the same. The name Edwin had come up during conversation. They had been talking about the new baby and the difficulty in deciding on a name and pleasing everybody. Alice and Iain had finally decided that the baby would be named after both grandfathers. George Edwin. George after Iain's father and Edwin after Alice's.

Alice had favoured David and in the end she got her way. The baby would be George Edwin David and would answer to David.

There was no turning back, she had come this far and she must see it through. Kate could only hope and pray that with the passage of time the past would have been forgotten. Why rake up something that was best left undisturbed? The man might make no connection between his son's girlfriend and Mildred, his one-time mistress. Even if he did the likelihood was that it would be ignored. In fact having the past dragged into the open would be the last thing he would want. Kate kept that thought with her.

Chapter Sixteen

Kate had suffered agonies since the invitation arrived from Roddy's mother and Ruth was surprised. She was also in danger of losing patience. The odd twinge of nerves could be excused but this was a lot more than that. It was as though Kate expected the visit to be an ordeal. For goodness' sake didn't the silly girl realise she had nothing to worry about. She had looks, charm and intelligence and if those weren't enough she was a young woman of independent means. Who could ask for more in a prospective daughter-in-law?

Roddy had noticed a tenseness and couldn't understand it.

'Kate, you can't be nervous about meeting my folks?'

'Of course I'm not nervous about meeting your parents, why should I be?'

'That's what I say to myself but something is bothering you and if not that then what is it?'

'Nothing, just your overactive imagination.'

'All right we'll leave it at that,' he smiled.

Roddy parked the car at the beginning of the Esplanade and they got out to take a leisurely stroll. Taking her hand in his they breathed in deeply of the fresh sea air.

'That should blow the cobwebs away.' He paused. 'Kate, this might be a good opportunity to tell you something about my family, not that there is all that much to tell, but you might as well hear what there is.'

'Fine, I'm listening,' Kate said lightly.

'As you must know yourself, Kate, a great many families have their darker side and are not keen to talk about it.'

'You don't mind?' she smiled.

'This is only for your benefit and let me say that mine is neither worse nor better than the average although there again that could be for you to decide.'

'I'll tell you once I hear about the dark deeds.'

'No murders, this is really quite tame. It concerns the family home, Craggy Point. We very nearly lost it, Kate, and the villain of the piece was my grandfather. If ever a man was cursed it was Edward Hamilton-Harvey. The old devil had a weakness for gambling and on the few occasions when he would be winning he hadn't the sense to stop. Instead he just went on and on until he lost the lot and by that I do mean the lot.'

'Don't be too hard on your grandfather, Roddy. Aunt Ruth was told by a doctor friend that compulsive gambling is an illness and needs treatment like any other sickness.'

Roddy gave a hoot of laughter. 'Try telling that to my father. I wouldn't like to repeat what he called my grandfather for leaving behind him the God-awful mess he did.'

'At the end of the day you still had Craggy Point.'

'Thanks to my mother and the money she brought with her when she and Dad got married.'

'That was only to be expected, a wife helping out.'

'There would have been no marriage if she hadn't.'

'Roddy, that's brutal and a terrible thing to say about your parents.' Kate was shocked.

'Nevertheless it happens to be the truth. You have to understand, Kate, that theirs was not a love match although my parents get on very well. I would even go as far as to say they have a stronger and happier marriage than some couples who have professed undying love.'

'You could be right,' she said but not sounding very sure.

Roddy squeezed her hand. 'We're different, Kate, what we have, darling, is very, very special but let me get on with this tale now that I have started. My mother declares with more than a touch of pride I think, that she comes from a very ordinary family but ordinary or not they had the good sense and foresight to see that fortunes could be made in jute. When my father began to court her she was in no doubt as to the real reason. She was no beauty as she told us – she called herself a plain Jane.'

Kate smiled. 'Maybe she was waiting for you to deny that.'

'Not Mother. She isn't beautiful but she has a lovely nature.'

'Roddy, should you be telling me all this, I mean I'm not family?'

'Soon you will be and it is better to let you know what you are getting yourself into,' he laughed.

'Not fair if I've kept my dark secrets from you.'

'You haven't any. I'm sure there are no skeletons in your cupboard.'

Kate didn't answer. Maybe he was about to find out.

'Mother, bless her, can be embarrassingly honest as we all know to our cost. If Alice hadn't kept badgering her it wouldn't have come out but Alice, trust her, pointed out that family history should be handed down. Mother was inclined to agree with that.'

'And your father, did he agree?'

'He wasn't present, had he been the bits that showed him in an unfavourable light would have been glossed over. And now to get back to the romance that never was. Dad cut quite a dashing figure in his younger days and Mother decided this was her chance to get what she wanted.'

'Which was?'

'To marry into an old and respected family.'

'And for that your mother was prepared to risk entering a loveless marriage?' Kate said incredulously.

'They were both taking a chance but it worked out.'

'The price of keeping Craggy Point in the family?'

Roddy was silent so long that Kate thought her words must have caused offence.

'Craggy Point,' he said slowly, 'is only a house but to my father it was and is everything. It would have broken his heart to see it go. A marriage of convenience wasn't too high a price.'

'Does Craggy Point mean as much to you, Roddy?'

'That's difficult to answer, Kate, I've often tried asking myself. Certainly it wouldn't be an obsession like it is with Dad but that said I would hate to see it going out of the family.'

'I suppose it is possible to love a house.' Kate was thinking of Aunt Sarah and of her love for Oakdene.

There was no one nearby at this time of the evening. Only a man down at the water's edge throwing a stick for his dog to fetch.

'I could have affection for a house but love – love is what I have for you, Kate.' They had stopped and were gazing out to sea. 'I love you so very, very much.'

'And I love you too,' Kate said huskily, 'never doubt that Roddy.'

'Why would I doubt it?'

'I don't know, just don't that's all.' They began walking.

'I might as well go on with this. When Alice and I appeared on the scene Mother considered she had done her duty and from then onwards it was separate bedrooms. Am I embarrassing you?'

'Why should I be embarrassed? I'm not a Victorian maiden,' Kate said a little crossly.

'Good, I won't have to watch my words. With it being separate bedrooms Mother had to accept that Dad would look elsewhere for his comforts. She raised no objections to him taking a mistress provided he was discreet about it. She could hardly do otherwise since she was opting out.'

Kate felt choked as though she could hardly breathe and it was with difficulty that she got out the words, 'I can't believe your mother would have wanted you and your sister to know this – it's so – so personal.'

'Sweet, innocent Kate, we weren't shocked and you have to remember that we were of an age to understand. Maybe I was slower to notice what was going on but Alice had always known she said.' He eyed her keenly. 'Please don't run away with the idea that my father was a womaniser, he was never that. Whoever she was, his mistress I mean, must have pleased him for he kept the same one for many years.'

There was no doubt in Kate's mind that Roddy was talking about her mother. It gave her a queer little feeling in the pit of her stomach. A part of her wanted to scream to Roddy to stop, she didn't want to hear any more but the other stronger part wanted him to go on. She had to know it all.

'What – happened to her?'

'Who? His mistress you mean?'

'Yes.'

'I wouldn't know, disappeared from the scene I suppose,' he said in a voice that dismissed something so unimportant. 'Mind you Alice always maintained that Mother was jealous of this woman who had become such a large part of Father's life.'

'Did you believe that?'

'I wasn't sufficiently interested to give it any thought. She was no threat after all.'

'I can't help sticking up for the underdog so forgive me if I ask about the mistress. You can't know how she came to be in such a situation.'

Roddy seemed mildly irritated. 'Kate, don't waste your sympathy, her kind can take care of themselves. A woman who is prepared to become a man's mistress knows the score. She knows it can't last for ever and takes what she can while the going is good.'

'She is no longer valued once she loses her looks.'

He shrugged. 'That's fair enough, it would be the attraction in the first place.'

'How callous that sounds.'

'And how surprised I am to hear you championing women who have so little self-respect that they sell themselves.'

'I wasn't championing them, Roddy, but none of us should condemn another before we know the full facts.'

The weather was damp and misty when they left Muirfield but the visibility had improved greatly by the time they reached the outskirts of Broughty Ferry. The popular seaside resort had the added advantage of being a good shopping centre with quality shops. During the summer months and if the weather was sunny and warm the beach would be packed with families complete with buckets and spades and all the rest of the paraphernalia necessary for a day at the sands. Some would have accommodation for a week or maybe two, others had just come for a day at the seaside. The busy months and the money that came with the visitors was much appreciated by the shopkeepers and the boarding house ladies. The locals were tolerant but glad when they all went home and Broughty Ferry became theirs again.

'Dad was sorry, Kate, he was looking forward to meeting you and he asked me to be sure to tell you that.'

'It's all right, Roddy, I do understand and I'll be meeting your mother.'

'Of course and there will be other opportunities for you to meet Dad.'

'Yes, I'm sure there will be.'

'Glad that wretched mist has lifted, I hate having to peer ahead and I'm not mad enough to take any chances, not with you in the car.'

'Not at any time, Roddy,' Kate said severely. 'I have

the distinct impression that on your own you would step on it.'

'Whatever gave you that idea?' he grinned.

Being a Sunday the roads were quiet and only became slightly busier when they drove through the centre of the 'Ferry' and took the road away from the beach. They passed farms and farmhouses followed by a cluster of cottages and then came green field after green field.

'Not far now, Kate. I'll slow down and you'll see Craggy Point through the trees.'

Kate sat forward seeing nothing and then it came into view. An ivy-covered mansion house. Asked for her first impression she would have said the house looked dignified. She was as much or maybe more impressed with the gardens. Even so late in the season – it was nearing the end of October – the shrubs were still in bloom. Roddy slowed down to a crawl and she caught a glimpse of smooth lawns and well-kept flower borders. Here and there in the rose garden were hardy blooms that had defied the severe early morning frost which in a single night could cause such ruination to plants and flowers. Kate could imagine the gardens in the height of summer, the blaze of colour and the heady perfume from the roses.

'The gardens look lovely, Roddy, I bet it takes an army of gardeners to keep it looking that way.'

'No, not really, we only have one true gardener, the others are just helpers and come when they are needed. Old Tim, he's quite a character as you will discover, sees to it that they put in a good day's work. No leaning on a spade and gazing into the distance if they want to keep their job. They may not know a flower from a weed when they arrive, Kate, but by heavens they very soon do. He must be coming up for seventy but he works as hard, maybe harder, than a man twenty years his junior.' Roddy smiled. 'Mother likes pottering about which did not please Tim at one time. He could hardly say anything but his disapproving look said it for him. Tim would have considered it an affront to his professional standing. Now he doesn't mind, recognising that Mother is quite knowledgeable about plants and she gives him his place by asking his advice.'

'A wise woman your mother,' Kate laughed.

'She's that all right.'

Roddy parked at the front of the house and was round very quickly to open the passenger door and help Kate out.

'You look very lovely, darling,' Roddy said giving her a quick kiss. Together they went up the stone steps. The heavy oak door with its lion's head for a knocker, was open a few inches and Roddy pushed it wide. Kate found herself in a vestibule with shelves holding a great many plants. 'Far too much greenery, makes you think of a hot house.'

'I like it.'

The stained-glass door led into a spacious hall and a maid who smiled at Roddy took charge of Kate's coat. Kate had given a lot of thought to what she should wear. Typical man, Roddy had been no help.

'Anything does, my mother isn't one for dressing up.'

In the end she decided on a dark blue calf-length dress with a bolero in a paler shade and the binding dark blue. Ruth agreed that it was neither too dressy nor too casual, the kind of outfit suitable for any occasion. Her navy court shoes had a small heel and her stockings were pure silk. Kate still thought pure silk stockings an extravagance but worth the money for that exquisite sensation that only silk next to the skin can give.

A tall, thin woman in a drab brown dress that accentuated her sallow skin came to greet them with a welcoming smile on her face.

'Here comes Mother,' Roddy smiled.

'Heard you arriving and this is Kate,' the woman said before Roddy got a chance to introduce them. 'My dear, I'm just so delighted to meet you,' she said extending her hand.

'How do you do, Mrs Hamilton-Harvey,' Kate smiled as they shook hands, 'it was very kind of you to invite me.'

Gwen Hamilton-Harvey had been looking forward to meeting this girl who had stolen her son's heart.

'Come along to the drawing-room, my dear. Roddy will have told you about my husband being called away unexpectedly and since it was very important I'm afraid he had no choice but to go,' she ended apologetically.

'Roddy did tell me and I do understand.' Kate had known a tremendous relief, yet it was no more than a postponement. The ordeal of meeting Edwin Hamilton-Harvey face-to-face was still there. Perhaps it would have been better to have got it over and done with, then she would know where she stood.

Like most mothers of a much loved son, Gwen worried that Roddy might choose unwisely but that worry disap-peared as soon as she saw the girl. She was exceptionally pretty but natural with it, no silly little mannerisms to draw attention to herself. Gwen liked the quick genuine smile and the hint of shyness. On further study her shrewd eyes detected a nervousness the girl was at pains to hide. That did surprise her. One would have expected someone blessed with such good appearance to have plenty of self-confidence.

'How very nice you look, my dear,' she said kindly.

'Told you Kate was a beauty,' her son said proudly.

'So you did and I can only agree.' She went ahead and into the drawing-room making for the bell once she was inside. 'I'll ring for tea to be brought, I'm sure like me, Kate, you are ready for a refreshing cup.'

Kate gave a smile of agreement.

'We have dinner at seven o'clock, does that suit you?'

'Yes, thank you.'

They exchanged pleasantries and then Gwen turned to her son.

'Roddy, I think I can hear Brenda with the tray, be a dear boy and open the door before she attempts to knock.' Roddy got up to do his mother's bidding and Gwen said sotto voce to Kate.

'A very obliging girl but a little clumsy. We have had one or two unfortunate accidents but as I tell my husband, who is less tolerant than I am, everyone has to learn and Brenda is just taking a little longer about it.'

Kate liked that. Many a mistress would have got rid of a maid who didn't give satisfaction but Roddy's mother was making allowances.

Brenda came in breathing heavily and put the tray on the table. She was a small, thin, pale-faced girl with an anxious look about her. The weight of the tray had probably sapped her strength.

'Want me to pour, ma'am?'

'No, thank you, Brenda, that will do nicely.'

Gwen waited a minute or two then poured the tea and Roddy made himself useful by handing the plate of biscuits to Kate.

Gwen drank some tea and put her cup down. 'Alice, my daughter, and I have been teasing Roddy about this girl he has been keeping secret from us.'

'Not true. Kate was the one who was taking her time. I thought I was never going to be invited to meet this aunt of hers.'

'That true, Kate?'

'I didn't want to rush things,' Kate laughed.

'You certainly didn't do that and as for your Aunt Ruth, a nicer lady you couldn't meet. Has a good sense of humour too.'

Kate's face softened to hear Roddy praising Aunt Ruth. On entering she had taken a quick glance round and now she could study the room at leisure. Everything was solid, old-fashioned and in good taste and Kate thought that few changes had been made over the years. Many with the means to do it would have replaced the shabby carpet yet the worn patches took nothing away from the room. Rather they added to the homeliness. The high ceiling had attractive cornices and light flooded in from the wide double windows. The nights were drawing in and come darkness when the plum-coloured, floor-length velvet curtains were closed and a good fire burning in the Adam fireplace, the room would look invitingly cosy.

There were numerous chairs set around and a large sofa which at present was occupied by Kate and Roddy. There was a set of tables that had the look of having originated in the Far East. The two embroidered foot-stools had more of a Victorian appearance. A handsome bookcase held mostly leather-bound books and on the mantelshelf above the Adam fireplace was a black marble clock.

'You are a working girl, Roddy tells me?'

'Yes, I work in a solicitors' office in Dundee.'

'Same office as Milly Barclay, Mother.'

Gwen nodded. 'Good for Milly I said at the time. The poor girl had to put up with a lot of opposition from the family but she fought on and in the end proved that she was more than just a pretty face.'

Kate smiled. 'Milly told me it hadn't been easy.'

'How lucky you girls are today to have such freedom. Sadly when I was young one did not seek employment not unless one had to earn a living.'

'Mother, you've worked all your life.'

'Indeed I have and all of it behind the scenes.' She addressed Kate, 'You see, dear, there were many women like myself who had a good business head on their shoulders but in most cases they couldn't put it to use other than to keep the household accounts and sometimes not even those. My father would have loved a pretty daughter instead of the plain one he got but as he said himself he made the best of it.' She threw back her head and laughed. 'Father discovered my aptitude for figures and my wish to learn about the jute trade and decided I could be an asset to the firm just as long as I didn't show my face.'

'And he could claim the credit,' Roddy added. 'Old devil.'

'No, dearest, just a man of his time.' She looked at the tray. 'You could ring for Brenda.'

'I could but I'll let Kate see how useful I am about the house and take it to the kitchen myself.'

'I never doubted your ability,' Kate laughed. They watched him pick up the tray and Kate was at the door to open it.

'Obviously you didn't trust me to do this myself.'

Once Kate was back sitting on the sofa Gwen said softly, 'I'm not the one who should be saying it but Roddy is a dear boy. I don't recall him doing an unkind thing in his life. That isn't to say he is soft, believe me he is far from that.'

'I know, Mrs Hamilton-Harvey, and you have every reason to be proud of him—' She broke off as the man himself came in.

'Marvellous smell coming from the kitchen.'

'We have an excellent cook, Kate. Mrs Milne has been with us a long time and like most cooks she has her own funny little ways.'

'Mother means that if we forget to say how much we enjoyed the meal she is likely to go off in the huff.'

'No, she doesn't. She just likes to be appreciated but then don't we all?'

Dinner was served at seven o'clock sharp and in the dining-room at a very long table. The whole surface was covered by a snowy white cloth and the three places set at one end. Roddy sat at the end of the table in one of the carvers and Gwen and Kate facing each other.

It was a well cooked but not an elaborate meal. The vegetable soup and hot dinner rolls were followed by succulent tender lamb chops served with mint sauce. Kate was used to mint sauce with roast lamb but never with chops. It would be something to tell Aunt Ruth. The sweet was a mouth-watering almond pastry served with smooth creamy custard. Coffee was served in the drawing-room.

'This was very informal, Kate, when it was just the three of us. Next time you come we'll make it a family occasion. As well as Roddy's father you'll meet Alice and Iain and make the acquaintance of the youngest member of the family. Little David is a darling, we all adore him.'

Chapter Seventeen

November arrived with a bitterly cold sleeting wind chilling everyone to the bone. Kate was glad of the warmth of her winter coat and the tartan car rug wrapped round her legs. From the window she could see an expanse of deserted beach. Not a soul or even a dog could be seen. No one was prepared to venture out unless it was absolutely necessary.

'Why is the weather in November so often worse than we get in December?' Kate asked as they drove towards Craggy Point.

'Maybe we just think it is. In December, Kate, there is Christmas to look forward to and the new year whereas in November there's only the thought of the long, dark winter ahead.'

'I suppose you could be right. Will Alice risk bringing the baby out in this?'

'Why not? What harm could come to him? The wee lad will be well wrapped up and it is, after all, just door to door and exchanging one warm house for another.'

'Of course.' Kate knew she was talking too much and that wasn't like her, not in the car. She was more inclined to keep it to the occasional remark and let Roddy concentrate on his driving. Today nerves were getting the better of her and she seemed unable to stop talking. Telling herself to keep calm, that she was probably worrying about something that might not happen was easy, acting on that advice wasn't. The dread of the meeting ahead was building up. It was a small, tight knot in the pit of her stomach. Kate had even considered pleading sudden illness or feeling sick and it wouldn't have been far from the truth. Roddy, always considerate, would have turned the car at a suitable point in the road and driven her home. Home to Aunt Ruth who would not be taken in. What would be the use? She couldn't go on postponing this meeting with Mr Edwin Hamilton-Harvey. It had to take place some time. The one way, the only way out of it, was to stop seeing Roddy and that was unthinkable. She might as well give up living.

'Are you warm enough, darling?' Roddy turned his head to look at her.

'I'm fine, Roddy, and thank you for thinking of the car rug.'

'Alas, I can't take the credit for that. You have Mother to thank.'

Kate was making every effort to pull herself together and thought she must be succeeding when Roddy seemed unaware of her growing panic. As they turned into the entrance to Craggy Point she smiled brilliantly. Once Kate had been acclaimed for her part in a school play and told that she was promising material if she ever thought of making acting her career. She never had, but here was an opportunity to give the performance of her life.

'That's Iain's car, they've arrived ahead of us. Bet nobody hears us arriving, they'll be so busy fussing over the baby. Wonder if we got that kind of attention, Kate?' he grinned.

Kate just smiled. She was sure that Roddy would have had the same kind of attention when he was a baby as his nephew was getting. She, herself, had been warmly welcomed into this world and only later had troubled times brought so much anguish.

Kate was wearing a tweed coat in a heather mixture. It had a high collar and a long vent at the back. For this her second visit to Craggy Point, she and Aunt Ruth had gone shopping in Dundee. The fine knit dress she wore was in rose pink, a soft shade perfect with Kate's fair colouring. The style was simple and on a coat hanger it was doubtful if Kate would have given it a second look. The owner of the exclusive gown shop would have known this and had the dress displayed on one of the wax figures. Ruth had stopped beside it.

'Kate, that would be perfect on you.'

'You think so?'

'I do, don't you?'

'I'm not sure,' Kate said thoughtfully, 'it looks marvellous on the figure but on me it might be too plain.'

'Try it on, you won't be under any obligation to buy. Here's the assistant,' Ruth said dropping her voice.

'Lovely, isn't it?' the woman smiled. 'It needs someone tall and slim just like you. Take your time and have a good look round.'

'Thank you, we'll do that.'

There were some black dresses in various lengths that Kate had gone over to examine.

'In my young days black was for mourning and women couldn't wait to get out of it. What was that about black I read in one of your magazines?'

'You read that every modern girl should have a little black dress in her wardrobe.'

'Black isn't for you, Kate,' Ruth said firmly.

'Why not? I'm a modern girl.'

'Too young. Black would make you look old before your time. Very suitable and smart for young matrons or the mature woman but—'

'Not for me?'

'For you it should be—'

'Bright colours for a bright young thing,' Kate finished for her.

'Not only bright colours, that rose pink is a lovely warm shade and I think you should try it on.'

'All right, to please you I will.'

The assistant was already removing the dress and instructing one of the shop hands to bring a black cocktail dress to replace it.

'It's only Sunday lunch with Roddy's family and his mother dresses very plainly.'

'That doesn't mean you have to although you yourself described this as being perhaps too plain.'

'Did I?'

'Yes, you did.'

'Pink isn't my colour.'

'Then choose something else.' Ruth was becoming exasperated.

'No, I do like it and I think Roddy will.'

Ruth smiled. She was coming round. Ruth knew Kate so well. She would try on a few others but come back to this one or so she hoped.

'Have you decided on those you would like to try on?' the woman asked.

'Yes.'

Kate looked at herself in the two-piece coffee and cream but didn't much care for it. The cornflower blue dress with the full skirt she seriously considered and blue was Kate's favourite colour.

'Lovely, dear, but you need a change from blue.'

As soon as Kate slipped the rose pink dress over her head Ruth and the assistant exchanged smiles. Plain it might be but it was beautifully cut and showed Kate's slim figure to advantage. For a few moments she studied herself in the mirror and nodded to show that she agreed that this was her dress.

'Not having second thoughts are you?' Ruth asked as they left the shop carrying a dress box.

'No, of course I'm not. Admittedly I wasn't too happy about the colour but I'm all right now.' Kate hadn't been thinking about the dress but of the occasion when she would be wearing it. She just wished it was behind her and her worries had been for nothing.

'Roddy won't be able to take his eyes off you and that could go for his father as well.' It was a flippant remark, a joke, but Kate had paled and Ruth saw her positively flinch. 'What on earth is the matter, Kate? The very mention of Roddy's father and you get yourself into a state.'

'That's not true,' Kate flared, 'it's just your imagination and if we don't step on it we are going to miss the bus.'

'Then we miss the bus and get another. A cup of tea wouldn't go wrong and help pass the time.' Ruth could be awkward too.

'I'm sorry,' Kate said wretchedly, 'I'm being very silly but I can't help it. I *am* nervous about meeting Roddy's father.'

'Why? Have you been hearing things about him? Is he an awkward individual or something?'

'No. Why should Roddy's father be awkward?'

'I don't know but there is something troubling you, Kate, and I have a feeling it concerns that man.'

Kate was tempted, very tempted to confide in Ruth and if the name Hamilton-Harvey had registered something with her then she might well have done so. Aunt Ruth might have made the connection herself. And if she had it would have been all right, it would have been a trouble shared. What would Aunt Ruth have advised? To finish there and then with Roddy? Or do as Kate was doing and wait to see how things would work out? Telling Aunt Ruth now wouldn't serve any purpose, she had come this far and there was no turning back

'So nice to see you again, Kate,' Gwen Hamilton-Harvey said as she kissed Kate on the cheek. 'Isn't this dreadful weather but we're cosy inside. Here comes Alice to meet you.'

Roddy had helped Kate off with her coat and handed it to a maid then he introduced his sister. She saw that Alice had the same sallow skin and flat features as her mother but with her gorgeous auburn hair, Kate thought her very attractive. They stood talking for a few minutes then began walking slowly along to the drawing-room.

'I absolutely adore your dress, Kate, but then you have such a divine figure and if I'm sounding envious it is only because I am.'

'Your figure will come back, dear,' her mother said.

'I wonder.'

Roddy was shaking his head and laughing. 'Women!!'

'Ignore him, Kate – and Roddy go and join Iain and leave us to our talk.'

Roddy winked at Kate and left them.

'What was I talking about?'

'You were moaning about your figure, Alice, and you shouldn't. It is a very small price to pay for that wonderful baby,' her mother said severely.

'I know that, Mum. David is gorgeous but I do have to keep my husband happy and he won't want to see me looking like a sack of potatoes. For absolutely ages I've been wearing tents and now that I don't have to I'm finding that nothing fits me. This thing I'm wearing, Kate, used to hang on me and look I'm almost bursting the seams.'

'Don't exaggerate, Alice. Kate, come along or the men-folk will wonder what has become of us.'

'Is the baby sleeping?' Kate asked.

'Yes. Ellen is in charge of David. We brought her with us so that we could have lunch in peace without straining our ears for baby cries.'

'You should have engaged a qualified nursery nurse. Your father isn't at all happy about this arrangement but he accepts that it is none of his business.'

Alice laughed. 'He does *not* accept that it isn't his business which it is not. Ellen is as good and possibly better than a qualified girl. She is the eldest of eight, Kate, and more or less brought up the younger ones. A whimper from David and I'm panicking but Ellen is always calm and knows exactly what to do.' Kate and she exchanged smiles. 'She'll bring him down as soon as he wakens.'

As soon as she entered the drawing-room Kate saw him. He was standing to the side of the fireplace, a glass in his hand which he carefully placed on the corner of a small table. Kate had a moment or two to study him. A stout man who looked smaller than she remembered but didn't children always think that? All adults look tall to a child.

In that moment when Edwin Hamilton-Harvey saw Kate there was a distraction. Ellen had come into the room carrying baby David, bright-eyed after his sleep and all eyes were on him except those of Edwin Hamilton-Harvey. He was staring at Kate as though seeing a ghost. The colour had drained from his face and she saw his hand reach out to the chair in front as though for support. Kate didn't realise that he wasn't seeing her but the ghost of Mildred McPherson, his one-time mistress and the only woman he had truly loved. Those that followed didn't last long, they filled a need and no more. It is truly amazing how much can go through the human mind in a split second. For Edwin it had been like staring down a tunnel of memory and being transported to the love-nest he had shared with a lovely woman who had always been there for him. The vision passed, he was himself again and this girl could only be Mildred's daughter. This was Kate. Damn it, he had never heard her surname or perhaps he had and if so it hadn't rung warning bells. How lovely she was but not as beautiful as the Mildred he remembered. She looked cool and calm and he resented that. Of course she had the advantage, she had been prepared while he had been taken completely by surprise. Edwin bristled with annoyance and that helped to bring back the old arrogance. People like him didn't show their feelings, they were above that.

Roddy had left Iain in the middle of a conversation to hurry over to Kate.

'Sorry if I seem to be neglecting you, darling. I made the mistake of asking about the farm and once started there is no stopping Iain.' He put his arm round Kate, protectingly, lovingly and she could sense Edwin Hamilton-Harvey freezing with disapproval. Meanwhile, Roddy, totally unaware of the charged atmosphere was smilingly introducing the girl he loved to his father.

'Dad, this is Kate and Kate meet my father. He was very disappointed to have been called away last time you were here.'

Edwin took it from there. 'Indeed I was.' The perfect host welcoming his guest and that guest knowing full well that he wished her anywhere but in his home. The smile didn't reach his eyes as they shook hands. Was he, too, remembering the last time they had shaken hands? Then she had been a bewildered child of ten and he had wished her well and thought that would be the last time he would see Kate McPherson. What must be his feelings now? Would he be willing to forget the past as she was prepared to do?

'Ah, Edwin, you and Kate have met at last.'

'Yes, my dear.'

She was frowning and looking at him with some concern. 'Are you all right, Edwin, you look so pale?'

'Rubbish, do I look ill, Roddy?'

'Look the same to me.'

'There you are, you see. Fussing over nothing.'

'No, I'm not, but if you say you are fine we'll leave it at that.'

'The Lord be thanked for small mercies,' he said, smiling at his wife.

'Men never admit to health problems, Kate. Edwin, did I tell you that Kate is a working girl?'

'Not that I recall.'

'Kate works with Stephenson, Smith & Methven, the solicitors in Crichton Street.'

He nodded. 'I know of them.' Edwin was smiling and managing to look relaxed. It had been the initial shock that had so upset him and he hadn't had time to fully recover before Gwen bore down on them. Dear God, it was a situation that had to be dealt with but it was going to be far from easy with Roddy obviously besotted with the girl. No use trying to blacken her in his eyes not when his were blinded by infatuation. Some other way would have to be found. He would have to think of something, anything just as long as it resulted in the end of this relationship between his son and Mildred's daughter.

'Excuse us, Dad, Kate hasn't seen the baby.'

'Of course, on you go.'

Alice had taken the baby from Ellen and was looking at her tiny, perfect son with all the pride and joy of a new mother.

'Kate, there you are. Let me introduce you to my husband Iain and our little son David and please don't say whom he resembles,' she laughed, 'we are just hoping he gets the best from both of us, then he may have a reasonable chance of growing up to be handsome.'

'I think he is adorable,' Kate said and touched the tiny fingers. When the hand curled round her own finger she wasn't prepared for the rush of feeling. It was so lovely that she felt like crying and that was just silly. Still everyone was allowed to be sentimental over babies.

'Made a good job of him, didn't we?'

'A very good job, Iain.'

Alice raised her eyebrows as though to question Iain's part then with her mother present must have thought better of it.

'Take him, Kate.'

'Oh, no,' came from a clearly shocked Kate. 'I've never held a new baby, I wouldn't know how. He'll probably cry or something.'

'Not my son, he doesn't cry,' Iain said and taking the baby from his mother put him in Kate's arms.

Fright turned to a look of pleasure as she felt the warmth of that little body but all she could say was, 'Goodness, isn't he heavy?'

'What did you expect, Kate, he is after all a farmer's son. Roddy, you next.'

'Absolutely not. Give David back to Alice, he's not a parcel to be handed around.'

'Lunch will be served very shortly,' Gwen announced and Ellen went forward to take the baby with practised ease before escaping upstairs. Her charge had been good, not a whimper out of him and for that she took the credit. She had no time for the nonsense written in books about bringing up babies. Common sense, that was all it needed. Feeding, changing and cuddling that was about the sum of it. Ellen was well content with her lot, believing herself to be incredibly lucky. She didn't think she would marry even if she got the chance. Looking after other people's babies would suit her very well. She thought of it as the best of both worlds. No worries, a comfortable room to herself, good food and a very fetching uniform. Her wages were found money and as for status, for the first time in her life she had that. Ellen wasn't an ordinary maid, she was far from that, wasn't she in charge of the young master and nothing could be more important. In time there might be a little sister and another after that. Ellen, looking to the future, could see herself well established in that household.

The family and Kate sat around the long dining-room table and chatted happily. Edwin carved the roast meat with the skill of someone well used to that task. Kate ate what was before her but afterwards couldn't have said what she ate. She added little to the conversation, just enough not to draw attention to herself. Her quietness wouldn't be noticed, not even by Roddy. There was a lot of leg-pulling between him and his brother-in-law.

Gwen had announced at the start of the meal that politics was not to be discussed and there was to be no scare-mongering about the danger of war.

'It can get rather heated, Kate dear,' she said by way of explanation.

'That just leaves the weather,' her son-in-law said cheekily.

'Should suit you, Iain, farmers talk of little else.'

Alice came to her husband's rescue. 'Weather is impor-tant, too much rain or not enough sunshine and it'll be a poor harvest, then we'll all suffer.'

'Wise words from a farmer's wife,' Roddy said to general laughter.

No one else would notice, only Kate did. Edwin Hamilton-Harvey had done a great deal of the talking without once addressing or including her. She ought to have been relieved only she wasn't. The signs were not good. Had he been prepared to forget the past, and he must know she would prefer that, surely he would have made an attempt to put her at ease, make her feel one of the family instead of ignoring her.

After the meal Alice excused herself saying she wanted to check that all was well with little David and to make sure that a tray had been sent up to Ellen.

'Darling, I gave the instructions to the kitchen, a tray will have gone upstairs.'

'I know but I still want to go up for a few minutes.'

'On you go then, I'll hold back the coffee.'

When Alice came back she wasn't alone.

'Mrs Hamilton-Harvey, I do apologise for barging in—'

'Cynthia, you are not barging in, we are just delighted to see you. You'll join us for coffee?'

'Of course Cynthia will join us for coffee,' Edwin said smiling hugely.

'Thank you, I will, just a quick coffee and then I'll go. Mummy told me that Alice, Iain and the baby were coming and, of course, I just had to pop in and see him.'

'We'll drink our coffee and then I'll take you up to see little David though the chances are he'll be asleep.'

'Our offspring seems to spend most of his time sleeping.'

'Babies do that for the first few months of their life, Iain dear.'

'Thank you, mother-in-law, we are always learning,' Iain grinned.

'You must meet Roddy's friend. Kate, Cynthia.'

Roddy had been sitting on the arm of Kate's chair.

Friendly eyes turned to Kate. 'Pleased to meet you, Kate,' Cynthia said quietly and went over to shake hands.

'Hello, Roddy, you are quite a stranger these days. Mummy and Daddy were saying that they never see you and wondered if they had offended you in some way.'

'How could they do that, Cynthia? I can only say that life has been pretty hectic one way and another but I promise to look in one day soon.'

'Then see that you do.'

Kate thought she detected an awkwardness with everyone talking that little bit quicker and was it her imagination or did Roddy seem less at ease than usual?

'Kate,' Gwen said, 'Cynthia's parents are very old friends of ours.'

'As a child this was practically my second home. Thinking back I must have been a terrible nuisance.'

'Not at all, the three of you played happily together and only occasionally were there temper tantrums from Roddy when you touched his precious engines.'

'My railway set, Mother, and no wonder. Those two had no respect for it.'

In an unguarded moment Kate caught the expression when Cynthia looked at Roddy. The girl was in love with him, Kate was sure of it. Did that explain the awkwardness? Roddy would be uncomfortable if he knew and it was possible he did.

'Cynthia had a name for us, Kate. Our name is such a mouthful, particularly for a child, and she got round that by reducing it to the first two letters of Hamilton and Harvey and for a while Edwin and I were Mr and Mrs HaHa.'

Cynthia laughed along with the others. 'It didn't last very long, my mother put a stop to it.'

This dark-eyed attractive girl with her healthy colour was obviously a favourite with Edwin and Gwen. Edwin was laughing and teasing her and it was so within the family that Kate felt shut out. Roddy had done some of the teasing too and perhaps sensing she was feeling left out had tightened his arm around her. She should have been reassured by that but she wasn't. This was the girl Roddy was meant to marry and Edwin Hamilton-Harvey was as good as telling her that if he had his way Cynthia would become his daughter-in-law. Kate shivered. If she remembered correctly he was a man who always got his own way.

'Not cold are you?' Roddy said anxiously.

'No, not at all, how could I be? The room is lovely and warm.'

Cynthia declined more coffee. 'No, thank you, I enjoyed that and now I am going up to see this precious infant and then I'll go. Goodbye, Kate, I'm sure we'll meet again. And, Roddy, don't forget your promise.'

'I won't.'

The door closed behind her and Alice.

'Charming girl,' Edwin said to a murmur of agreement. Kate caught Iain's eye and thought she saw sympathy. She wondered if he had been readily accepted into this family or had they had other hopes for their daughter? Parental wishes wouldn't have played much part. They were obviously very happy together.

Kate saw Alice, who returned a little while later, and Iain exchange looks with no words necessary. Lots of married couples did it. The time had come to make their departure and it was Alice's place to make the first move. She did.

'Sorry to break up the family party, Mum. It's been lovely but we must be on our way.'

'So soon? I've hardly seen my little grandson. Why not stay overnight? Iain you could come and collect them some time tomorrow, couldn't you?'

Iain looked at Alice, leaving it to her.

'No, we'll go now,' Alice said firmly. 'David is sound asleep, he won't know he is being moved and . . .' She smiled at Iain. Words weren't necessary, she wanted to be with her husband.

Roddy got to his feet. 'Kate and I will be right behind you.'

Kate could have hugged him. She wanted away, the strain was beginning to tell and although Roddy couldn't have known the reason he must have thought her tired or a bit out of sorts.

The car left for Carnoustie and Kate was saying her thank you to the host and hostess. Gwen kissed her cheek and her husband moved away so that nothing was expected of him.

'That's that,' Roddy said when they were on their way.

'I enjoyed it very much,' Kate lied.

'Really?'

'Why did you say "really" like that?'

'You didn't look to me as though you were enjoying yourself.'

'Why? What did I do wrong?' she said stung at the suggestion that she had failed in some way.

'Kate, that wasn't what I meant and you know it. I don't know what got into Father, he can be an awkward customer when he wants.'

'You mean he didn't approve of me?'

'Don't be silly, of course he approved of you.' Roddy was getting angry. He felt under some strain himself. He wasn't particularly observant unless where Kate was concerned and it had been plain to him that his father was making no effort to welcome Kate into the family. Probably it was just the mood he was in and his mother could be right and maybe he was unwell. Pity Cynthia had arrived when she did, not that there had been anything between them, but it could have looked that way to Kate. 'You'll like Dad when you get to know him.'

I do know him, that's the problem. What would Roddy have to say to that?

'I like your sister and her husband.'

'Iain is a good sort and to the surprise of us all Alice is enjoying being a farmer's wife. She isn't above putting on a pair of wellies and helping out. Not lately of course but before that.'

'Cynthia seems nice.'

'She is.'

No harm in asking. 'Tell me if I'm wrong but I have a sneaking suspicion that Cynthia is in love with you.'

'Wrong, you couldn't be more wrong. We grew up together and remained good friends that's all.'

Kate didn't speak.

'Don't you believe me?'

'I think you might be blind to it but others aren't.'

'That imagination of yours is running away with you.'

'No, it isn't imagination. She is the girl your father wants you to marry.'

'Father does have a special fondness for Cynthia, as I said we all like her. That said,' Roddy laughed, 'don't you think I should have some say in the matter?'

Kate gulped. He was so nice and she was being horrid.

'I'm sorry, Roddy, I'm being awful. Blame it on tiredness, I didn't get much sleep last night.' That was true enough, she hadn't.

'An early night for you then and I'll get my head down to some long neglected work. Your fault with me wanting to spend so much time with you.' He took one hand off the steering wheel and brought hers to his lips.

'I love you and you love me and that is all that matters.'

'Yes, Roddy, that is all that matters.' She wished with all her heart that it could be the case.

Back at Craggy Point, Edwin was preparing to disappear into his study.

'On a Sunday?' Gwen sounded her surprise.

'Why not?'

'Because you never do, that's why.'

'Very well, I shan't then.' Edwin had felt the need to be alone to address this problem. Dear God! who would have believed this could happen?

Gwen was worried but knew better than to fuss. Edwin hated fussing. Even so it was hardly fussing to be concerned about her husband's health. She might have to have a quiet word with the doctor and between them make Edwin take care of himself. Men of his age had to be careful and not overdo it. Had he been short of breath? No more than usual but then she wasn't always with him.

Edwin liked a glass of whisky in the evening and Gwen a cup of tea. It was a routine they both enjoyed. A chance to discuss the day's events before retiring to their separate bedrooms.

'Alice could very easily have stayed overnight and Ellen could have had that small room in the attic.'

'Not much good her being up there if the wee lad is screaming for attention.'

'Alice could have coped, she isn't helpless.'

'Granted, but she obviously preferred to return with Iain.'

Gwen drank some tea and put the cup down.

'Kate is a delightful girl, didn't you think so? And very pretty. No wonder our son is head over heels in love.'

'She's pretty and Roddy is infatuated at the moment. It won't last.'

'I'm sure you're wrong.'

'I'm not. Cynthia is the girl for Roddy and we both know that.'

'Edwin, dear, I know how fond of Cynthia you are and I am too.'

'A perfect match.'

'No, I'm afraid not. Cynthia, I do believe, might be in love with Roddy but Roddy's feelings are not involved. He thinks of her much as he thinks of Alice, like a sister.'

'Nonsense.'

'Your trouble is, Edwin, that you only see what you want to see. Roddy happens to be in love with Kate and both Alice and I like the girl.'

'The lad isn't twenty-one yet.'

'Not far from it.'

'Too young to be serious.'

'Try telling that to Roddy. The young won't be dictated to.'

'More's the pity, but to get back to this girl. She could be nothing but a gold-digger. Remember she has to go out to work and with no family other than an aunt.'

'You appear to know a lot about Kate.'

'Only what was said in my presence.'

'Then you misunderstood.'

'Indeed, and how do you arrive at that?'

'Let me tell you. Roddy's happiness means everything to me just as it does to you.'

'Don't tell me you did some snooping?' Edwin said feeling the grip of fear.

'Not an expression I expected from you. I made some enquiries that's all.'

'And the result of these enquiries?' He tried to smile.

'For some years Kate lived with a spinster aunt in Silverbank and when she died she left everything to Kate. A considerable sum as it happens, Edwin, so you can discount the gold-digger.'

'Why go out to work if that is the case?'

'Many girls do. Not necessarily for the financial rewards, probably just pin money, most of all it is to prove something to themselves.'

'For a sensible woman you can talk a lot of nonsense.'

'No, I don't and I can understand it. The monotony of a woman's life, not to mention the waste, was quite appalling. It says a lot for this generation—'

'All right, Gwen, you've made your point.'

'Good. Now perhaps you'll tell me what you have against Kate.'

'She isn't right for Roddy.'

'Roddy will be the judge of that, it is his life.'

'Exactly and I don't want to see him ruin it.' He poured himself another whisky, something he very seldom did. Gwen watched him drink some and put down the glass with a hand that wasn't quite steady. Then he got up and began pacing the floor.

'Edwin,' Gwen said sharply, 'sit down and tell me what this is all about. I'm not a fool.'

'You're far from that,' he said and sat down.

'You are keeping something from me.'

'Why do you say that?'

'I haven't lived with you all these years without recognising the signs,' she smiled.

Edwin was silent for a long time, then he gave a deep sigh. 'Not in my wildest dreams did I imagine this could happen.'

Gwen waited not rushing him. It would all come out in his own time.

'It began a long time ago . . . you see, Gwen, Kate's mother was my mistress. Seeing Kate was like seeing a ghost.'

'Oh!'

'Mildred McPherson, Mildred,' he said and Gwen thought she heard his voice soften as he said the name.

Mildred McPherson, that had been the woman's name. Gwen's memory was excellent for detail particularly where Edwin was concerned and, painful though it was, she was always honest with herself. She knew she had always had her husband's respect but never his heart. Gwen had known jealousy and humiliation but managed to keep them well hidden. Had she been a proper wife to Edwin he would not have looked elsewhere. There was no one to blame but herself.

'Was Kate's mother a widow?' she asked in a strangled voice.

'Yes.'

'When – how old?' She shook her head and bit her lip. 'Would Kate have known?'

'About my relationship with her mother?'

'Yes.'

'Possibly, I'm not sure. Is ten old enough to understand?'

'For a bright child, I imagine so. She must have had some idea.'

Gwen's brain was working frantically. Kate couldn't fail to have connected the name. She must have known all along and decided to keep poor Roddy in ignorance. No wonder she had been nervous, she couldn't have been sure if she would get away with it. In the event her close resemblance to her late mother had sealed her fate. Another stab of pain. If Kate looked like her the woman must have been beautiful. Was it any wonder that Edwin had fallen in love with her.

He sighed. 'It's a mess.'

'Yes, Edwin, it is a mess.'

'What are we to do, Gwen? It has to be stopped at once but how to go about it.'

'I really don't know. She was such a nice girl or so I thought.'

Edwin was beginning to relax. He wasn't on his own. 'You do agree the affair can't go on?'

'I'm not sure we can do anything. Roddy has a mind of his own and he won't be dictated to. We could, of course, tell him the truth and that might put an end to it but we can't be sure of that.'

Edwin was shaking his head. 'No, not that, I would much rather that Roddy was kept in ignorance. Give me time and I'll think of something or you will.'

Chapter Eighteen

It had been a particularly busy day and the staff were tired. Kate covered her machine, tidied her desk and hurried along to the cloakroom to collect her coat. She called good night, heard an answering cheerio from Amy and Netta and ran down the stairs and out into Crichton Street. Before catching the bus home she wanted to go to the baker's in Union Street. Their pineapple tarts were special and Kate liked to take home a surprise treat.

'Kate!'

Hearing her name, Kate stopped and with a sinking heart looked at the man getting out of the car. She wondered why she wasn't more surprised. Perhaps she had been expecting something like this. After all, he did know where she worked. When she last saw him – was it just two days ago? – he had been dressed in a dark, tailored suit. Now he wore tweeds and looked every inch the country squire come to town. Broughty Ferry was seaside not country though Craggy Point had all the appearance of a large country house.

'Hello, Mr Hamilton-Harvey,' Kate said awkwardly. 'You must excuse me but I'm hurrying for my bus,' she lied. The pineapple tarts would have to wait for another night.

'We need to talk, Kate—'

'Not now, I'm sorry – but—'

'Kate, I've been parked here for a considerable time,' he

said frowning heavily and making it sound as though she were at fault. 'I assure you this won't take long and I'll drop you off at the bus station.'

Kate felt trapped with no escape possible. With a show of reluctance she got into the car and stared straight ahead. Roddy's father checked that the passenger door was properly shut then went round to take the wheel.

He angled out. 'We'll find a quiet spot.' They drove for a while until he found a suitable side street, parked neatly, then switched off the engine. He moved in his seat until he was facing her.

'Seeing you in my home, Kate, gave me a nasty turn, it was a very great surprise.'

'I'm sure it was an unpleasant shock.'

'Yes, I'm afraid that is exactly what it was. I had no idea you were Roddy's friend but you must have known all along that Roddy was my son.'

'You are wrong there,' Kate said coldly, 'when Roddy told me his surname I thought it possible that you might be distantly related but no more than that.'

'I hardly think so, Kate.'

She remained silent.

'I think you were reasonably sure from the beginning that Roddy was my son.'

'You can think what you like.' It was rude and quite unlike Kate but she had ceased to care.

'Are you trying to tell me that you came to Craggy Point unaware of the connection?' His eyebrows shot up.

'No, I am not. By then I thought it a very strong possibility,' Kate admitted.

He was looking at her and shaking his head. 'How cruel of you to do that to Roddy. Once you knew of the relationship wouldn't it have been kinder to stop seeing my son?'

He made it sound so reasonable, such a small effort on her part. It was what she should have done, she had known that herself.

'Why didn't you end it?'

'Because I love Roddy.' Kate swallowed painfully. 'You have no right to dictate to me, Mr Hamilton-Harvey. Whom I choose to go out with is my business and no one else's.'

'You are wrong, it is my business, very much my business. For goodness' sake, Kate, face facts, your late mother—'

'Your late mistress,' she put in quickly.

'I was trying to spare you that.'

'How very thoughtful of you,' Kate said sarcastically.

The man gave a deep sigh and seemed on the verge of losing patience. 'You aren't making it easy for me.'

'Why should I make it easy for you, Mr Hamilton-Harvey?' Anger was giving her courage. 'Roddy and I are not children, we are both responsible people and perfectly capable of making our own decisions.'

'There you are wrong. I'll remind you that Roddy has not yet come of age, he is only twenty.'

'Very soon he will be twenty-one.' Kate was shaking and took a deep breath to help calm her. 'What happened all those years ago is surely best forgotten. Why rake up the past? What possible good can that do? I had nothing to do with your relationship with my mother and Roddy can't be held responsible for your past conduct.'

The angry colour suffused his face. Kate saw it and smiled grimly, that had hit home. 'There is no reason that I can see why any of this need be disclosed.'

'Don't you? What if I were to tell you that it has already been disclosed?'

He was bluffing, he had to be. 'Why would you do that when you come out of it so badly?'

'But, my dear, I don't.' She saw genuine amusement in the smile. 'There, Kate, is where the difference in your upbringing shows. My reputation in no way suffers and I'm reasonably sure that both my children would have been aware that I was not always faithful to their mother. I'm sure too that they would not have been unduly concerned.'

Kate felt like slapping that arrogant face but knew that he only spoke the truth. Roddy had been very matter-of-fact about his father's peccadilloes as he would have described them.

'I find that very sad, Mr Hamilton-Harvey, that your children should accept such a situation.'

'You have a lot to learn about life, my dear.'

'Some of it I would rather not know.'

'What we can't change we must accept. Life is unfair we all know that. Men are permitted, indeed in some circles it is expected, that a man have a relationship outside marriage. It doesn't threaten the marriage in any way, rather it often strengthens it. Sadly for a woman it is very different. Once she takes that road her reputation is in tatters.'

'You ruined my mother,' Kate said bitterly.

'No, Kate, I did not. Your mother came to me of her own free will. There was no pressure from me and had she said "no" then that would have been the end of the matter and you and I wouldn't be sitting here.'

Kate had to try and salvage something out of this.

'She did it for me.'

'I can well believe that. Mildred was a lady, a very lovely lady and if she were here to advise you she would tell you to give up Roddy.'

'I'm not so sure.'

'I am. I knew your mother very well and it was the saddest day of my life when she died.'

She nodded and swallowed the lump in her throat. Kate liked him for that. They were both silent, busy with their own thoughts. She saw him make an arc of his fingers and she remembered him doing that when she was a child.

'We do agree on one thing.'

'Do we?' she said sharply.

'Yes, Kate, we both want Roddy's happiness.'

She nodded feeling the tears close. She hadn't expected to win, not really.

'Let him go, Kate. Make it a clean break, nothing else will do.'

'I can't do that,' she whispered, 'and Roddy would never accept it.'

'He would. I know that it is asking a lot but if you truly love him and I believe you do, you'll find the courage.'

'It would be so cruel and he would be so hurt,' she said brokenly.

'One has to be cruel to be kind in some cases and this is one. Whatever you do decide to say to Roddy, or there again a letter would make it easier, it must mean the end. Roddy has his pride and if you make it abundantly clear that you want nothing more to do with him he'll leave you alone. Roddy won't run after a girl who doesn't want him.'

Kate felt numb. He had it all worked out and she was just expected to agree. He was talking again.

'My wife would find it difficult, impossible, to welcome you into our family.'

'You didn't have to tell her.'

'Roddy's mother is a very astute lady. She knew I had a mistress, it was never a secret. All that was secret was the woman's identity.'

'I don't want you ever mentioning my mother again,' Kate said agitatedly. 'What if I told you she left me a letter explaining everything.'

'I wouldn't be in the least surprised.'

'She loved my father, she didn't love you. You used her—'

'And she used me, Kate. Kindly remember that I put a roof over her head and bread on the table.' He was breathing heavily. 'I do believe she had affection for me or if I'm wrong she must have decided that pretending something she didn't feel was easier for her than facing poverty.'

'She would have faced that if it hadn't been for me.'

'You could be right. She could have married again and as a beautiful young widow had her pick. As a young mother that was more difficult. Men do like to father their own children rather than have to bring up someone else's.' He switched on the engine. 'I'll drive you to the bus station. Give careful consideration to all I have said, Kate. A wrong decision on your part could cause a great deal of heartache.'

Outside the bus station she opened the car door and all but stumbled out. He said something and she muttered a reply but later she couldn't recall those final words.

When Kate dragged herself up in the morning, Aunt Ruth took one look at her and ordered her back to bed.

'I'm not ill,' Kate protested, 'I'm just tired that's all.'

'I'm a nurse and I know a sick person when I see one.'

Kate gave in and went back to bed for in truth she did feel awful. Sleep had been far away as she tossed and turned and went over in her head all that had been said in the car. Roddy was to be in Edinburgh for a few days and she was glad of that. The letter would be waiting for him on his return. The sleepless night had given her plenty of time to think and she was in no doubt now about what she should do. What to put in the letter was the big problem. She had to make it crystal clear that she had no wish to see him again.

The longing to confide in Aunt Ruth was great but she must resist. Aunt Ruth was perfectly capable of taking the matter into her own hands and that could mean Roddy learning all the sordid details. She didn't mean sordid details not when it concerned her mother, but he would hear what she would like to keep from him. Knowing Roddy he would say that none of it mattered but deep down would he really think that? Family was important and he was proud of his. He couldn't be happy about their future children having a grandmother who had been a kept woman.

Aunt Ruth was out and Kate had the house to herself. Page after page was crumpled and thrown aside as she tried to compose a letter that would free her and not be too brutal. She tried again.

> *Dear Roddy,*
>   *This is a very difficult letter to write and I'm too much of a coward to tell you face-to-face. The truth is, Roddy, that*

though I like you enormously, I don't love you. Someone I truly love has come back into my life. There were misunderstandings that made us both miserable for a time but happily we are together again.

Thank you for the good times we enjoyed and try not to think too badly of me. Maybe you and Cynthia are right for one another. If not there will be someone else.

Please do not reply to this or make any attempt to see me. It would do no good. A break when it does happen should be clean.

My best wishes and forgive me.

Kate

She was far from satisfied with what she had written and reading it over she was appalled. How could she write such a letter to someone she loved so much. Should she tear this one up and try again? No, what was the use, as Roddy's father had said sometimes it was necessary to be cruel to be kind. Before she could change her mind Kate sealed the envelope and was putting a stamp on it when Aunt Ruth popped her head into the bedroom.

'That for posting?'

'Yes.'

'If I go now I'll get it in the letterbox before the collection.'

'Thank you.' There was no use having second thoughts now.

The weather got colder, very much colder. In the mornings the grass had a delicate lacy covering for all the world like a giant spider's web. The trees, stripped of their leaves, were stark against the clear sky. It was the beginning of January 1939 with the wind restless as always, then gathering momentum to rip the slates off roofs and in a frenzied anger set windows rattling dangerously.

Kate barely noticed the world around her, every day was

so empty. She had known Roddy wouldn't answer but even so hadn't she hoped. Everyone knew that she had stopped seeing Roddy but something in her face stopped them asking the questions they longed to ask. Kate made a big effort to act normally and her work didn't suffer. Keeping herself busy helped to take her mind off her heartache.

Aunt Ruth was worried out of her mind seeing the change in Kate. The laughter had gone and in its place was this terrible lethargy. In the evenings she would just sit around, sometimes staring into space and at other times with a book in front of her and no pages turned.

'This won't do, Kate, it is pure selfishness.'

Kate's eyes filled with tears but Ruth ignored the pleading in them, she would have her say.

'This has to do with Roddy and I don't care who is to blame. If I had my way I would knock both your heads together and see if that brought you to your senses. If the lad is half as miserable as you then I'm sorry for his parents. You, my girl, have to pull yourself together unless you want to make yourself ill. Then it is hospital for you, I am not going to look after someone who has made herself ill.'

Kate was half laughing and half crying. 'Would you really do that?'

'If I thought it would bring you to your senses I would.'

Kate was feeling ashamed. She had been so wrapped up in her own misery that she hadn't given thought to the effect it was having on others, particularly Aunt Ruth.

'I needed you to talk to me that way, I have been selfish but – but—'

'Never mind the but. One day you might get round to telling me what went wrong between you two but I'm not going to pester you. We all have to rise above our troubles and this is you, I hope, about to do that.'

Kate nodded.

They had been sitting at either side of the fireplace with a cup of tea beside them. Ruth picked up the newspaper, sighed, and put it down again.

'It makes depressing reading.'

'Do you believe we might be on the brink of war?'

'I think it is a strong possibility but I pray to God I'm wrong.' She gave a sad little smile. 'You've heard me going on about our politicians being a set of ditherers and some of them are just that.'

'I have.' Aunt Ruth could be scathing about those in power.

'Having said that, Kate, I would hate to be in their shoes and forced to make decisions that could affect every man, woman and child in the country.'

The weeks turned into months and Kate was getting on with her life. She went out with her friends and accepted invitations. There was the occasional date but none that lasted more than a week or two. Ruth was relieved but not taken in. Kate was putting on a good act but Ruth had seen the fleeting sadness when the girl thought herself unobserved.

Chapter Nineteen

Voices were raised in the drawing-room at Craggy Point, a rare occurrence.

'Why in God's name did you do it?' Edwin Hamilton-Harvey was shouting. 'Do you want to get yourself killed?'

'Not especially but I'll take my chances with the rest.'

'If you had to do it why the Royal Air Force and not the Army? Tell me that.'

Roddy and his father were both standing. Gwen was seated in a chair beside the window and looking from one to the other.

'I think this war is going to be won or lost in the sky.'

Edwin's eyes were bulging. 'What kind of damned, stupid answer is that? If we're drawn into a war and it is still a big if then, of course, we'll win and no question about it.'

'The arrogance of the British,' Roddy muttered.

'What was that?'

'Nothing. Just calm down, Dad, will you. I've volunteered for the Air Force because that is what I want. Training pilots takes time and I'm not sure we have all that much of it. We're teetering on the brink of war.'

'It isn't inevitable, the talking isn't over.'

'More talk, more pieces of paper signed, delaying tactics that's what they are,' Roddy said disgustedly. 'It isn't any good burying your head in the sand and pretending it isn't going to happen.'

'The young are so sure of themselves, they think they know it all. To hear them, experience counts for nothing,' Edwin said bitterly. He unfolded a clean white handkerchief and wiped his mouth. 'What about the mill? Have you given any thought to it or is it that you couldn't care less?'

'I have given thought to the mill and yes, I do care,' Roddy said quietly.

'It doesn't look much like it.'

'The mill, Dad, like so many other mills will be taken over by the government and become part of the war effort.'

'Gwen?' Edwin was appealing to his wife to come to his assistance.

'I rather think Roddy could be right, Edwin dear. We will have no say or very little and we will just have to do what we are ordered to do.'

Edwin was obviously taken aback. Her answer was unexpected and did not please him in the least. So much for a wife's support, he thought angrily, she was taking Roddy's part.

'You're taking a gloomy outlook I must say and as for being ordered – ordered indeed,' he spluttered, 'that is preposterous. It happens to be *our* mill.'

'War is preposterous, Dad. We are in this mess because a jumped-up little nobody is calling the tune. The warnings were there but the powers-that-be chose to ignore them and look the other way. A few who did read the signals correctly tried to make their voices heard but were silenced and ridiculed.' Roddy looked across the room to his mother. 'What do you think, is war inevitable?'

Gwen didn't like to upset her husband but she had to be honest.

'There may be a slim chance of avoiding war. No,' she shook her head, 'not avoiding, just postponing. To my mind it has all got out of hand and I don't see any way out of it.' She frowned at Roddy. 'You should have waited and talked it over with us. We are both upset, your father and I.'

'I'm sorry you're upset but talking it over would have been a waste of time since my mind was made up.'

'We might have persuaded you to give more thought to the matter before taking such a drastic step.'

Roddy shook his head. 'There was no chance of me changing my mind.'

'Time enough to go when you were called up I would have thought,' his father said gruffly.

'It's done and we can't make a better of it.' Gwen smiled bravely. 'I haven't told you yet that I had Alice and little David here in the afternoon. War, or the possibility of it, is being discussed at the farm too. Iain is quite convinced that we will be at war before very long.'

'Alice won't have to worry, her husband is in a reserved occupation. The country has to be fed.' He was fiddling about on the coffee table and scowling. 'Where are those damned matches?' he said irritably, 'I can never find them when I want them.'

'Try looking under your tobacco pouch, dear,' Gwen said in the long-suffering voice of a woman frequently accused of removing or hiding whatever he was suddenly in need of.

He grunted, found the matches, lit his pipe and took a few puffs.

'Farmers are exempt from military service,' Gwen agreed, 'but that won't stop Iain doing what he believes to be his duty. Alice says, should it come to war, Iain is determined to get into uniform.'

'More fool him. It isn't a game for God's sake. I'm as patriotic as the next man but it would be sheer folly for Iain to neglect the farm. Does he forget he has a wife and child to consider?'

'Iain isn't likely to forget that. He is far from stupid and he'll have someone in mind to take over in his absence.'

'A very great risk that would be. That person he has in mind may work well under supervision but left in charge it could be a different story. Making the wrong decision could be costly. He might not have a farm to come back to.'

'Edwin, you seem to forget there is Alice.'

'What good is she? What does Alice know about farming? Damn all.'

'Not so, you underestimate your daughter. Alice is taking a very real interest in the farm. Iain has her looking after the books and, as he says himself, making a better job of it than he did.'

Roddy smiled. 'It's true, Dad, Alice takes after Mother, she has a good head for figures.'

'Huh!'

Mother and son exchanged smiles. 'You could be right and Alice is getting her chance. War is dreadful as we all know but if there was one good thing to come out of the last it was the opportunity given to women to show their worth. Not that they had ever doubted it but others were to find out. There was nothing those women wouldn't turn their hands to and what they did then their daughters or granddaughters will do now and in far greater numbers.'

'Fine words and I wouldn't dispute what you've just said. There may well be a need for women to do a man's work in wartime but come the end of hostilities a man wants to return to a comfortable home and a wife content to look after him and their children.'

'I managed both, Edwin, I hope I did.'

'You did but then you are the exception not the rule.'

Roddy hid a quiet smile. His mother was getting her oar in.

'Glad to hear you say that, Dad. With due respect you have always enjoyed the best of both worlds. Mother was always the brains behind the business, she worked hard but she never neglected you or us.'

'Thank you, Roddy dear, but your father has always done his share,' she said loyally.

'The devil I do,' he barked.

Roddy knew that not to be the case. His mother didn't

seem to mind having the heavy end of the stick, she never complained. It could be that she felt she had nothing to complain about.

Roddy wasn't far off the truth. His mother didn't feel hard done by. She considered herself fortunate to have Edwin as her husband and Craggy Point as her home. As for her children they were the greatest gift of all. Not many plain women, even those with money, got their heart's desire.

At this moment she was deeply concerned about her son. She had a sneaking suspicion she hadn't shared with Edwin that Roddy had volunteered for the Air Force to get away from home. Edwin had been so sure that a few weeks would do it and he would have forgotten Kate. A few weeks hadn't done it, Gwen had never seen him so unhappy and guilt was tearing at her. She wasn't proud of her part in all this. For her own selfish reasons she had wanted Kate out of their lives and Kate had gone quietly and completely. Roddy never mentioned her name and he had even snapped at Alice when she asked in all innocence what had become of Kate. He had gone around with a closed look on his face and was seldom at home, coming in after they had retired. At breakfast he was polite but said little.

Hearing that Kate was no longer on the scene, Cynthia began to call at Craggy Point which pleased both Edwin and Gwen. Roddy treated her as he always had and Cynthia, seeing no future for her with Roddy, gradually faded out of the picture.

Edwin's anger turned to pride. He began boasting about his son joining up to train as a pilot. Gwen was dreading the time when his training would be over and her real worries would begin. She tried not to think too much about it and envied Edwin who could, even now, convince himself that war could be averted and if the worst did come to the worst then it would all be over in a matter of months. The veterans he met up with at the club were of the same opinion.

An intelligent woman, Gwen could read between the lines. This was a country caught unprepared and what was happening now were panic measures. According to those who were in the know, Hyde Park was being dug up for air-raid shelters. In Gwen's opinion and not only hers, if Londoners were digging up their precious park then the position was grave indeed.

Over in Muirfield in Ashgrove Cottage, Ruth listened to the nine o'clock news on the wireless and despaired that world events were worsening by the minute. Did nobody learn from history that there were no winners in a war? War solved nothing, it only increased the bitterness and stored up trouble for the future. In the Great War, her war, the war to end all wars, the legacy for each side was a whole generation of young men wiped out in the trenches. This war if it happened would be very different. Bombs would drop from the sky on helpless civilians, on women, on children, on the old and infirm. And our boys, our pilots, would be doing the same to other helpless civilians. Ruth felt a terrible sadness that the lessons of the Great War should be so easily forgotten.

On a warm day in September the rumours ceased to be rumours. A clearly distressed Mr Chamberlain explained to a hushed country that everything possible had been done to prevent war but without success and we had to accept that our country was at war.

Talking about the possibility of war was one thing, being plunged into it was another. People came out of their houses and huddled in groups as a wave of fear swept the country. Mothers clutched their children and gazed fearfully into the sky as if already enemy planes were on their way to unload their cargo of destruction.

In a small community people look for a leader and in Muirfield Ruth McPherson was the obvious choice. She was a trained nurse, a mature woman and highly respected. As well as those qualities she had a nice way with her. She could persuade the less confident to tackle jobs they were convinced must be beyond them.

Black blinds, the roller type, were almost impossible to find and black-out curtains were the next best thing. Those who owned a sewing machine were much in demand. Blocking out the light was the first priority and the curtains had to meet strict requirements. Even the smallest chink of light showing, Ruth emphasised to a well-filled village hall, could have devastating consequences. That small light might be seen by an enemy plane looking for a target to drop its bombs on before returning to base. They didn't want to linger in dangerous skies any more than our boys did when they were over Germany. Ruth knew she was alarming the good people of Muirfield, she could see the fear in their faces, but if it got the message across then it was worth it. This was war.

Just as it had been in the Great War, the community spirit was very much alive and for those who wanted it there was always a helping hand. Tearful mothers who had seen their sons off to war were given cups of tea and comforting words. Older women, some of them housebound, got out the knitting needles and very quickly produced an assortment of knitted comforts to be distributed by various organisations. Everyone wanted to play their part. Men, long past the age of being called up, became visibly smarter as they reported for duty with the Home Guard or became air-raid wardens.

The fear, mixed with excitement, began to lessen when nothing much was happening in those first weeks. No bombs fell, there were no battles in France and the soldiers were becoming restless and bored waiting for the action. When the real conflict did begin there was some relief, the popular opinion being that the sooner they got stuck into the enemy the sooner it would be over and they could get home. Most believed it would be a short war and that was probably just as well. What would it have done to morale if they had known the struggle was to continue for six long, difficult years?

Fear was rekindled when the locals, Ruth and Kate

among them, presented themselves at the village hall to be issued with a gas mask. Each gas mask was contained in its square cardboard box with a string attached for easy carrying. Folk eyed this monstrosity with disbelief and prayed that they would never be called on to wear them.

Kate had taken over most of the cooking to Ruth's relief.

'Would you, darling?' she had said when the offer was made. 'That would be such a help.'

Kate smiled. 'I can't promise a high standard.'

'Kate, dearest, a high standard would be quite impossible with the shortages but your best will be a lot better than mine.'

'We are lucky compared to some.'

'Yes, Kate, we are and we should try to remember it. Those of us in the country have very little to grumble about.'

It was true. The country folk had many advantages over the town's people. The hens continued to lay and there were fresh eggs to be enjoyed for breakfast. Rabbits were plentiful and if properly cooked could taste as good as chicken. Nurse Ruth as she was usually addressed would occasionally have a rabbit handed in at the back door or left on the outside door mat. After that first time when she had looked at the dead, furry beast with some misgiving, the others had arrived skinned and ready for Kate to deal with. Potatoes and vegetables were there for the taking and nobody went hungry.

In the town it was a different story, the housewives formed queues for everything. It became a way of life. So much so that women seeing a queue forming outside a shop would automatically join it without knowing what was on offer. Whatever it was would be a scarce commodity and no one could afford to let a chance go by. A fresh egg was a luxury not enjoyed by many of the town's people. They had to make do with egg substitute which, when fried, tasted like boot leather. New recipes began to appear in newspapers and magazines suggesting ways to produce nourishing meals using those ingredients still available. In the evenings Kate studied the recipes and amazed herself by finding most of the dishes quite tasty.

Office life continued as before with only occasional changes. Milly was the first to give up her job and return home to prepare for her wedding to Tony which had been brought forward. Very little preparation was necessary, this was to be a quiet wedding and a far cry from what it would have been in normal times. Tony was a second lieutenant with the Black Watch and shortly to be going overseas with his regiment. They would all miss Milly.

Kate arrived at her usual time and Amy and Netta a few minutes later. Amy was looking glum.

'What's the matter, Amy, you don't look too happy,' Kate said.

'My sister is being sent to Birmingham. We don't agree about anything but I'm going to miss her.'

'No one to fight with,' Netta said. 'I know someone else who is going to Birmingham,' she continued as she took out the postage book in readiness to add up the column of figures. 'She's going to a munitions factory.'

'Isn't that careless talk?' Kate said. The villagers had been given several lectures on the danger of speaking unwisely.

'Not between us for heaven's sake.'

'Never know who might be listening at doors,' Amy grinned.

'In a solicitors' office, don't be so daft. You know this, every time I add up this column I get a different answer.'

'You can't count that's your trouble.' Amy paused. 'I'd like to join the services but if I suggest it my mother will hit the roof.'

Netta gave up on the columns and put down her pencil. 'Your mother will just have to hit the roof, you'll have to go when you get your calling-up papers.'

'She knows that, Netta, my mother just doesn't want me rushing off.' Amy looked at Kate. 'What about you?'

'I'd like to join up.'

'Which service?'

'I don't know though I might favour the WAAFs.'

'What is your aunt going to say to that?'

'Nothing, she'll leave it to me. She was a nurse in the Great War.'

'Was she? That seems ages ago but older people, like your aunt, must remember. Must be awful for them living through two wars.'

'Aunt Ruth was in France,' Kate said sounding very proud. 'So was my father.'

'Your aunt and your father were brother and sister?'

'No.'

'The relationship was on the other side?'

'Yes,' Kate said too quickly. This was just casual conversation with Amy but didn't it show how family secrets could come to the surface in unexpected ways? One would always have to be on guard and it would be a never-ending strain. That's how it would have been if Roddy and she were still together, Kate thought. The awful emptiness was always there but now she was better at hiding it.

'If it isn't your aunt, what *is* holding you back from joining up if it is what you want?'

'Amy, I'd feel so guilty leaving Aunt Ruth just now when she is so terribly involved. I don't know how she gets through the work she does and if I wasn't there to make a proper meal I don't think she would bother about eating.'

Netta looked scornful. 'If she was hungry enough she would make the effort to cook something. And if it is bad as you say why doesn't she demand help?'

'Good question, Netta, I've been asking that myself. It's always the willing horse that gets the heavy load. Still the broad hints a few of us are dropping are beginning to get results. One or two are looking a bit uncomfortable and hopefully they'll have the decency to offer assistance.'

'Leaving the way clear for you?'

'I suppose so. Everyone isn't accepted you know.'

'They'll take you like a shot. Shorthand typists are always in demand, even typists without shorthand. Wish I could type.'

'Then learn for heaven's sake,' Amy said. 'Milly's machine is there doing nothing.'

'Would I be allowed to practise on it?'

'I can't see why not, you're not going to break it are you?'

'Of course not.'

'Netta, I'll help you,' Kate said, 'but once you know the fingers to use it is just a case of practise, practise.'

'Thanks, I'll take you up on that.' She clapped a hand over her mouth. 'Nearly forgot to tell you both, mind you I wasn't listening I just couldn't help overhearing.'

'That'll be right,' Amy grinned. 'Come on out with whatever it is.'

'Our Mr White is leaving to join the Army, officer of course.'

'Good for him,' Amy muttered, 'not so good for the Army.'

'That's not fair, Amy, and I bet he'll look handsome in his uniform.'

'Most men do, it does something for them.'

Kate nodded as though to agree. She had had no further trouble with Andrew White but for all that she wouldn't be sorry to see the back of him.

'Miss Howard will be happy,' Amy said, 'she won't have to retire, the partners will want her to stay on.'

Kate smiled. 'I'm glad for her, it must be awful to have no interests outside work.'

'Netta for heaven's sake give me that postage book and I'll add it up.'

'Thought you'd never offer,' Netta said handing it over. 'Incidentally, when do I get my first typing lesson?'

'What typing lesson?' All eyes went to the door. Netta went pink and swallowed and Kate came to her rescue.

'It was my suggestion, Miss Howard. I thought seeing

that Netta was so keen to learn she could practise during quiet times.'

'Or during my lunch break,' Netta added eagerly.

'I have no objections to that at all, Netta, in fact I am extremely pleased. Since we haven't replaced Milly we could do with another typist. If you show promise it might mean promotion for you. It is always easier to employ someone straight from school to be office junior.'

Netta looked as though someone had handed her a five-pound note.

'This will only happen if you show aptitude,' she said and went away smiling.

'Too true I'm going to show aptitude whatever that might be.'

Miss Howard returned a few minutes later. 'All that about typing put it out of my head. There was a gas mask left in the office overnight. I saw it when I arrived in the morning.'

'Mine, Miss Howard,' Netta owned up, 'I forgot it.'

'That was very careless of you.'

'Sorry, Miss Howard, but honestly nobody bothers now.'

'It is a government order that gas masks must be carried at all times,' the woman said severely.

'I know girls who use the box for carrying other things.' Cosmetics she could have added but didn't.

'That is quite dreadful. Silly, stupid girls. What happens if there is a real emergency?'

'No one believes there ever will be.'

'No one knows, Amy, and it is our duty to be prepared.'

Amy shook her head. 'My dad says it was a panic measure. After a while the rubber deteriorates.'

'Surely not?'

'It'll be true, my dad knows about these things. He says just another example of money wasted.'

'My dad said the same.'

'Maybe they are next to useless, Netta, I wouldn't know.

However I shall continue to carry mine until we are told otherwise,' Miss Howard said primly. 'Just make sure, Netta, that you don't leave yours behind in the cloakroom. If you do I shall have to reconsider your chance of promotion.'

'Yes, Miss Howard.'

The woman went out closing the door behind her.

'Think she meant what she said?'

'Yes, Netta, she meant every word,' Kate said as she began on a pile of work.

When Kate got home it was to find a hastily scribbled note propped up in front of the clock. She read it then sat down abruptly feeling her legs weak with shock. Her thoughts were in tumult: Tommy Nicholson, the boy who had pestered her for a date when he was home on leave. She had gone with him to the cinema but reluctantly. Afterwards they had gone for coffee and she had agreed to write to him. Then he had asked for a photograph or snapshot. All he had to look forward to, he said, were his mother's letters and great though they were it wasn't like one from a girl. And as for a photograph that would be something to look at last thing at night. She had laughed and said she would. Tommy could be very persuasive and he did understand that it was nothing more than friendship. Or she hoped he did.

Would he have received her letter? It was highly improbable, the mail didn't get through very quickly when you were on the high seas. Tommy would never read what she had written nor see the snapshot taken in Milly's garden one summer. Tommy wouldn't be coming home. She read the note again.

Sorry, darling, awful news. That nice boy, Tommy Nicholson – a telegram has just arrived to say he has been lost at sea. From bits of information received it appears his ship was torpedoed and there are believed to be no survivors. Poor Mrs Nicholson, as you can imagine, is in a

dreadful state and as for Tommy's father the man has just gone to pieces. Relatives are on the way but I must stay until they arrive. Eat your meal and don't wait for me.
  Aunt Ruth

Kate's eyes filled and the tears rolled down her cheeks. She tasted the salt as they touched her mouth and she began searching in her sleeve for her handkerchief. Tommy Nicholson wasn't the first war casualty in Muirfield but the one best known to her. Thinking back she felt such relief that she hadn't denied him her company and she could so easily have done so. There would never be anyone like Roddy but she couldn't go through life longing for something that wasn't going to happen. She didn't want to go through life alone and when this war ended she wanted a husband and children.

Kate made herself a cup of tea then set about preparing the meal. She would wait for Aunt Ruth and the minute she heard the click of the gate she would put on the oven. It would mean having to wait until the meal was cooked but better that than making something now and having to reheat it.

The war was going badly there was no hiding that. Hearing the voice of the newsreader no one could doubt the gravity of the situation. Some even switched off rather than listen. They could cope better not knowing the true position. No one doubted that victory would eventually be ours or if they did they had the good sense to keep that to themselves.

Chapter Twenty

'Darling, why couldn't they have stationed you a bit nearer to home?' They were in the kitchen with Ruth washing the dishes and Kate drying them.

'So that I could pop along any time, you mean?' Kate smiled.

'No, that would be too much to hope for. But you could have come for short leaves, twenty-four hour or whatever they call them.'

'Perhaps there is method in their madness and they won't want home to be too near. I bet the girls from down south are sent up here.'

Ruth was frowning. 'I just wish RAF Miltonwells wasn't so near London.'

'It's not all that near.' Kate's face betrayed her alarm. 'You won't tell anyone where I'm stationed?'

'I hope I have more sense. Anyone who does ask will be told you are stationed somewhere in the Midlands and have to be content with that. This plate is going to have to steep for a while, I'll leave it in the water. Most folk,' she continued, 'appreciate how dangerous careless talk can be and just to remind them there are plenty of posters about.'

'Including one in our very own village hall,' Kate teased.

'Including one there,' Ruth smiled.

'I wonder who was responsible for that?' Kate said raising her eyebrows. She knew very well that one of the visiting WVS ladies had left one behind and Ruth had asked the air-raid warden to hang it up in a prominent position. 'Seriously, Aunt Ruth, when I'm not here to look after you—'

'Darling child, I'll manage.'

'I don't doubt it but you must ease up or your health is going to suffer. And,' she continued before Ruth could interrupt, 'learn to delegate. I'm always telling you that and you won't do a thing about it.'

Ruth lifted the plate out of the water to examine it. 'Whatever is stuck to this is stubborn, I'll leave it a while yet.' The plate went back into the water and Ruth dried her hands on the kitchen towel. 'Kate, dearest, you are not to worry about me. I am not silly enough to neglect my health and as for delegating, I'm doing that already.'

'Funny how I haven't noticed.'

'You've been too busy yourself to notice anything. Tell me again what you are training to be?'

'A teleprinter operator.'

'You won't be making use of your shorthand and typing? That seems a shame.'

'Not shorthand, but it won't be difficult to get my speeds back if I need to.'

'That's not so bad then.'

'A teleprinter operator, Aunt Ruth, is no more than a glorified typist. There won't be much training required because the keyboard is the same as a typewriter except there is no shift key and all the letters are the same size. What you do have to be is a touch typist since you don't see what you are doing.'

'You mean you could be making mistakes without knowing?'

Kate smiled. 'If you are, the operator at the other end will let you know about it.'

Ruth looked puzzled. 'Why does it take two operators for one machine?'

Kate was wishing she hadn't got started on this.

'Aunt Ruth, it is a bit complicated to explain. The best way I can describe it is by saying the machine transmits messages by typing over the telephone exchange system.'

'My! My! What will they be inventing next? Oh, did I tell you old Mr Cruickshanks was in Dundee and the poor soul walked into sandbags in the dark and gave himself a terrible fright?'

'Was he hurt?'

'A bit of bruising, nothing serious. The shock upset him more than anything and I'm sure the language must have been colourful.'

'They *are* a menace in the dark, thank goodness here in Muirfield we don't have that problem,' Kate said as she put the clean dishes in the dresser.

It was true the folk in Muirfield didn't have to contend with sandbags but getting about could be extremely difficult and not just in the dark. Country roads could look the same in daylight and with all the signposts removed there was no telling which direction to take at a crossroads. A stranger might ask a local for directions but there was no guarantee he would be given the correct information. Strangers were treated with caution at the best of times and in wartime with suspicion. There was no means of knowing who was on genuine business and who was up to no good.

The long suffering townsfolk got used to the stacks of sandbags set at regular distances on the pavement. Come darkness they were cautious. One had to be extra careful where one walked and if there was a warning, it was only the slightly darker shadow that loomed ahead. The young were quick to cope with the inconveniences and without fear went to dance halls and other places of entertainment. The war had its advantages for them. There were lonely soldiers far from home who were looking for companionship, a light flirtation or perhaps more and the girls were very happy to help them forget the ugly side of war.

Jokes were told and laughed over. Many were about dangerous encounters with sandbags. A favourite was the

one about a man leaving a public house after a 'few',
bumping into a stack of sandbags and apologising profusely.

Kate decided she needed her hair cut. It wasn't long but
she thought she ought to have a bit taken off to be on the safe
side. The regulation was that hair had to be above the collar.
When she arrived home from the hairdresser, Ruth had
been nearly in tears.

'What have you done to yourself?'

'Nothing, just got my hair cut.'

'I can see that. She hasn't left you with much.'

Kate fingered her hair or what remained of it. 'My usual
hairdresser left last week and I told the new girl I was joining
the WAAFs and I had to have my hair short.'

'She's gone mad with the scissors. Why didn't you stop
her?'

Kate had been about to when she saw what was being
taken off then decided it was too late and closed her eyes
until it was done and a junior was sweeping up her blond
curls from the floor.

'I couldn't once she'd started. Never mind I'll get used to
it and it'll grow again.'

Kate had to grit her teeth as folk looked at her, shook
their head and gave their comments, none complimentary.

'Your bonny hair, who did that to you?'

'It'll grow and I have to have it short, it looks neater
under a cap.'

'Ah, well, it's your hair,' Mrs Wallace said, 'but your
aunt won't be all that pleased. And this is you going into the
services?' That was followed by several shakes of the head.
'Taking the laddies you would have thought would be
enough without taking the lassies too. Your aunt will miss
you, Kate.'

'I'll miss her too.'

'That goes for most of us. She would be sorely missed if
she was to take herself off.'

Kate looked puzzled as well she might. 'What do you
mean take herself off? Where to?'

'There's no saying is there? Her being a trained nurse and not all that old the powers-that-be may decide to make use of her in one of the hospitals. I mean all those wounded coming home to be nursed. Still we've all to make sacrifices, there's a war on.'

'Yes.'

'Terrible times we're living through.'

'Yes, I must—'

'Where is it all going to end, tell me that?'

'Mrs Wallace, I really must—'

'The government must think us all daft, the rubbish they come out with and expect us to swallow.'

'That's to keep our spirits high.'

'Huh! not mine, the opposite more like. Give it to us straight and less of the mollycoddling, the British don't need it, that's what I say. There I go not letting you get a word in edgeways.'

Kate had been trying to get away. 'I must go, Mrs Wallace.'

'Me too. I've a few bits of shopping to do before the shelves are emptied. Best of luck, Kate, if I don't see you before you go.'

Kate was leaving Muirfield with mixed feelings. It would be wrong to say it was all for King and country. Those left behind were doing every bit as much for the war effort but not everyone appreciated that. Kate's own reason for joining up was her need to get away and give herself a new challenge. Leaving would be difficult but staying could be worse. There were too many memories here. New faces, new places, would take up her attention and leave less time for her own thoughts. Where was Roddy? What was he doing? Was he miserable or had he forgotten her already?

She said goodbye to all at Stephenson, Smith & Methven of Crichton Street and her friends and neighbours in Muirfield. Time was supposed to be the great healer or was it that the level of pain couldn't last? There was just so much one could stand. Kate likened her own suffering to toothache. First the sharp, unbearable pain which somehow one endured then the dull, never-ending ache that followed. Nagging, nagging never giving peace. The only sure cure for toothache, when it defied all else, was to have the offending tooth removed. What Kate was doing was removing herself to where there was little or no chance of meeting Roddy. Away from reminders of happier times, the restaurants and cafés where, from across the table, they had gazed into each other's eyes. The Palais where they had danced cheek-to-cheek and the country lanes where they had strolled hand–in–hand.

That first railway journey to England would long remain in Kate's memory. She had been lucky to get a seat at Dundee and had said her goodbyes to Aunt Ruth on the platform. From Dundee station onwards there had been a rush to get on that bordered on pandemonium. The corridors filled up with exhausted soldiers, sailors and airmen sleeping in any space they could find. The blinded windows of the coach shut out any landmarks and the raising of the corner of the blind gave no assistance. Kate wondered and worried how she would know when she reached her destination. No one spoke, it was as though there was nothing left to say, or they were too tired to make the effort. Only the loud roar told Kate when they were entering a tunnel and the rushing noise when they were leaving it. Each time the train slowed down and stopped at a station, doors were opened and voices gave shouted instructions that few could make out. There was near panic as those wishing to leave the train had to battle their way out by stepping over bodies and bulging kitbags. Kate sent up a silent prayer that there would be less of a stampede when the train reached her destination and more important that she wouldn't go beyond it.

*   *   *

Back in Muirfield, Ruth was in the narrow hall ready to swoop on the letter as it fell from the letter box on to the mat. Had it not been from Kate her disappointment would have been great. But it was and Ruth smiled. There was something pleasurable about delaying a treat, holding it back to enjoy at leisure. She had been in the middle of breakfast when she heard the gate open and was immediately on her feet knowing it could only be the postman. Taking the letter back with her to the table, Ruth looked at the familiar writing then refilled her cup and buttered her second piece of toast. Just a scraping was all she allowed herself, there was something virtuous about keeping within her ration. Her standing in the village would have allowed her a little extra had she sought it but she hadn't. There were those who never went short of anything, they had bargaining power and used it. Even those considered upright citizens were involved in a small way in the black market. For the real black marketeers it was a way of life and a business enterprise that could be very profitable and worth the risk of being found out and punished.

Ruth put on her spectacles, opened the envelope and withdrew two pages of small, neat writing.

Dearest Aunt Ruth,

You will, I hope, have received my previous letter which was just a hastily scribbled note to let you know I arrived safely. The journey down was a bit nightmarish, or so I thought, but I was quickly assured that what I experienced was the norm and didn't I know there was a war on!

I do love my uniform and feel so proud to be wearing it. The girls I will be working alongside and sharing accommodation with, introduced themselves. They are all English and talk so fast that I am hard put to understand what they say. A one-to-one isn't so bad but a crowd of them together laughing and talking and the noise is unbelievable. Aunt Ruth, sometimes I feel like the country cousin come to town. I exaggerate of course, should those same girls happen to visit our village hall and hear the tongues wagging they would think we spoke a foreign language.

The WAAFs I've met are a friendly lot and helpful to a new recruit. One of them a Cockney girl has gone out of her way to explain everything. Her name is Dorothy Brooks. She is an absolute scream and can swear like a trooper but somehow it doesn't sound bad coming from her. Her home is in London with her grandmother. Dorothy never mentions anyone but her grandmother and there are those who think her family may have been wiped out in the blitz. Friendly though she is there are parts of her life not for discussing. I like them all but if I had to choose a friend, someone I could trust with anything, it would be Dorothy.

Teleprinting holds no terrors for me. I've discovered it needs a lighter touch and now that I've mastered that I find it to be less tiring than pounding a typewriter. What I do take bad with is the noise they make which I can only describe as a racket. Apparently everybody finds this to begin with and I was told that after a few days I wouldn't even notice. Silence would make a bigger impact and this proved to be the case. A fault developed and all the machines stopped. The silence was absolute, eerie even and we found ourselves whispering. Then the fault was corrected and the noise back. Just goes to show, doesn't it, that one can get used to anything. So much for the work, now for the accommodation. Let me say first of all how I miss my comfortable bed in Ashgrove Cottage.

This isn't too bad and we shouldn't complain. The very first lot, WAAFs I mean, had to make do with wooden huts with corrugated roofs and the most primitive of living conditions. I can't believe it could have been as bad as they say but you never know. The RAF didn't exactly welcome the WAAFs though that can't be said now. I was telling you about the accommodation. We are in this huge station and I do mean huge. Our living quarters, or should that be sleeping quarters, are in a red brick building put up in a *hurry. I'm lucky to be sharing a room with two others when I might have been sharing with a great many more. The beds have iron bedsteads with a metal locker for each bed. Amazingly I get off to sleep quite quickly.*

Some of the WAAFs have bicycles and I may buy myself a good second-hand one. Now I come to the social life and there seems to be quite a bit of that. Dances are held regularly and there is a place to meet, have a refreshment and maybe a game of ping-pong if there are any table-tennis balls available. The local Rotary or maybe it was some other organisation, gifted a piano. It gets a lot of rough treatment by those who think they can play and bash away making as much noise as possible.

London, I gather, is still the place to go and draws the crowds. Dorothy says shortages don't affect the top hotels and restaurants. Luxury food is still there for those who can afford it.

If this letter is a bit disjointed blame the many interruptions. There is no such thing as a quiet corner around here.

I miss you, I miss my comfortable bed and I miss my own cooking. The food isn't too bad but lacks imagination. Maybe the huge amounts puts the cooks off trying something different.

Write when you can and do include all the silly bits of gossip. It will bring home and you a little bit closer. Take care.

> *Lots of love,*
> *Kate*

Ruth was smiling as she laid aside the letter. Kate was settling in and sounding reasonably happy. It was a relief to know she was beside nice girls but Kate was the kind of person who would fit in anywhere. Ruth was pleased to learn that the girls had a social life within the station and didn't have to go out looking for it. Her dearest hope was that Kate would meet a nice airman who would take her mind off Roddy. She hadn't been fooled that the girl was over it. She was far from that but with all her life before her, Kate would have to forget her first love. One day there would be someone else. How easy it was to say that but Ruth hadn't found it to be so. She had loved with all her heart and had known such jealousy, thankfully hidden, when it had been obvious to her that Robert and Mildred were deeply in love. Why had she tried so hard to blind herself to that? How selfish she had been, and how ashamed when she looked back. She didn't deserve Kate but God worked in mysterious ways. He had forgiven her and put a precious life in her hands. Whatever the future held Kate would always be her main concern. She wanted her happiness above all else.

Chapter Twenty-One

In the 1914–1918 conflict class had been important, whereas in this war people were more united. The class barriers were still there but folk were less intimidated by position or rank. The dream of a classless society would always remain a dream. It could never be, it wasn't in the order of things. What was evident was the new togetherness. There was a willingness to give a helping hand to strangers. Women began to take a greater pride in themselves and not only in appearance. Gone was the little woman left behind in tears and despair, in her place was a woman, still fearful for her husband's safety, but making her own contribution to the war effort. Some went into the munitions factories and, working side by side with others, soon made friends. They wore a scarf tied round their head, turban fashion to protect their hair and reduce the danger of accidents. Others served in canteens, manned first-aid posts and females driving ambulances and other vehicles no longer raised an eyebrow.

Women were making an important contribution and at the end of the week there was a pay packet and the satisfaction that brought. The family didn't suffer, there were those who remained at home and willingly took charge of a neighbour's family. The money they were paid was welcome and where was the trouble in looking after a few more bairns? The older girls could be relied upon to take charge of the younger ones. It had always been that way. Everyone was content or appeared to be.

Kate was enjoying life in the services and finding it no more demanding than working in a solicitor's office. There were frantic busy spells when they were kept hard at it then would come a slack period when they could relax and have a gossip.

Kate did not attend all the dances. She preferred having time to herself to read a book, there were always some left about to be picked up, read and replaced or there would be letters to write. She wrote weekly to Aunt Ruth with every scrap of news she could gather. The replies were hilarious and a joy to read. The letter would be started on a Monday and a bit added each day, then the pages gathered together and posted on Saturday. Any interruptions were detailed, the identity of the caller and what was said and the same with phone calls. The goings-on in the village were described and no doubt greatly exaggerated and had Kate laughing.

Amy from the office wrote to say she had been accepted for the ATS and was having problems with a tearful mother selfishly considering only herself and refusing to see it that way. Milly's letters were very short, only a single page written on one side. She had no news she said and wrote as though she were both worried and angry that no letters had arrived from Tony. She didn't say for how long, only that it was ages. Kate tried to tell her that Tony's letters might have gone astray or that if he was moving about he might be unable to write. The reply had been typical Milly. 'Kate, I know all that, I hear it every day from my parents and I realise it could be true. But it isn't helping me. What if Tony isn't writing because something has happened to him? It's the not knowing, that's why I'm between anger and despair as the days turn into weeks and no word.'

★   ★   ★

'I'm not in the mood.'

'Then put yourself in the mood. They've got hold of a good band and it's much more fun when there is a crowd of us. That apart who knows what might walk in?'

Dorothy Brooks, the Cockney girl, had wandered over. 'Our Kate being awkward, Vera?'

'No more than usual.'

'I'm not being awkward,' Kate protested. 'You two would go dancing every night of the week if you could.'

'Too true we would. Come on, Kate, we needn't stay until the end unless we want.'

'All right, I'll come,' Kate said resignedly.

The dances were popular and well attended and occasionally some of the officers wandered in but seldom stayed long. Too long for the ordinary airmen who could see them far enough. They couldn't compete with the glamour boys.

A group of them were together laughing and talking. Kate wasn't doing much of the talking, rather she was listening and smiling. Those talking were having to shout to make themselves heard above the band.

One of the girls facing the door suddenly made a hushing sound.

'Don't all look now but the real talent has just shown up.'

'And how,' someone answered as three tall, handsome pilot officers came through the door and stood for a moment as though considering whether they should come in or go away again.

Kate was slow to turn and when she did she found herself looking straight into the eyes of Roddy Hamilton-Harvey. They were staring at each other and standing stock-still as though glued to the spot. Curious eyes watched them, then the girls tactfully moved away.

Roddy was the first to recover and with a polite smile he crossed over to where she was.

'How are you, Kate? I could hardly believe my eyes.'

'Nor I,' she managed to get out.

'Don't tell me you are stationed here?'

'Yes, I am. I've been at Miltonwells for – oh, quite a while.' She couldn't think for how long, her brain had seized up.

'Strange that we should meet like this?'

'Yes.'

'Life is full of surprises, is it not?' he said drily.

'Yes. Yes, it is.' She was trembling and hoped he wouldn't notice.

As for Roddy he felt as though the breath in his chest was being squeezed.

'You've cut your hair.'

She smiled. 'Regulations, I had to.'

'You suit it that way though I prefer it longer.'

They were alone standing not far from the door. The others had drifted away to dance or to queue up for a refreshment. Roddy looked at Kate's left hand.

'No ring, Kate, I *am* surprised.'

'Wh-what?' she stammered.

'The name, I fear, has escaped me, that is if I ever knew it – I'm talking about the lost love who so suddenly reappeared in your life.'

She looked at him blankly then reddened. 'I'm sorry, Roddy, I wasn't thinking.' She stopped and bit her lip.

'Somebody you made up? There was no one, Kate, am I right?'

She didn't answer. What could she say?

'It was just an excuse to stop seeing me. You could have told me face-to-face instead of resorting to untruths. I thought better of you, Kate.'

'It wasn't like that,' she whispered.

'Wasn't it?'

There was a whiteness about his mouth and a strained look that brought her close to tears. Had she done this to him?

'No, Roddy, it wasn't. It wasn't like that at all.'

'Then suppose you tell me what it was like.'

Why shouldn't she? Why shouldn't she just do that?

'Was it because you fell out of love? It happens, Kate,' Roddy said quietly. 'I wouldn't have held it against you.'

'Roddy, I never stopped loving you, not for a single moment.' There it was out and she had no regrets. The old reasons didn't apply in wartime, perhaps they should never have mattered at all, at any time.

'If he isn't going to ask you to dance may I have the pleasure?'

Kate turned to see who had spoken. It was one of the officers who had arrived with Roddy.

'Push off, Derek, will you? Kate and I are old friends and we have a lot of catching up to do.'

Derek smiled good-naturedly. 'Nice to have met you, Kate, another time perhaps?'

'Of course,' she smiled back.

'Come on,' Roddy said almost roughly, 'let's get out of here. Trying to carry on a conversation through that noise is impossible.'

Kate made no objection when he took her arm and led her out into the darkness. Once outside he stopped and drew her close but it wasn't an embrace.

'Never rush out into darkness, Kate, always take time to let your eyes grow accustomed. It's a tip worth knowing.'

'Yes, I know, my aunt always does that. She says the pitch black becomes dark grey.'

'Mrs McPherson, how is she?'

'Very well, thank you.'

'Take my arm and we'll make better progress.'

She tucked her arm in his and it felt just right as though that was where it belonged. 'Where are we going?'

'Not very far. Somewhere where it is quiet and peaceful and we can talk. There is a lot I don't understand and I hope we are going to put that right,' he said grimly.

'You still haven't said where you are taking me?'

'Don't you trust me?'

'Yes, Roddy, I have complete trust in you.'

'We are going to my flat.'

'Your flat?' she said disbelievingly.

'I don't own it. It's furnished and I rent it. If you want to know how I came by it—'

'Only if you want to tell me,' Kate said hastily.

'One of my fellow officers took it so that his wife could be near him.'

'And he's gone, been transferred?'

'You could say that.'

Something in his voice alerted her to her mistake. She should have been more careful. More than likely whoever it was had been one of the unlucky ones who hadn't returned from a raid. Her stomach lurched with fear for Roddy.

'I'm so sorry, Roddy.'

'It's all right, you couldn't have known.'

'I should have thought before I spoke.'

'No, Kate, we can't tiptoe round everything. If we all thought before we spoke there wouldn't be much said.' He paused. 'I don't spend a great deal of my time in the flat but it is there when I want my own company. High jinks, and there is plenty of that, can be a bit wearing. A little does me.'

'I know, there are times when I long for a bit of peace and quiet. Sometimes I think I'm a round peg in a square hole if I've got that right.'

She felt his smile. 'You, a misfit, never. Here we are, this is us arrived. I'm afraid we have to go through a bit of a performance. When I open the door nip inside, then stand quite still while I shut the door then find the switch for the light.'

She giggled. 'Didn't you think about investing in a torch?'

'No, have you one?'

'No, I haven't, but I would if I was coming to a place like this in the dark.'

'I know my way around. You all right?' Roddy's voice floated across to her.

'Yes, I haven't moved a muscle.'

'Give me a minute, I'm making sure the black-out is in

placc before I switch on the light. Seems to be all in order,' he said as the light went on in the hall. Kate moved from the vestibule and saw Roddy turning on two lamps in what turned out to be the sitting-room. Then he bent down to switch on a bar of the electric fire.

'This is very nice,' Kate said coming into the room.

'I like it, it suits me.' He smiled. 'An inspection can be arranged for later. Meantime make yourself useful and help me move this sofa nearer to the fire.' He took one end and she the other.

'Heavier than I expected.'

'That was why you were called on to help. Sit down, Kate, on the sofa and I'll join you once I get the percolator going. The percolator belongs to me not the flat. It was a case of buying one or drinking Camp coffee which I dislike. Coffee suit you or there's beer and tea, of course.'

'Coffee please.'

He came back and sat down but made no move to touch her. All he did was half turn so that he could see her face.

'Kate, did I imagine it or did you really say you had never stopped loving me?'

'That's what I said.'

'And did you mean it?'

'Yes, Roddy, I meant it. I meant it with all my heart.'

'And yet you put me out of your life. Why?'

'I had to, at the time I was convinced I was doing what was best.'

'You aren't so sure now?'

Her eyes met his. 'I'm not sure of anything any more. What was important then doesn't seem nearly as important now. The war has done that.'

'The war has done a great deal,' Roddy said heavily. 'And I want to know what was so important then. I think I'm entitled to some explanation.'

'So do I.' Kate knew there was no turning back. Once she got started she would tell Roddy everything, leave nothing out. What he would make of it remained to be seen.

'You're taking a long time to get started.'

'I'm wondering where to begin.'

'I would suggest the beginning.'

No, not the beginning, she thought, that would come later. Kate took a deep, shaky breath. 'That second time I visited Craggy Point, you remember I met your sister, Alice and her husband and the baby?'

'And my father.'

'Yes, and your father.'

'That was when it all went wrong, Kate?'

'Yes.' She paused. 'Before meeting everyone, you and I sat in the car and you told me a little of your family history. About your grandfather and his gambling—'

'What has that got to do with it?' he said impatiently.

Kate continued as though he hadn't spoken – 'and how it nearly cost your family Craggy Point. After that you told me about your parents' marriage, that your father had not always been faithful to your mother—'

'I can't for the life of me—'

'Roddy, this is difficult enough for me without you interrupting. Everything I'm telling you has a bearing on what happened to us.'

'Sorry.'

'You spoke about your father having had the same mistress for many years.'

'I remember telling you that but I wish I knew where all this is leading.'

'I can't rush this, I have to tell it in my own way. If I remember correctly I must have been showing some sympathy for the mistress and you said that she didn't deserve any, that her kind would always survive. You said that type of woman had no self-respect and they were only out for what they could get. You do remember saying that, Roddy?'

'I may have.'

'You did, I assure you.' Kate gave a hard little laugh. 'Well for your information, Roddy, that woman who earned your contempt was my mother.' She moistened her dry lips. 'You don't have to look so shattered, most others would agree with what you said. I might have shared your opinion had I not known better. You see, Roddy, my mother was the kindest, sweetest person you could hope to meet. She never hurt anyone and as for your mother, my mother knew the position and therefore could feel no guilt. What she did was for me, to give me a better chance in life. Had I not been born her life would have been very different.'

'Kate, I don't know what to say,' Roddy said looking and sounding distressed.

'Let me go on, I can't stop now. The details are complicated and I won't go into them yet. Just let me say that when my father died there was no money and because of the circumstances my mother was not entitled to a widow's pension. You are looking sceptical but I can assure you that was the case. One day I would like you to read the letter my mother left for me when she knew she was dying. She told me everything, Roddy, and left it to me to judge her. I have to be completely honest and tell you that though I understood the reasons for doing what she did, it didn't stop me feeling she had left me a legacy of shame. Incidentally if you are wondering, she, my mother, never had a bad word to say about your father.'

Roddy was looking agonised. 'Why in God's name didn't you tell me all this? You've put us both through hell for what – because you thought it would make a difference to me—'

'What's that noise?' she said sharply, her nerves on edge.

'The percolator, I'd forgotten about it. No harm done.' He got up. 'Give me two ticks and I'll get the coffee. I think we need it in the absence of something stronger.'

Kate sat forward. The electric fire gave out a good heat and was more than sufficient for an evening in late summer yet she felt chilled to the bone.

'There you are, Kate.' He handed her a plain white cup and saucer.

'Thank you.' She put them down on the table Roddy had brought forward before he went to see to the coffee. When he came back with his own she was warming her hands on the cup.

'That the way you like it?'

'Yes, thank you, you remembered how I take it.'

'I remember everything about you, Kate.'

She smiled.

'I don't need to hear any more.'

'You do. A half story is no good and you have to hear what made me do what I did.' She took a drink of coffee then kept the cup in her hands. 'Aunt Ruth says I take after my mother in appearance and I think I must.'

Roddy was nodding. 'My father, I gather, saw the resemblance and that shook him. Of course it did,' Roddy said jerking himself upright. 'My mother remarked about how pale he was and he was irritated at her saying it.'

'When he saw me there I have a feeling that he was seeing the ghost of my mother. Then, of course, he realised I was Mildred's daughter.'

'Did you know?' Roddy said quietly.

'Know what?'

'That we were father and son?'

'Not at the very beginning, though when I heard your name I had to wonder. It was wishful thinking, I was hoping you would be a distant relative, very distant. It was a very slim hope and I knew then that I shouldn't have agreed to see you again. My only excuse was that I desperately wanted to.'

'Not as desperately as I wanted to see you. For me it was love at first sight and I wouldn't have let you go, not without a struggle.' He looked in her cup. 'Finish that and I'll get the table out of the way and we'll have more room for our legs.'

'Thank you, that was a good cup of coffee.'

'Pride myself on that. Kate, when were you sure we were father and son?'

'When Alice's baby was born and David was to be named after both grandfathers. There was no doubt in my mind after that.' Kate smiled but without humour. 'I called your father Uncle Edwin until I was ten years of age and until my mother died. That was when he informed me that he wasn't my uncle, that we were in no way related, and it had been my mother's wish that I should address him that way. It was about that time he told me that my mother had been his mistress.'

Roddy looked as though he couldn't believe what she was saying. 'He did that? You are telling me that my father told a child of ten, a recently orphaned child, that her mother had been his mistress? That was monstrous and I can't believe we are talking about the same man.'

'Don't think too badly of your father, Roddy, he was never unkind to me.'

'If that wasn't unkindness I don't know what is.'

'You have to remember he was awkwardly placed and looking back I can appreciate his difficulty. In the event I did go and live with my Aunt Sarah but at the time my mother died no one was claiming me.'

'My poor Kate.' He pulled her close to him.

'Mr Hamilton-Harvey just wanted me to understand that I wasn't his responsibility. He went as far as to try and get a foster home for me but by then I had been in touch with my Aunt Sarah.'

'I still say it was monstrous. At the tender age of ten did you know the meaning of mistress?'

Kate's lips quirked with amusement. 'Your father asked me that and I felt so insulted that he should think me ignorant. I told him quite forcefully that I did and I can recall how relieved he looked.'

'Did you know?'

'Absolutely not, I was a little innocent. I knew that my father had died when I was a baby and I just accepted that the man who came about the house was Uncle Edwin. We were never very comfortable with each other and I can understand that. Your father wanted my mother's complete attention and so did I.'

Roddy nodded.

'I overheard my mother being described as that man's mistress and something about the way it was said made me think there must be another meaning for mistress. I had connected it with headmistress or the mistress of the house. Anyway I asked the woman who had been looking after my mother when she was ill if mistress had another meaning, a bad meaning. Poor soul, she must have been terribly embarrassed. Looking back it was quite funny. I thought she didn't know and I was going to tell her.'

'Oh, Kate!'

'She did tell me in the nicest way she could. Am I making sense?'

'Just about. What a difficult life you've had, my darling.'

'I didn't think so not until I went to live with my Aunt Sarah. She was very much of the old school, believing a child should be seen and not heard. And never be idle, there were always jobs for me to do. I got a rude awakening I can tell you.'

'Obviously it did no lasting harm.'

'I'm not so sure. I felt cheated of my childhood.'

'Kate, let's go back to that Sunday at Craggy Point. I can't believe all that was taking place and I noticed nothing.'

'Not too surprising. Little David was getting all the attention and later on you had a visitor.'

'Cynthia.'

'Your father made a big fuss of her and I think that was for my benefit.'

'No, Kate, he always did.'

'She was the chosen one for you.'

Roddy's anger had been building up and now it exploded.

'Chosen for me, indeed! Am I supposed to have no say about my own future? Cynthia has never had any encouragement from me and she knows it. I've only ever wanted you, Kate, and when you dropped out of my life it was the end of my hopes and dreams. I wonder if you have any idea of what you did to me?'

Roddy was thinking back to his own despair and the pain of rejection. How empty and meaningless his life had become. Had it not been for Kate and the hope he might be able to forget her, he would never have joined up when he did. Most certainly he would not have trained as a pilot. Had it been a death wish? Hardly that but the danger must have attracted him. He hadn't much cared what happened to him and in joining up at least he was doing something for his country. He had been proud to gain his pilot's wings but he had known from the start that he wasn't cut out to be a pilot in wartime. Essential though it was Roddy hated what he was doing. Others got satisfaction from seeing an enemy plane disintegrate and fall apart. They were the men whom the climate of danger suited. They could watch men bailing out and on fire and mark it up as a victory. One less to return another night. Roddy couldn't watch. It just gave him a sick feeling in the pit of his stomach for that poor devil and the fear that the same fate could be waiting for him.

Kate felt a spurt of anger. 'What I did to you? What about what you did to me? I suffered every bit as much, perhaps more since I was the one who had to break it off.'

'That's the awful part of it, you didn't need to. Why for God's sake couldn't you have trusted me? What kind of person do you think I am?'

Her blue eyes flashed pure anger. 'Hear me out. On the Tuesday evening, after that Sunday I mean, your father had parked his car in Crichton Street and he was waiting for me outside the office. He remembered where I worked or maybe your mother told him. Whatever, there he was. I didn't want to go with him, I made that perfectly clear, but he was equally determined that we should talk. He said we had to.'

'You should have walked away.'

'That would have been rude. I got in the car and he drove

to a quiet side street and parked. He did practically all the talking and I listened. I remember looking straight out of the window rather than look at him. That was rude of me, I know.'

'Never mind that.'

She swallowed. The telling was more painful than she had imagined but it was the time for the whole truth. 'He, your father, began by saying how upsetting it had been to see me at Craggy Point and the shock it had given him. He said I was very like my mother when he first met her and what I did was cruel or words to that effect. What I personally think annoyed him was that I should be prepared for the meeting and he not. I wouldn't argue with that. What he didn't know, or didn't want to know, was the agonies I had suffered at the thought of meeting him. For weeks I had wondered what I should do and that was why I took so long to introduce you to Aunt Ruth.'

'Mrs McPherson must have known of the connection?'

Kate shook her head. 'I had thought she might when she heard your name but she has always been hopeless with names. Actually I did think about telling her and asking her advice.'

'But you didn't.'

'No, I didn't.'

'Afraid she would make you see sense and insist on you telling me about your mother and my father?'

'Yes, Roddy, I was afraid of that. I thought it was unfair on you. Knowing you as I do I was fairly sure that you would say it made no difference.'

'Exactly what I would have said, I'm glad you give me credit for that.'

'Don't, Roddy,' Kate said hearing the hint of sarcasm in his voice. 'What I was afraid of—' she stopped.

'What were you afraid of?'

'That in years to come you might regret it, particularly if there were children.'

He laughed, a genuine laugh. 'I see what you mean, the

complications over the grandparents? Adds a bit of colour to the family history wouldn't you say?'

'It's not a laughing matter,' Kate said indignantly then began laughing too.

'There can't be any more?'

'Not much. What I found most hurtful was Mr Hamilton-Harvey telling me that I had deceived his son all along.'

'You had deceived me, Kate,' Roddy said quietly.

'That's why it hurt, knowing that I was guilty.'

'Your intentions were good.'

'All along I hoped that none of it need come out. That was naïve of me, I should have known better.'

'Let sleeping dogs lie, I would have been for that.'

'Before I got out of the car I made one last attempt. Not with much hope of success I may add but I had to try. I said no one need know, it could be our secret, that I had no wish to rake up the past and I felt sure he wouldn't either.'

'What had Dad to say to that?'

'That it was too late and that he wouldn't have gone along with that anyway. He had told your mother and she agreed that it was impossible, totally impossible, that I could become part of your family.'

'The only person who appears to have no say in my future is me. God! I don't know which is the stronger, anger or humiliation.'

'They didn't want you to make a mistake that would ruin the rest of your life, and Roddy, this is the end I am coming to and what made me decide to get out of your life—'

'This I must hear,' he said heavily.

'He said if I really loved his son I could show it by going out of his life for ever. That in time we would both forget and meet someone else. The someone else was for me. I knew very well whom he had in mind for you and that Cynthia would be warmly welcomed into the family.'

Roddy swore under his breath. 'The hypocrite, my happiness didn't enter into it, he didn't want his own past intruding.'

'He wouldn't, would he? I would have been a constant reminder.'

Roddy fell silent and she lay back on the sofa exhausted. The telling had taken a lot out of her.

'Kate, I think there might be a little more to this and that my mother is aware of it,' he said slowly. 'You are very lovely, Kate, just as your mother must have been. I think my father was in love with your mother. How else would he have kept the same mistress all those years and one with a child?'

She looked at him and thought he probably spoke the truth.

'My poor mother,' he said softly, 'she must have been jealous of the woman who had held her husband's affections for so long. She must have wondered about her, pictured her in her own mind and now seeing you, Kate, she didn't have to imagine. My mother is not a vindictive woman, far from it but she has human failings like the rest of us.'

'I liked your mother very, very much.'

'And she liked you, Kate. What she would find difficult to accept was knowing that it had all been her own fault. She had failed my father and he had looked elsewhere.'

'We have to let the past go.'

'She will in time, if not, they will lose a son. I won't let you go, Kate. Fate or whatever you like to call it has given us another chance.'

'Yes, another chance,' she whispered. Her finger traced the wings of his tunic. 'I'm very proud of you, Roddy. Our boys in blue are all so brave.'

'I'm not brave, Kate, for much of the time I'm afraid.'

'Admitting to it is brave and you still do what is expected of you.'

'We have our share of daredevils and they are brave in a careless sort of way and as though they welcomed danger. To some of them it is a game. We need them, Kate, for the majority of us are just plain scared. I see it in their faces and they must see it in mine.'

'Doing what you do is dangerous and needs a great deal of courage.'

'The strange thing is that when I'm actually flying I'm not in the least scared. I suppose my mind is one hundred per cent on what I am doing and there is no time to be afraid. The worst time for me is landing safely, getting out of the plane and knowing I have to do it all again and wondering how long my luck is going to last.'

Kate shuddered, fear for Roddy's safety gripping her. 'You're going to be all right,' she said fiercely, 'nothing is going to happen to you.'

He smiled. 'It won't, not now I have you.' They looked at each other and then she was in his arms, pressed to him. Their lips met in a long kiss that left Kate breathless and she laughed joyously as she came up for breath.

'You do love me, Kate?' He needed constant reassurance.

'With all my heart.'

'Never, never to be parted?'

'Never, never to be parted. Roddy?'

'Mmmm.'

'You were going to show me round your flat.'

'That won't take long. Come on then,' he said pulling Kate to her feet and giving her another kiss when they were facing each other. 'You've had your chance to study this room.'

'Not in detail.' She eyed it as though she were a prospective buyer. Whitish walls showed up the pictures which were of still life, two with a bowl of fruit and two with flowers and falling petals.

'No great appreciation of art,' he grinned.

'Or imagination. Still you have to admit they look rather attractive against the white walls.'

'Whitish grey walls.'

'True they could do with a freshen up.'

'Have to wait for that until the war is over.'

'Like everything else.'

The chintz-covered sofa and armchairs gave a cottage

look to the room, and the only jarring note for Kate was the vase of wax flowers on a spindly-legged table.

'I'd get rid of those,' she laughed and pointed to the offending flowers.

'No mistaking them for the real thing. Kate, I can't throw them out, they are part of the furnishing and I have signed for the complete contents.'

'You can't throw them out I accept that but you could shove them in a cupboard out of sight.'

'Why didn't I think of that?'

'Men never do think of the obvious,' she teased.

There were white painted shelves in an arched recess holding an assortment of books and paperbacks.

'Those will be yours?'

'Yes. A few old favourites I brought from Craggy Point and the paperbacks are mostly detective stories.'

He went ahead to stand in the small square that was the vestibule.

'This is where I left you in the dark.'

'I remember it well,' she laughed.

Halfway down the hall was a walnut, half-moon table with a mirror and a clothes brush hanging to one side. The kitchenette was similar in size to Aunt Ruth's. There was a rather ancient cooker, a double sink, one much smaller than the other and a refrigerator that looked to be the last purchase before the owner had decided to make her home elsewhere for the duration of the war. The wall cabinets were white.

'Too clinical for my taste, Kate, for our home we'll have something a lot more cheerful.'

'I like white.'

'Oh, dear, we'll have to toss up for it. Seen all you want?'

'Yes.'

'Finally the bedrooms,' he said throwing open the door.

Kate stood at the door and looked in. Everything was neat and tidy, the bedcover perfectly placed on the double bed. There was the usual bedroom furniture and a rather handsome white sheepskin rug over beside the bed.

'That's a reasonable size but come and see this,' he said opening the door opposite. 'You see the single bed has to be hard against the wall to make room for that slim wardrobe and tiny dressing-table. No chair.'

'You're expected to sit on the bed. No prize for guessing which one you use?'

'None,' he smiled. 'And in case you are wondering, let me say quickly that I haven't suddenly acquired domestic skills.'

'Somehow I didn't think you had.'

'With the flat I inherited a cleaning woman. I have never once seen her. She has a key and comes in to do the necessary. I leave her money on the mantelshelf and when she needs cleaning materials she gets those and I pay for them. A very honest woman is Mrs Lambert, she accounts for every penny she spends and should I leave behind any valuables I can be sure they will be there when I return. Comments?'

'All very nice.'

They returned to the sitting-room and had been sitting on the sofa her head on his shoulder when he suddenly gave a gasp. His eyes were on the clock and then went to his watch. 'Heavens above! I had no idea of the time. Come on, Kate, I've got to get you back. I take it you have a late pass?'

'Yes.'

'Even so you're going to be horribly late.'

'I know,' she said cheerfully.

'You don't appear to be worried.'

'I'm not. You are going to be late too.'

'Not me, I have twenty-four hours of blissful freedom.'
He closed his eyes and Kate saw the tiredness, the strain of what the war was doing to him and she knew exactly what she was going to do. It went against all the teachings and what she was proposing would have her Aunt Sarah turning in her grave. The war had brought a greater tolerance, a

more broad-minded attitude to sexual behaviour. A feeling of live for today for we know not what the morrow might bring.

'Kate, on your feet, my girl, unless you want to be on a charge, desertion of duty or AWOL.'

'You are not going out of this flat, Roddy.'

'If you think for one single moment I would allow you—'

'I know you wouldn't.'

'Then how do you propose getting back?'

'I thought I might stay,' she said looking down at the carpet.

'Stay? You mean stay here in the flat with me?'

'If you want me and I'm beginning to think you don't.'

'Kate, are you suggesting what I think you are suggesting?'

She nodded happily, enjoying seeing the changing expressions on his face.

'I want you, I've never stopped wanting you, but I'm not selfish enough to get you into trouble.'

'There may not be trouble. Don't imagine I'm the first to do this. In fact I've covered up for one or two of our girls and I'm pretty sure they'll do the same for me.'

'If they know.'

'They would have seen me leaving the dance hall with you and if I didn't show up they would—'

'Assume the worst?'

'Draw their own conclusions.'

'Can this really be the Kate McPherson I once knew?'

Kate became serious. 'A few short hours ago I wouldn't have believed it of myself.'

'You make me feel very humble.'

'All I want is to make you happy.'

'Kate,' he said cradling her in his arms, 'you are the most wonderful girl.'

'I'm not.'

'You are sure? I mean I wouldn't want this to be because you think you owe me something?'

'It isn't.'

They found enough in the fridge to make a meal. Kate drank tea and Roddy had a bottle of beer. They talked well into the night and it was like uncovering layer after layer, learning more and more about each other. They had thought they knew all there was to know but then it had been boy and girl, now it was a man and a woman.

'With the blackout blinds it feels as though it is just the two of us in a world of our own.'

'I only wish it were.'

'You're tired?'

'Not really,' he lied.

'Yes, you are.'

'A bit then.'

'They ask far too much of you. Haven't you done your share of missions? Isn't there a certain number—'

'Not so strict about that now. More is expected of us.'

'Why?' she demanded.

'Because, Kate my darling, as you very well know it takes time to train pilots and we've lost quite a few. I shouldn't be telling you this.'

'Yes, you should, we must tell each other everything. I want to help you.'

'You are doing that by being here, by coming back into my life. You were the only one with whom I could share my thoughts.'

'What were you going to say before I interrupted?'

'About the training? They are cutting down drastically on the training time and I can't but think that is a mistake. Apart from the cost in human life there is the loss of planes. Mind you, Kate, that said I wouldn't like to be the one having to make the decisions.'

'Nor I. When is it going to end, Roddy?'

'Sometimes I think I can see a glimmer of hope, that things are changing for us, changing for the better and then comes another setback. Still it can't last for ever, someone has to give in and it won't be us.'

'The Germans will be saying that too.'

'Yes, Kate,' Roddy said heavily, then with a burst of sudden anger, 'This war is wrong, it should never have happened.'

'Hitler started the war, Roddy.'

'Yes, but he should have been stopped long ago. We aren't blameless.'

'I know we aren't, but we are a peace-loving nation and we just didn't believe it would happen. The Germans are much more aggressive than the British.'

'Not the ordinary German man and woman. Hitler worked his magic, or his evil, on the very young, the impressionable and we all know how easily influenced we were when we were fresh out of school.'

Kate yawned. 'Sorry.'

'I'm boring you to tears.'

'No, you are not. I may not agree with everything you say—'

'I wouldn't want that. An argument is healthy and now, my darling, I think we should be turning in. I only hope they haven't sent out a search party for you.'

'They won't have done that.'

Kate was feeling embarrassed. She was regretting nothing but it was not knowing what to do. Did she excuse herself and get undressed in the bedroom or was that something they did together?

Roddy saw her uncertainty and wondered if she was having second thoughts. Kate had an expressive face, she couldn't easily hide her feelings.

'There are two bedrooms, Kate,' he said gently.

'No, it isn't that.' The colour rushed to her face.

'Kate, my dearest one, there is no need to be embarrassed. We are going to be married, aren't we?'

'Yes.'

'Then we are engaged. We'll find a decent jeweller and get you whatever ring you fancy.'

'I wasn't pushing for that,' she said looking hurt.

'I know that but it is what I want.' Getting up he disappeared and came back with a dressing-gown. 'Take it. You go ahead, I have a few things to see to here.'

'You must think I'm an idiot.'

'The nicest kind of idiot.'

'I've never done this before.'

'I have to say I'm happy about that.' He gave her a quick kiss and a push towards the bedroom. 'On you go before we both fall asleep on our feet.'

Kate was nervous, fumbling with buttons, then chided herself. How the other girls would laugh if they could see her. They didn't have her inhibitions. That didn't mean they were promiscuous. It happened usually before the favoured one was sent overseas. Kate had been amazed at the openness of some of the WAAFs. They didn't know the meaning of embarrassment.

She had undressed and before that had folded back the bedcover. Picking up her slip Kate decided to wear it as a nightdress. Shivering a little she went below the bedclothes. She heard Roddy walking about then he came in. Only a dim light came from the bedside lamps and she was aware that he was undressing.

The light went off and in a moment he was reaching for her and drawing her close. She lay in his arms and smiled into the darkness. There was nothing to be afraid of, not with Roddy. He made love to her showing great tenderness and in a little while they were both asleep, arms around each other and their breathing regular.

The drone of planes could be heard as they returned from another raid.

Chapter Twenty-Two

'Open your eyes, Dotty,' Vera called to what appeared to be a lump in the next bed. 'The shameless hussy has just come in.'

'Sh! Sh!' Kate said putting a finger to her lips. 'Don't advertise my arrival. I think, I hope, I got in without being noticed.' And then in a surprised voice, 'What is Dorothy doing in my bed?'

The lump moved. Dorothy gave a huge yawn and struggled to a sitting position. 'You look positively glowing, Kate my love, staying out all night suits you.'

Kate's cheeks were flushed from her hurried walk in the cool of the morning.

'Never mind that, what are you doing in my bed? What is wrong with yours?'

'Nothing and what a show of gratitude. If you cast your eyes in the direction of mine you'll find the body is a pillow supposed to be me.'

'But—'

'But nothing, I was saving your skin. Since your bed happens to be the first to be seen by anyone checking up, it was surely sensible to have it occupied. Fortunately I sleep with my head under the blankets and Vera's snoring accounts for her.'

'What a cheek, I do *not* snore.'

'No one ever admits to it. And as for checking on me,

Kate, there was no need, I saw to that. I made sure that our miserable sergeant knew I was around at midnight and after. In other words, Kate McPherson, I saved your bacon.'

'I *am* grateful.' Kate sank down on a corner of her own bed and let out a long sigh of relief. 'I thought I might be for the high jump.'

'AWOL is a very serious offence, very serious indeed, McPherson,' Vera said in a fair imitation of one of the WAAF officers, 'I hope you have a satisfactory explanation for your non-appearance last night.'

'I'm afraid I didn't notice the lateness of the hour and by the time I did it seemed wiser to stay where I was.'

'Which was precisely where?'

'I would rather not say, ma'am,' Kate said getting into the spirit of the game. Dorothy and Vera were good friends to have and would have gone to no end of trouble to save her from a severe reprimand or worse.

'That won't do McPherson, you will kindly answer my question.'

'My young man has a flat and that is where I spent the night.'

'Is that true, Kate?' Both girls were agog and making no attempt to hide their curiosity.

'Yes.'

'Come on, spill the beans. You surely don't expect us to be satisfied with that after all the trouble we went to.'

Dorothy Brooks smiled. She was the one who understood Kate best. 'We won't pry too much . . .'

'I know but give me a minute. I've hardly got my breath back.'

Both girls were open about their own love life, too open Kate often thought, or maybe she was the one out of step. They were fond of Kate, saw her as a girl who had been strictly brought up and still lived by a set of rules. In a way they were protective of Kate as they might have been of a younger sister going out into the big wicked world for the first time.

'Want a biscuit before you get started?'

'Wouldn't mind. Keep the hunger away until I get breakfast.' Kate got up to accept a plain Abernethy from a tin Vera kept in her locker. 'I'll eat this then give myself a proper wash.'

'Not so fast. Story now wash later.'

'All right,' Kate said resignedly.

'Presumably the dream-boat was in the flat.'

'He rents it.'

'Very nice,' Vera nodded. 'You know, of course, what we are dying to ask and managing not to?'

'I haven't the faintest,' then blushed furiously.

'I would say we've got our answer,' Dorothy grinned. 'Good for you, Kate, I didn't think you had it in you.'

'A dark horse that one.'

'Do we get to know his name?'

'Pilot Officer Roddy Hamilton-Harvey.'

Vera pulled a face. 'Double-barrelled name no less. I've never met anyone with one of those.'

'You don't move in the right circles, Vera. For that matter neither do I.'

'I knew Roddy before I joined up.'

'Going steady were you?'

'Yes.'

'Something went wrong?'

'You could say that.'

'Lovers' tiff, happens all the time,' Vera nodded as if she knew all about lovers' tiffs. 'A God-almighty row about nothing at all, I suppose, and neither of you willing to make the first move.'

It hadn't been like that at all but it would do and Kate nodded.

'At least you've made it up?'

'Yes, everything is fine.' That much was true.

Vera was sitting cross-legged on the bed struggling to undo two pipe cleaners from her hair. She always slept with two in the front to give some bounce to her fine hair.

'How come he has a flat hereabout and more to the point how did he persuade you to stay?'

Kate stifled a giggle. The pair of them would collapse with shock if she were to tell them that it hadn't been Roddy's suggestion but hers. As it happened she didn't have to answer. Vera had suddenly become aware of the time and shot out of bed like a scalded cat.

'Holy Moses! the time, you could have told me. Kate McPherson this is all your fault.'

Kate was glad she was back on duty and away from the questions, good-natured though they were. First thing in the morning there was usually a rush of work to be dealt with then a lull. Kate used the welcome break to think back. In the space of a few hours her life had been turned upside down. There had been the experience of waking up in a strange bedroom, too dark to see and the only sound the steady breathing of someone in a deep sleep. Someone so near that she could touch. She remembered the first moments of feeling confused and disorientated followed by near panic when she realised what she had done. It was different in wartime was the usual cry and she had believed that to be no more than an excuse for immoral behaviour. How smug she had been and how mistaken. How could it be wrong to love when there might be so few tomorrows? I'm growing up, she thought. The noise of a message coming through brought her back to the present. She taped it on to a form, initialled it and put it aside for collection.

Again her mind returned to the morning and her anxiety not to be missed. Searching for and finding the switch on her bedside lamp, she had been able to read the time. Six thirty. Kate immediately got up. Carrying her clothes to the bathroom so as not to disturb Roddy, she freshened herself, dressed and pulled a comb through her tangled curls. Back in the bedroom Kate was relieved to see that Roddy hadn't moved and rummaging in her bag she found a notebook and tore out a page. A further rummage produced a few remnants of pencil and selecting one with a half decent point she sat down to scribble a note to Roddy. He would get it when he awoke.

> *Darling,*
> *You looked so peaceful that I hadn't the heart to disturb you. Don't worry about me, my friends will have done their best to cover. If they haven't succeeded I'm not too worried. AWOL or whatever, it was worth any risk. Rest assured I have no regrets, none at all. I love you,*
> *Kate*

For a few moments she watched Roddy in sleep then with a smile she hurried away. Last night in the darkness she had had only a vague idea of where she was but in the light of morning she wasn't long in getting her bearings. Then she was half running, desperate to get back. For all her brave words to Roddy her stomach was churning with nerves. She had never before broken any of the rules, had never wanted to. And here she was breaking the most important rule of all. Absent without leave, staying out all night. She didn't have the excuse of missing the train or the last bus. She had no excuse to give and if she was caught it was going to be a very black mark against her name.

She was still thanking her lucky stars that she had got away with it and so grateful to Dorothy and Vera.

Would Roddy be up and out of bed now? she wondered. Would he have reached for her and found emptiness? Perhaps. Then he would have found her note and understood her haste to get away.

Life was stranger than fiction, Aunt Ruth always said that. Her aunt would be so happy to hear that Roddy was back in her life. It was all so wonderful, so amazing, so unexpected but now there was a constant worry. She was so afraid for him. Fighter pilots took such terrible risks. One man and his plane against another in his. A battle to the bitter end. A plane spiralling out of control and the other returning to base satisfied that there was one less plane in the skies.

Death and destruction and all for what? Because countries couldn't agree. Two young men with similar interests, who might have been friends instead of which their fate would be decided by speed and manoeuvring in the sky. Kate, like the other girls, was used to hearing the planes going over and they always crossed their fingers for their safe return. Some would count the number going over and again on their return. Kate didn't and it was generally frowned on. Not all returned at the same time, there were stragglers who somehow managed to limp home in a damaged plane. Hope lived on for as long as possible.

Kate had a key to Roddy's flat and could come and go as she pleased. Arranging their time off together was always a problem but they made the best of the hours they had. Tonight they were in the flat and sitting on the sofa, her head on his shoulder.

'Not a decent jeweller around here, we'll have to go further afield.'

'Like where?' she smiled. The main jeweller's shop had closed down due to lack of business and the small one remaining concentrated on the cheaper goods. Once the High Street in Miltonwells had been a busy, bustling thoroughfare but now it was shabby and run down. The shops seemed wearied like the assistants behind the counter with not much left to sell. The wonder was that they bothered to remain open all day but it would not have occurred to them to shut up shop early. They would work their hours as always.

It was worse here than at home, Kate thought. It saddened her to hear about the housewives standing shivering in long queues and often when it came to their turn it would be too late. The consignment of whatever it was would have been small, made smaller by the amount put aside for favoured customers who could not be expected to take their place in a queue. It would all have gone and there was no saying when the next supply would arrive. Once that would have brought angry exchanges but anger needed energy and there was little enough of that. The defeated just walked away with their empty shopping bags.

'Like where? Like London. How does that appeal to you?'

'It does. I've been meaning to go there with Dorothy or one of the others but something always got in the way.'

'Your first visit? Then we must make it a day to remember.' He eased himself away to reach for a cigarette and Kate picked up his lighter and handed it to him.

'Every day with you is a day to remember,' she said quietly. 'I belong to you, Roddy, I don't need a ring to show it.'

'I know, darling, we belong, we always have but I thought all girls liked to have an engagement ring.'

'I didn't say I wouldn't like one, I said it wasn't necessary.'

'Yes, it is necessary, for me it is. Why the thoughtful expression?'

'I was thinking of my Aunt Sarah.'

'The one you went to live with after your mother died?'

'Yes. She was terribly strict and good living.'

'She would be shocked to know what her niece gets up to,' he grinned.

'Shocked? She would be scandalised, horrified. I'm a fallen woman. Like mother like daughter.'

'She doesn't sound like my favourite kind of aunt.'

'She wasn't mine either. There were times, Roddy, when I was near to hating her. I wanted to run away but there was no place to run to.'

Roddy stubbed out his half-smoked cigarette and drew her close. 'My poor little Kate.'

She snuggled in. 'Later, when I was older, I understood her better but I was never able to love her. Not the way I love Aunt Ruth.'

'She's rather special.'

'Yes, she is. There was a good side to Aunt Sarah but she didn't show it very often.'

'Why is she in your thoughts now?'

'She would be so disappointed in me. She had a soldier boyfriend in the last war. We, Aunt Ruth and I, found a photograph and some little trinkets he sent or we think they were from him.'

'Was he killed?'

'He might have been.'

'Maybe she lost him because she couldn't show her love.' He smiled. 'And perhaps lived to regret it.'

'We'll never know. I think I wanted Aunt Sarah to think well of me. She left me everything in her Will.'

'She must have thought a lot of you to do that.'

Kate paused. 'I'm very comfortably off.'

'Are you? How glad I am I proposed marriage before I knew you were a wealthy young woman,' he teased.

'I didn't say wealthy, I said comfortably off.'

'That's nice.'

'It is nice, it's very nice. I won't ever go hungry or without a roof over my head.'

'Lucky girl.'

'I would say lucky boy. The Hamilton–Harveys haven't had to count the pennies, not in your father's time,' Kate said drily.

'Seriously, Kate, our fortunes could be changing. Mother is the one with the business head and though she doesn't say much I think she is very concerned. To begin with she wouldn't allow herself to think the impossible, jute has been her life, and now she is seeing the writing on the wall.'

'Perhaps it won't be as bad as all that.'

'Maybe not. It's the uncertainty that is the worst, not knowing how we will be placed when this war is over.'

'A common worry,' Kate said. She didn't have a great deal of sympathy for the Hamilton-Harveys.

Chapter Twenty-Three

Euston was crowded with travellers and loud speakers blared out announcements that no one could properly hear for the hissing of the engines and the general noises of a busy station. Roddy took Kate's arm and guided her through the crush to the exit and outside to where the sun was shining. A few heads turned to look at the handsome pilot officer and the tall, attractive WAAF with him.

Kate started to look around her with interest. 'So this is London,' she said smiling. 'Is it always as busy as this?'

'Most of the time.'

She had expected crowds but nothing like this. The city was positively throbbing with life and there were uniforms everywhere. Most would appear to be bent on having a good time, a determination perhaps to live it up before they had to return to the horrors of war. Thinking of that brought back her own worries about Roddy and she shivered.

'Cold?'

'No, not at all.'

'I thought that was a shiver.'

She shook her head. 'How could I be cold, it's a lovely morning.'

Roddy's suggestion had been to take a taxi or cab as they called it here, to let her see a little of London but she hadn't wanted that.

'No, I'd rather walk, Roddy, but I wouldn't say no to a cup of coffee, I'm parched.'

'Could do with one myself.'

They found a small café with a few tables just inside the door, one of which was unoccupied. 'This do, Kate?'

'Perfect, I only want coffee.'

The coffee came quickly along with two pink wafer biscuits. Roddy didn't want his and Kate ate both.

'You don't mind if I have a smoke?'

'When have I ever objected? Of course I don't mind.'

'No one has persuaded you to start?'

'Not as yet.'

'Don't, it can quickly become a habit.' Roddy brought out his silver cigarette case with his initials on the corner. He opened it and took one out, At the third attempt the lighter worked.

'Must try and remember to fill this thing.'

'You hardly ever smoked before, just the occasional one.'

'Maybe I didn't need to then.'

And now you do, she thought. Perhaps they all did. Most of Roddy's fellow officers were heavy smokers, some were chain-smokers. Was it to calm their nerves? Kate thought it very likely.

Leaving the café, Kate watched the road as lorries, buses, cars and London cabs streamed by. The noise at times was deafening. No wonder Londoners made for the parks when they could or was that now denied them?

'Roddy, is it true that the parks are closed?'

'Why, did you want to go there?'

'No. Vera thought they might be.'

'She could be right, I don't know. A sensible precaution I would have thought with the ever present threat of time-bombs.'

She nodded. London was a dangerous place.

'We ought to have planned our day,' he said.

'No, Roddy, let us do what we want, when we want. It'll make a change.'

'Provided we don't forget the main purpose of this visit.'

'As if I would! I've thought of nothing else.'

'First port of call the jewellers, then the day is our own.'

'Until it is time to get the train back.'

'Yes.' For a moment his face was grave then he smiled the old familiar smile. 'Following that, the jewellers I mean, my darling, we are going to have a very special lunch. I've been provided with the names of several black-market restaurants where one can get just about anything.'

Kate thought of those struggling by on rations and did feel some guilt but not enough to have her raising objections. This was, after all, a very special occasion and she could be excused.

'Money talks in every language.'

'The way of the world, Kate. Maybe money doesn't bring happiness but it sure makes life more pleasant.'

She laughed. 'I have to agree with that.' She paused a moment. 'My friends swear by the Corner Houses.'

'I'm not knocking Lyons Corner Houses, don't get me wrong. I've had some jolly good meals but one doesn't go there to celebrate.'

Hand-in-hand they strolled along the streets, just happy to be together. Where the bombs had fallen there were ropings-off of dangerous tracts of the road. Passers-by would glance over at the emptiness without showing surprise or much interest. It had become a commonplace sight. Away from the pleasure-seeking crowds, Kate saw the real Londoners and admired their spirit. With grim determination they were going about their everyday duties. Those who worked in offices, shops, banks and restaurants showed the strain of fatigue. Sleep was a luxury denied to most. A few snatched hours if they were lucky before the wailing of the siren got them out of a warm bed to grab clothes and run for the nearest shelter. Some preferred to take the risk and remain in their own home. A cupboard or under the stairs might give some protection, the choice was open. The fatalists, with their beliefs, stayed put. What was for them wouldn't go past them. Others were grateful to be alive knowing that some would never again see the light of day. The previous night's raid might have robbed them of home and possessions but they had been spared and life was precious.

Kate and Roddy stopped to look at the devastation and were joined by a middle-aged man who looked like a city gent in his dark business suit and carrying a rolled-up umbrella.

'Never without it,' he smiled, 'marvellous for stopping traffic you know. I discovered that walking on to the road with it held out in front of me is guaranteed to stop the traffic. Never fails and, of course, others seeing it take advantage and cross with me.'

'Must remember that,' Roddy laughed.

'Pilot I see. You boys are giving it to them I hope?'

'Doing our best, sir.'

'Fighter pilot?'

'Yes.'

'Proud to be talking to you, lad. I hope when this is all over we don't forget the debt we owe you.' He paused. 'See that man,' he indicated an old man sitting on a bit of broken wall, 'and those others wandering about like lost souls? Habit, you see, they can't stay away. This is where they once lived and they are drawn to it. Sad! Pathetic! Human nature though.'

'The homeless, where do they go?' Kate asked.

'There are places and volunteers who help them. The war has done that, brought folk closer, it's a family feeling almost. Just here for the day, you two?'

'Yes.'

'Won't have seen the underground or have you?'

'No, we haven't.'

'That's where they congregate, a lot of them. Feel safer there than in their homes. Cheerful too, there's usually a sing-song before getting the head down for a bit of shut-eye.' He seemed suddenly to have become aware of the time.

'Here's me talking to you as if I had all day. Nice to have met you and good luck to you both.'

'Thank you,' they said together and smiled as he hurried away waving his umbrella.

'People talk more to strangers than they ever did,' Kate said as they continued their stroll, 'even back home they are freer.'

'Not a bad thing, we Scots need to open up.'

'Not too much, it would be out of character.'

'Next stop, the ring.'

Kate was nervously excited as they entered the shop. The interior was in quiet good taste and the gentleman who came over to serve them seemed to fit into his surroundings. The dark, well-tailored suit worn with a white shirt and subdued tie was in keeping. He spoke softly.

'Good morning, how can I be of assistance?'

'We would like to see engagement rings.'

'Please be seated and I'll show you what we have.'

He went about the task unhurriedly but with the air of one who knew exactly how it should be done. Kate watched as he covered a section of the counter with a black velvet cloth. On it went a display of engagement rings, their stones sparkling from the light above. Kate, pink with excitement, kept looking at Roddy. She wondered if he was feeling the same excitement and thought, no, it would be different for him, different for a man. An engagement ring was so special for a girl. A token of love she would keep for the rest of her life.

'Select the rings you want to try on,' Roddy said.

'Don't worry if they don't fit that can be seen to,' the assistant smiled, 'and let me tell you that a ring should not go over the knuckle with too much ease otherwise you might draw it off with a glove and lose it.'

Kate looked alarmed. 'That would be quite dreadful.'

'As you say but sadly it does happen.'

'I'll make sure mine is the correct fit.' She had picked out three and was trying first one and then another and each time Roddy was asked for his opinion.

'Very nice but do you prefer a coloured stone or just diamonds?'

'Diamonds. Three diamonds, Roddy, that is what I would like.'

'If the lady prefers diamonds, excuse me and I'll bring another selection.'

He disappeared and returned with a tray which he placed alongside the other.

'The young lady must take her time and choose carefully.' There was no sales talk. His training had seen to that. Only an amateur in a cheap establishment would resort to persuasion in order to procure a sale. Customers were put off by that.

As soon as she saw it, Kate knew it was her ring and just prayed that it would fit. An adjustment would take time and she wanted to wear her ring now. She wanted everyone to know she was engaged, to shout it from the roof tops that she was engaged to be married to the most wonderful man in the world.

'This one, Roddy.' She slipped it on her finger and sighed with relief when it required a little persuasion to go over the knuckle.

Roddy looked at the ring with its three diamonds. Kate had nice hands with long, slim fingers. He, himself, would have gone for something more eye-catching.

'Quite sure?' He sounded doubtful.

'I am. Why, don't you like it?'

'Of course I like it but the diamonds aren't very big.'

The assistant smiled, how like a young man. 'If I may say so the lady has made an excellent choice. Diamonds are not valued by their size but rather by their quality. These are very fine diamonds.'

Roddy laughed. 'I'm won over. And now with that settled we had better have a wedding ring to go with it.'

'Roddy,' Kate protested. 'The wedding ring could wait until later.'

'Might as well get them at the same time.'

The assistant was already removing the trays of engagement rings and replacing them with a selection of gold and platinum wedding rings. Kate chose one that suited her hand.

'Will that be everything, sir?'

'Yes, thank you.'

'No, my turn now,' Kate said and turned to Roddy. 'A ring for you.'

'Not necessary.'

'Meaning you don't like rings, you don't want to wear one?'

'Rings are becoming much more fashionable for young men.'

Kate beamed at the man. 'Please, show us what you have.'

'You don't have to wear it, Roddy, if you'd rather not,' Kate whispered when they were alone.

'What's the use of buying it then?' he said reasonably.

'Because I want you to have it. You can keep the ring in your pocket for luck.'

His face twisted into a wry smile. 'In that case I gladly accept.'

The man walked with them to the door and bowed slightly. It had been a pleasure to serve them he said and added his best wishes. Then he returned to his duties of polishing the silver until the arrival of another customer. It had been a good morning so far.

Once outside on the pavement Roddy hailed a cab and gave the driver instructions. In less than ten minutes they were in Soho. There was a steady stream of people entering and leaving restaurants. Young women, beautifully made-up and expensively dressed, hung on to the arms of American servicemen. Kate saw our boys look with loathing at those they blamed for taking their girls and with contempt at the girls who could so easily be lured by the promise of nylons and the luxuries so long denied the British. Kate hoped the girls felt ashamed. She did on their behalf.

An officer's uniform was the passport to one of the best tables and Kate and Roddy found themselves shown to one nicely secluded. They exchanged smiles as they sat down. This was just perfect.

'It is quite dreadful you know, Roddy, the preferential treatment you get just because you happen to be in officer's uniform,' she teased.

'I'm not complaining and you shouldn't either.'

'I'm not but I bet anything if I came here on my own I wouldn't be shown to one of the best tables. Lucky if I even got served.'

Roddy's face split in a grin. 'My dear Kate, this is Soho, there would be a mad rush to join you. No well brought-up girl would dare enter on her own. Don't you know its reputation?'

'I never thought to ask. I'm safe with you?'

'Absolutely.'

'When I'm with my friends we'll stick to the Corner House.'

'Do that but even there be careful.'

Roddy spent a long time over the wine list but eventually he chose a wine he thought would suit Kate. He knew she drank it to be sociable and not from enjoyment. In time, he thought, she would learn to appreciate a good wine.

They both decided on Dover sole and when the wine was poured, tested and given the nod of approval, Kate's glass was filled and then Roddy's. The waiter departed and Roddy, producing the ring, leaned over the table and slipped it on to Kate's finger.

'We are now formally engaged.'

She nodded, feeling the tears close. Why did happiness make you want to cry?

'Yes,' she whispered, 'we are formally engaged.'

Roddy got up, came around and kissed her. There was a ripple of applause from nearby tables and Kate blushed with embarrassment. She had expected Roddy to be embarrassed too but he didn't appear to be. The old Roddy would not have kissed her in such a public place. The war was changing everyone.

Every few minutes Kate was examining her engagement ring and thinking it was impossible to be happier than she was today.

'Roddy, I'm so happy, I think I'm going to burst with happiness.'

'I feel a bit like that. Kate, why wait,' he said urgently, 'what is there to wait for? We'll get married right away or I mean as soon as possible. I'll have a word with the padre—'

'You are going too fast for me,' Kate protested.

A shadow crossed his face. 'Don't you want to get married, I thought you did.'

'You know I do. More than anything in the world I want to belong to you completely but you have me breathless.' She gave a shaky laugh. 'Let me get used to being engaged first.'

'Is everything to your and the lady's satisfaction, sir?'

Roddy turned at the interruption. 'Everything is just fine, thank you.'

Kate had barely touched her wine but Roddy's glass was less than half full. The waiter topped it up, covered the bottle and went quietly away.

'Kate, I want to get married quickly and quietly.'

'Why quickly and quietly?'

He didn't answer. 'Two witnesses that's all we need. No fuss.'

'What about our own people and our friends?'

'You can forget my parents,' he said bitterly, 'they did their damnedest to keep us apart.'

'You can't do that, Roddy.'

'Can't I? Kate, I'll continue to send my few lines home every ten days or so but you won't be mentioned. You'll be my wife and they won't know a thing about it until I'm good and ready to tell them. And that, believe me, could be a long way off.'

Kate felt her happiness drain away. This wasn't the way

she wanted it. It was no way to start married life, war or no war.

'What about Aunt Ruth?'

'Mrs McPherson is different,' he smiled. 'You must tell your aunt. Did you think I wanted to exclude her? No more talking, Kate, until we finish this sole and choose what we want to follow.'

When they had finished a delicious sweet and were at the coffee stage, Kate had decided to humour Roddy. He was excitable in a strained sort of way that worried her. She wanted nothing to spoil this day and if she showed a reluctance to go along with his marriage plans, it would put a dampener on it. Roddy, she was finding, liked his own way.

When she wanted, Kate could be stubborn too and suddenly it had become very important to talk everything over with Aunt Ruth. Kate was disturbed by Roddy's almost feverish haste to tie the knot. She could understand his anger at his parents. She couldn't easily forgive them for what they had put her through but at least she was prepared to try. What was the use of hiding their marriage? They couldn't go on doing that. And given a chance Mr and Mrs Hamilton-Harvey might come round to accepting her as a daughter-in-law. It would be that or losing their son and Kate felt very sure they wouldn't risk that.

If Roddy was surprised at her decision to spend a long weekend at home with Aunt Ruth he gave no sign of it.

'Give Mrs McPherson my best regards.'

'I'll do that.'

'I'll miss you.'

'I'll miss you too but it's only a weekend and I haven't seen Aunt Ruth for ages.'

'She's very welcome to come to the wedding, be sure to tell her that.'

'Yes.'

'Getting married in wartime does save a lot of trouble. Just think of what we will be spared.'

Kate swallowed. Before her eyes swam a picture of a bride, a vision in white and a handsome bridegroom standing outside the village church and the well-wishers ready with the confetti. Then it faded.

He was waiting for her to say something and she smiled and nodded.

Aunt Ruth looked no different. She was craning her neck the better to see who was coming off the train and when she saw Kate she gave a huge smile. In another moment they were hugging.

'Marvellous to see you, Aunt Ruth.'

'And you, my darling. You look wonderful just as a newly engaged girl should but we mustn't linger, Mr Brownlow volunteered transport when he heard you were coming.'

'How very kind of Mr Brownlow. Petrol coupons are pure gold – how did he manage it?'

'We won't go into that,' Ruth said hurrying Kate to the exit and to where the car was waiting. Bob Brownlow, an ARP warden and proud of it, beamed at Kate.

'Grand to see you Kate and smart as paint you look in that uniform. Never thought the day would come when I'd admire a lass in uniform, too mannish you see.'

'Do *I* look mannish?' Kate teased.

'You look – what do they say in the films?' He appealed to Ruth.

'A million dollars is, I think, the expression you are searching for.'

'That's it. In you go to the back, the pair of you, and have your chat. I've no doubt you've a bit of catching up to do.'

Bob Brownlow dropped his passengers off at Ashgrove Cottage and waved away their thanks. 'Your aunt does a power of work in the village, Kate, I'm just glad to be of assistance.'

'You are appreciated, Aunt Ruth,' Kate said once they were inside.

'We all pull together. The kettle is filled, I'll just put the gas below it and we'll have a cup of tea in no time.'

The serious talk began after Ruth had admired Kate's lovely ring.

'Kate, something is troubling you,' she said once they were seated and a cup of tea in front of them.

'Not exactly troubling me, Aunt Ruth. I think I need to talk things over with you.'

'I'm a good listener.'

'Yes, you are.' She paused to drink some tea. 'Roddy wants us to get married now, as soon as arrangements can be made.'

'And you are not in favour of such haste?'

'No, I'm not, I see no reason for it. That's not to say I want a long engagement, I don't . . .' She sighed and spread her hands.

'You don't want to be rushed. Have you told Roddy that?'

'I've tried to. He's usually so reasonable but not about this. Maybe I'd better tell you everything.'

'I think that would be advisable if I'm to be of any help.'

'Roddy doesn't want his parents to know, he isn't going to tell them. They don't know we are together again,' Kate said wretchedly.

'You mean they, Roddy's parents, don't approve of you?'

'That's what I mean.'

'May I ask what they could possibly have against you?'

Kate bit on her lower lip.

'I gathered something wasn't quite right after that visit to Roddy's home, but you would never tell me what it was.'

'I wanted to, then I thought it would be better to keep it to myself. You see, Aunt Ruth, it was all so long ago.'

'I see nothing yet. You'll have to do better than that.'

Kate gave a strangled laugh. 'When I told you Roddy's name I was so sure you would make the connection.'

'Should I have?'

'Oh, yes, you should.'

'You know yourself how bad I am with names. I was never all that good but I believe it got worse – I suppose from the time in France when I lost my memory.'

'Aunt Ruth, my mother and Roddy's father—' Kate paused – 'she was his mistress.' It came out in a rush.

Ruth looked shocked. 'Oh, my dear, how dreadful for you, for you all.' Her brow puckered. 'Why did it have to come out? But, of course, I am forgetting you were old enough to remember him. Did you connect the name?'

'I did wonder but I just hoped Roddy was no more than a distant relative and I went on hoping though to be honest I was almost sure before—'

'Before that visit? That's when it came to a head?'

'Roddy's father saw the resemblance to my mother.'

'That must have given him a turn?'

'I think he thought he was seeing my mother's ghost.'

'My dear, why didn't you tell me about this?'

'I wanted to but I was so sure you would side with Roddy. He wouldn't have given me up,' she said proudly.

'He most certainly would not, not the Roddy I used to know.'

'Later on I thought he might come to regret his decision especially if there were children.'

'I'm not with you.'

'Then you should be,' Kate said tartly. 'Think about the grandparent situation and no matter what Roddy says family is important to him.'

'I would expect family to be important but you to be more important. You've burdened yourself with all this and I'm not only angry, I'm deeply hurt.'

'I'm sorry,' Kate said miserably.

'Maybe I'm beginning to understand or I'm trying to—'

'You haven't heard it all.' Kate took a deep breath and told Ruth everything. By the time she had finished her voice had sunk to a whisper.

Ruth got up. 'I'm well organised in the kitchen for a change. Sam, the new lad in the butcher's, brought round a steak pie, not a word to anyone mind—'

'How often have I heard that,' Kate grinned.

'All I have to do is heat it up, boil the potatoes and see to a vegetable. You could set the table and no, Kate, I'm not ignoring what you've just told me. I need time to think about it so no more until we have eaten. Meanwhile I'll regale you with the latest village gossip.'

'Juicy?'

'Naughty! Naughty!'

'That was lovely,' Kate said putting her knife and fork down on the empty plate, 'and I'm sore laughing.' Over coffee they were back with Kate's problems.

'Kate, one question and this is the crux of the matter. How much do you love Roddy?'

'With all my heart,' she said simply.

'Then if you want my advice, marry the lad as soon as he has the arrangements in hand.'

Kate didn't think she was too surprised. 'Two witnesses and the padre to marry us, that's all it will be.'

'You would feel cheated?'

'More disappointed than cheated. Not that I wanted a big fuss but it seems so – so cold somehow.'

'Kate, you are a romantic as most young girls are but you know there is quite a lot of glamour about a uniform wedding. Roddy handsome in his officer's uniform and you looking lovely in yours. Someone said not so long ago that Ruth McPherson's niece would look bonny in a dish cloot.'

'I'm not sure how to take that,' Kate said laughing.

'Joking apart, Kate, war makes us all very aware of the dangers we face and in this war that includes civilians. Take happiness when it is offered, grab it with both hands. An engagement isn't enough for Roddy, he needs to know that you belong to him.'

'I've been selfish.'

'No, just muddled.' Ruth's eyes grew soft. 'I would have gone to the ends of the earth with your father. Robert wasn't dashing like your Roddy, he was quiet and serious but with a magic that was all his own.'

Kate was touched. They were both feeling emotional.

'Roddy sends you his best regards and I have to tell you that you are most welcome at the wedding.'

'Nice to know I'm wanted,' Ruth said brusquely.

'You'll come?'

'No, Kate, I won't but I'll be there in spirit.'

'It won't be the same.'

'Darling, I'm being selfish and I make no apology. You will be surrounded by young people and I imagine the witnesses or whatever they are called will be close associates of yours and Roddy's. I would feel very much out of it and a nuisance into the bargain.'

'You could never be that.'

'Who is to be your witness – no, I won't call her that I'll call her your bridesmaid.'

'I'll ask Dorothy.'

'The Cockney girl?'

'She's my best friend.'

The wedding took place with Flying Officer Timothy Winters and Dorothy Brooks as witnesses. After they were pronounced man and wife Kate expected there would be a toast and then they would leave for four days in Edinburgh. Instead there had been secret moves to have a surprise celebration for the newlyweds. Kate was absolutely taken by surprise when she saw the spread and the number of people all smiling and clapping as they entered. Roddy was less surprised, he had gone into too many rooms when the conversation had broken off abruptly not to know something was afoot.

If there were any shortages the officers' mess knew little about them. Kate was thrilled with the cake. There was icing, not make-believe but real icing and a cardboard bride and bridegroom on the top. A number of the WAAFs had been invited and were cheerfully accepting drinks while the happy couple cut the cake.

'Not quite what you expected, darling,' Roddy said when they were on the train to Edinburgh.

'Roddy, I was never so surprised in my life when I saw everybody. And the cake, I wonder whose idea that was? Hope they don't eat it all, I want to send a piece to Aunt Ruth.' The words were falling over each other in her excitement. 'Did you know?'

'I suspected there was something going on but not on that scale. They did us proud wouldn't you say?'

She could see how pleased he was. 'I do, it was magnificent.'

'One or two of your girls were throwing them back. A few sore heads tomorrow I fear.'

'Don't you believe it, our girls are built of stronger stuff than that.'

The train filled up with a few standing in the corridors. Kate and Roddy had been sitting close together and were even more tightly squeezed when another body forced itself in. One woman glared, another one smiled painfully but no one uttered a word.

The train half emptied at Edinburgh and Kate and Roddy, not troubled with too much luggage made their way to Princes Street by foot and to a hotel almost opposite Sir Walter Scott's monument.

'Chose it because it was central. Maybe I should have gone for somewhere quieter.'

'No, I like this. In a small hotel I'd feel conspicuous as a newly-married, here no one would notice.'

'Or care?'

'Or care,' she smiled as more people arrived.

After signing the register, Roddy was given a key and a young boy in the hotel uniform showed them to a room on the first floor.

'Thank you, sir.' The boy gave a satisfied smile for the generosity of the tip.

'This suit you, Mrs Hamilton-Harvey?'

'Very nice indeed.'

Roddy bounced on the bed. 'Springs seem to be in order,' he grinned.

'What did you expect? This is a highly recommended hotel.'

'Even so you can still get a sagging mattress. Food, I think, Kate, we both need a decent meal and if we wait too long there may not be much of a choice.'

'I hardly expected there would be. You, my darling Roddy, are used to the best of everything. You should see what is served up to us poor WAAFs.'

'Complain.'

'Do you think that would do any good?'

'Probably not.'

The meal served to them in a well-filled dining-room, was good and well cooked. They were both hungry and after it Kate had to stifle a yawn. It had been a very full day with an early start. She was tired but she wasn't going to admit to it.

Kate had no regrets about having slept with Roddy before the gold band was on her finger. That night had been very special and tonight and all the other nights would be too. She was discovering that there was no hard and fast rule. What was right for one wasn't necessarily right for another.

'Four whole wonderful days when it is just you and me,' Roddy said sitting down on the only armchair and pulling Kate on to his knee.

'Aren't I too heavy?'

'No, my dearest one you are not,' he murmured as he kissed her. 'You are very lovely,' he said huskily, his kisses becoming more passionate as he felt her responding. By the time the hotel quietened for the night they were asleep in each other's arms.

The all too short days were spent wandering about the lovely city. They had both seen its main attractions but Edinburgh had so much more to offer. The cold east wind that so often swept the city had been stilled and many like Kate and Roddy were enjoying a leisurely stroll through Princes Street gardens. Later, after a refreshment, they would take the popular walk down the Royal Mile and on to the Palace of Holyrood House.

'A perfect honeymoon, Roddy,' she sighed.

'Much too short though.'

They were back in their hotel and doing their packing.

A shadow crossed her face. She had always been terrified for Roddy's safety but now it was ten times worse. This was what marriage did – brought two people so close that they became one. Anything that threatened that union was too awful to be contemplated.

'Roddy, the war news is a bit better. You think so, don't you?'

'The worst could be over, darling.'

'Light at the end of the tunnel?' She was almost pleading.

'Oh, definitely that.'

Chapter Twenty-four

'On your way, Kate, you're wanted in the office. I'll take over here.'

'Thanks, Myra.' Kate got up and the red-haired girl with the cheeky grin sat down.

Being able to make the change from teleprinter back to typewriter with little trouble meant that Kate was often singled out to help in the main office when things got hectic. At first there had been some resentment at what the other WAAFs considered favouritism but when they discovered it was hard work with no chance for a gossip, they decided that Kate was welcome.

Kate knocked and on being told to enter opened the door. She was surprised to find herself being led through the main office and into a smaller one she knew to be the province of the First Officer. First Officer Anne Wilkinson was behind her desk, a pen in her hand which she put down. A calm woman who didn't fluster easily, she was held in some awe by those in her charge. She also had their respect for being strict but scrupulously fair. Kate felt bewildered and gave an uncertain smile. Over at the window, where he had been looking out, the padre turned round.

'Sit down, Kate,' the First Officer said and Kate's brain registered that the woman had never before addressed her by her Christian name. The chair was near to but not beside the desk. Once she was seated the padre lowered his long, thin body into the chair beside the window. To Kate it seemed like a film in slow motion, a build-up. She waited with her hands in her lap, refusing to let her brain accept what was screaming in her head.

'It's bad news, I'm afraid,' the woman said, her eyes full of sympathy.

'Roddy hasn't come back, he's missing, that's what you're going to tell me?' Kate was amazed at how calm she sounded. The words came out as a statement, not a question. She looked over at the padre as though for confirmation.

The Rev. Charles Cuthbert had volunteered for the services at the outbreak of war and should by now be well used to dealing with and comforting the bereaved. He had the training and the right words as well as a natural sympathetic manner. Yet in those first moments he found he couldn't speak. How do you tell a young wife that her husband is dead? He who only two short months ago had married them and wished the attractive couple a long and happy life together. After the ceremony he had joined in the celebrations and some celebrations those had been. Now he was faced with the heartbreaking task of informing this lovely girl that her beloved husband had given his life for his country.

'I'm afraid it is true, Roddy hasn't come back,' the padre said it with difficulty. How calm and composed she appeared, but he knew she was neither when he saw the whiteness of her knuckles.

'He will though, he'll come back. Missing doesn't have to mean . . .' Her eyes were pleading.

'In this case I'm afraid it does. Kate, you have to accept that Roddy is dead. There is absolutely no doubt.' The words were brutal and she must have thought so by the resentful look she gave him, but they were necessary. To cling to hope where none existed only added to the agony. The padre had seen it all before, the slow dying of hope. Let Kate start her mourning now.

'I'll have someone bring in tea.' The First Officer got up and left the room. There was nothing she could do at present. Better to leave the girl with the padre. Arrangements could be put in hand for compassionate leave.

'Miracles do happen, you should know that,' Kate said harshly.

'Kate,' he straightened himself in the chair, 'if there was even the smallest hope I would be down on my knees praying with you.'

Her face clouded. 'What happened? Please, I need to know.'

'I don't have all the details but apparently there was a midair collision, both planes caught fire and went out of control. The others saw it happen, Kate, and were of one voice. No one could have survived that.'

'An enemy plane?'

'Yes.'

As if it mattered. The other pilot's family would be suffering the same pain. The tea arrived, two cups and saucers on a tray together with a sugar bowl and milk jug. It was left on the desk. The padre got up to do the necessary. Two heaped teaspoons of sugar went into Kate's cup and rather less into his own.

Kate watched his rather clumsy efforts and found she could think of ordinary things. Sugar was in very short supply and that amount wouldn't have been far short of someone's ration for the week. She remembered Aunt Ruth telling her about one household she visited where everything was meticulously measured. No one member of the family got more than another. The butter was divided equally and put into small dishes before each place at the table. If they had been rather generous to themselves then it would be dry bread until the next ration was due. Kate recalled giggling about it and thinking that was taking rationing too far.

'Drink that, Kate,' the padre said, handing her the cup then keeping hold of it when he saw her hands were shaking.

He held the cup to her mouth and made her drink the sweet tea. She made a face. 'Too sweet I know but it does help.'

'Thank you. I'll manage now that it isn't so full.' She took the cup between her hands and forced herself to drink more. 'That's all I can take.' She gave him back the cup and he put it on the tray with his own untouched. 'You get all the unpleasant jobs to do.'

'Some are – difficult, but others are a pleasure.'

'Like our wedding?' she smiled.

'Like that and the celebrations that followed.'

'It was a surprise.'

'I know, I was in on it.'

She looked at him thinking what a kind face he had. 'Do you really believe in us all being reunited in heaven?'

He didn't immediately answer. 'Perhaps not quite in the way you mean,' he said slowly, then saw she wasn't satisfied. 'People think more about religion after losing a loved one.'

'I was ten when my mother died and I thought of heaven as being more like another world, a better and happier world with everyone going about much as they do in this.'

He smiled. 'At the time did it help?'

'Oh, yes. Now I'm more inclined to think of it as a spiritual reunion, a meeting of souls. Does that make sense?'

'Yes, Kate, it makes sense. None of us knows for sure but we have our beliefs and these we must hold on to.' The Rev. Charles Cuthbert ran his fingers through his thick, greying hair. A remarkable young woman, she looked calm, was putting on a brave front but inside she was weeping. It was there in her pain-filled eyes.

'You've been very kind. Roddy always said you were very approachable.'

'I like to think I am.' He paused. 'Kate, anger is not uncommon, anger at God for allowing it to happen and if you experience this don't feel guilty. It will pass and you will realise that there is a purpose to everything that happens in life.'

'No use asking why – we have to have a sort of blind trust?'

He smiled. 'With that enquiring mind of yours I imagine you and Roddy had many a discussion.' It wasn't an answer to her question but maybe he didn't have one.

'I'm going to miss him so much.'

'I know. You and Roddy had something very special. Not too many can say that. There are some who go through life never having loved or been loved,' he said gently.

She nodded. There had been a time in her own childhood when that description would have fitted her. 'May I ask you something?'

'Of course.'

'Have Roddy's parents been notified?'

'I believe so.'

She was worrying her bottom lip. 'They, Roddy's parents I mean, don't know about our marriage. They didn't approve of me you see.'

He didn't see. He couldn't imagine anyone not approving of Kate. He had been blessed with two sons and if there had been a daughter he would have hoped for one like Kate.

'I find that hard to believe. They can't know you well.'

'Well enough,' she said a little bitterly. 'I only ask because I've just thought of – of Roddy's—' she faltered.

He helped. 'Roddy's personal effects,' he said gently. 'They'll come to you, of course.'

'Send them to his parents. They would expect to receive them.'

'In the circumstances they would but perhaps you should give more thought to this.'

'It won't change anything.'

'Don't you want something?'

'I would have liked to keep the ring I gave Roddy, we had our initials engraved on it and the date we got engaged.' She smiled and her face lit up. 'Roddy wasn't keen on wearing a ring but I said he could keep it in his pocket for luck.' She choked. 'It didn't bring him much.'

There was a light tap on the door and the First Officer came in with a clearly distressed Dorothy. The girl had been told to report to the senior WAAF and in fear and trembling had gone along wondering which of her sins had been found out.

When told the news Dorothy had gone hot and cold with shock.

'That's awful, just awful but maybe—'

'No, Brooks, no maybe. Pilot Officer Hamilton-Harvey is dead. Don't encourage your friend—'

'Give her false hopes you mean?'

'Yes, Brooks, that is what I mean.'

'Poor Kate. Her parents are dead.'

'Yes, I do know that. Arrangements are being made for Kate to travel home but meantime I would be glad if you would look after her.'

'I'll do that and gladly.'

'Thank you. I imagine she will still be with the padre. You had better accompany me.'

The Rev. Charles Cuthbert shook hands with Kate and patted her shoulder. He nodded and smiled to Dorothy then left them.

Dorothy didn't utter a word, she just took Kate's arm and they walked out of the office along a corridor and then outside and along to the WAAF quarters. Thankfully no one was around.

'Oh, God, Kate, what can I say?' They put their arms about each other, drawing comfort, and for a long time they stood like that. Then without warning Kate gave a choking sob and the tears came. Hot scalding tears followed by huge painful sobs that tore at her throat until she was almost retching.

'I'm so – so – sorry,' she said when the paroxysm of weeping stopped.

'Don't be,' Dorothy said furiously. 'This bloody, bloody war. Howl, scream, do what you like, anything is better than bottling it up. I should know, that's what I did.'

Kate raised a tear-blotched face. 'You never told me!'

'Never told anyone.'

'Never told anyone what?'

'Lost my family in the blitz, our street got a direct hit.'

Kate was looking at Dorothy with horror, her own tragedy put aside for the moment. 'And you kept that to yourself?'

'My way of coping. I feel like telling you if you want to hear?'

Kate nodded.

'I'll never forget that night, never. We were used to bombings or as used as you could ever be. After the all-clear I told my gran I was going home. I could see the bombers had been very close and I began to run. Kate, I couldn't believe my eyes, I think I became hysterical. Where our house had been there was nothing but rubble. I remember seeing a piece of the living-room wallpaper fluttering in the wind and clouds of dust. There were screams joining my own but not from the rubble, not from the devastation. They were from people like me who had hurried from wherever they had been to check on their family.'

'Oh, Dorothy . . .' Kate was shaking her head as though she couldn't take it in, it was beyond belief.

'Six of them, Kate, they had been there one minute and gone the next. My parents, my two sisters, my little brother and my Aunt Violet, she had been staying with us.' Dorothy stopped to wipe a hand over her eyes. 'It should have been seven.'

'Don't say that, Dorothy.'

'Why not when it is the truth? I'd had a blazing row with my parents and I'd stormed out saying I was never coming back.'

'You didn't mean it.'

'No, I didn't mean it. My mother wouldn't have been too bothered, she knew where I would be. At my gran's. That was always where we went if we'd had a row. Not that we got much sympathy but Gran would listen, give us something to eat and by then we would have recovered.' She gave a wistful smile. 'If my mother said anything at all

339

on our return it would have been – so you've decided to come home, have you?'

'That's a real family, Dorothy, I never had that.'

'You don't appreciate what you have until you lose it. That's why it is just Gran and me, we are all that's left. She tried to talk me out of feeling badly but it will always be there. I'll always feel regret that my last words to Mum and Dad were said in anger.'

'Your gran is right you should stop feeling badly. Your parents wouldn't want you tormenting yourself with regrets, they would want you to remember the happy times.'

Dorothy nodded. 'The same goes for you, Kate, you have to remember the good times.'

'Roddy was so tired of it all. The killings and the awful devastation. Treasures lost for ever, never to be seen by our children.'

'The bloody Germans, they have a lot to answer for.'

Kate smiled. She had been deeply shocked to hear Dorothy using that word but now it didn't bother her. She thought there were two kinds of swearing. One that sounded coarse and horrible and the other that came close to being accepted. She would never use that word herself but that was because she and Dorothy had had a very different upbringing.

'Roddy didn't blame the ordinary Germans, they wouldn't have wanted war. They had no more choice than we had, he said and I think that has to be true, Dorothy.'

'I'm not so generous, I hate them one and all.'

'No, you don't.' They were sitting on Kate's bed. 'I don't remember when Roddy said this but he told me he had a sneaking admiration for conscientious objectors. He didn't see them as cowards, quite the opposite. He said it took a lot of guts to stand up for your beliefs especially when you were spat upon and became an object of hate.'

Dorothy looked thoughtful. 'Some suffered through no fault of their own. We had an Italian family living near us. They had a shop and I used to have a crush on the eldest son.

We liked them because they were always so pleasant and obliging and of course they stayed open late. Then along comes the war and without warning the shop is closed and the father and the elder son interned. I don't know what became of the others.'

'Overnight they became the enemy yet they probably saw themselves as more British than Italian.'

Dorothy laughed. 'The family couldn't even speak the language, they were educated here.'

The news about Roddy got round very quickly and everyone was shocked and upset for Kate. The usually boisterous WAAFs went about quietly and spoke in hushed tones.

'I haven't been able to think straight,' Kate said to Dorothy. 'There are things I should be doing but I don't seem able to concentrate.'

'That's only to be expected. I'll do anything, you've only to ask.'

'I know. You can't know the comfort it is just having you beside me.' She paused. 'Aunt Ruth has been notified, I wonder who did that?'

'That would have been done officially.'

'I'm going home tomorrow.'

'That would be best. You and your aunt are pretty close?'

'Yes, we are. She was very fond of Roddy and this is going to upset her terribly. Oh, God!' Her hand went to her mouth.

Chapter Twenty-Five

'Aunt Ruth, I don't want to sound ungrateful, please don't think that, but I would rather not see anyone.'

'Then you needn't. They are all concerned about you and when I tell them they'll respect your wishes.'

'I just want to think,' Kate said apologetically, 'and I can do that best here in the house with you.'

'Peace and quiet is what you need.'

Kate thought long and hard and by the next morning she knew what she was going to do.

'You seem more rested,' Aunt Ruth said at breakfast time.

'That's probably because I've made up my mind.'

'I rather thought so. This is about Roddy's parents?'

'Yes.'

'You are going to see them?'

'Yes, I've decided to do that.'

'It's bound to be an ordeal,' Ruth said worriedly. 'Do you feel equal to it?'

'No, but that won't stop me going.'

'Would a carefully written letter not be enough?'

'No, I need to tell them myself.'

'When will you go?'

'Today, before my courage fails.'

'Would you like me to come with you?'

Kate smiled and shook her head. 'That's good of you to offer but this is something I have to do on my own.'

'I understand.' She looked across to the window and seemed satisfied with what she saw there. 'You should get there and back dry, that looks like a settled sky.'

'How are the buses these days?'

'The timetable hasn't been too badly affected.'

As Kate set out, smart in her uniform, Ruth watched from the window and her heart felt heavy. Robert's child had known such a lot of heartbreak. Why was it that some suffered so much while others seemed to have a charmed life? At times her own faith was sorely tried and it was difficult to believe that it was all for a purpose. What purpose? Our standing in the next life? If one could be sure of that it would go some way to help.

What kind of reception would Kate get? Ruth wondered. Never in her wildest dreams could Mildred have imagined her liaison with Edwin Hamilton-Harvey could have caused such havoc in the lives of so many people.

Kate tried not to think of those other two occasions when she had come this way. Then it had been in Roddy's car and she hadn't seen as much of the drive as she was seeing now. There was a difference. In war how could it not be? Only the old or those unfit for active service were available to work in the gardens and where once flowers had grown in abundance there were rows of vegetables. At Craggy Point standards might have dropped but the grounds still looked cared for. Kate thought that Mrs Hamilton-Harvey would often be on her knees weeding and trying to keep the gardens tidy.

It was all so peaceful, no one was around and Kate wondered if she would find Roddy's parents at home. Then she thought it very probable. People didn't venture far from home these days. The nearer she got to the big heavy door the more her heart hammered and she had to force herself not to turn round and run down the drive and get as far away as she could. Two deep breaths restored her a little and before she could change her mind her hand was on the knocker. At the same moment she saw the bell-pull and decided that would be more likely to be heard. After the ring had died away she had what seemed to her to be a long wait. Then she heard footsteps, a woman's she thought and the door opened. Kate was taken aback, she hadn't expected the mistress of the house to open the door. Both women stared at each other.

'You are – it is Kate? The uniform – forgive me.'

'Yes, I'm Kate. May I come in Mrs Hamilton-Harvey?'

'Of course, I'm so sorry. Do come in. It was the shock you see.'

Kate stepped inside and the woman shut the heavy door. Then she went ahead to lead the way.

'We are in the morning-room, that's where we spend most of our time. We did have evacuees, a mother and four children.' She turned to face Kate. 'That was quite an upheaval.' She closed her eyes as though it hurt to remember. 'The children would have settled given time but not the mother. She asked how I could stand the awful quiet, that she would lose her mind.'

'They left,' Kate smiled.

'To everyone's relief, yes they left. There is word of us having to give up part of our house to three Polish officers. Nothing more is required of us other than the accommodation. They have a batman to deal with everything.'

She was talking non-stop and too fast. Kate thought it was to hide her unease. The door was ajar and the woman pushed it open.

'Edwin, we have a visitor,' she said ushering Kate in.

Kate had never been in the morning-room and had the impression that it was now a sitting-room. She recognised articles of furniture that had come from the drawing-room.

'Who is it?' he said blinking.

'Kate.'

'Kate?'

'Yes, dear, it's Kate and in uniform.'

They had both aged, she thought. There was a lifelessness

about them as though each day was just another one to get through.

'Sit down, Kate, would you like something? Tea or coffee?'

'No, thank you.' Kate sat down. 'You must be wondering why I am here?'

'I suppose we are.' She paused and the tears welled up in her eyes. 'Roddy was killed, did you know that?'

'Yes, it is the reason I'm here.' Kate swallowed the lump in her throat. 'We – we were stationed at RAF Miltonwells, both of us were stationed there,' she added unnecessarily.

'That was a – a coincidence?'

'Yes.'

'How extraordinary.'

'We thought that too.'

Edwin Hamilton-Harvey hadn't spoken since asking who the visitor was.

'Is that what you've come to tell us?'

'No, I came to tell you that Roddy and I were married two months before he was killed.'

There was a stunned silence. Husband and wife looked at one another.

'I – I don't believe what I am hearing!'

'I'm sorry, I didn't think to bring proof, Mrs Hamilton-Harvey, but you won't find that difficult to get.'

'Forgive me I didn't mean it that way. You see, Kate, Roddy never mentioned you or marriage.'

'I know. Does that surprise you?' Kate said bitterly. 'And please don't try to blame me, it wasn't my wish that you were kept in the dark. I didn't approve of what Roddy was doing but I could understand it. He blamed you both for keeping us apart.'

'Which means you must have told him.'

'Yes, Mrs Hamilton-Harvey, I did.'

'You broke your promise.' It was the man who spoke.

'There was no promise and I did what you asked. You made us both miserable, Roddy because I had said there was someone else and me because I had been forced into that position by you.' Kate smiled. 'Roddy and I were still in love and we both felt that fate had brought us together.'

'So Roddy knew,' the woman said and a strange little smile played round her mouth, 'all that for nothing.'

'Yes, it was for nothing. Roddy insisted on being told everything and I felt no need to hold back. If war does nothing else it does put things in perspective. I discovered that what happened all those years ago was unimportant. Roddy agreed, he said he couldn't care less. We had our life to live and the sins of the father –'

Edwin Hamilton-Harvey gave a gasp and half rose from his chair but one look from his wife and whatever he was about to say was never uttered.

'How right you are, none of it is important. Too late I am realising that too. Kate, if it is any consolation I would give anything to turn the clock back,' Roddy's mother said.

'We made a mistake,' Edwin Hamilton-Harvey said getting the words out with difficulty.

'And now we are paying the price for it,' his wife said bitterly. 'To lose our only son was very dreadful but to learn that he died perhaps hating us . . .' Her voice trembled.

'No, you mustn't think that, Mrs Hamilton-Harvey, Roddy was quite incapable of hating. He was angry and disappointed but he never stopped loving you. In his own time he was going to tell you about our marriage and those were his own words. He – it was his way of punishing you.'

'Thank you, that does make it a little easier. We can all make mistakes.' Her eyes were sad. 'Such a short time you had.'

'Yes, but we were happy, very, very happy. That is what I cling to, knowing I made him happy . . .' Kate had to stop, the tears were too close and she didn't want to break down. 'I'll go now,' she said getting to her feet.

'Don't go, please don't go just yet. My mind isn't clear, I'm trying to think.'

Kate sat down but on the edge of the chair as though poised for flight.

'By right you should have Roddy's – they were sent here.'

'I know, I asked them to be sent to you.'

'Why?'

'I don't know.'

'I'm grateful. Kate, you are our daughter-in-law . . .'

Only because fate took a hand, Kate thought but without any bitterness. They had wanted the best for their son but had gone the wrong way about it.

'Yes, Kate,' her husband joined in, 'we must not forget that fact. You are part of this family.'

'No, I am your son's widow, no more than that.' Kate got to her feet and smoothed her skirt.

'Won't you keep in touch?' Roddy's mother said wistfully but knowing the answer before it came.

'No, I'll never return to Craggy Point. I've done what I came to do and now I'll say goodbye.'

Kate was surprised when Roddy's father got up and came over to shake her hand. 'Goodbye, Kate,' he said heavily, 'and I am sorry.'

'I'll see you to the door,' his wife said.

'Is Alice well?' Kate asked politely.

'Yes, and very busy. Alice has two land girls who have turned out to be a great help. Iain is a prisoner-of-war.'

'Yes, Roddy told me. Poor Iain, I hope conditions are not too bad.'

'He says not, that it is mostly boredom. That, of course, could be for Alice's benefit.'

'At least he's safe.'

'Yes, that is what Alice says. We are very proud of our daughter, the way she is keeping things going for Iain's return. And she has David, he's a bright lad.'

They were at the door. The woman fumbled to open it then managed. Kate held out her hand and Roddy's mother grasped it in both of hers.

'Goodbye, Mrs Hamilton-Harvey.'

'Goodbye, Kate, it should have been all so different. I would never say this to my husband but sometimes I wonder if we were partly responsible for Roddy's death. Joining up when he did was out of character, he wasn't an impulsive person and volunteering to train as a fighter pilot . . .' She shook her head.

'Maybe I was partly responsible too but I'm not going to think that way and you mustn't have these thoughts either.'

'God bless you, Kate, I hope one day there will be someone else for you and that you will know great happiness. It's what Roddy would have wanted.'

Kate nodded and smiled through her tears. Almost blinded she hurried away. She didn't turn back but knew that the woman watched her and then in a curve in the drive when she would be lost from sight, Kate heard the door shut and the noise of a bolt being shot into place.

Ruth had been unable to settle, her thoughts constantly with Kate and she had come home early. Kate's face when she came in told her nothing.

'Well?' she said a little impatiently. 'Was it very bad?'

Kate sank down on a chair. 'No, Aunt Ruth, it wasn't bad just sad, so very sad. They have their daughter, Alice, and little David but even so it is like a light has gone out in their lives.'

'That is exactly what it is. Death is a light going out.'

'They wanted me to keep in touch. They meant it then but later when they thought about it what good would it do?'

'Perhaps to bring their son nearer, to make up in some small way. Did you think of that?'

'No, I didn't. We were all a bit emotional, how else could we be? I had given them a big shock.'

'Yes, it must have been that all right.'

'Separation is best.'

'I'm inclined to agree with that.'

'Something is burning.'

'Dear heavens, take your eyes away a moment . . .' She hurried into the kitchenette and Kate's laughter followed her. Aunt Ruth was a disaster in the kitchen.

Chapter Twenty-Six

Kate's compassionate leave could have been extended had she wished it but she hadn't. She wanted to get back into a routine, to fill every waking hour and hope that sleep would claim most of the night time.

Another ordeal had to be faced and it was better she should get it over. The rental for the flat had been paid until the end of the month and there was no reason for Kate to keep it on. What she must do was remove Roddy's belongings and her own. How would she feel, she wondered, going into the flat where they had spent so many happy hours?

'Don't Kate, don't put yourself through that. It isn't as though you have to. You said there was a cleaning woman?'

'Yes, there is.'

'Get her to clear out the wardrobes and the drawers and collect anything lying about. She'll know what belongs to the flat and what doesn't.'

'I expect so,' Kate said wearily. Even thinking needed energy and she had so little of it. She had never understood the expression 'dead tired' until now.

'Well, then—'

'Dorothy, you are a wonderful friend to have and I've used you shamelessly.'

'Nonsense, I've done no more than anyone else would have done.'

'A great deal more.' Kate smiled sadly. 'It isn't just the

removal of our belongings, Dorothy, I have to say goodbye. Roddy and I thought of the flat as our first home, a place we could call our own.' She paused. 'Tell you though, you could help in one way if you didn't mind.'

'Name it.'

'Once I pack the things you could help with the carrying.'

'Sure thing. You could ask about transport, worth a try.'

'No, I won't do that. Neither of us kept very much in the flat. The only bulky thing, the thick dressing-gown Roddy wore sometimes, didn't belong to him. It was hanging on the back of the door when he took the flat and since it fitted . . .'

'He decided to make use of it?'

'Yes.'

'What is there in the way of cases?'

'A suitcase and I seem to remember a hold-all.'

'Put some in each and we'll carry them between us.'

So often Kate had walked this way, sometimes with Roddy, sometimes alone. Even before they were married she'd had her own key and could come and go as she pleased. Reaching the flat, Kate took the key from her pocket and opened the door. The musty smell so often present in an unoccupied house was missing. The cleaning woman would be coming in as before to open the windows, let fresh air blow through the rooms and do whatever else was necessary. Stepping inside Kate wondered if it had always been this quiet. Perhaps and she hadn't noticed. The silence was different, deeper as though the house was showing respect for another brave airman who would not be returning.

'Roddy,' Kate whispered to the empty room. 'This is to say goodbye properly. I wanted it to be here where we became lovers. Marriage sealed our happiness, that was what you said. And I agreed with that though I was yours with or without the gold band. How I have changed, and Aunt Sarah would have said not for the better. There will be no more weeping, my darling, I have no tears left. What is left and what I will never lose are the memories. I'll treasure those for always. Whatever the future will hold for me, Roddy, you will always have a place in my heart.'

Kate went round the room touching the furniture and then crossing to the window to play with the blind-cord. Roddy had done it so often and jokingly she had blamed him for the cord being frayed in places. He had promised to see about a replacement cord but he never had and now he never would. Whoever followed would have to deal with it.

In the bedroom the open suitcase was on the floor beside a Gladstone bag Kate suspected came from Craggy Point. Time to get started, beginning with the larger wardrobe. Not everything was to be taken, Roddy's bedroom slippers and a spare pair of shoes he kept in the flat were put aside to be disposed of. Other articles of clothing were added until a small pile had grown. Kate looked at it then scribbled a note and left it beside the bundle. The woman might have a use for them.

Dorothy had said an hour was long enough for the task she had set herself and just as Kate looked at her watch the doorbell rang. Dorothy was punctual.

The weeks went by, September gave way to October and there was a gradual lifting of spirits as better news filtered through. No one dared to read too much into it but it was a welcome change from setbacks. They were claiming advances but really they were just reclaiming what before had been lost.

The signal room was buzzing with activity. Kate and Dorothy were sitting together, Kate's fingers flying over the keys and Dorothy dealing with the tape coming through the teleprinter. They could talk through the noise of the machines.

'Kate, I'm a bit concerned about my gran.'

'Why, is she unwell?'

'Don't know. If she is she'll keep it to herself. She can be a stubborn so-and-so when she wants. The neighbours are good but she doesn't welcome too much interference, calls it nosiness which it isn't and even if it is where's the harm?'

'A small price to pay for a helping hand?'

'That's what I would say. Mrs Maxwell, she's the most attentive and the one Gran likes best – heavens! what am I doing?' she said quickly as she broke off the tape at the wrong place and had to do a patching job. 'Where was I?'

'Mrs Maxwell.'

'The woman must be worried when she went to the trouble of finding my address and writing here. Her worry seems to be that Gran won't budge when the siren goes and no one can force her.'

'Not everyone thinks the shelters are safer.'

'The sensible ones do,' Dorothy said tartly. 'Think I'll have to go and see Gran. I'm due a twenty-four hour.'

'So am I come to think about it.' Kate didn't want to go to London, it was probably the last place she wanted to go but she must stop thinking about herself. Dorothy had done such a lot for her, surely she could do something in return. 'Want company?' she said casually.

'You mean you would come?' Dorothy said in a disbelieving voice.

'If you want me.'

'As if I would turn down an offer like that.'

'Provided we can get our time off together.'

'Leave that to me,' Dorothy said cheerfully. 'Gran has a spare room with two single beds, actually it's my room and when I'm there I take time about with the beds.'

'Why?'

'Don't know, Gran's idea, save dampness though I don't think there is any. It's not the Ritz but a sight better than we have here. We'll just arrive and surprise her.'

London had had a raid the previous night, but not on the scale of those that had gone before. Kate and Dorothy got off the early morning train and once out of the station set off at a brisk pace. The October sunshine was fitful and the rain clouds hadn't completely dispersed. In the distance smoke could be seen rising from the ruins. A few more made homeless, more pain, more misery.

Dorothy was proud to call herself a Londoner. 'You know, Kate, we can take a battering night after night and still manage to keep going. Londoners don't give in.'

'Not only Londoners,' Kate corrected her.

'No,' Dorothy conceded, 'we've had the worst but others are catching up, is that what you mean?'

'I suppose I do.'

'Stop here, this is where we queue for the bus, funny how we all queue, we never did that before. We shouldn't have long to wait.'

'You hope,' a voice came from somewhere and there was a ripple of laughter.

Dorothy lowered her voice. 'Folk are so different. A lot of them fled London the minute war was declared and most returned because they couldn't stay away.'

'Same as where I come from. The city people couldn't stand village life, not enough for them to do. Glasgow and the Clyde area suffered badly and there was a big move to get the children away. Our village, together with others, had evacuees, some mothers came with them.'

'Played havoc,' Dorothy grinned.

'Some did, others settled quite well. My Aunt Ruth said the mothers, not the children, were the problem. They had no interest in village life, didn't want to know, and after a few weeks a lot of them packed their bags and went home.'

'Found the quiet worse than the bombs?'

'So it would appear.'

The bus came and they got on. They got seats but not together. The conductress punched two tickets and Dorothy signalled to Kate that she had them in case Kate bought another two. It seemed a fair distance to Kate but as Dorothy pointed out it was the number of stops they made and the slowness of some people to get on and off that made it appear a long journey. When it came to their stop it was a short walk to a street of brick houses all with a small front garden and no railings, just the holes where they had been.

'Removed the railings for the war effort.'

'We lost ours too.'

'Bet it was a panic measure and they don't make use of them,' Dorothy said.

'That would be a shame. I mean no one would object to losing their railings if it helped to bring the war to an end but to find piles of them lying about doing no good . . .'

'Makes me mad too,' Dorothy said then stopped opposite number 12 of the terraced houses. It had a dark maroon door badly in need of a paint. 'Never locks the door you see.' Dorothy turned the knob and went in to a small vestibule, opened another door and then shouted. 'It's only me, Gran, don't be alarmed.'

Kate shut the outside door and followed slowly. A stair with a well-worn carpet led up to the two bedrooms. There was a living-room, a large kitchen and a scullery off it. Some years ago a bathroom had been added out at the back using up most of the garden.

'Lord's sake, you'll be the death of me, girl, giving me a fright like that. I'm sitting here in the kitchen.'

'Shouldn't keep your door unlocked, it isn't safe.'

'Not much to steal unless you think I'm worth the bother. Who is that behind you?'

'Kate. Come on in, Kate, and meet my grandmother,' Dorothy said after giving the woman a hug and a kiss. 'I told you about Kate,' she said as though willing her to remember.

'How do you do, Mrs Brooks,' Kate smiled. 'I hope you don't mind me coming with Dorothy.'

'Mind? I'm delighted,' the woman said taking Kate's hand in a firm grip.

'We're staying the night, Gran, unless you've let the room to lodgers,' Dorothy said jokingly.

'No, pet, that's your room for as long as I'm here. Kate, you'll have to forgive me not getting up. It's not that I haven't the use of my legs, just a stiffness that makes getting around difficult. I'm not complaining, there's many a one worse than me and as for the house—'

'You can't keep it the way you used to,' her grand-daughter interrupted. 'As if it mattered.'

'Oh, I can still see to the fire, make myself a bite to eat and take a duster round.'

'Everything looks fine to me,' Kate said, feeling she should be contributing to the conversation and then won-dering if she'd said the right thing. The old lady would, she thought, be in her seventies. She was thin with grey hair and her face was devoid of colour. Not a healthy paleness, there was a touch of yellow about it. She wore a grey cardigan over a dark dress and there were a few stains on the dress.

'Give me a minute to get on my feet and we'll have a cup of tea.'

'Stay put,' Dorothy ordered, 'I'll see to the tea.'

'May I help?'

'No, Kate, not yet. You sit and talk to Gran.'

'That's what to do, dear, bring your chair nearer. I nearly said nearer to the fire but I won't put a match to it until later. The sun warms the kitchen for much of the day but by night it can be chilly.'

'How do you manage for coal?'

'It's a case of having to manage,' she smiled. 'I eke out my allowance with logs but they've become almost as scarce. Bed with a hot water bottle is what it sometimes comes to. You in there, is that kettle boiling yet?'

'Yes, and the tea is made. Some folk have no patience.'

'Try and get matching saucers for the cups seeing as we have a guest.'

'Odd ones will do me,' Kate laughed. To begin with she had felt awkward as she did in any strange situation but not now. Dorothy's grandmother had a dry sense of humour and there was a kindliness about her that Dorothy must have inherited. She made no mention of Kate's loss yet Kate could feel the sympathy. It was like a reaching out where words were unnecessary.

The tea refreshed them and they ate a Rich Tea biscuit which was all that was in the house. 'Practically lives on those she does. There never was much of her at the best of times but now she's just skin and bone.'

'That'll be me you're talking about?'

'Yes, it's you. You aren't eating enough.'

'I don't starve myself but when you don't have an appetite food isn't all that important.' She looked at Kate's cup. 'More tea?'

'No, thank you but I enjoyed that.'

Dorothy had got up and was wandering about opening drawers and closing them.

'What are you hunting for?'

'Your ration book.'

'Has to be somewhere.'

'I know that but where? You can be the limit, Gran. Have you lost it?'

'How could I manage that?'

'Very easily. You never remember where you put your purse or your keys.'

'In the end I find them. Try the scullery.'

'I have.'

'Then have another look.'

Dorothy came back holding aloft the ration book. 'Know where I found it, in the vegetable basket. Come on, Kate, we'll do some shopping. Not far there's a shop at the corner.'

'Henry Wallace. If you tell him it's for me he'll see you all right. Get me my purse, you'll need money.'

'I've enough.'

'Changed days. Forever scrounging off me that one was.'

'That was a long time ago, my scrounging days are over.'

They were both laughing when they went outside.

'I like your gran, she's a real character.'

'She's the best,' her granddaughter said.

The bell pinged as they entered the shop and a man came from the back to see what they wanted. His smile broadened.

'It's you Dorothy. This'll be a bit of leave?'

'All of twenty-four hours. Meet my friend Kate.'

He nodded and she smiled.

Dorothy put the ration book on the counter. 'Not taking her ration is she?'

'No, there's a fair bit due. She hasn't been in for a while.'

'I'll take it all now and anything else you can spare.'

'I'll see what I can do. Funny old world this. Before the war I had a well-stocked shop but times were hard and folk had to watch the pennies. Now there's a bit more money about and precious little to spend it on.' All the time he was talking he was going back and forward to the shelves to get what was required.

'That it all?' Dorothy asked.

'More than you're due.' He gave a broad wink. 'You wouldn't say no to a pork pie would you?'

'I wouldn't say no to three pork pies.'

'That's asking a bit much but seeing it's you and you have a friend to feed . . .'

'Thanks very much.'

He went to the back and brought three individual pork pies and put them beside the groceries.

'I had better not forget bread and milk and a packet of Rich Tea.'

'Give me your shopping bag and I'll pack it for you.' When he'd finished he covered it with a square of white paper. 'Keep that over it in case someone sees what you have there.'

'I'll do that.'

'If you don't my life won't be worth living.'

'Thanks a lot, Mr Wallace.'

Kate had money in her hand, more than enough to pay for the groceries.

'There you are Dorothy,' he said handing over the shopping. 'Now let me add this up.'

Before Dorothy had time to get her purse out Kate had paid for the groceries.

'My regards to your grandmother,' Mr Wallace called after them.

'Yes.' They were outside. 'You shouldn't have done that, Kate, but I'll square up with you when we get back,' Dorothy said severely.

'No, you won't.'

'I didn't invite you—'

'I invited myself.'

'Same thing. I don't expect you to pay for the food.'

'I want to. I couldn't think what to bring your grandmother so please, it's my pleasure so don't spoil it.'

Kate was glad that Dorothy hadn't objected too strongly. She didn't imagine the old lady was hard up but one never could tell with old people. Their pride got in the way of asking for help. Dorothy was never flush of cash, perhaps she sent money home.

Mrs Brooks had her rest in the afternoon and Dorothy with Kate's assistance, gave the downstairs a good clean.

'She used to be so particular and my dad would say no spider would dare show itself in our house. Me now, I do what is necessary. I like everything clean but I can't get any enjoyment out of polishing. My mum once told me that when she got really mad at my dad or some of us she would get rid of her temper by putting all her energy into polishing.'

'When I lived with my Aunt Sarah I got the job of cleaning the brasses and she had masses of the stuff all over the house.'

'Put you off brass for the rest of your life?'

'It has and I'm not joking.'

The old lady had been upstairs and lying on her bed for the best part of two hours and Dorothy was on the point of going up to see if she was all right when she appeared. She had changed into a brown skirt and a hand-knitted twin-set in pale pink.

'You've changed?'

'As you can see I've changed. Had you told me you were coming I would have been changed and ready to receive our guest,' she said with some dignity.

'Our guest just wants to be part of the family and that means taking us the way she finds us. Isn't that right, Kate?'

Kate was laughing. 'Yes, that's right.'

Mrs Brooks grew serious. 'I've rested more than usual because I want to stay awake longer to enjoy your company. You cannot imagine the joy it gives me to have you both here and staying the night.'

Dorothy exchanged a look with Kate but neither of them answered. Instead Dorothy set the table and put a pork pie at each place. 'A treat for you, Gran.'

'I won't manage a whole one.'

'Of course you will.'

'I won't. When you get to my age you don't eat so much. A half will do me and I'll enjoy that.'

'If you insist.' Dorothy gave Kate and herself the extra quarter. After that they ate new bread and jam and thoroughly enjoyed the makeshift meal.

By half past ten the old lady's head was nodding but she was determined to last it out to eleven, the time she had promised herself to turn in. Earlier in the evening Dorothy had put fresh sheets and pillowcases on the two single beds and opened the window an inch at the bottom.

'Nearly eleven, Gran, and time all good people were in bed.'

The woman had been about to answer when there was the sudden wail of the sirens. For a brief moment Kate and Dorothy looked at each other then Dorothy was all action.

'The shelter, Gran, come on there's no time to lose.'

'Leave me, I'm not moving from here.'

'You've got to.' Dorothy made to drag the woman from

the chair when there was the drone of bombers followed by the first explosion.

'Leave me and go, both of you.'

'Not without you. For God's sake move.'

Kate was trying to help Dorothy by taking the woman's arm when she found herself being pushed and propelled into the space below the stairs. She crawled in, believing Dorothy was behind her and, discovering she wasn't, Kate shouted.

'Dorothy, where are you?'

'Stay there, we're com—' The rest of the word was lost in a screeching whistle and then an explosion, the sound of which was enough to burst the eardrums. The house shook then slowly began to disintegrate. Kate felt a paralysing fear, something cracked down on her head and everything turned black.

Ten minutes later the bombers had gone, mission accomplished. A row of houses that had been home to so many families was no more. Just rubble, broken glass and gaping craters. A burst pipe spouted a jet of water into the air like a miniature fountain.

There was the sound of running feet, of shouting, of panic, of orders yelled and the terrible, terrible screams that went on and on. The survivors, bloodied and filthy, wandered around bewildered and dazed, not knowing where to go or what to do.

Desperate hands pulled at the rubble, dragged at bricks and plaster, uncaring of their bleeding hands. There could be people under that, trapped and unconscious or choking to death in the clouds of dust. The grim-faced men who had seen it all too often, had a plan of action and worked in groups. They didn't rush at it and were especially careful of what they moved in case they brought down a wall or part of the roof.

The fire engine had already arrived followed by ambulances. Bodies lay among the wreckage like broken dolls. One ambulance left with the seriously injured on stretchers while another took away the walking wounded, some still whimpering with terror.

The maroon door with its number 12 still in place, was splintered and a helper kicked it out of the way then looked in horror at what had been below.

'Oh, my God.'

'Jim!' It was a sharp command. 'Don't look, there is nothing can be done for them.'

'No one could survive this,' someone said.

'You never know,' replied another, 'better to make absolutely sure.'

'Over here.' It was an urgent voice. 'I'm not sure, yes I am, I can see an arm.'

As always there was the natural leader who took charge and gave instructions to those willing but in need of guidance. George Sturrock was that man. They were looking at him. George was a big man with broad shoulders and he stopped what he was doing to weigh up the situation. No one knew the danger better than George, of moving timber or a beam that might be giving slender support. One careless move could bring the whole lot down on them. And it could be for nothing. There was no knowing at this stage if whoever was trapped was dead or alive. More than likely dead but where there was a glimmer of hope one had to try unless the risk was too great.

'Lads, I'll need volunteers for this.'

'You have them,' someone muttered gruffly.

'The way I see it is this. We move this a fraction at a time until we are sure or reasonably sure . . .' He went on to explain what he proposed doing. 'That clear?'

There were grunts.

'No bloody heroics, remember. The second you feel the thing giving way, get the hell out of it.'

Slowly, oh, so slowly, the beam had been moved along with some of the masonry. The girl could be seen but was still firmly wedged. A doctor and a nurse had arrived on the scene and confirmed that the girl was alive but only just.

Fearful that they wouldn't get her out in time everyone concentrated and not an unnecessary word was spoken. Only when she was pulled out and gently placed on a stretcher, did they breathe freely. It was too early for cheers, she might not survive the journey to hospital.

Chapter Twenty-Seven

Ruth was grey-faced with shock but a part of her brain was still working as she went about cancelling her patients and her other commitments. There was no telling how long she would be away. She saw herself staying in London until Kate was well enough to travel home.

What had seemed so important before was forgotten, swept away with this dreadful news about Kate. It was serious but how serious she didn't know. The call had come from RAF Miltonwells and the bad line had made it difficult to hear all that the woman at the other end was saying. Some of it had to be repeated but even then she hadn't got it all. What Ruth made absolutely sure about was the name and address of the hospital in London. She had taken it down very carefully and then repeated it.

'How – how badly is Kate hurt?' she had asked in a shaken voice.

'Her condition is—' It sounded like 'critical' but the line had crackled again and even worse this time.

'I'll get the overnight train.'

'That would be advisable, Mrs McPherson. I'll phone the hospital to let them know.'

'Thank you.'

Ruth replaced the receiver. Then she sat beside the telephone with her eyes closed and her hand to her mouth. Kate was desperately ill, that was what kept hammering in her brain. She could be dying and she was so far away. Ruth's brow puckered. What had Kate been doing in London? Not for amusement that was for sure. Kate had said in her letters that she was merely existing, filling her days with work, keeping herself busy so that there was less time to think about Roddy.

She thought of all the kindness being shown to her. Kate was well liked and the villagers were anxious to help in whatever way they could. They were both concerned and distressed to learn that Kate had been badly hurt in an air-raid.

Ruth's next-door neighbour, Edna, was proving to be a tower of strength and had taken charge. Ruth, usually so calm in time of trouble, was acting out of character.

Edna had put a cup down in front of her.

'Try to relax, Ruth, and drink that tea. I'll see to everything.'

'Thank you, Edna, this isn't like me, is it?' she said wrapping her cold hands round the cup.

'No, it is not but very understandable. Kate is as close to you as a daughter.' She frowned. 'Drink that, please and I'm going to make you something to eat.'

Edna phoned the railway station to find out about trains and as she so often did blessed the day when she and Ruth had decided to have the phone installed. Train times could be erratic and no one depended on them running to time or indeed running at all. Edna was informed by a weary-sounding clerk that the overnight train to King's Cross London was expected to run at the scheduled time but that it could be late.

'Ruth, what are you doing about accommodation?'

Ruth hadn't given it a thought and she shook her head. That was the least of her worries. Once she had been to the hospital and seen Kate then she would go in search of a boarding-house preferably in the vicinity of the hospital. If that turned out to be fruitless she would sleep in the station waiting-room or join the many Londoners who nightly went to the underground where they felt safer.

Edna had frowned when she heard this but wisely said no more, Ruth would put her own comfort last. Edna's husband, Norman, was on the late shift in the factory where he was employed on war work and at considerable inconvenience to himself had offered to drive Ruth to the station. Edna had said she wanted to go and Norman could drop her off at home before going on to his work.

With all that arranged, Ruth packed a small suitcase with a change of clothing, an extra pair of shoes and a pair of slippers. She got a sponge bag from the bathroom and put in those toiletries she would require. That done she gathered together all the money she had in the house and her bankbook to draw on when necessary.

Edna's husband was a careful driver who sat hunched forward in his seat. Some said Norman was too cautious which usually indicated a lack of confidence. Ruth wished he would get a move on, step on it and Edna, sitting with Ruth in the back seat, could feel her agitation.

'Norman, dear, could you go a little faster?' his wife said with a hint of apology in her voice. He was, after all, being very obliging and risking a reprimand for turning up late for work.

'I could, Edna, I could, but there is no need. The train won't go before its time and I'll have Ruth there long before that,' he said in the slow, measured voice that Ruth thought would drive her mad if she had to live with him.

It was a cold night with a starry sky and people were milling about the station when Norman parked the car. He went round to the boot, opened it and took out Ruth's case.

'Thank you, Norman,' she said taking it, 'I'm very grateful. You have both been wonderful and I don't know what I would have done without you.'

He dismissed that with a wave of his hand. 'It would be very sad indeed if we couldn't help at a time like this. And, Ruth—' as she was making to go.

She stopped.

'Worrying yourself sick about Kate isn't going to help the lass. She'll expect her aunt to be her usual calm self.'

'I know, Norman, it's the advice I'm quick to give to others but I'm finding it difficult to take myself.' She smiled. 'Goodbye, both of you.'

'Safe journey and we'll be thinking of you. I have your keys and I'll keep an eye on everything,' Edna said for at least the third time.

'I'll phone when I get the chance.'

'Do that.' They were walking away lengthening the distance between them. Ruth gave a final wave then, carrying her suitcase, hurried away. The clock told her she had twenty minutes to wait and her own watch confirmed it. There were a few waiting at the ticket office and she joined them. When it came to her turn Ruth asked for a single to London King's Cross.

She had a forty-minute wait. The train steamed in twenty minutes behind time. Ruth got a seat and somebody took her suitcase and put it on the rack above her head. She was so tired, an exhausted tiredness, and she thought she might sleep. She did drift off only to be rudely awakened by a shuddering stop with more bodies pressing to get on an already overcrowded train.

At long last they were steaming into King's Cross Station and the same man who had put her case on the rack, now took it down.

'Thank you very much,' she smiled.

Ruth had wondered about getting a London cab and visualised many waiting for very few cabs. In the event she had only ten minutes to wait since she was one of the first to arrive at the stance. Half an hour later the cab was outside the hospital. Ruth paid the driver, added a tip and lifted the case he had put down beside her.

'Visiting someone?' he asked as he pocketed the money.

'Yes, my niece.'

'Big place, easy to get lost, ask at the desk,' he said

helpfully then whistling cheerfully got back into the cab and drove away.

Ruth crossed to the hospital main entrance and went inside. There was another door which she pushed open to be met by the usual hospital smell of ether and strong disinfectant that some people found so sickening. Ruth had known cases where some folk had been quite unable to go beyond the door.

Accustomed as she was to hospitals, entering this one was proving to be an ordeal. What would she find? What sort of condition was Kate in? Ruth gave herself a mental shake and walked determinedly to the reception area and enquired of the woman at the desk how she would find Ward 22A.

'I'll direct you but first why don't you leave your case with me. It'll be perfectly safe.'

'Would you? That would be helpful. I've just come off the overnight train from Scotland and came straight here.'

'Travelling at the best of times is exhausting but these days it's nothing short of an ordeal. Ward 22A you said?'

'Yes.'

She pointed. 'Go right down the corridor then left and left again. That's Ward 22 and 22A is a smaller ward off it.'

'Thank you very much.'

The woman had turned to deal with an elderly man who seemed to be confused as to whether or not he had come to the right hospital.

Passing doors left open temporarily, Ruth caught glimpses of mummy-like forms in some beds and white-bandaged patients sitting up in others. There were sling pulleys, cages, drips and other medical equipment, some in use, some not. She heard a few groans and a few whimpers among the noises ever-present in a busy hospital. There were vases of flowers on tables and a dressing-gowned young man sat glumly on a chair beside his bed staring into nothing.

Ruth walked the length of Ward 22 wondering how the imagination failed when it came to decorating. There was no move to get away from the depressing bottle green relieved only by two narrow stripes of cream paint to something more cheerful. Yet it was generally accepted that colours had a definite effect on patients.

Before she reached Ward 22A a stiffly starched senior nurse stopped her.

'Who are you looking for?' The voice was sharp, businesslike and Ruth felt a vague annoyance although readily accepting that the nurse was perfectly within her rights. The question was acceptable, the manner was not.

'I'm on my way to Ward 22A to visit my niece Kate Mc—' She had been about to say McPherson and hastily changed that to Kate Hamilton-Harvey.

'Oh!' The manner changed and was that a sympathetic look? 'Please wait here a moment,' she said and hurried away.

It left Ruth feeling uneasy and with no reason for it. A very ordinary request surely to be asked to wait a moment when she was here outwith normal visiting times. Why then did she, a mature, experienced nurse, get this chill along the spine, this terrible foreboding that she was about to hear bad news? Was she too late?

'Are you all right?'

Ruth started. She hadn't noticed the arrival of the white-coated figure, obviously a doctor.

'Yes, I'm all right,' she managed to smile. 'Blame it on tiredness,' and worry she could have said, 'I've been travelling all night.'

He smiled sympathetically. 'Nurse tells me you are a relative of Catherine Hamilton-Harvey?'

'Kate is my niece, her parents are dead,' she said by way of explanation.

'I'm Dr Anderson.' He waited for Ruth to say her name.

'I'm Mrs McPherson, Ruth McPherson and I'm Kate's only relative.' They shook hands. 'How is she? I didn't get much information over the phone other than that her condition is serious.'

He nodded gravely. 'We'll go along to my room for a

few minutes then I'll take you to see your niece. I should say at this point that Kate, it is Kate?'

'Yes.'

'Kate is not my patient. She is Dr Morton's but he is off duty at present.'

'You can tell me how she is? Dr Anderson, I am a qualified nurse, I don't need protecting.'

'Very well. It was touch and go whether your niece would survive the journey to hospital and all I can say now is that she is holding her own.'

'There is hope?' she said unsteadily.

'Oh, yes, Mrs McPherson, there is hope.' He was a small man of about middle age, inclined to stoutness and losing his hair at the front. He had kind eyes.

'Come along, Mrs McPherson, the nurse will have finished now, if not, in your case it wouldn't matter.'

'Is she – is Kate conscious?'

'No. No, she isn't,' was all he said.

Ward 22A was a small ward set aside for the most serious cases. A few of the beds, including Kate's, had a curtain round them. When they approached the nurse was smoothing the cover.

Ruth caught her breath as she looked at the still figure in the bed. Kate's head was bandaged and what could be seen of her face was chalk white.

'Her face isn't damaged other than a few cuts and bruises.'

Ruth nodded.

'I believe your niece belongs to one of the services?'

'The WAAFs.'

'Mrs McPherson, I think you should sit down, you look all in. A cup of tea would help I'm sure?'

Ruth smiled faintly. 'A cup of tea would be very nice.'

'Dr Morton, a fellow Scot I should tell you, will be here shortly. Excuse me, I'll get a nurse to bring that tea and now I must leave you and get back to my patients.'

'Thank you, Dr Anderson, you have been very kind.'

He went out leaving Ruth alone with Kate. Ruth got up, leaned over the bed and spoke softly.

'Darling, I'm here. You're going to be all right, do you hear me? We'll fight this together, Kate. I'm going to will you to get better and you have to do your bit. You're strong, you've had to be and you're a fighter, and a real fighter never gives in.'

A very young nurse with a lovely pink and white complexion, carefully put down the tray on the bedside table-cum-locker then looked at the strained face of the woman who had been talking to the patient.

'It's no good,' she said softly, 'she won't hear you.'

'Perhaps she does, nurse, none of us can say for sure.'

'But she's unconscious and has been like that since she came in.'

'I know. Even so she might recognise my voice.' Ruth looked at the tray. 'Thank you, I'll enjoy the tea.'

'I put milk in it, not very much, I hope you take it like that,' she said anxiously, 'and that's all the sugar I could find, just two lumps. You wouldn't think hospitals would be rationed but we are for some things and sugar is one.'

'I don't take sugar,' Ruth smiled as she sat down on the chair at the side of the bed.

'We call her Catherine.' The girl seemed in no hurry to get back to her duties.

'Catherine is her real name but she always gets called Kate.'

'Kate,' she said and nodded. 'Dr Morton is ever so good with her.' She lowered her voice. 'He even comes and sits with her when he is off duty.'

Ruth didn't encourage her to say any more, she didn't approve of gossip no matter how innocent. The slight frown must have warned the girl. She bit her lip.

'Sister keeps telling me I talk too much and worse that I should think before I speak.'

'Sister is very wise.' She smiled to soften what had been a reprimand.

'I'll come back for the tray, had to use one because I don't have a steady hand and some of it would have been in the saucer. Oh, excuse me, I'll take the sugar cubes since you don't want them.' She gave Ruth a beaming smile and left her.

She was a nice child and she would learn. It brought back memories when she, too, had been new to nursing.

Edna had given her a small packet of biscuits for the train and she'd only eaten one. She would have the others now and that would keep her going until she got a bite of food somewhere. In London there were always restaurants or cafés open.

No one asked her to leave. Dr Anderson must have informed Sister that Mrs McPherson was a nurse and to be trusted.

Just after midday when the patients were being fed, Ruth was served with a plate of soup and a slice of bread. It had been a long wait and she didn't know when she had enjoyed a meal so much. She said so when the tray was removed. A little later a tall, loose-limbed young man in a white coat came in and introduced himself as Dr Morton. Then he went over to the patient and stood looking down at her for some moments.

'No change,' he sighed softly, 'or maybe, just maybe Catherine's breathing is a little easier.'

'It's Kate, she's always called Kate,' Ruth said once again.

'And you are? Dr Anderson couldn't recall the name, only that you are an aunt of the patient's.'

'I'm Mrs McPherson, Ruth McPherson.'

She saw a huge, incredulous smile light up his face.

'That's it! That's it! Now I've got it.'

Ruth looked at him in amazement. 'Got what?'

'The name. You see Catherine Hamilton-Harvey meant nothing to me but her own name—'

'Kate McPherson.'

'As soon as she was brought in I knew there was something familiar about the face, that I had seen her before but try as I might I couldn't get the connection.'

Ruth smiled. 'And now you do?'

'Now I do. Mrs McPherson, Kate and I were at school together. Oh, I'm a bit older. I would have been in my senior year and Kate possibly in her third.'

'Small world as they say. So we come from the same neck of the woods or near enough. When she was at school, Kate lived with her aunt, a maiden lady, a Miss McPherson in Silverbank. She died some years ago and Kate has been living with me in Muirfield.'

'I know it. Our team used to play cricket there.'

'Weather permitting,' Ruth smiled.

'Yes, weather permitting.' He paused. 'You came here on the overnight train from Dundee?'

'Yes.'

'No wonder you look exhausted. Have you eaten?'

'Yes, thank you, everyone has been very kind but – but there are so many things I don't understand. I mean I don't know what happened to Kate and why she should have been in London.'

'Didn't someone at RAF Miltonwells tell you?'

'Not very much or maybe I just missed it. It was a terrible line and I couldn't keep asking everything to be repeated.'

He took another look at the motionless figure in the bed.

'We'll open the curtain so that the nurses can check on Kate and we'll talk with more freedom when we are away from here.'

In the room, the same one Ruth had been in earlier with Dr Anderson, they sat facing each other. Ruth thought what a nice-looking young man he was. He had thick jet-black hair, a thin clever face and grey-blue eyes. Young though he was there was an air of authority about him and a kindliness that would put patients at ease. So many doctors, excellent in other ways, allowed a show of impatience thereby destroying the very important doctor–patient relationship.

'Shall I tell you what I know?'

'Please.'

'From what I understand and the information we have came from one of the WAAF officers, was that Kate and another WAAF were to visit the other girl's grandmother.'

'That would be Dorothy. Kate spoke a lot about her Cockney friend.'

'The street was bombed and that particular house or one close to it got a direct hit. According to those who rescued her it was a miracle Kate was alive. Getting her out had been extremely dangerous for those concerned. There are many unsung heroes, Mrs McPherson, I correct that to heroes and heroines.'

'I know, I have seen it myself. That other war, the one that was to end all wars, we saw it then too.'

'You were a nurse?'

'Yes, in France.'

'What about Kate's husband? Is he overseas?'

She had thought he would have known. 'Roddy is dead. They were only married for two months.'

'I'm so very sorry.'

'Roddy was a fighter pilot.'

'You can't get braver than that.'

'Kate said Roddy never saw himself as brave.'

'The really brave never do.'

'He hated war.'

'I go along with that. My own war was very short. I was overseas where I managed to pick up some infection that laid me low. Instead of being an asset, I became a liability and at the first opportunity I was shipped back to the UK. Once I was fit and well I would rejoin my unit was what they said.'

'Instead of which they decided to keep you here.'

'Looks that way. The truth is I haven't been declared a hundred per cent fit and there appears to be some concern that the trouble could flare up again. I don't agree but one cannot argue with the top brass as I wasn't long in finding out.'

'Do you know what happened to Dorothy, I'm sure that's who it would be and her grandmother?'

'Yes, I do know. I'm afraid they were both killed.'

'How dreadful.'

'How long do you intend staying, Mrs McPherson?'

'For as long as Kate needs me. I'll stay until I can take her home.'

He nodded but didn't say anything.

'How bad are her injuries?'

'The right leg was a mess—'

'She won't lose it?'

'There was that possibility but we are fairly sure it won't come to that.'

'Thank God.'

'Her whole body is a mass of cuts and bruises.'

'Those will disappear through time. Is there something more serious?'

He nodded slowly. 'There could be internal damage, that can't be ruled out.'

'And her head?'

'We aren't too worried about the head wound. Something heavy caught her a blow but given time that will mend. Mrs McPherson, when we say Kate was lucky we mean that it was nothing short of a miracle that she got out of that house alive.'

'If only she was conscious, if only she would speak,' Ruth said despairingly.

'That could happen at any time and you must know that,' he said gently.

Ruth also knew that it didn't always happen. 'I have to keep reminding myself.'

'Have you fixed up accommodation?'

'Not as yet, but I must do something about it. I was hoping to find a boarding house within walking distance of the hospital.'

'You must have some luggage.'

'A suitcase, the receptionist has it.'

He nodded. 'There is the Lennox Boarding House, a ten-minute walk from here I should think. They might have a room. Or there are others in the district you could try. The hospital keeps a list of boarding houses and private houses for those who might require overnight accommodation.'

'That sounds hopeful.'

'I'll come to reception with you.' They walked together to the desk and the woman looked up and smiled.

'You want your case?'

'Not just at the moment Mrs Maitland,' Dr Morton said, 'Mrs McPherson requires accommodation and I wondered about the Lennox.'

'I'll phone and check.'

'Thank you.' He smiled at Ruth. 'Mrs Maitland will try and fix you up, Mrs McPherson, and I suggest you try and get a good night's rest. I'll see you tomorrow some time.'

'Thank you, Dr Morton, you have been more than kind.'

The receptionist was dialling a number. 'He's nice and always so obliging. Oh, is that the Lennox? This is the Weldon Hospital, do you happen to have a single room available? You do. Just a moment the lady is here I'll ask her.' She covered the mouthpiece. 'One night or longer?'

'Longer. I can't say for how long.'

'Longer but the lady can't say more than that. The name – Mrs McPherson. Thank you.' She rang off.

Ruth frowned. 'I should have asked, is it bed and breakfast?'

'Bed and breakfast and they do evening meals if required. Now shall I give you directions?'

Ruth felt that if she had any walking to do her legs would buckle.

'If you could phone for a cab I would be very much obliged.'

'No trouble. The cabbies all know where the Lennox is. Better to take your case and sit near the door.'

'Thank you, I'll do that.'

The cab driver was pleasant and talkative. 'This you visiting someone?' he asked.

'Yes, my niece.'

Scottish, aren't you?'

'Yes.'

'Fair distance to come.' He swore happily at another cab driver who was making a manoeuvre and holding up traffic. 'Do that myself but that's different,' he laughed.

She smiled from the back seat.

'Relative of mine in the Weldon. Blitz victim, only eighteen Peter is and lost a leg.'

'How awful.'

'As you say but he could have been killed and that would have been far worse. He's a plucky one, he'll cope.'

'My niece is a blitz victim, she's still unconscious.'

'That's worrying for you, but just try and remember this, the healing process is going on all the time and when she comes to she'll be that much better.'

He was trying so hard to help. 'I do hope you are right.'

'Terrible times we are living in but we're winning.'

'If we can believe all we hear,' Ruth said wearily.

'Take my word for it, peace will be declared before very long. We cabbies have a sixth sense, you know. And here we are at the Lennox. You'll be fine there.'

Ruth paid him and added a reasonable tip which he acknowledged. Then case in hand she went up the three stone steps to the door with its shining brass letterbox and doorknob. It was a street of tall Victorian houses. Two called themselves guest houses and the others appeared to have been made into superior flats. Ruth rang the bell and it was answered straightaway by a maid with a duster in her hand.

'Yes?'

'I've come about accommodation.'

'Margery, I've told you before that answering the door is not one of your duties.'

'I only did it because I was next to it,' she said cheekily and with a toss of her head walked away.

The woman was shaking her head. 'Sign of the times.

Before the war she wouldn't have lasted a day now we are lucky to get anyone. You've come about a room?'

'The hospital phoned—'

'Mrs McPherson, do come in, I hadn't expected you so soon.'

Ruth stepped into a vestibule with a coloured glass door leading into a spacious hall.

'Just leave your case down here. Yes, there will do nicely. Margery can bring it up if the room is to your satisfaction. We just have the one room vacant.' She went ahead up a thickly carpeted stair and Ruth followed.

'Here we are.' She opened the door, had a quick look inside, probably to check that everything was as it should be, and then they both went in.

'This will do me very nicely, I'm sorry, you didn't say your name?'

'Neither I did, blame it on Margery, she always manages to upset me. I'm Miss Hunter, Miss Emily Hunter. My sister Joan and I run the boarding-house between us. Joan does the cooking and I'm more or less in charge of the rest.'

The room was small but adequate for her needs. It held a single bed with a patchwork quilt, a narrow wardrobe with a mirror door, a very small kidney-shaped dressing-table, a wooden chair with a thin cushion tied on with four tapes and at the window a black blind and pretty floral patterned curtains. The floor was linoleum-covered with a square of carpet covering most of it.

'Do you wish an evening meal?'

'What time is it served?'

'Seven o'clock.'

'Yes, I would like that. I'm not sure about other evenings—'

'Provided you tell me at breakfast, that will be all the notice I require.'

Ruth thought she should give a little information about herself. 'My niece was badly hurt in an air-raid. She is still unconscious—'

'How very distressing for you. Poor girl, you will be spending as much time at the hospital as you can.'

'Yes.'

'You look tired,' she said kindly. 'I'll bring up your case myself. Margery is never there when I want her. This is about my time for a cup of tea. How do you take yours?'

'A little milk and no sugar.'

'You can come again,' she laughed. 'Sugar is a problem, at least it is with my men boarders, it doesn't appear to have sunk in that we are rationed and I have to close my eyes when I see how much goes into their tea. By the way, if you are to be here for some time I would need to have your ration book.'

'I have it with me. I'll let you have it at dinner.'

'Thank you, Margery, you brought up the case.'

She didn't answer, just dumped the case inside the room and departed.

'Thank you,' Ruth said.

'I'll leave you and get the kettle on. Would you like your cup of tea downstairs or would you prefer it in your room?'

'In here, please.'

Ruth opened her case and put away her clothes. The ration book she put on the dressing-table. A good thing Edna had reminded her or she would have forgotten.

There was a light tap at the door. 'Your tea, Mrs McPherson, and a piece of home-baked cake. My sister can do wonders with dried eggs and all the other peculiar things we are supposed to use. Do you have the same shortages in Scotland?' asked Emily Hunter.

'In the towns and cities but in the country or small villages we do rather better.' She smiled. 'The hens still lay for us.'

'Don't,' she said looking pained. 'A fresh egg for those of us who rarely see one, is a treat.' She walked to the door. 'Worry and strain take a lot out of one. Drink your tea then lie down and rest. Don't worry if you fall asleep, I'll give you a knock half an hour before I serve dinner and make sure you answer.'

'Thank you, that'll let me relax.'

Chapter Twenty-Eight

After a good night's sleep, Ruth felt refreshed and less worried than she had been the previous day knowing that Kate was in good hands. She had eaten and enjoyed a breakfast of crisp bacon, tomato and black pudding followed by toast and butter and a tiny portion of marmalade. The only other occupants of the dining-room were two businessmen, well into middle-age, who looked up when she entered, smiled, said good morning then quickly returned to what they had been doing. There would be no conversation and Ruth was glad she wouldn't have to make the effort. One of the men had returned to his morning newspaper and the other looked as though he might be checking on his calls for the day.

It was a pleasant walk to the hospital, part of it tree-lined, and it took Ruth about a quarter of an hour. She felt the better for the exercise. Miss Hunter had given her a note of approximate bus times and clear instructions to the nearest picking-up point. All buses passing that way stopped at the hospital gate, she was told. Ruth thought she would continue to walk when the weather was good but take advantage of transport when it rained.

Going in the door she saw Dr Morton walking along the corridor in conversation with a colleague. As soon as he saw her he excused himself and came over to speak.

'Good morning, Mrs McPherson, did you get fixed up?'

'Yes, I did, thank you. The Lennox had a room and I'm very comfortable.' She paused. 'Dr Morton, have you seen Kate this morning?'

'I have. When I left, your niece looked much the same but there is a chance she could be coming round. The night nurse reported what she thought had been a small movement and a flickering of her eyelids.'

'That's wonderful.' Ruth's face lit up.

'Too early to be sure but I felt I should share it with you. You have the experience to know . . .'

Ruth nodded and sighed. 'It could be imagination, especially during the night hours.'

'I'm afraid so. On the other hand, the nurse in question, is reliable and she would be fairly sure within herself before putting it in her report.' He made to leave her.

'Before you go – I don't want to hold you up, Dr Morton.'

'You aren't. I'm only on my way to a rather late breakfast.'

'I would like to be with Kate as much as possible and I would also like to offer my services.'

'That's extremely kind of you. I'll mention it to Sister and I'm sure she will be grateful for any assistance.' He smiled and hurried away.

There was a lot of coming and going with everyone appearing to be in a hurry. Ruth quickened her pace and was soon at Ward 22A. She removed her costume jacket and put it on the back of the chair. Then she went over to look at Kate, remaining there for a long time and praying that the night nurse hadn't been mistaken.

'Mrs McPherson?'

Ruth turned away from the bed to see that Sister had arrived, Dr Morton hadn't put off much time. He must have spoken to her before going into breakfast.

'Good morning, Sister.'

'Dr Morton tells me you are anxious to be of assistance. I do know that you have nursing qualifications which makes the offer all the more welcome. We should both sit down I think.' She sat down and Ruth did too.

'I spoke to Dr Morton only a moment ago,' Ruth smiled.

'Yes, I met him going into breakfast. We do have a number of very willing volunteers, some of them extremely good I may add, but very few have nursing experience.'

'Provided I am always available for Kate, I would be prepared to do anything,' Ruth said carefully.

The woman looked thoughtful. 'If you were to help with your niece and give a hand with the other patients in 22A it would free one of the nurses for other duties. I'll have to have a think about what would be best.'

Ruth nodded. To share Kate's nursing was what she wanted, but had hardly dared hope that it would be granted.

'In return for your generous offer you must feel free to take your meals in the staff dining-room or if you would prefer it, they could be brought to you here.'

'Thank you.'

Sister got up. She was a severe-looking, straight-backed woman who tolerated no nonsense but gave praise where and when it was due.

'My nurses will be informed that you are a qualified senior nurse working as a volunteer. That should save any misunderstandings.'

Ruth smiled. Sister was a wise woman who could see ahead and thus avoid the pitfalls.

Another day had gone by and then another. Ruth worked quietly and efficiently and there was no resentment from any member of the nursing staff. Far from it, they welcomed an extra pair of capable hands that made their own workload lighter. The younger nurses, particularly the nervous ones, had started to go to Ruth if they were unsure about something. Mrs McPherson had a friendly manner and explained to them whatever they were unsure about without making them feel foolish. What was easy for one wasn't so easy for another and some of the hierarchy were slow to realise that.

Ruth had been writing a letter home to Edna and when she glanced up from it she was startled to find herself looking into a pair of blue eyes. The writing pad fell from her knees as she got up.

'Kate! Oh, Kate! you've wakened up at last. You clever, clever girl.' She was babbling and the tears were running unchecked down her cheeks.

'Aunt Ruth.' It was the softest of whispers but surely, for Ruth, the most wonderful words to hear. Footsteps were approaching but Ruth didn't turn round, she couldn't risk it in case in that split second, Kate returned to her silent world.

Whoever it was had noticed. There was a gasp and then the sound of hurrying feet. In a little while Dr Morton was there and Ruth thought his excitement matched her own. She made to move away from the bed but he stopped her. 'Let Kate see you and hear you. Strangers would only confuse her.'

There was a ripple of, if not exactly excitement, something very close. A patient in a coma, particularly when it is a young patient, is always a source of interest. They wonder aloud how long the patient will be in that state and when he or she comes out of it how much will be remembered. When it is a blitz victim the interest is all the greater.

Kate's eyes flickered then closed and Dr Morton nodded as if satisfied.

'She'll sleep naturally and hopefully Kate is now on the road to recovery.'

The thought of internal injuries had worried Ruth but her mind was put to rest when she was told there was no lasting damage. The bruising was already beginning to fade and the cuts would slowly mend. The leg would take longer. No bones had been broken but the damage to it was considerable.

There had been regular enquiries from RAF Miltonwells as to Kate's progress and knowing how concerned they were

Ruth took it on herself to phone the officer-in-charge with the latest news. Cards began to arrive and requests as to how soon Kate would be allowed visitors.

'Not at present.' Dr Morton had been adamant about that. His patient wasn't ready for visitors. She had her aunt and she needed no other until she was stronger. He had confided in Ruth that he was waiting for Kate to relive her experiences and once she had that behind her the healing process would commence. One also had to accept that Kate may have no recollection of the night of the bombing. 'We must just wait and see,' he said.

'Better that she should relive them?' Ruth made it a question.

'Yes, I would be inclined to say so.'

Ruth was there when Kate showed the first signs of distress.

'What is it, darling?' Ruth said leaning over the bed and watching in dismay as Kate's head began turning from side to side. Her eyes were wild and she looked terrified.

'Kate,' Ruth said soothingly, 'you're safe, it's all over and you're safe. I'm here beside you. Aunt Ruth is here.' She was speaking as though to a child but that's what Kate was – a terrified child.

The head stopped moving and Kate became quite still.

'Dorothy? Where is she?' Kate asked in an agonised voice. 'She was coming when the – she was coming with the old lady.' Hands gripped Ruth's blouse and the eyes were demanding an answer.

Ruth had no answer to give. How could she tell Kate that her friend and the old lady were both dead?

The look on Ruth's face told her – it might have been that or her not answering. Whichever it was Kate knew. When it came it was a pitiful sound, part small scream, part strangled sob. She began to struggle to get up.

'No! No! No! Not Dorothy. Please, not Dorothy.'

The cries brought two of the nurses running to see what had happened. Mrs McPherson was clearly distraught as she shouted to them to get Dr Morton or any doctor only to be quick.

Dr Morton must have been nearby and he came rushing in. One look at his patient and he was preparing something to quieten her. The two nurses left to resume their duties.

'What caused that?' the doctor demanded sharply.

Ruth had recovered, her professionalism restored. 'Kate must have been reliving the moments before the bomb fell. She wanted to know if her friend Dorothy was all right. I didn't say anything, Dr Morton,' Ruth said quietly.

'No doubt your silence spoke volumes. Don't blame yourself, Mrs McPherson, there was nothing you could do other than tell an untruth and that would have been all the worse in the long run.'

'Poor Kate, she's going to take a long time to get over Dorothy. The girl was so supportive when Roddy was killed and Kate said had it not been for Dorothy she would have gone to pieces. I didn't believe that, not for a moment. Kate is a survivor. Even so Dorothy was very special, Kate called her her funny Cockney friend. The others were very kind but it was Dorothy she depended on.'

'Don't worry too much. Kate obviously came to terms with her husband's death realising there was nothing else she could do. Given time it will be the same with her friend.'

'I hope so.' Ruth looked almost angry. 'I wonder to myself why life is so hard for some of us yet others seem to live a charmed life,' she said bitterly.

'I don't have an answer to that, no one does.'

For the next few days Kate was quiet but there were no more distressing scenes. Gradually she was beginning to take an interest in what was going on in the ward and she perked up when Vera and another WAAF called Georgina, arrived and tiptoed over to the bed in case, they said, some of the patients were sleeping. They each came with an armful of flowers and Vera had a beautifully wrapped box of chocolates that she said came from Janice's American boyfriend and which Janice wanted Kate to have. They were careful not to stay too long for fear they might not be welcome another time. Promising to come again and give her all the gossip, they tiptoed out, blowing kisses as they went.

'Aunt Ruth, how long have you been here in the hospital?'

'Three weeks all but a day.'

'What about the house?'

'It won't run away. Edna is looking after everything.'

Kate nodded. 'How will the village be managing without you?'

'Perfectly well. No one is indispensable, Kate. We are all brought down to size when we find that to be true. According to Edna everybody is doing that little bit extra.'

'All the same you must be getting wearied to be back home?'

'Kate, I am not wearied, anything but. I am here with you where I want to be. You are making good progress, my dearest, and it won't be too long before we are on that train taking us to Muirfield.'

'I wonder about the days when I was in a coma.'

'What about them?'

'Is that like being dead, do you think?'

Ruth looked startled. 'Kate, you do ask the most peculiar questions.'

'I know and I like answers.'

'You are getting better,' Ruth smiled. 'As to your question, I wouldn't think so. Death is very final, it is leaving this world for another. To be in a coma is more like being in a deep sleep. Satisfied?'

'I think so.' She paused. 'Aunt Ruth, don't be alarmed, I'm not going to get myself into a state, I promise you that.' She swallowed. 'I need to talk about this and you are the only one I can tell.'

'If you need to talk then you must.'

'Dorothy saved my life.'

'Did she?'

Kate nodded. 'It was all hazy before but now I can see it clearly. Dorothy's grandmother was such a lovely old lady and funny, you would call it droll. Dorothy was like that too.' She smiled as though remembering.

'Kate, why did you go to London? That was what I couldn't understand why you should be there.'

'I only went because Dorothy was worried about her grandmother. I offered to go with her, Aunt Ruth, she didn't ask me.' Kate stopped as though to get her thoughts together. 'The old lady, Mrs Brooks, could be very stubborn.'

'Old people can be.'

'I know. When the air-raid siren went she refused to leave her home for the shelter. She wanted us to go but to leave her.'

'And, of course, you wouldn't?'

'As it happened there wouldn't have been time to get there.' She shivered. 'There was this awful, whistling noise, that's the only way I can describe it. Dorothy was trying to pull her grandmother out of the chair then suddenly she stopped and she was pushing me under the stairs into a cupboard-like place. I thought they were both coming and I moved to see if I could help.' She started to cry.

'You promised and here you are upsetting yourself.'

'I'll be more upset if I don't tell you. Just give me a minute.' Kate dried her eyes and began again. 'I think I was crawling out when the – the whole house began to move. It was absolutely terrifying and the next thing I remember is something hitting me and then nothing more.'

Ruth held her close. 'It was a dreadful experience, dear, you've told me about it and now you must try and put it out of your mind.'

'Easier said than done.'

'Nevertheless you must try. Dwelling on it will only hinder your progress and you are doing very well.'

'I won't ever forget Dorothy,' she said fiercely.

'I wouldn't expect you to.'

'I'll never, never forget Roddy because I loved him so much and I'll never forget Dorothy because she was very special.'

Sharing her agonies had helped and though progress was slow it was steady. She was getting up to sit in a chair for a little longer each day.

'Dr Morton is really, really nice, isn't he?' Kate said when he had left the ward.

'Yes, he is, very nice and Dr Morton has been very attentive to you.'

Ruth had a sneaking suspicion that the doctor was attracted to Kate though there was no evidence of it. He was very professional. Ruth had been amused, though she had been careful not to show it, when he'd asked her not to say anything to Kate about them both attending the same school. He said he would like to do that himself when he decided the time was right.

'I know, he couldn't be more attentive.' She smiled. 'I bet half the nurses are in love with him.'

'I wouldn't be at all surprised.'

'Do you think he is married?'

'I have no idea.'

'I think he must be.'

'Why?'

'No one that good-looking would escape,' she said mischievously.

'You could ask him. Bring it in casually.'

'I couldn't do that,' Kate said sounding shocked. 'It would be intrusive and whether he is or not is none of my business.'

'Quite,' Ruth said and earned herself a sharp look.

It was early afternoon and Kate was sitting in a chair beside the bed and wearing a dressing-gown. The dressing-gown had come from RAF Miltonwells along with some of her clothes. Ruth had requested that some be sent to the hospital

since that would be easier than having Edna going to the
bother of sending some on from home.

'What will I do about clothes when I get out of here?'
Kate wanted to know.

'I have quite a lot of clothing coupons and once you
decide what you want I'll go on a shopping trip for you.'

'How long before I go back?'

'To Miltonwells?'

'Yes.'

'You are officially on sick leave but to be honest I don't
see you having to return.'

'Why not? I thought I was almost recovered,' Kate said
sharply.

'Indeed you are almost recovered, you have taken me up
wrongly. What I meant was that the war news is good, it
could be that the war is coming to an end.'

'I must start reading the newspapers. How awful I don't
seem to know what is going on outside the hospital.'

'You haven't felt like reading.'

'No, I haven't. I enjoyed being a WAAF but I'll be glad if
I haven't to go back.'

'I can understand that,' Ruth said gently.

'Too many memories. I'll be able to cope better with
them at home.'

'Here is Dr Morton to see you and it is time I was seeing
to my own rounds.'

'Hello, Mrs McPherson, keeping you busy, are they?'

'Yes, but I don't mind, in fact to be honest I'm rather
enjoying it.' She was off to see to a fractious old lady who
was giving the young nurses a hard time. A talking to, kind
but firm, was probably all that was required.

'And how is my patient today?' the doctor asked as he
drew up a chair. 'Leg giving you any trouble?'

'Sore when I move it but much, much better than it was.'

'Good. You're doing fine, carry on like this and you'll
soon be on your way home.'

She smiled. 'That's good to hear.'

'A word of warning. When you do leave here you will have to take it easy for a while. You've come through a lot, Kate, physically and mentally.'

She nodded.

'The body needs time to recover.'

'You've been so kind, everybody has.'

'Easy to be kind when you have a model patient.'

'Have I been that?' Kate said sounding both surprised and pleased.

'With you being a fellow Scot I can be excused for giving you that little bit extra attention.'

'By your accent I would say east coast.'

'Silverbank near Dundee is home ground.'

'I don't believe it,' she said looking amazed.

'Why not?'

'Because I went to school there.'

'I know.'

She looked at him quickly. 'How could you possibly know unless—'

'Unless what?'

'Unless Aunt Ruth told you. Did she?'

'No, she didn't although she did confirm it for me.'

'I'm lost, I don't understand any of this.'

'Then let me try and explain. When you were brought in the name Catherine Hamilton-Harvey didn't strike a cord – but when your aunt said you were always called Kate and her name was McPherson' – he smiled – 'then I knew where I had seen you before.'

'David Morton,' she said after a long silence, 'that's who you are?'

'That's who I am. I have to confess to feeling a little peeved that I should have been so completely forgotten.'

'Not completely, there must have been something. I remember saying to Aunt Ruth that it was as though I had always known you.'

'That's my bedside manner,' he grinned. 'We are taught to relax the patient.'

'You were a senior and we were just third-year girls. You were our pin-up boy. I remember blushing if you as much as noticed me.'

'I noticed you all right. Knew then you were going to be a beauty and I am proved right.'

'Now you are embarrassing me.'

'Here comes the trolley,' he said as a nurse wheeled it over to each bed.

'Dr Morton, do you want a cup?' she asked when the trolley reached them.

'Yes, please, I'm not on duty so I can afford to relax with a cup.'

They were allowed to sugar and milk their own tea then the trolley was trundled to the other side of the ward.

'I'm so sorry.'

'What for?'

'Taking up your time when you are off duty.'

'Talking to you is a pleasure.'

'Wait until I see Aunt Ruth, I'm going to have a word with her.'

'Don't blame your poor aunt. I asked Mrs McPherson to say nothing, that I wanted to tell you myself. I've been looking forward to this.'

They lifted their cups at the same time and drank some. He made a face. 'Why does hospital tea always taste stewed?'

'Because it takes a long time to get round to everybody. We must all be grateful for small mercies.'

'Who said that?'

'My Aunt Sarah, not about tea,' she grinned, 'but in general. I lived with her you see, Dr Morton—'

'Doctor when I'm on duty, David when I'm not.'

'She, my Aunt Sarah, would have had me being grateful for the very air I breathed. No, I am being too hard. She was strict and she was difficult but I discovered before she died that there was a softer side to her.'

'There usually is, maybe she had a hard life.'

'David, are you married?'

'No.'

'That's surprising.'

'Why?'

'Most doctors marry young or youngish.'

'Came close to taking the plunge.'

'What stopped you?'

'Something was missing, the right person hadn't come along.'

'Whoever that turns out to be, she'll be very lucky,' Kate said earnestly. 'You deserve to be happy, David, and one day you will be, with the right person.'

'I hope so,' he said very quietly and looked at her for a long moment. 'I'm sorry this conversation has made you sad. I should have thought.'

'You didn't bring up marriage I did. David, for a long time after Roddy was killed I couldn't think about him without a great wave of – of grief gushing out. Now I can talk about him, I like talking about him. He was a truly wonderful person but not without faults. When someone dies people talk about them as though they had lived a perfect life and that is so silly.'

'Don't talk ill of the dead,' he smiled.

'We shouldn't talk ill of the dead, I go along with that, but neither should we talk about them as though they had led a blameless life.' Kate looked a bit shamefaced. 'Some of that is Aunt Ruth talking.'

'I thought it might be. My mother talks about some folk being the salt of the earth and I think your aunt could fit that description.'

'Thank you.' Kate was touched. Aunt Ruth did such a lot of good and much of it went unthanked.

The great day had arrived. After seven weeks Kate was ready to leave hospital. She was leaving with mixed feelings. Hospital routine had become a way of life and the faces familiar. Leaving David was worst of all, she couldn't believe how much she had come to look forward to his visits, to their talks. He must never know – know what? Know that she had fallen in love and how could that be so soon after losing Roddy? What kind of a person was she? Vulnerable that's what she was. There was nothing unusual about a patient being a little in love with her doctor, it happened all the time. Doctors were trained how to deal with the situation though in most cases the 'symptoms' disappeared once the patient was discharged and home life took over.

Kate and Ruth had said their goodbyes, their cases were at the hospital door for the cab driver to deal with. Kate was to stay overnight at the Lennox Boarding House and from there they would get the early morning train to Scotland. Having said their farewells they had expected to slip away quietly but instead they were to be sent off in style. Waiting for them were a number of the nurses and the receptionist with whom Ruth had become friendly. She was there with one eye on the desk. Standing a little apart was Dr Morton and Kate didn't know whether she was glad or sorry. What she had thought to be their final goodbye had been difficult enough. She hadn't wanted him to see how near to weeping she was though no doubt he would have put that down to weakness. She still felt a bit fragile.

It was Ruth who gave Kate a little push towards David.

'All packed and ready to go?'

'Yes.'

'You look very smart.' It wasn't what he had wanted to say. What he wanted to say was – you look very lovely and I'm going to miss you.

Kate was wearing a herringbone coat which Ruth had purchased for her. It would not have been Kate's own choice and when she first saw it she hid her disappointment. Then she tried it on and changed her mind. It really was very attractive as well as being a suitable garment in which to travel. Her hair was as long as she had once worn it and it curled becomingly. Maybe she would get it cut short again or maybe not. The maybe not would please Aunt Ruth.

'Thank you.' She held out her hand and he took it in both of his.

'Take care of yourself.'

'And you,' she said awkwardly. He looked tired but was that surprising considering the amount of work he did? As far as she could make out there was very little time off.

'That's the taxi drawing up, Kate,' Ruth said giving them both a smile.

'Goodbye, Kate,' he said quickly and kissed her on the cheek. The nurses would make something of that, he thought disgustedly. Give it an hour and it would have gained feet and legs. 'Goodbye Mrs McPherson, safe journey and thank you for all you have done.'

Their last glimpse of Weldon Hospital was of nurses waving to them from the doorway.

The journey northwards on the crowded, unheated train had to be endured but at least they had seats. They also had a vacuum flask and some sandwiches. Edna had written at length to tell Ruth that the house was ready for their return and Norman, or if not Norman, someone else would be at the station to meet the train. They were all looking forward to their return.

Chapter Twenty-Nine

Kate was still a little pale and thinner than she used to be but otherwise she was in good health. The leg, the last part of her body to heal, was giving no trouble and in time, she was told, the ugly scars would fade though they wouldn't entirely disappear. Kate wasn't too bothered – she thought it a small price to pay for being alive.

As for the war, the news was good, very good. People were waiting confidently to hear that hostilities had come to an end and that victory was ours after six long years of pain and suffering. The boys would be coming home and the POWs released. There would be no more running for the shelters at the sound of the air-raid sirens and folk would be able to sleep in their beds at night without fear.

In the towns and in the country there were victory parties with bunting-draped streets and flags flying from windows. The war was over – peace had been declared. Muirfield celebrated but in a quiet way or rather a quieter way. They were mindful of those whose loved ones would not be returning and thought how hard it must be for them. Instead of laughter there would be tears behind closed doors.

Ruth and Kate had gone along to join in the festivities and smiled at the excitement generated among the children and their wide-eyed wonder when they saw the spread. Makeshift tables had been set up and covered with table-cloths or sheets or whatever came to hand. Cupboards had been raided and what could be spared went towards the common good. It was a mouth-watering display and the villagers were justifiably proud of what they had achieved.

Nurse Ruth and her niece were made very welcome, like special guests and no one thought the less of them for staying only a short time. Not with Kate having lost her husband so tragically. Poor girl, what a lot she had come through and how must she be feeling?

Kate's thoughts were of Roddy and she felt a renewed anger at the waste of a young life. And all for what? The ready answer would be that it had brought peace. If that was so and this was to be a lasting peace, then the loss of those lives would not have been in vain. But was it to be a lasting peace? The same had been said in 1918. And didn't the Bible say very clearly that there would always be wars?

She thought about Roddy's parents and felt a wave of sympathy for them. In due course Alice would have her husband returned to her and though she would mourn the loss of a beloved brother there was the prospect of a joyful reunion with Iain. Over at Craggy Point two elderly people would be grieving the loss of a son they had loved dearly and hurt so badly.

Kate was becoming frustrated and annoyed.

'Aunt Ruth, I am *not* an invalid.'

'I know you aren't.'

'Then kindly don't treat me as one.'

'I don't. What I do and intend going on doing is to see that you take care of yourself.' She paused to look at the mutinous face. 'I know you think I am an old fusspot.'

'That is the last thing I would describe you as. What you are is overprotective of me.'

'Perhaps I am. We always are of those we hold dear.'

'I know and I'm sorry, it's just . . .' She sighed.

'You're bored. You want to get back to work, back to the office? Is that it?'

'I'm not sure what I want and I think that is half the trouble. I could, I suppose, go back to Stephenson, Smith & Methven but I won't. It just wouldn't be the same.'

'Nothing does stay the same,' Ruth said gently. 'Just remember, my dear, that you are in the fortunate position of not having to work for your daily bread.'

'I know that.' Kate smiled. 'I must say it helps.'

'Kate, you are no different from many others. We were used to war, that is a terrible thing to say but it happens to be true. Peace has come and folk are taking time to adjust. They are unsettled, not quite knowing what they expected and curiously disappointed. And that makes them feel guilty. Does that make sense?'

'You always make sense, Aunt Ruth.'

'Thank you, my dear. What saddens some is that there will be no magical return to the days of plenty. Rationing, I'm afraid, is here to stay for the foreseeable future.'

'At least it is the fairest way.'

'Without a doubt. I would say that rationing is very necessary.'

The showery morning had given way to a lovely, warm afternoon with the gentlest of breezes. Ruth and Kate were sitting in the back garden with Kate reading and Ruth enjoying the luxury of doing absolutely nothing.

Kate looked up from her book. 'Did I hear the doorbell or was that my imagination?'

Ruth was about to say 'your imagination' when this time they both heard the ring.

'I'll go,' Ruth said getting up.

Kate returned to her book. More than likely it would be someone wanting her aunt, it usually was.

'A visitor for you, Kate.'

Kate looked up, then put down her book and got to her feet quickly. She had gone very pink. How often had he been in her thoughts but she had never expected to see him again.

'David, this is a surprise, how lovely to see you.' She

knew she was smiling foolishly but she couldn't help it. She was in his arms and they were hugging for a few moments. Had he opened his arms for her, she wondered. Or had she just rushed into them? If that was the case what must he be thinking of her? More than likely this was David having a few days at home and maybe to fill in the time he had decided to look in on his former patient.

'Couldn't be in the district and not look you up. And let me say how well you both look.' He was smiling. 'You know, for a few moments I thought no one was going to answer the door and that you were both away from home.'

'I'm afraid we don't always hear the bell when we are in the garden,' Ruth said apologetically. 'The folk around here know to keep their finger on the bell until the sound does penetrate.' Ruth laughed. 'Dr Morton—'

'Maybe you could make that David?'

'Delighted to. I was going to suggest we went indoors or would you prefer sitting out here? I'll bring an extra chair.'

'If you don't mind, Mrs McPherson, and if Kate feels like a walk – it's a lovely day, shame to waste it,' he said waiting.

'I'd like that,' Kate said breathlessly.

'Then off you go, the pair of you. When you come back I'll have afternoon tea ready.'

'Don't go to any trouble for me.'

'David, it is no trouble. I want to hear all the hospital news. You will recall, I hope, that I was practically a member of staff.'

'Unpaid and much appreciated. You are remembered with fondness. Incidentally, did you say news or gossip?' he grinned.

'A mixture would do very nicely.'

'I must change,' Kate said looking down at her blue and white dirndl skirt which she was wearing with a short-sleeved white blouse. Her arms were quite brown.

'Don't. You look very nice.'

'Take a cardigan,' her aunt said.

Kate frowned. 'I don't need one.'

'Take it over your arm,' David said recognising the signs. There was going to be a battle of wills here.

'Very well. To please you I'll take it but I most definitely won't need it.'

Ruth smiled and Kate went indoors to collect her cardigan. Whilst there she took the chance to comb her hair and put on a trace of lipstick followed by a light dusting of powder over her nose. She was ready.

Kate gave a little shiver of pleasure. How well he looked and how relaxed. She thought he looked younger without the white coat. Maybe without it he shed some of his worries. Sharing a joke with Aunt Ruth he looked both handsome and casual in grey flannels, white open-necked shirt and navy blue blazer.

'Ready?'

'Yes. See you later, Aunt Ruth.'

'Enjoy your walk.'

'We'll go out the back door, David.'

'You lead, I'll follow,' he said when he saw the narrowness of the path.

Kate opened the wooden gate that led into the lane. 'You know Muirfield, didn't you say you played cricket here?'

'That was years ago and I didn't see much more than the field where we played and a quick look at the village main street from the bus window. By the way, make this a stroll not a brisk walk.'

'Not feeling energetic?'

'No the energy isn't lacking but strolling and talking go together.'

'Then a leisurely stroll it shall be. We'll cut across the field, it is allowed, and go round by the church. It's a favourite walk of Aunt Ruth's because it's mostly on the flat and it is pretty.' For a few minutes they walked in silence then David spoke.

'I missed you very much when you went home.'

'Did you?'

'I did.'

'I missed you too.'

'Honest? Or are you just being polite?'

'I'm being both.'

'I wanted to write to you, Kate.'

'Why didn't you? You had my address.'

'I wasn't sure if you would want it.'

'I would have replied.'

'I know you would, a kind-hearted girl like you.'

'Seriously, David, I didn't expect to hear from you because you have such a busy life but I confess I was hoping.' She stopped, thinking she had already said too much. 'Is this you on holiday?'

'In a way. I'm considering taking up an appointment with Dundee Royal Infirmary and, of course, coming up was a chance to see my mother.'

'DRI. That's great, David. I hope it works out but – but—'

'But what?'

'I seem to remember you saying you always wanted to be a GP.'

'I did say that and I suppose I still do but one can't always get what one wants. No, that isn't altogether true, I could go into general practice—'

'In the town or do you want to be a country doctor?' Kate interrupted.

'Country or village would do, I'm not so keen on the town.'

'Then why are you considering DRI?'

'My future wife might not take kindly to the country life. I mean there are no set hours just disturbed nights and all the rest of it. It's no picnic, Kate, and I have to bear that in mind.'

What had she been hoping? That David was interested in her? How silly of her to think that. They were friends, no more than that. She swallowed and her voice came out normal.

'David, go for what you want. The lucky girl who is to

share your life would tell you that. She won't find it a hardship if she loves you. Have you asked her?'

'Not yet.'

'Well do so and I think you might be pleasantly surprised.'

'Kate, I hardly dared hope when I came today that – or maybe I've got it all wrong.'

'Got what wrong? This is all as clear as mud.'

'Why did you think I came to see you?'

'Because I like to think we are friends and friends are for asking advice.'

'Was I asking advice?'

'About your lady love and whether . . . weren't you?'

He was shaking his head in bewilderment. 'I think we should start over again. I haven't got a lady love.' He stopped and turned her to face him. 'I'm making an awful mess of this and it really is perfectly simple. I love you, Kate. From the moment you were brought into the hospital when I tried and failed to place you, I had a feeling you were going to be special to me. When that turned to love I don't know. What I do know is when you left us to go home it was like a light going out of my life. Am I making myself clear enough?'

'Oh, yes, David,' Kate said tremulously, 'I thought there was somebody, I never thought that somebody was me.'

'Now you know?'

'Yes,' she said with a hint of tears in her voice.

'It's too soon I know that.'

'Because of Roddy?'

'Yes, Roddy. I accept that he was and always will be your real love but you are young, Kate, and you can't want to go through life alone.'

'David, stop there a moment. It is true that I loved Roddy very, very much and he will always have a place in my heart. I didn't think it would be possible to love again but I was wrong.'

'Then you do care—'

'I more than care. I love you Dr David Morton, so please get that into your head. I love you, not more than Roddy, not less than Roddy. Just different.'

There was no one about. The only sounds the whistling of the birds and the quiet gurgle of the burn making its tortuous way through the village and eventually to the river.

He drew her to him, kissed her gently then hand-in-hand they continued their stroll.

'I'm not going to rush you into marriage, Kate. I'll wait until it is right for you. There are others you will want to consider. I'm thinking of Roddy's parents.'

How kind he was, Kate thought and there was a lump in her throat. He was always thinking of others. It made her decide there and then to tell David her life history, to have no secrets from him.

'Mr and Mrs Hamilton-Harvey won't mind, David. Roddy's mother did say to me that she hoped I would meet someone else and be happy.'

'That was generous of her.'

'Yes. Yes, it was,' Kate said quietly. 'David?'

'Mmmm?'

'Let's sit over there on that big flat stone. We don't have to hurry back and I do want to talk.'

'Fine by me. You can sit on your cardigan – see you have got a use for it,' he smiled.

'True,' Kate said as she spread it over the stone. They sat down and David slipped his arm round her shoulders.

'What are we going to talk about? Our future?'

'Not yet, not until I've dealt with the past.'

He looked at her sharply and saw by her face how serious she was.

'I'm not concerned with your past,' David said, equally serious. 'I love you, Kate, I always will and nothing is going to change that. Whatever it is, please believe you don't have to tell me. If, however, the telling will make you happier then I'm listening.'

'It would. I want you to know everything and for that I

have to go back to when I was a baby and my mother was left alone to bring me up. There was very little money and it was because of that—' She stopped, swallowed and stared ahead to the gently sloping hills. Then she turned to face him. 'David, until my mother died and that was when I was ten years of age, she was – she was Mr Hamilton-Harvey's mistress.'

'You mean,' David said slowly and sounding incredulous, 'you mean—'

'I mean, David, that Roddy's father and my mother—' She stopped and bit her lip.

'That must have been awkward,' David said quietly.

'Very awkward,' Kate said drily, 'but you need to know the whole story to understand.'

'All right, you tell it in your own way, take your time and I promise I won't interrupt. Once you have told me, my dearest, that is the end of it. The past is the past and it can't be altered.'

'I know. Once I've told you I can put it all behind me.'

'Good girl.'

Kate found the telling easier than she had expected. Maybe that was because she could feel David's sympathy reaching out to her. He hadn't once interrupted the flow but his arm tightened round her making her feel safe and protected.

At last she reached the end. 'That's it, David, that's the story of my life.'

'I'm proud of you, my darling,' David said huskily, 'life has not been easy for you, but you have faced up to it bravely.'

'Aunt Ruth was my saviour, she has been wonderful to me.'

He nodded. 'You two are very alike, not in appearance, but the way you face up to difficulties. In the hospital we were all very impressed with her.'

Kate made a move and grimaced. 'David, I'm stiff.'

'I'm not surprised. A hard stone isn't the most comfortable thing to sit on, even with a cardigan,' he laughed. Getting up he pulled Kate to her feet and for a few moments he held her close, his lips brushing her brow. Then they began walking back to Ashgrove Cottage.

'Don't think badly of my mother, she was good and kind,' Kate said almost angrily.

'I'm quite sure she was.'

'David, I feel so guilty.'

'Why?'

'Because – because though I loved her dearly I still felt ashamed and angry.'

'That was natural, Kate, we all feel mixed up at times. You find it quite impossible to imagine yourself doing what your mother did. But who are you to judge, how can any of us judge another? To my way of thinking your mother was a very courageous woman. She knew she would be ostracised yet she was prepared for that humiliation to give you a decent start in life. I have only admiration for her.'

'You really mean that?'

'I do. Strong characters, the women in your family.'

They were both laughing. 'David, you are good for me.'

'Of course I am, we are a well-matched pair. Seriously, darling, forget the past and concentrate on the present. You are going to marry me?'

'Yes, please.'

'Shall we wait or announce our engagement when we go in?'

She dimpled prettily. 'When we go in, I don't want to wait.'

'Bit of a shock for your aunt.'

'A pleasant surprise, she is very fond of you, you know,' Kate said as she opened the door. 'Here we are, Aunt Ruth.'

'Goodness, I was about to send out a search party,' her aunt said popping her head round the door. 'Now that you're here I'll make the tea.'

'No, wait until you hear our news.'

Ruth came into the room and looked from one happy face to the other.

'David and I are going to be married,' Kate said in a rush.

'Oh, my dears, I couldn't be more pleased.' She was beaming as she hugged Kate and then David. 'I'm not surprised you know, I saw the signs long ago.'

'Did you?'

'Yes, Kate, I did along with half the hospital staff,' she laughed.

David laughed too. 'You can't hide much from that lot.'

'What about your mother, David? Will she be upset at the suddenness?'

'Not a bit of it. She's heard all about you and being a local lass she'll consider that a bonus. You'll meet her very soon and I know she'll love you. I can see you both getting on well together.'

'Kate, what do we have in the drinks cupboard?'

'Precious little, I can tell you that without looking.'

'Must be something. David, go and help her look, I'll go and boil that kettle again.'

The sherry bottle was quarter filled, enough to fill three glasses. Ruth raised hers.

'May you always be as happy as you are now. Kate and David – your future health and happiness.' There were tears in her eyes and Kate felt her own brimming. She was so lucky. For a moment she closed her eyes. If Roddy was looking down she knew he would be happy for her.